DREAMING UNDER AN ISLAND SKYE

LISA HOBMAN

Boldwood

First published in Great Britain in 2021 by Boldwood Books Ltd.

1

Copyright © Lisa Hobman, 2021

Cover Design by Head Design

Cover Photography: Shutterstock

The moral right of Lisa Hobman to be identified as the author of this work has been asserted in accordance with the Copyright, Designs and Patents Act 1988.

All rights reserved. No part of this book may be reproduced in any form or by any electronic or mechanical means, including information storage and retrieval systems, without written permission from the author, except for the use of brief quotations in a book review.

This book is a work of fiction and, except in the case of historical fact, any resemblance to actual persons, living or dead, is purely coincidental.

Every effort has been made to obtain the necessary permissions with reference to copyright material, both illustrative and quoted. We apologise for any omissions in this respect and will be pleased to make the appropriate acknowledgements in any future edition.

A CIP catalogue record for this book is available from the British Library.

Paperback ISBN: 978-1-80280-933-6

Ebook ISBN: 978-1-80048-873-1

Kindle ISBN: 978-1-80048-874-8

Audio CD ISBN: 978-1-80048-880-9

Digital audio download ISBN: 978-1-80048-872-4

Large Print ISBN: 978-1-80048-875-5

Boldwood Books Ltd.

23 Bowerdean Street, London, SW6 3TN

www.boldwoodbooks.com

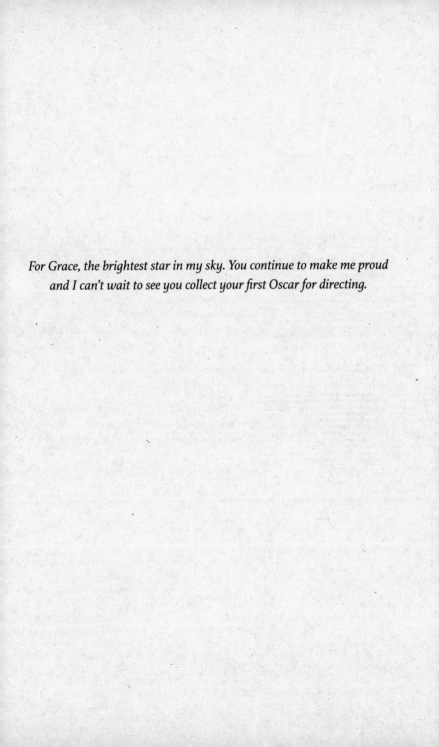

For Grace, the brightest star in my sky. You continue to make me proud and I can't wait to see you collect your first Oscar for directing.

PROLOGUE

Through gritted teeth, Juliette cursed the Victorian architect who'd had the monumentally stupid idea of utilising every inch of the high-ceilinged room for storage. If they'd been subject to health and safety regulations back then, there's no way ladder access to shelves – that were ridiculously high in her opinion – would have been allowed. Although it was a stunning library, with its ornately carved oak posts and arches, it was simply not practical any more. In fact, she couldn't imagine it being practical back in 1873 when it was originally constructed. But, of course, the University of Gloucestershire was proud of its heritage, and rightly so, Juliette reasoned. Who was she to demand changes, but a twenty-six-year-old former student turned librarian?

This wasn't how she was expecting to spend her day, that was for sure; clinging precariously to the location where she had just replaced copies of *The Modern Judge*. Her fingers ached and her toes were going numb as she clung on for dear life and tried to formulate a plan. She could jump, but as there was probably fifteen feet between her and the floor, that would possibly result in bone breakages, muscle sprains or, worst-case scenario... death! Her alternative

was to hold on and either: one, shout for help, or two, simply hope
it manifested by chance, sooner rather than later.

Friday lunchtime was usually Juliette's favourite time in the
library. It was the one time of the week when no students were
allowed in and the librarians were able to catch up on restocking
the shelves with returned books. To be surrounded by millions of
pages of knowledge just waiting to be soaked up... and, oh, the
bibliosmia – was there a better smell anywhere in the world than
old books?

There were usually at least two members of staff, but today,
typically, her boss, Nancy, had gone home ill and her colleague,
Claire, was on holiday, meaning Juliette was alone.

All alone.

Completely by herself.

Which would be fine if she wasn't stuck up a bookcase, sans
ladder, wearing a floaty skirt.

Bloody typical.

Anger and embarrassment heated her skin in equal measure as
she realised the security guards would have a field day if they
watched back the footage of this utter debacle. She could imagine it
now. The two main ones, Bill and Ben, as Juliette liked to call them,
sitting there in front of the surveillance screens, a mug of some
steaming brew resting on each rotund belly as they stuffed biscuits
into their gobs. Then, she imagined crumbs spraying everywhere as
they were overcome with the hilarity of watching the ladder fall
leaving Juliette dangling from the top shelf of the Law Reference
section like something off bloody *You've Been Framed*.

She was still unsure how the *attached* ladder had become
*de*tached and had fallen to the floor, leaving her stranded and terrified. She would have serious words with the caretaker or, if
anything bad was to happen, she'd be haunting the ratbag; those
things were certain. What *wasn't* certain, however, was how she was

going to circumvent the small issue of the fifteen feet of air between her current location and the floor.

The lack of space at the edges of the lower shelves annoyed her. Nancy had obviously been tidying again. The woman had an aversion to spacing and each book was butted up to the edge, as well as being tightly packed in, making it virtually impossible to retrieve anything in order to use it but, more importantly now, it meant Juliette was unable to find a foothold.

So... climbing down isn't an option, she huffed.

The door to the library gave the familiar high-pitched squeak as it was pushed open and Juliette closed her eyes. She couldn't see the door from where she was, but she prayed it wasn't one of the obnoxious new caretaking team she'd encountered in recent weeks. If it *was*, she could be sure this would all end up on YouTube with a gazillion views, meaning she wouldn't dare show her face in public again.

She held her breath for a moment and listened intently for noises that would indicate the identity of the visitor.

When none came, she opened her eyes and cleared her throat. 'Ahem... hello? Who's there, please?' she shouted with as much dignity as her situation would allow.

There was a pause and then, 'Erm... It's Laurie... erm Professor Fairhurst... Laurence.'

Oh shitty, shitty, shit. It just had to be him, didn't it?

She had nursed a secret crush on the gorgeous, yet shy, man since the day she had started work at the university a year before and first laid eyes on him. The resemblance he bore to Superman from the DC movies wasn't lost on her. She had noticed the lack of a wedding ring and had tried on so many occasions to pluck up the courage to speak to him; to actually have a conversation that *wasn't* work-related. But, up to that point, the courage she sought had evaded her. And, much to her dismay, their relationship had been solely based on professional politeness and courtesy when he came to sign out a research book for his latest thesis.

She squeezed her eyes shut again and she called out, 'Professor Fairhurst, it's Juliette, I'm one of the librarians?' – in case he didn't remember her – 'This is rather embarrassing, but... could you possibly come to the Law Reference section, please? I'm in a bit of a pickle.'

'Sure! On my way.' From the speed of his footsteps, he'd evidently sensed the urgency in her voice.

A couple of seconds later, she opened her eyes and turned her head slowly to find the handsome English professor staring up at her in bemusement. As always, he was immaculately presented in a tweed jacket, pressed shirt and co-ordinating tie, smart trousers and matching waistcoat. His dark hair was parted to the side and swept back in that Clark Kent way, and she tried her best not to swoon.

He shook his head. 'How... I mean... *why?*' From the way he held his hand over his mouth, it was clear he was trying not to laugh. *Great.* 'Hang on, am I supposed to recite Shakespeare to you at this point, *Juliette?*' He gave into the laughter he'd been holding back.

Anger flared inside her and her cheeks, by now, she guessed, would be a delightful shade of scarlet. 'It's not a laughing matter, Professor Fairhurst,' she snapped.

His face squirmed and contorted into an expression of solemnity. 'No, no, you're right. I apologise. And, please, call me Laurence. Now, what exactly has happened?'

'Well, *Laurence*, I think the ladder fixing is broken. The ladder fell when I reached across to grasp it and...' She didn't need to finish the sentence.

Laurence dashed to the offending article and lifted it up to rest beside her, but the top section was broken in two. 'Ah, yes. It appears to have broken further in the fall. We can't risk you climbing on it. Okay...'

Juliette prayed that her footless tights were not the ones with the hole under her left buttock that she'd meant to throw out. If they *were*, the Professor was getting an eyeful.

He took off his jacket and rolled up his sleeves, then scratched his chin and glanced at his surroundings, seemingly trying to formulate a plan. 'Right. Okay...' He returned his attention to her and pursed his lips as he appraised her, hanging there.

She was on the verge of pointing out the fact that time was of the essence when he spoke again.

'You're quite small, really, which means I can easily catch you... I'm... I'm pretty *sure* I can.'

Juliette scowled down at him, and with a distinct wobble to her voice, she said, 'In spite of your positive assertion, the delivery of it leads me to believe the contrary.'

He squared his broad shoulders and took a wide, arms-open stance beneath her. 'No, no, I *can* do it. Just be sure to push *off* the shelf so you don't hit yourself on the way down. I'm ready when you are.'

She gulped. 'If anything... you know... *bad* happens, my diary and my phone are in my bag, which is under the main desk. My emergency contacts are in both.'

'Nothing bad is going to happen, I promise.'

She peered down at him and saw sincerity in his beautiful eyes. Eyes that she had longed to gaze into ever since she first laid *hers* on him.

He smiled. 'I promise I won't tell everyone you fell for me.' His smile turned into a grin, but it quickly disappeared as if he realised he had been rather inappropriate. 'I mean... I didn't...' He appeared to be scrabbling around his mind for the words to undo his comment and blurted, 'I'll take you to the refectory for a cake when you're down here, shall I?' His colour drained, telling her he felt he'd made the situation worse. 'I-I only mean because sugar helps with shock, I-I've been led to believe.'

Her heart melted at his awkwardness and she thought to herself. *You can tell everyone I've fallen for you... it is the truth, after all.* Instead, she said, 'I'm holding you to that offer of cake,' in the hope it would let him know she wasn't offended.

'Great. I'm quite partial to death by chocolate.' He cringed again and she guessed it was at his mention of death. He clearly chose not to dwell on his faux pas. 'Now, come on, before they run out.'

She nodded with determination. 'Okay. I'm letting go now.' She took a deep breath and released her grip on the shelves...

1

EIGHT YEARS LATER

Why the hell didn't I drive into town? Why the hell did I come in the first place? Stupid, stupid woman. Why didn't I realise going on a date was a mistake of epic proportions? Juliette pondered the answers to these and many other questions as she hid in the alleyway beside the upmarket restaurant.

She'd given up wiping at her eyes now. The icy rain that battered against her skin mingled with her tears so no one would even realise she was crying. Not that anyone could see her. The walls surrounding her were shielding her from public view but doing nothing to protect her from the deluge. For goodness sake, she couldn't even *hide* properly.

Every time she thought of the confused expression on Peter's face, and the way he glanced around in embarrassment as she completely lost it, her own face crumpled again. What the hell must he have thought? The poor, *poor* man. He hadn't asked to date a neurotic, snivelling loony. He hadn't asked for his date to freak out before the food was even ordered. But, then again, Juliette hadn't asked to be a widow at the age of thirty-four.

A breeze whipped its way down the alley, curling around her bare legs, causing her to wrap her arms tighter around her body and ruffling her freshly straightened, mousy brown hair.

So much for spring.

Earlier in the evening, she had stood before her full-length mirror, but the reflection staring back was one she hardly recognised. Gone were the curves she had owned proudly when Laurie was with her. Gone were the bright eyes filled with hope and happiness. Now she was gaunt, pale and clothing that had once clung in all the right places hung shapelessly from her fragile-looking frame.

As she had riffled through her wardrobe, the only thing that had seemed suitable for a night out was her little flimsy summer dress. It hadn't appeared to be such a problem when the sunshine had cast a merry gleam over everything outside her bedroom window. Her long, natural waves had been tamed with a straightening iron and she had even applied a little blush and lip gloss to detract from the bizarre glow her almost translucent skin cast.

'I look like a bloody vampire,' she had whinged as she stared into the eyes of the woman in the mirror.

Her best friend, Millie, was having none of her negativity. 'You look absolutely stunning, Jules. Peter will almost certainly fall for you. And if he doesn't, he's gay and in serious denial.'

Now, though, standing outside in the alley in the pouring rain, Juliette felt like a complete and utter arse. Not only was her dress inappropriate for the inclement weather that had descended, but she had made a total fool of herself on her first date since Laurie had died two years ago.

Who the hell has a meltdown over the bloody wine list?

Of course, it was nothing whatsoever to do with the wine list, but Peter wasn't to know that. Nor were the nosey buggers sitting on the other tables. Oh, the judgment in their eyes; the pity and the amusement too. She'd be the talk of Mistford, no doubt, when the news reached there.

Her whole body juddered as she dialled Millie's number. She wasn't sure if the shaking was due to the Icelandic blast surrounding her, or the utter shock of what had just happened. Or, more to the point, what she had *allowed* to happen. She was crazy to think she could make such a bold step. In fact, she was verging on idiotic to think she was anywhere near ready to do such a thing.

More tears fell as Millie answered her call. 'Hey, honey. Why are you calling so early? I thought you'd be—'

'Please, Millie, can you c-come and g-get me? I just can't... He was...' she sobbed and her words became inaudible blubs and mumbles.

'Juliette, why are you crying?' Millie only ever used her full name when she was peed off or worried. 'You're at Alessandro's, right?'

'Yes,' Juliette managed to reply, and she prepared to explain as briefly as possible. 'You see—'

'Stay there. I'll get to you as soon as I can.' The words rushed out and Juliette could hear the urgency in her best friend's voice. There was definitely conclusion-jumping afoot.

Dammit, she needs to know... But before Juliette could respond or, more importantly, explain the situation, the line went dead.

Millie would be in a blind panic now. All manner of terrible things would be going through her mind about what Peter had done to upset her so much.

Shitty shit. God, why am I such a drama queen? She slumped against the wall and let her head fall back onto the wet bricks. She clamped her eyes shut and fought the frustrated scream threatening to escape from her throat.

The evening *really* hadn't gone according to plan.

Juliette gripped the silver locket with the robin engraved on the front that always stayed round her neck – a gift from Laurie – and wished she could simply turn back the clock.

* * *

The short journey to Millie's was reasonably calm, apart from the initial barrage of questions: 'Did he insult you?' and 'Did he smell?' and, finally, 'Did he *hurt* you? Because if he did, I'll make earrings from his—'

'No, nothing at *all* like that. He was the perfect gentleman.'

'Well, we'll get you back to mine and you can tell me all about it.'

'You can drop me at home, I'm fine, honestly,' Juliette insisted.

'You forget how long I've known you. You're clearly very shaken so you're coming home with me. No arguments.'

Juliette didn't protest any further. There was no point. Millie was very protective over her since Laurie's death, and she was grateful to have such a loving friend on her side.

Millie and Juliette had been friends since the first day at university, when, like a fish out of water, Juliette found herself in Gloucestershire to embark upon the next stage of her life, studying English and Creative Writing. It was a far cry from the little village outside the North Eastern city of Durham where she had grown up, and the moment she walked into orientation, she wondered if she had made a *huge* mistake moving so far from home.

Any worry was short-lived, however, when a well-spoken, smiley blonde girl had informed her, 'I'm Millie. You and I are going to be best friends, I can just feel it!' and had subsequently linked arms with her and given her a squeeze. They had been virtually inseparable ever since. Over the years since leaving university, Juliette becoming employed in the library there, and Millie beginning a career in marketing, the friends had grown so close, they considered each other as family. They'd shared student digs and then a rented house; the house where Millie still lived and ran her freelance business from, in fact. Juliette wasn't sure how she would've coped without her since losing Laurie.

Once they were back at Millie's and Juliette was dried off, she stepped into the cosiness of a pair of her friend's fleece pyjamas; the picture on the front was a cartoon chicken wearing a nightcap and the slogan read *It's Motherclucking Bedtime.* She couldn't help giggling as she thought about Millie's obsession with pyjamas. For most women, it's shoes and handbags. Not Millie. Give her a cute pair of PJs and she was as happy as a pig in poop! In fact, she probably had a pair with that very slogan on.

When Juliette walked back into the living area, she found Millie sitting curled up on the sofa, wine glass in hand. She too wore pyjamas, but hers were accompanied by an expectant expression. She patted the seat beside her. 'Come on, I've poured you a glass. Tell me what happened.'

Juliette plonked herself down and picked up her glass. She took a large gulp of the ruby-red liquid before recanting the events of the evening...

Alessandro's was the best Italian restaurant in the area. It was a quaint former pub that was located on the main street of Bourton-on-the-Water, the next village to her home of Mistford, and overlooking the River Windrush. Fairy lights were strewn across the exterior and Italian music drifted out of the open doors. Their home-made pasta was to die for and their desserts orgasmic. She and Laurie had eaten there on numerous occasions over the years and it held many happy memories for Juliette. Mistake number two, after accepting the original offer of a date, had been agreeing to meet *there*.

She'd recently met her date, Peter Wilsden, through her colleague, Claire, a happily married mum of two. Her husband was a high-school PE teacher and Peter was his divorced colleague. The photo of him on the school website – eagerly displayed to her by Claire – showed a fairly handsome man with cropped dark hair and smiley eyes. He wasn't drop-dead gorgeous, but Juliette knew better than to expect perfection again after having it once with Laurie. He was a science teacher and, apparently, a really lovely man who had been through a tough divorce the same year that Laurie had lost his battle with cancer.

They had exchanged phone calls and emails and things seemed to be going swimmingly. So, when he suggested dinner, she couldn't think of an excuse why she shouldn't go. She'd tried to come up with reasons, but none made much sense and were all down to her own insecurities.

It was strange to be back 'out there' and Juliette still had niggles of doubt in the back of her mind. But she knew she didn't want to be single for the rest of her life and even Laurie had made her promise she would move on. Admittedly, at thirty-four, the prospect of being alone *forever* was daunting; but not quite as daunting as meeting someone new.

The date had been set and Juliette had done the obligatory internet searches to make sure Peter Wilsden wasn't a wanted, axe-murdering psychopath disguised as a science teacher, but as nothing had come up, she figured he was either *not* a criminal *or* he was an extremely good one that hadn't been caught yet.

Millie had encouraged her to agree to his offer of dinner. 'You never know, Jules, this might just be the one.'

Of course, she'd had to pull her up there. She'd had her shot at '*the one*' and he'd died after three wonderful years of marriage.

Following her return to work and the realisation that she would never see Laurie in her library again, grief had descended into clinical depression and it had taken a lot to get to where she was now. She was quietly proud of herself and grateful for the help she'd had to come through the other side but she knew there was still a long way to go, and meeting Peter may just be the next step on that journey, she'd figured.

Dinner was arranged for the last Saturday in May and Millie had come around to help her get ready. Although the help had consisted of copious cups of tea and, 'Ooh, can I borrow this frock, Jules? And this top... ooh, and these shoes!'

Juliette had arrived at Alessandro's a few minutes late – on purpose. There would be nothing worse than arriving early and appearing desperate. The maître d' had shown her to the table, but, as she had approached it, she'd felt a little uneasy. The man sitting at the table was almost the spitting image of Laurie. How had she not noticed this before? Was this her mind playing tricks on her now that she was taking the first brave steps towards moving on?

The more she watched him as she walked, the more she tried to see past the initial similarities. He wasn't Laurie and that was that. However, a niggle in the back of her mind insisted that, from the hairstyle to the clothes, he could have been Laurie's twin. Except for the fact Peter wasn't wearing glasses. That was something, at least. If he'd worn spectacles, the man would've been a doppelgänger for sure and she wouldn't have coped with that at all.

He greeted her with a kiss to both cheeks – very fancy – and had even pulled out her chair. A whiff of his aftershave sent her stomach into knots. She'd recognise that Hugo Boss fragrance anywhere. She'd spent the two years since Laurie's death inhaling it from the dregs of the bottle in the bathroom cabinet, with her eyes closed and fond, yet heart-breaking, memories charging around her mind.

Determined to not let this spoil what could potentially be a pleasant evening, she sat and smiled, answering his questions about her journey and others that pertained to the usual small talk.

The waiter had offered them a wine list and Peter gestured to Juliette. 'Oh, I think the lady should choose,' he said with a handsome smile.

She'd held up her hand. 'Oh, no it's fine. I'll drink most things.' She cringed, regretting her words immediately. *How to make yourself sound like a lush in one easy step.*

Peter had nodded and grinned. 'Okay. I'd better put my specs on then, or I'll be ordering a bottle of milk or something equally inappropriate.' He'd chuckled and reached into his inside pocket. He pulled out his black-rimmed glasses and placed them on his nose. 'Now, I've had the Shiraz here before and found it quite palatable. What do you think?'

Unable to articulate her thoughts at that precise moment, Juliette widened her eyes and gasped. *Oh no, glasses too? And they're black, just like Laurie's. I think I'm going to faint.* Her heart had thumped in her chest and she'd rapidly lost the ability to pull air into her lungs. No words would come, and she felt the blood drain from her cheeks. She presumed the strange choking noise was coming from her and could feel the eyes of every patron boring into her.

Peter had leapt from his seat and rushed round to her side. 'Are you okay, Juliette? You've gone so pale. Breathe, please breathe!' Panic was evident in his tone. 'Can anyone help?' he'd shouted to the people uselessly watching the debacle unfurl in front of them.

Stars had danced before Juliette's eyes and the room had swayed to and fro as she'd gulped in desperation. The background music had seemed to lose its key and everything became a strange echo. She'd stared at Peter, unable to explain *why* it had happened or what the matter even was. She could hear people talking loudly.

'Is she choking?'

'Does anyone know the Hendrick's manoeuvre?'

'It's *Heimlich*, Geoffrey. The *Heimlich manoeuvre*. Hendrick's is *gin*, for goodness sake, you silly old fool.'

'Could it be a heart attack?'

'Should we call an ambulance?'

Someone had thrust a paper bag into her hand and a soft Irish accent had said, 'It's a panic attack, here, love, breathe into this.' A smiling, older woman came into view as she crouched before her. 'Try to slow your breathing, love. In through your nose... out through your mouth. Nice and easy. That's it. You're doing grand. You'll be fine. Just keep your eyes on me and listen to what I'm saying...'

Doing as she was instructed, Juliette's breathing began to calm, but she was then overtaken by pained sobs; a combination of embarrassment at the crowd around her and horror at the fact she had chosen to go on a date with a carbon copy of her dead husband. This only went to prove that she *hadn't* moved on at all. She hadn't made the inroads into recovery that she'd thought. She'd felt foolish and incredibly guilty for putting Peter through this whole disaster.

The woman, who introduced herself as Linda Clancy, a retired mental health nurse, had comforted her and tried to reassure her that she had no reason to be embarrassed. That these things had a habit of creeping up on you even if you weren't noticeably feeling anxious. Linda had tried to explain things to Peter too, but he didn't appear to be taking it in; nodding blankly as he sat there, pale and clearly shaken by the whole ordeal. Juliette guessed he was probably mortally horrified, wondering what kind of nutjob he'd been set up with.

Once she was reasonably calm, and everyone had gone back to their own conversations, Juliette had excused herself to go to the bathroom. Once she had splashed her face with cold water and examined her blotchy, swollen reflection, she'd realised she couldn't face Peter again. He'd no doubt never call her again after this anyway, so she'd decided to make it easier for him. She snuck out of the restaurant and darted into the adjacent alleyway, finding herself in the midst of a torrential downpour.

When Juliette finished recounting the horrendous evening, Millie reached across and squeezed her hand. 'Oh, honey. I'm so sorry I pushed you into it. I feel terrible. Here I am trying to sort out your love life and I can't even *find* one of my own.'

Juliette shook her head. 'No, no it's not your fault. I should've known better than to think I was ready. I thought two years was a good length of time to grieve. Although now I'm not entirely sure there *is* a time limit on such things.' She wondered silently to herself if, in fact, she would ever really get over losing Laurie.

There were so many firsts for a married couple: first dance as man and wife, first anniversary, first child if they were lucky, but for Juliette, she was still facing all the firsts that come when you lose someone you consider to be a part of yourself. She would never get used to the empty side of the bed. When she woke each morning, the first thing she wanted to do was to snuggle up to her husband, only to be brought back to earth with a resounding thud when reality hit and she remembered that would never happen again. She would never get over the fact that she wouldn't hold their first-born child as he gazed lovingly at them both, because that chance had been stolen from them by his cancer. She would never get used to the times when something funny happened and she was momentarily taken with the urge to text Laurie to tell him all about it, only to remember that there was no one holding his phone at the other end of the airwaves. She would never get used to watching a sad movie and having no one there to pull her into his arms to soothe her sadness and kiss away her tears. Because now, all that remained was the empty space that her husband used to occupy, both on the earth and in her heart. The Laurie-shaped hole that would never heal.

Millie opened her mouth as if to speak but closed it again and took a sip of her wine.

Juliette could tell when her friend had things to say and wasn't willing to let it go so easily. 'Come on, Millie, out with it.'

Millie placed her empty glass on the coffee table. 'It's just that... the more I think about it, the more I wonder if you really *did* grieve. You threw yourself back into work. You carried on volunteering at the Shelter charity shop on your weekends. You didn't really take time for *you* until your mental health forced the issue. And then you were so busy dealing with depression that I don't think you really had a chance to grieve.'

She possibly had a point. 'I thought keeping busy would help. Clearly, I was wrong about that too, considering I almost had a nervous breakdown.' After nursing her sick husband, Juliette had descended into the type of depression that consumes and devours. Medication and counselling had followed, but it had been a long journey.

'Exactly. Maybe you need to *really* deal with it. Allow yourself some time away, perhaps?'

Juliette tried to make light of the situation. 'You're just trying to get rid of me because I keep forcing my cooking on you.' It was true. Spending time alone wasn't something she enjoyed, and she invited her older brother, Dexter, who also lived locally, and Millie around at every possible opportunity. It was a shame her cooking wasn't improving in the slightest, even with all the practice.

Millie laughed good-naturedly. 'You know that's not what I mean. Maybe you need to head off somewhere warm and relaxing?'

'You mean like every holiday Laurie and I ever took together?'

Millie cringed. 'Okay, fair point. Maybe go snowboarding in the

Alps or something then? But just take the time and space to let yourself heal. You nursed Laurie through his illness, but now you need to take care of you.'

Again, she was making sense and Juliette resolved to seriously consider Millie's suggestion. In the short amount of time she'd had with Laurie, they'd sunk their toes into the soft white sand of Caribbean beaches and had experienced the pretty wooden huts and the crystal-clear, turquoise waters of the Indian Ocean. Perhaps a trip somewhere completely different was a great way of moving on? Of becoming *Juliette Fairhurst* instead of *Professor Laurence Fairhurst's poor widow*.

As Juliette lay in Millie's spare bed later that night, she thought about her parents. How much she'd missed them since she had moved away from County Durham to Gloucester. How easy things were when she was a little girl sitting on her mum's lap as she serenaded her with the enchanting words and tune of the 'Skye Boat Song'. Her mum used to tell her many stories of her childhood growing up on the Isle of Skye until her own parents moved to the mainland when she was ten. From a young age, Juliette vowed to one day visit the island of her mother's birth to discover the magic for herself, and had talked about it with Laurie on so many occasions. Sadly, he was given a terminal diagnosis which put paid to further holidays. Even though he promised he'd take her one day.

* * *

The following morning, Juliette was sitting in Millie's lounge, drinking her first cup of tea of the day, and she picked up a magazine from the coffee table. An article titled *Does It Always Rain in Scotland?* caught her eye and she thumbed through the pages until she reached a stunning photograph of the Cuillin Hills on the Isle of Skye. The backdrop of the naturally sculptured rocks was an almost cloudless, cobalt sky. A lone person stood in silhouette, arms outspread, head tilted towards the sun, and a shiver travelled along Juliette's spine. It was as if the article was meant to be seen by her. It was as if Laurie was saying, 'Yes! Do it! Go to the place we never got to visit.' And she knew she would listen.

2

The summer break was looming, which meant Juliette's hours at the university would be drastically reduced for several months. It was time she could use to her advantage if she were to arrange to take the whole summer off. And the more she thought about it, the more she realised that Skye would be the perfect escape for her. She knew no one there, so she could reinvent herself, but she still had family ties to the island, albeit historical ones. It wasn't a million miles away, but the distance was sufficient for her to need to rely only upon herself again. And, most importantly of all, there were no memories of Laurie there to catch her off guard.

Having emailed Peter the Sunday after their non-date to explain her panic attack and tell him that she was going away for a while, she received a pleasant enough response that eased her conscience. It turned out he too, had realised that he wasn't yet ready for dating – although she guessed he just wasn't ready for dating *her*. They ended things on a friendly note with the agreement to keep in touch. She knew – and she guessed he did too – that it was highly unlikely their paths would ever cross again.

Whilst still on the computer she opened a new tab and

searched for the village of Glentorrin on Skye where her mother had been born. Her heart skipped as she flicked through images of the coastal village with its whitewashed houses and mountainous backdrop. Her mind began to whir with possibilities.

Back at work on Monday, Juliette managed to avoid the whole conversation with Claire about why her date with Peter hadn't gone well. Apparently, Claire had workmen in at home and spent most of the day responding to calls and messages from the foreman. Some of the calls became quite heated and so Juliette decided that avoiding her was the best option.

After lunch, whilst Claire was out, Juliette took the plunge and knocked on her boss's door. 'Nancy, could I have a moment of your time, please?'

'Absolutely, dear, do come in.' Nancy epitomised every stereotype going when it came to librarians – the one thing Juliette had promised herself she would never do – from her neatly styled grey bun to the spectacles dangling from a chain round her neck and the sensible shoes on her dainty feet. She was a lovely woman but very serious and, on occasion, dour in appearance. 'How can I be of help to you, Juliette?'

Juliette twisted her hands in her lap. 'Well... the thing is... I'm thinking it might be a good idea if... I mean, obviously, I understand if the answer is no, but—'

Nancy tilted her head inquisitively. 'My dear, whatever it is, please don't be afraid to just come out with it.'

Juliette nodded and inhaled a deep, calming breath. 'Okay... okay... The thing is, I'd like to take a long-term unpaid leave of absence over the summer.' She exhaled. There, it was said. Out in the open. Dealt with... kind of. 'I've been doing some family research and I'd very much like to spend some time in the village where my mum was born, on the Isle of Skye. It's a cute little place called Glentorrin. I've never been, but I feel a kind of connection to the place. Something's pulling me there and...' Realising she was rambling, she allowed her words to trail off.

Nancy nodded slowly. She leaned forward, folding her hands on the desk. 'I see. I see. Can I be frank with you, dear?'

Uh-oh. This doesn't sound good. 'Of course.'

'I think it's about time you did this. In all honesty, I was so surprised when you returned to work so soon after Laurence's passing. Especially seeing as you're surrounded by memories at every turn here. Your tenacity was admirable, and I certainly appreciate your commitment to your work, but really... no one expected you to just *get on with it*, dear. We're two years on and I've been waiting for this day to come. I've left you to come to the decision yourself, of course, but I had a feeling you would, eventually.'

Juliette opened and closed her mouth, a little stunned by what she'd just heard.

Nancy held up her hands. 'Please, don't get me wrong,' she continued, 'you're a most valuable member of the team and we certainly don't want to lose you, but you must take care of yourself, too. I think it's an excellent idea to take some time away. Obviously, I'll need to run it by management, but as far as I'm concerned, it's a yes.'

Well, that was easier than she expected. 'Oh... wow... thank you.'

Nancy eyed her with curiosity. 'You don't sound convinced that it's what you really want.'

Juliette scrunched her brow. 'No, it's not that. I just... I wasn't expecting you to be so understanding.'

Juliette witnessed a first: Nancy rolled her eyes. It was thankfully accompanied by a wide smile. 'Goodness me, Juliette, I'm not an ogre. The health of my team is of paramount importance to me. I would've hoped you'd known me long enough to realise that.'

'Oh yes,' Juliette backpedalled. 'I didn't mean to insinuate the contrary. Not at all. I think I just expected there to be more hoops to jump through.'

'Well, hopefully it should be a relatively hoop-free process. Now, let me have the dates and the length of time you wish to take, and I'll see what I can do.'

* * *

Juliette sat in the window seat of her cottage, watching the children playing in the park opposite as she chatted to her mum on the phone. 'Nancy was great about the whole thing. It was a relief and terrifying all at once, Mum. This means I actually have to *do* something now.'

'Well, I think it's a wonderful idea. And I'm so glad you've chosen Skye. It's a shame we never took you there as a child. Your dad loved our family holidays abroad though. Can you imagine if I'd insisted to your father, the sun-worshipper, we should go somewhere where it rains a lot?' She laughed. 'He's just the same now. Give him a pool and an ice cold beer and he's sorted.'

She had a point though. Dad loved nothing more than to sit under a parasol, on a sunlounger with a good book while she and Dexter built sandcastles and ate helado and sandía.

'I do regret it now though,' her mum continued. 'All the holidays we had and not one to the place where I was born.' She sighed. 'I've only visited since to attend a couple of family events when me and your dad were first married. It's such a beautiful island, sweetheart. You'll love it.'

'So, you don't have any living relatives there at all now?'

'None that I'm aware of. There may be some distant ones. After all, your granny and grandpa grew up there, so there may be someone with a distant connection, if nothing else. Neither had siblings though, so finding relatives isn't likely, but think of the fun you could have researching. Oh, it will be so wonderful for you. Do you have any particular place in mind?'

Juliette didn't need to think much about this. She was desperate to visit the village her mum grew up in. 'I'm going to try to find somewhere to stay in Glentorrin.' There was a silent pause and then she heard a sniff. 'Mum? Are you okay?'

Her mum cleared her throat. 'Sorry, love. I'm a silly old fool. I'm getting all emotional at the thought of you visiting my little village. I wonder if it's changed after all these years.'

Juliette wasn't sure what she would find in Glentorrin but now that it was feeling a little more real her stomach knotted with excitement. It was a good sensation and one she hadn't felt since before Laurie had died.

* * *

The following Friday was supposed to be Millie and Juliette's *girls'* night. Of course, Dexter, being at a loose end since his split from his girlfriend of two years, had managed to muscle his way in and the three of them sat round the laptop at the kitchen table, searching the internet for suitable accommodation on Skye whilst eating snacks and drinking wine.

Eventually, Juliette gave an exasperated sigh. 'It's no use. There's nothing in Glentorrin, or anywhere close to it, that's available for a long enough period. Well, nothing that I can afford anyway.' She huffed and folded her arms across her chest like a petulant child. 'I'll have to rethink the whole thing.' Devastated didn't cover it. She'd geared herself up to go away. The management team at work had approved it. Her friends and family supported her. But it was all a moot point now.

'Erm... Jettie, what about a working holiday?' Dexter asked as he stared at the screen on his phone. The pet name he called her had stuck since they were tiny and he couldn't pronounce his new baby sister's name.

Juliette scrunched her brow. 'I hadn't really thought about a *working* holiday. Why? What have you found?'

'Millie, search up Skye Jobs dot com,' he instructed, and Millie typed the address into the search engine on the laptop. 'Now, click on the one that says Lifeboat House Museum.' Again, she did as requested.

Juliette's interest was piqued. 'Museum? What's that all about?'

Dexter nudged her. 'Well, sis, they're these places where people go to find out things.' He guffawed at his own joke.

Juliette whacked him, almost knocking him from his chair to a loud 'Oi!'

'Seriously, what does it say, Millie?' Juliette asked, curious.

Millie leaned towards the screen, cleared her throat and began, 'Glentorrin Lifeboat House Museum is currently seeking a volunteer to oversee the running of the establishment for a period of three months. This will take place from the first of July and will finish at the close of the season on the thirtieth of September. The museum houses a unique collection of artefacts not only connected to the old lifeboat and its crew but also about Glentorrin and the wider areas of Skye. Accommodation will be provided, and utilities are included. Please note, however, this is an unsalaried position, suitable for a retiree or someone with the freedom to relocate to the village for the period of cover. An interest in history is essential and willingness to learn about the artefacts is a must. Application by emailed CV with a covering letter. Interviews to be held via telephone. All necessary checks will be carried out.'

It sounded wonderful, but Juliette was pretty sure she had no chance. 'They'll fill that locally. Why would they accept someone from so far away?'

Dexter pondered her words for a moment. 'Actually, they maybe won't get anyone close by who's willing to work for nothing. It's a big ask in today's economic climate.'

Juliette scrunched her brow. 'No, I reckon someone will jump at the opportunity.'

Millie, who had been silent since she finished reading the job ad, swivelled in her chair. 'Actually, Dexter might have a point. And you could always apply. Nothing to lose really. And maybe he could stay here while you're away?' she shrugged.

Juliette thought about it for a moment. 'What do you think, Dex? Fancy a change of scenery?'

'Hell, yes. It'll be nice to live alone for a while. Living with Buzz is okay, but he has no concept of personal hygiene.' He held his nose as if to emphasise his point. Jacob 'Buzz' Busby, Dexter's friend and colleague at the garage, had taken him in a month before as a lodger after he split from his girlfriend.

Juliette felt butterflies of excitement come to life in her belly. 'Okay. Why not? Go and open another bottle of vino while I email them.'

Twenty minutes later, and with Dexter reading her email over her shoulder, Juliette hit 'send' on her application.

'Well, that's it. Just a waiting game now.' Juliette was already prepared to carry out more searches the following day, certain in her assumption that she would receive a 'thanks but no thanks' response.

* * *

The following morning, Juliette was rudely woken by her landline. Her head was fuzzy, thanks to the copious amounts of wine she had drunk the night before, and her mouth tasted rancid, as if she had been licking dustbins. Not that she knew what that *actually* tasted like, but she guessed it was pretty close.

She expected to hear her brother's voice when she reached to the bedside table and lifted the receiver. 'It's Saturday, you know, dingbat. I like to sleep in sometimes.'

'Oh, my apologies, I can call back later,' an unfamiliar male voice replied.

Juliette sat bolt upright, sending the room into a three-sixty-degree spin that caused her to close her eyes immediately. 'I'm *so* sorry. I thought you were my brother. Who's calling?'

'This is Reid MacKinnon. I'm wanting to speak to Juliette Fairhurst.' He had a lovely, lilting Scottish accent and a deep gruff tone to his voice.

'S-speaking. I mean, yes, this is she. How can I help?'

'Good. Good. I'm on the board for the Lifeboat House Museum on Skye. You emailed an application last night?' he replied as if she should have automatically *known* it was him calling.

'Oh, gosh, yes. Hello. I'm so sorry, I wasn't expecting to hear anything so soon.'

'Evidently. Anyway, I wanted to double-check your address. It appears you live in the Cotswolds?'

She cringed before answering. 'That's right, yes, but I'm hoping to visit the area and—'

'Ah, right. I see. Well, thank you for your application, but we're really looking for someone a little more permanently local. The last thing we want is to be left in the lurch if you were to be called back home for a family emergency or something.' His tone was terse and clipped.

She scowled. 'With all due respect, Mr... Mr...' *Shit, what was his name?*

'MacKinnon. Reid MacKinnon.' By the exasperation in his tone she could imagine the eye roll that accompanied it.

'With all due respect, Mr MacKinnon, you could be left in the lurch by someone who lived closer. Surely, it would make no difference to you the fact that they had further to travel home?'

Silence descended over the airwaves and Juliette scrunched her eyes tight. *Urgh, I've well and truly blown that now.*

'That's as maybe, Ms Fairhurst, but we'd *prefer* someone more local. Someone with a genuine interest in the area.'

She was surprised at how disappointed she felt at him brushing her off so easily. 'Excuse me for contradicting you again, but I *do* have a genuine interest in the area. I love history and my mother—'

'Really? I didn't see mention of your love of history on your application.' She heard a shuffling of paper and fingers tapping on a keyboard.

'Well, it was there, along with my connection to the place,' she snapped, knowing instinctively that she wasn't making her case any better for doing so.

'I see. I see. Well, my apologies. However, we do have some other interested parties in the local area, so I'm afraid we won't be requesting an interview. Thank you for your interest in the Lifeboat House Museum.'

It was clear that his mind was made up and no amount of cajoling would change that. And in any case, if he were to be her boss, perhaps she'd dodged a proverbial bullet. 'Okay. Thank you for your call.' Feeling utterly deflated, she hung up the phone and flopped back onto the mattress, promptly pulling the duvet over her head.

* * *

The next time she was woken by her landline, Juliette checked the clock. It was almost one in the afternoon. She figured she must have needed the sleep. Again, she sat and lifted the receiver from its base, the room had thankfully ceased its rotation. 'Hello?' she asked, carefully this time.

'Jules, sweetie, it's Mum. I have some news.'

'Oh, hi, Mum.' She yawned. 'What news?'

'Well, I made contact with Marjorie Dawson from church. She goes to Skye on holiday quite a lot. She's given me the details of a bed and breakfast place, called Thistle House, on the outskirts of Glentorrin. It's within walking distance of the village and they apparently have vacancies for the first week of July. It could put you up and you could find somewhere longer term whilst you're there, maybe?'

Juliette perked up. 'Aw, Mum that's great. Thank you. Give me the details and I'll call them asap. The way things seem to get booked up there, I need to strike whilst the iron's hot.'

She'd call the bed and breakfast and Mr Grumpy MacKinnon could stick his museum...

3

Juliette sat in the chair before a huge gilt mirror. People around her were reading magazines and drinking coffee, their hair wrapped in tin foil. She felt like she was in some bizarre space-age café or a weird Christmas lunch vignette from a film noir.

Charmaine, the stylist, stood behind her, running her fingers through her wet hair. 'Are you sure you want it all off, Jules? It's a drastic step, especially with the change of colour too. I mean, brown to blonde is a brave move on its own.'

Juliette inhaled a shaking breath. 'I'm sure. I have to reinvent myself and this seems like the perfect way. New hair, new location, new me.' She hadn't had her hair cut in so long and it was now midway down her back; the coffee-coloured strands a little lacklustre, to say the least.

'Okay, well, I'm going to take a quick before pic for the Facebook page, if that's okay? People love these dramatic transformations.'

Juliette shrugged. 'Why not?' Months ago, Juliette would've been horrified at the prospect of people seeing her and potentially judging her. Now, however, she was finding the prospect of these changes empowering; exciting even.

Millie had offered to accompany her to the salon. 'You hate being the centre of attention, honey. I'm happy to come and keep you company.'

But she had refused point blank. 'No. I need to do this by myself. For myself. Thank you, though. But it's time I show everyone I can stand on my own two feet again.'

Millie had hugged her. 'My brave, gorgeous friend.'

With her antidepressants down to the minimal dosage, she had chatted to her grief counsellor on the phone the day before the hair appointment. He hadn't been surprised at all about her desire for change, which in itself surprised Juliette. He encouraged her to take the next step in her life journey. So here she was, her hair looking bizarre in its tin-foil hat under an orange light, a pile of magazines in her lap.

Two hours later, Juliette stood before the same gilt mirror, her mousy hair replaced with shoulder-length waves in several shades of blonde. Just this one change to her appearance had given her a boost.

She smiled at her reflection. 'Wow! Charmaine, you're a miracle worker!' She hugged the stylist, who happily snapped several photos for the 'after' version of the makeover.

With her stunning new locks and an unfamiliar but enjoyable bounce to her step, Juliette embarked upon a mission to purchase new clothes for her trip. Luckily, Millie arrived for coffee and, after gawking at her in a speechless stupor for a good three minutes, offered to help with the search.

This was a whole new chapter to Juliette's life and it saddened her that Laurie wasn't here to share it with her. But this was something she simply had to do, even though it meant going it alone.

* * *

A few weeks passed like minutes and preparations for Juliette heading to Skye were almost complete. Work had given her a tea party to wish her bon voyage. Gifts had included insect repellent and a transparent 'rain mate' hat, which had caused great hilarity, especially when she had modelled it.

She visited the cemetery to lay fresh flowers for Laurie and chat to him about her impending trip. 'You'll always be in my heart, Laurie, no matter where I go. And I'll always wear my locket,' she told him as she gazed at the lettering carved into the stone plaque. Walking away that day had been hard and she wondered, very briefly, if she could actually go through with it. But she knew that she wouldn't just be letting her family and friends, and Laurie, down if she didn't, she'd be letting herself down, so she was determined to follow her plans through.

Before she knew it, packing day had arrived and Juliette giddily folded yet another pretty new sweater and placed it neatly in her suitcase with the rest. Rain and cold weren't things she was averse to. Growing up in a small northern mining village had meant she was used to puddles and grey days. But they didn't mean her childhood had been dull. Far from it. She had so many fond memories of woodland walks with her parents and Dexter. Bright wellingtons and raincoats were wardrobe staples. As well as some scorching-hot summers in her childhood, she remembered visiting the beach at Scarborough on wet winter days to build sandcastles and eating fish and chips on the seafront. Knowing this meant that whatever weather Skye threw at her, it would still be an opportunity to make more wonderful memories.

These days, however, she was more of a ballet pump flats girl, but she had invested in walking boots for this trip. It wasn't a total step into the unknown, but she knew she had to consider her wardrobe carefully. She glanced up and caught sight of her reflection in the mirror. Her newly coiffed hair looked a little statically charged and dishevelled thanks to the effort of trying on *every* item she packed.

A deeply huffed sigh briefly distracted her, and she turned to where Millie sat, brow creased, on the bed. 'I know this is the right thing for you to do, but I'm going to bloody miss you.'

Juliette stopped packing and walked across her bedroom to her friend. She bent slightly, placed a hand on each of her shoulders and looked her straight in her familiar green eyes. 'I'm going to miss you too. But I think it's just what I need, and it's only a few months. It'll fly by.' She kissed her friend's forehead and hoped Millie would think of a few months as no time at all.

She turned and yanked open the sticking door of the large pine wardrobe, then stood, hands on hips, assessing her hanging garments with bewilderment.

After a few moments of silence from Millie, she piped up again. 'I have to say, though, I can't believe that arsey man turned you down for the job. And I'm worried about you only having some-where to stay for the first week. What will you do if you can't find anywhere? Will you come home?'

Juliette sighed. It was concerning her too, but the last thing she needed was to worry Millie further. 'I'm sure I'll find somewhere. Word of mouth is probably the best way and I need to be there to hear of a place. If all else fails, I'll move on and find something somewhere else. Honestly, don't worry. I'm a big girl, you know.' It was all rather scary, but a flutter of excitement skittered inside her at the thought of the adventure to come.

Since Laurie had died, Juliette had felt as though she was living in a kind of bubble. It'd been just over two years and she *still* felt as though people didn't really know how to speak to her. It was as if they thought she was made of glass and she'd shatter at the mere mention of his name, so they avoided her altogether and she was tired of it. She wanted things to be *normal* again; to just be somewhere that no one knew her as *poor Jules, the widow*. If only for a little while.

Millie pulled her lip between her teeth and sat silently for a moment. 'I'm sorry, chick. I know how hard this last couple of years has been for you. Laurie's death was just awful... so bloody unfair. And I know I encouraged you to do this, but... I just... I don't want you to feel you *have* to run away.'

Juliette smiled and sat on the bed beside her. 'I don't feel that, honestly. This is the first thing I've felt excited about in ages. It just feels like... like something I *need* to do. Ever since I was a kid, I've been fascinated by Skye. My mum was born there and when I was little I didn't understand how she could've been, since there are only clouds up there.' She giggled at the memory. 'When I realised it was actually an island, I built it up into this mysterious, beautiful place. And that silly meltdown at Alessandro's made me realise I just need to get away. Going to Skye will give me that chance, plus I'll get to see where Mum grew up. I can't quite believe I've waited this long, to be honest.'

Millie's eyes glistened with tears. 'Just make sure you come back, okay? Don't go falling in love with the place and buying a bloody house up there.'

Juliette wrapped her arms around her. 'I'll definitely be coming home, don't you worry. You can't get rid of me that easily. And, anyway, Mistford is my home now. You're here, Dexter's here. My job is up the road. So, you see, there are too many reasons to be here.'

'Don't you ever think about moving back up north to be closer to your mum and dad? You could rent this place out now that the mortgage is paid off.'

Juliette laughed and nudged Millie with her shoulder. 'On the one hand you're telling me to hurry home and on the other you're giving me ways to leave. I can't keep up.'

Millie smacked her palm into her forehead. 'God, it does sound confusing, doesn't it? Sorry. I just mean... well, you relocated here for university, but I know how much you miss your parents. After Laurie's death, I think I expected you to want to go back home.'

'Dexter moving down here made that easier. And I have *you* too, silly.'

Millie hugged her. 'You certainly do. And we've had some laughs, haven't we, over the years? I know how hard losing Laurie has been for you. And I miss the fact that you were always smiling when he was around. Perhaps this trip will help you to regain that sparkle. I really hope so, my lovely.'

Juliette swallowed the ball of emotion that threatened to restrict her voice. 'I hope so too,' she whispered.

'Has Dex said much since it's all been confirmed?' Millie asked, turning to face the window and trying to hide the fact that a few tears had escaped her eyes.

'He's all for it. I think he'd have jumped at the chance to escort me, truth be told.'

'Aww. He's such a good big brother. It wouldn't surprise me if he ended up going there too.'

'That thought had crossed my mind.' Juliette giggled as she folded another top.

'And I suppose getting away from things is on his mind since Brid cheated on him. I still can't believe she did that. All I can say is that it's a good thing they never got married.' Dexter had been devastated by the discovery. The couple had been together for two years and Brid had always seemed so committed to him. But it was evidently true that you never know what was going on in the background.

Juliette had sensed that Brid wasn't *the one* for her brother but seeing how hurt he was initially over the split had really upset her. 'I know. He didn't deserve it. But I think he's coping well now he's got used to things.' Juliette paused mid-fold and pursed her lips as she contemplated her brother's situation. 'Although, when I think about it, he did seem rather *too* insistent about coming to Skye to *look after* me, as he put it. Maybe he's *not* coping all that well.' A niggle of guilt tugged at her insides when she realised she could have been paying more attention. After all, he had been her rock through Laurie's illness and subsequent passing.

Millie grabbed a pair of jeans and began to help. 'I should think he's finding it very hard to move on, especially as he sees her at work every day. I don't know why he doesn't just get a job elsewhere.'

Her mechanic brother had relocated to the area after Juliette's graduation and he had met Brid when she had accepted the receptionist position at the garage. 'I agree. But *she's* the one who cheated, so maybe *she* should bugger off somewhere else.'

Millie laughed lightly. 'Good point. Anyway, have you got something comfy to travel in?'

Juliette held up a pair of trousers and a sweater. 'Sorted.'

'I still can't believe you're driving all the way to Skye. Can't you fly or something?'

'I'm actually looking forward to the drive. It's part of the adventure and the Skye terrain is exactly what *Wolfie* was created for.' Jules had always adored her old four-wheel drive, even if it did guzzle fuel. The nickname, whilst she was never sure how it happened, had stuck since she bought the vehicle with the money her parents gave her after university. Thanks to Dexter, a mechanic and lover of all things rusty and oily, it was almost a new car due to all the parts he'd changed.

Millie grinned. 'So, how long will it take you to get there?'

'It's over twelve hours, so I'm stopping off at Gretna to break up the journey.'

Millie placed her hand over her heart. 'Oh, honey, didn't Laurie always want to visit there?'

Unable to speak, Juliette nodded.

'Well, I'm sure he'll be with you in spirit,' Millie said and grappled her into another hug.

Laurie's death had followed a year-long illness in which Juliette had watched him become weak and frail; the complete antithesis of the strong, handsome English Professor she had fallen in love with. Before they officially met, she'd had to be satisfied with secret glimpses of him as he came into the university library to take out books for a paper he was writing on the literary greats. He was incredibly handsome in a classic way: tall, dark hair, chiselled jaw, glasses, and broad shoulders.

The day they officially met everything changed. It was like something out of a romantic comedy movie and she loved to replay it in her mind and imagine some beautiful soundtrack playing in the background. From that ridiculously embarrassing first meeting, they struck up a friendship. They would visit a local coffee shop and share their love of books. He would advise on the best classic titles to read, depending on what Jules was in the mood for, and as a qualified librarian with a penchant for finding new authors, Juliette would share her love of modern literature, from the captivating story of loss in Donna Tartt's *The Goldfinch* to the mystery and scenery of Ann Cleeves' Shetland series. Her tastes varied, but the more gripping, the better the ride, she insisted.

Despite her feelings for him she never expected they would fall in love. Especially considering there was a definite indentation where a wedding ring had once sat. But their friendship grew and before long there were little signs that this was no longer just platonic. Laurie would find excuses to touch her: an eyelash on her cheek, a hair across her face. She would catch him watching her with a serene smile curling his perfectly shaped lips.

Over time, Juliette discovered that Laurie was thirty-six – a mere ten years her senior – and was divorced. His dedication to putting in many extra hours at work had allegedly caused a rift between him and his ex-wife, but he promised he had made changes and learned from that mistake. He was a gentleman, a passionate and kind man. He encapsulated everything Juliette could've ever dreamed of and he made her so happy.

Fast-forward eight years and their short but perfect relationship was in the past: six years together, three of which were spent blissfully happy as a married couple, and then a painful two years since, without him.

Juliette had been a widow for a whole twenty-four months, three days and eight hours and, following her recovery from an almost crippling fight with depression, she had vowed never to let herself fall so low again. This trip was to be part of that vow, not least because, lately, she had felt like a stranger in the pretty little village of Mistford that she and Laurie had called home.

Oh, how she had loved it when she was newly wed, with her whole life ahead of her. And how cruel it seemed now to be living that life without the man she loved. Her stone cottage had lost its warmth. The heart had been ripped out of it, along with her own, and she longed to revive both but knew that without Laurie it would be nigh on impossible.

She needed a change of scenery; a different kind of fresh air; a new location to recharge her batteries and help her to decide what she wanted to do with the rest of her life now that Laurie wasn't in it. She was too young to settle for the loneliness that had been weighing her down. Through counselling, she had discovered that thirty-four was no age to give up on life and she was determined now not to do any such thing.

Laurie had insisted as much when he was seriously ill. 'Promise me, Jules,' he had whispered breathlessly. 'Promise me that you'll do something you love when I'm gone. Something that makes you smile. You have such a beautiful smile. Don't waste your life grieving and missing me. Go out and *live*. Fall in love again. You have so much love to give. Don't waste it. Learn to throw caution to the wind. Learn to fall like you did on that day in the library.' His eyes had shone. 'Promise me.'

She had chewed the inside of her cheek to abate the threatening tears and had replied, 'I promise, Laurie. I promise.' At the time, she hadn't meant it. How could she even consider life without him? Let alone plan a future.

So, despite her promise, her future had been put on hold as she fought to come to terms with her loss. But now... *now* was different. Now she was stronger. Not *strong*. But she was at the stage where she could smile through her tears when she remembered his whacky proposal in the middle of the boating lake at Mistford Park. Or when she closed her eyes and imagined waking up to find him smiling down at her, ready to take her into his arms.

She had realised she needed to escape. To find her place in the world again. And something deep inside told her that Skye was the key.

4

As Dexter loaded the final piece of her luggage into the back of the car, Juliette hugged Millie tightly. She felt sure her friend would feel her pounding heart drumming at her ribs as she held her. 'I'll message as soon as I get to my first stop, okay?'

Millie clung to her. 'You do realise you're doing that creepy smile, like some kind of mad scientist who has made a dastardly discovery, don't you?'

Juliette pursed her lips and tried to eradicate *the smile,* but it was no use. 'I can't help it. I'm excited. And are you saying happiness looks creepy on me?' she said with a scowl.

Millie smirked. 'Just look in the mirror, chick. It's there. And I have to say it's wonderful to see. Creepy but wonderful.' Her smile faded. 'Where are you stopping first?'

Juliette rolled her eyes. 'I'll contact you when I take a break at Preston, okay? Then again when I get to Gretna.'

Memories sprang to mind of Laurie telling her about the young couples who escaped there to marry. 'We could go and renew our vows there,' he had suggested. Such a romantic. 'Imagine standing there, before the anvil in a place where so many people have stood throughout history.' He'd had a wistful look in his eyes, but she had laughed at the time and reminded him they hadn't been married that long anyway. 'I'd marry you over and over without a shred of doubt in my mind,' had been his reply.

Juliette shook away a momentary feeling of sadness. 'Anyway, I should get going.'

Millie held Juliette at arm's length. 'Be careful, okay? I'll be worried sick until I hear from you.'

Juliette managed to refrain from rolling her eyes again. 'I'll be fine. I'm a big girl, remember?'

She stepped towards her big brother and he ruffled her hair as he always did.

'Oi!' She laughed and immediately reached up to smooth her, already untidy, blonde waves. He had a mousy-coloured mop, the same as Juliette's, prior to her salon visit, only his was a mass of unruly curls with a beard to match. She always joked that he was a bear in a former life and he simply growled along with it.

He grappled her into a hug. He was the best hugger and his huge frame swallowed her up, making her feel safe and loved. 'Have an amazing time, Jettie. Mum and Dad say you've to ring when you get there. Behave, and don't forget I can head up on the bike any time if you need me.'

'I will. And, honestly, there won't be any need for you to follow me. I'm sure it will be everything I've dreamed of and more.' She narrowed her eyes suspiciously. 'You're just looking for an excuse to do your Valentino Rossi up the motorway, aren't you?'

He held up his hands. 'Guilty as charged.' He kissed her head and locked his bright blue eyes on hers. 'Anyway, the offer's there. Now bugger off. I've seen you twice this week and that's plenty.' His grin hid the worry she knew he was feeling. He had been by her side during Laurie's illness and had been instrumental in getting her to seek help when her downward spiral had begun. He'd driven her to therapy appointments and had held her for hours as she'd cried. He'd sat in silence with her, just to be there when he knew she needed him, and he'd forgiven her for the times she'd lashed out at him. He'd been her rock and her saviour. And she knew she owed him so much... maybe even her life.

She had been on the road to recovery for a while now and secretly hoped that this trip would help *everyone* to realise that she was fine – broken-hearted and a little lost, but fine all the same. And she knew she'd find herself again. It was just a matter of time.

She clambered into the car and slammed the door before winding down the window. 'See you in three months!' She waved eagerly and hoped her ebullience was contagious.

'There's time to change your mind!' Millie blurted and immediately covered her mouth, as if the words had fallen out by accident.

Dexter scowled at her and gave her a nudge with his elbow.

She shrugged, sheepishly. 'What? I'm only saying.'

'Speak soon! Love you a squillion!' Juliette shouted the saying that had been a part of her family since forever as she started the engine and put the car in gear. The CD player sprang to life and she grinned as she spotted the double jewel case on the passenger seat complete with the label *Songs for the Road*.

Dexter had made one of his famous compilations for her journey and she couldn't wait to hear what songs he'd chosen. *This should be fun.*

She pulled away from her little cottage to the lilting guitars of 'Good Riddance (Time of Your Life)' by Green Day and couldn't help grinning and shaking her head at his choice.

* * *

The first leg of Juliette's journey took her through some pretty, yet familiar scenery. The early-morning sun was cresting over the tops of the houses in the rural idyll of Mistford, casting a peachy glow through the haze. The town was nestled between Gloucester and Cheltenham and had been her home since she married Laurie. The main street was quaint, with its olde-worlde charm: little stone buildings with bay windows, narrow pavements and wrought-iron lanterns atop black lamp posts – the kind of place you saw in traditional Christmas card scenes. There was a butcher and a bakery. In fact, all that was missing was the candlestick makers and you'd have had the hat-trick. There was, however, a traditional sweet shop that did a roaring trade during the school holidays.

She passed the Hope and Anchor pub on the edge of town; the local watering hole and a place where she had spent some hilarious evenings with Millie, Dexter and, of course, Laurie. And the Mistford Theatre on the opposite side of the road where there had been a variety of performances over the years by MIAOWS, or *Mistford Independent Amateur Operatic Welcome Society*; their little emblem was of a white cat curled around the letters. She smiled as she remembered Dexter saying he'd join if it wasn't such a *catty* group. As always, he'd laughed at his own joke, whereas the others had simply rolled their eyes and groaned. Their favourite show was always the annual Christmas panto. Even as adults, they'd all got heavily involved in the loud shouts of 'He's behind you!' and had booed and hissed along with the children in attendance.

After hours of driving, Juliette made a brief stop in Preston for lunch and to stretch her legs. She checked in with Millie, her parents and Dexter, as promised, but she was soon back in the car and able to lose herself in the music once again. She tapped the steering wheel and yelled along with the band, Fun, as they sang a rousing anthem about being young and setting the world alight. Drivers of passing cars gawked at her as she belted out the loudest parts. She didn't care what other people thought. She'd always found singing cathartic; a kind of release that allowed her emotions to take flight in a positive way.

Just after five o'clock and tired from the journey, Juliette crossed the River Sark, which forms the border between England and the county of Dumfries and Galloway in Scotland. A little further on, she pulled into the parking area at the front of the modern hotel at Gretna that she would be calling home for the night.

From the car park, Juliette could just make out the blacksmith's shop along the road that was famous for illicit nuptials dating back hundreds of years. These days, it was a fashionable place to wed, as opposed to the necessity it had once been for some. She smiled as she gazed over towards the hotel to see a newlywed couple still in their finery, kissing just beside the doorway and smiling lovingly at each other.

Those were the days, she thought as she climbed from the car and walked round to retrieve her overnight bag from the boot.

The early-evening sunlight glinted on the windows causing a kind of ethereal halo effect around the couple, and for a moment she regretted her choice of hotel and location. The air of romance around the place exacerbated the sadness tugging at her heart. Evidently, this was a place you visited with the one you loved, not alone with a grief-stricken soul.

Juliette held her breath, closed her eyes for a moment and rallied. She was embarking upon something good; something on which Laurie would have fully supported her, and that fact alone made it feel like he was there with her.

With fresh resolve, she opened her eyes and, after she'd closed the boot and locked the car, she headed eagerly towards the entrance, inhaling a couple of lungfuls of the chilly air.

Pushing through the revolving door into the reception area, she was greeted with contemporary black and grey décor and comfy-looking sofas. A door to the left opened and she caught a brief glimpse into the dining area, where smartly dressed couples and families sat eating mouth-watering dishes – the smell of which made her stomach grumble.

Once checked in, she made her way to the allocated room and opened the door. The room was just as contemporary as the reception area, with clean lines and a minimalist appearance. The colour scheme was muted tones of beige and touches of dark oak, and there was a seating area that led through to a balcony. Out in the grounds, there was another wedding party; the bride and groom posing with glasses of champagne and their friends and family snapping photos on their smartphones.

Juliette sighed as she remembered her own small ceremony with Laurie at the church in Mistford. The old vicar must have been about eighty-five. He was *definitely* way past retiring age and she felt sure he was going to nod off as he spoke to the congregation. Every so often, he seemed to drift elsewhere in his mind, and he'd go off at a tangent, talking about things that had no connection to the bride or groom, or even marriage. There was one part of his sermon where he started talking about lobsters mating for life and then ended up telling the congregation about an episode of food poisoning from shellfish. Not only was he factually incorrect about the crustacean's mating habits, but the details of his sickness were a little too graphic, to say the least. Although, the gathered wedding party had found it hilarious and, as Juliette had dared to glance around, she noticed there wasn't a single person whose shoulders were still, or whose face wasn't contorted with the effort of stifled laughter.

At the altar, Juliette and Laurie had squeezed each other's hands tightly and had tried their best not to giggle.

At the end of the ceremony, the vicar forgot to announce that they could kiss, and Dexter had chimed up in his unmistakeable Durham accent with, 'Go on then, Laurie, give her a snog, mate!'

The whole congregation had erupted in laughter as Laurie had taken her in his arms and kissed her tenderly...

Laurie had looked so ridiculously handsome on that day – as he did every day –and knowing they were making this vow to be with each other until death made her feel like the luckiest woman alive. However, neither of them had expected the vow to be so short-lived.

Back in the present, Juliette decided she couldn't quite face entering a packed dining room filled with wedding guests, so she ordered room service and, whilst she waited for the food to arrive, she decided to make some calls home. After the first call to her parents, she dialled her best friend's number.

Millie answered on the second ring. 'Hey, beauty. How's it going? What's it like? Are you okay? Have you eaten?'

Juliette laughed. 'Blimey, okay... It's going well, the hotel is really pretty, I'm fine and I've ordered room service.'

'Well, I don't blame you for getting room service. I'm not sure I'd be happy, in my single state, to be amongst all that sickly *coupliness*.' An audible noise of disgust could be heard across the airwaves.

'No, and anyway, I'm tired out. I just want to sleep, which is precisely what I'll be doing when I've eaten.'

'Call me tomorrow when you get to Skye, okay?'

Juliette saluted even though Millie couldn't see her. 'Understood, cap'n. Bye for now. Love you.'

'Love you too, chick... oh and, Jules.'

'Yes?'

'I think you're so brave to be doing this. And you should be proud of yourself.' Her voice wobbled slightly.

A lump formed in Juliette's throat and she swallowed it down before answering. 'Thank you. That means such a lot. Goodnight.' She ended the call and closed her eyes, trying to fight off the threatening tears.

* * *

The following morning, after showering, Juliette descended the stairs to enter the dining room for breakfast. Fortunately, she had woken early enough to be one of the first seated, meaning she could eat and have a little wander along to the blacksmith's shop before she got back on the road to begin this new adventure she arranged for herself.

'Ah, you're a loner too, are you, dear?' an elderly man said as he passed her table.

She looked up into his wizened old face and smiled. 'I'm afraid so.'

He shook his head. 'I'm looking forward to getting back to my own little village and sleeping in my own bed. I never sleep the same in hotels,' he said, as if they'd known each other for a while.

'Oh yes, I'm the same.'

'Are you here for the McAndrews wedding?'

Juliette shook her head. 'No, I'm not actually here for a wedding; I'm just stopping off on my way to Skye.'

He raised his eyebrows. 'Oh, that's smashing. I live on Skye. Beautiful place. No husband or... *wife* with you?'

'Sadly, no. My husband passed away two years ago. I'm going it alone, as they say.'

The man placed a gentle hand on her shoulder. 'Oh, my dear, I'm so sorry. My wife died forty years ago, and I miss her to this day. Do you have plenty of family and friends?'

Juliette smiled warmly. 'I do, thankfully.'

'Ah, that's good. There's nothing worse than loneliness.'

Her heart squeezed for the poor man. 'No, you're absolutely right there.' She placed a hand over his where it sat on her shoulder as empathy caused her throat to constrict.

'Not that I'm lonely, I suppose. I've a big family. But I miss having a best friend.'

She knew exactly what he meant. She had Millie and Dexter, but being with Laurie was completely different. They had finished each other's sentences, laughed at the same crazy things. Knew what the other was thinking.

'You know, I envy those in our situation who are lucky enough to fall in love and marry again. But not me,' he said.

'You didn't meet anyone?' Juliette asked, curious.

He shook his head. 'No, I spent so much time dwelling on the worry of betraying my wife that the chance passed me by.'

Her eyes stung a little but she forced a smile. 'Never say never, eh?'

He chuckled and his eyes brightened. 'My advice to you, young lady, is don't shut out the idea of meeting someone in the future. You don't want to get to my age and realise it's a bit too late, and all the single folk your age are more interested in *Countdown* and a cup of tea than romance.' He winked and she had the urge to hug him. The elderly man sighed and looked briefly towards the ceiling. 'Oh, listen to me; you'd think I was here for a blasted funeral, not to see my grandson be wed to his fella.' He shook his head. 'Pay no heed, dear. Now, you go off to Skye and, you never know, I might see you again. It's only a wee island in the great scheme of things.' He turned to go but stopped. 'You know, there's this saying you should keep in mind, it goes *"What's for you will not go by you."* So, you go and make some new memories, eh?'

Juliette nodded and smiled as she watched him turn when he heard, 'Grandad! Save me a seat, would you? I'm famished. I think it's nerves.' A handsome young man with white blond hair was walking towards the old man and hugged him when he arrived. He may have been without his beloved wife for forty years but he was still, clearly, loved.

5

Gretna was beginning to wake when Juliette stepped outside. It had rained overnight, and the sun glinted on the puddles like tiny diamonds – fitting for the location. She wandered up the road to the old blacksmith's shop and was surprised to find people already buzzing around, making preparations for the day's events. Fresh flowers were being carried one way and chairs in another.

The low whitewashed building was a little reminiscent of the village hall in Mistford with its black paintwork. She spotted the famous black and white sign with the words *Gretna Green Since 1754* standing just outside, waiting for the next happy couple to be photographed there. She snapped a photo of the kissing gate topped with horseshoes and caught a glimpse of the wedding room as a door was propped open in readiness. Old carved pews lined the aisle and the anvil sat centrally at the front on the old stone flagged floor. The place was virtually untouched on the inside and she could definitely see its appeal; the history, the romance.

Juliette stood at the information board, twiddling her locket between her fingers, and read about the origins of Gretna's wedding history that she knew already. Laurie had read all about it and told her they simply must visit one day. Yet, here she was. Without him.

* * *

Juliette loaded the car once again. This time, the journey meandered around the outskirts of the bustling city of Glasgow, with its industry, concrete structures and hotels and then on along the shores of Loch Lomond. The scenery here was a vast improvement on the city and she was now surrounded by the silvery waters of the loch on one side and imposing trees and purple-hued hills on the other. There were log cabins a little further on and some people sailing kayaks on the still surface of the loch, their brightly coloured life vests a luminous contrast to the earthy colours of nature. A sign informed her she was in the Trossachs National Park. It was otherworldly. A vast array of colours formed the palette before her, and she could feel a strange pull; a kind of longing.

Eventually, she found herself on the outskirts of Fort William and, on discovering a supermarket with a café, she pulled in to call her brother.

'Hey, Dex, just letting you know I'm at Fort William.'

'Hi, Jettie, how's the journey been so far?'

'Not too bad. It's so beautiful up here. Just like Mum said it would be.'

He sighed. 'Do you think I'd like it?' Dexter didn't sound his usual cheery self and worry niggled at her.

She frowned at his question. 'Yes, there's nothing to *not* like. But why do you ask? I thought everything was okay with you?'

There was a pause before Dexter answered rather too breezily, 'Yeah, course it is. I'm great.'

She could tell he was lying. 'I've known you my whole life, don't forget. What's wrong?'

'Nothing... well... Brid has been making things tricky at work. She keeps hanging around me and saying she wants me back. And she's turned up at Buzz's too. Thankfully he didn't tell her where I'm staying.'

'Please, tell me you're not considering taking her back, Dex.'

'Oh, don't you worry. Once bitten and all that. No, I just wish we didn't work together. Life would be so much easier, that's for sure.'

'I know. Have you thought about... I don't know... looking for work elsewhere?' She cringed as the words left her mouth, especially remembering her comments to Millie when *she'd* suggested the same thing.

'For the first time since I started there, I actually have been thinking about a change, yeah.'

Bloody hell, it must be bad then. 'I hate what this is doing to you when *she's* the one in the wrong,' Juliette admitted.

'Anyway, enough misery. Bugger off and get to your B and B, will you? I'm far too busy to be sat here chatting to you all afternoon.'

She laughed and shook her head. 'Whatever, big brother. Speak soon. Love you a squillion.'

'Speak soon, love you a squillion,' he replied with a little more natural lightness to his voice than he'd had earlier. She wished there was something she could do for Dexter, after everything he'd done for her, but right now all she could do was be at the end of a phone for him, and she promised she would do just that.

Once she was refuelled, Juliette set off once more towards her destination. She switched from the CD to the local radio station, *Radio Skye*, with its presenters who spoke in the most wonderful, melodic accents, and before long she was surrounded by the jagged, mountainous vista to one side and another picturesque loch on the other. The early-afternoon sun danced on the water, sending dazzling shafts of light hovering above it as though the twinkles were alive. The tiny puffs of luminescent cloud above were a striking contrast to their cerulean backdrop.

After passing through Kyle of Lochalsh, Juliette forged ahead with an excited anticipation fluttering in her stomach. The arc of the Skye bridge loomed before her and she knew she was mere minutes away from the start of something spectacular. A few people stood at the centre point of the bridge, taking advantage of the vivid azure sky overhead, with the pretty village of Kyeleakin below.

A twinge of melancholy tugged at her once again. Laurie would've loved it here and she wished more than anything he could be alongside her for the trip. But just as she had before, she stopped the sadness from brewing; she knew he was there in spirit. And she thought of her mum and how fondly she talked of the island. It was bizarre, but the family connection gave her a strange sense of belonging before she even officially arrived.

She followed the road until her satnav instructed her to take a left turning, indicating that her destination could be found on the left. Thistle House bed and breakfast was situated beside a pub that would be handy for dinner, she thought. As she focused on the pretty stone house with its array of purple-headed thistle bushes, she mused that it wasn't hard to see where it got its name. She slowed, looking for suitable parking, when a series of loud thuds came from the front of the vehicle and she slammed on the brakes, her heart almost leaping from her chest.

A tall, auburn-haired man wearing paint-spattered trousers and an equally paint speckled T-shirt had slammed his hand on the bonnet of the car. His hair was a little wild and unkempt and there was a stripe of blue paint on his cheek. His face was scrunched in anger and he pushed his glasses up his nose, glaring at her as he shouted, 'Watch where you're going, will you?' He had a rather rich, deep voice and, of course, that accent she loved – shame about the aggressive tone of it though.

She immediately wound down her window and with wide eyes spluttered, 'Oh, my word, I'm so sorry! I didn't hit you, did I?' The fact that she was only driving at walking pace didn't really register when she saw the red-faced man scowling at her.

'No, but you could have!' he shouted. Then, he mumbled something about, 'Bloody tourists,' as he stormed off in the direction of Glentorrin.

Juliette took a deep breath and glanced around to see who else had been witness to her act of careless driving, but thankfully no one else was in the vicinity. Once her heart rate had calmed, she parked the car and took her overnight bag inside. The tiled hallway was painted in a calming sage green colour that complemented the parquet flooring. To the left was a dining room, to the right a small lounge and the staircase led up in front of her.

An older lady, perhaps mid-fifties, with neat, grey hair and wearing an apron appeared from a door along the hall, wiping her hands on a tea towel. 'Hello there. You must be Mrs Fairhurst,' she said with a warm smile.

Juliette held out her hand and shook the offered one. 'Yes, but please call me Juliette or, even better, *Jules*.'

'Well, it's lovely to meet you, Jules. I'm Morag. I'll show you up to your room, then you can come down and have a cup of tea and some home-made shortbread if you'd like. I say home-made, but it was Caitlin at the bakery that made it.' She chuckled.

'Sounds lovely,' Juliette replied as she followed Morag up the stairs.

'Here you go. You've a pretty view over the village from here. En-suite through the door in the corner and you've a kettle and some tea-making things on the tray over on the dressing table. I'll let you get settled and I'll go and put the kettle on. Pop down to the kitchen, last door along the hallway.'

Once she was alone, Juliette glanced around the cosy surroundings. The room wasn't huge, but it was sufficient for a week. The double bed was covered in what her mum would call a candlewick bedspread, in pale blue, and the rest of the furniture was painted white, giving a fresh and bright appearance to the room. Fresh flowers sat in a small glass vase on the dressing table and beside that was the tray Morag had mentioned.

After she'd unpacked her belongings, she made her way back downstairs and to the door she presumed was the kitchen.

'Ah, come away in, Jules. I've made tea. Or do you prefer coffee?' Morag said as she stood there, teapot in hand.

'Tea is just fine, thank you.'

'Have a seat. What brings you to Glentorrin?' Morag asked.

Juliette sat at the old pine table that showed aged signs of plenty of family gatherings. 'It's a long story really, but I'm here on a kind of sabbatical from work. My mum spent some of her childhood here, so I thought it'd be a nice place to visit.'

'Oh, how lovely. What's your mum's name? Might I know of her?'

'She left when she was a young girl, but her maiden name was McLeod. Lorna McLeod.'

Morag tapped her chin. 'Hmm, it's certainly a well-known name on the island, but there are none in Glentorrin just now. You might want to ask around though, someone may remember her.'

'That's what I'm hoping. Although I thought I might start in the museum.'

Morag sat opposite her and her smile disappeared. 'Ah, now I'm afraid you won't be able to do that. The museum is closed at present.'

Juliette was both disappointed and intrigued by this news. 'Oh? How come?'

'Oh, where do I begin?' Morag sighed heavily. 'I won't bore you with the ins and outs of it all, but, to cut a long story short, we advertised for volunteers to run it over the summer months but had no appropriate applications.'

Knowing she had been one such *inappropriate* applicant, Juliette's heart sank. 'Oh dear. That is a shame.'

Morag folded her arms across her chest. 'Aye, it is. The wee museum is owned by the village co-operative, you see, we rely on donations to keep it going and we all used to take our turns in running it, but things haven't exactly been going to plan lately. Everyone has their own businesses, meaning no one has enough time these days. My husband, Kenneth, and I have this place and the shop, and the others are in similar situations. Not enough hours in a day. I'm not sure of its fate at the moment.' Sadness was evident in the woman's eyes. 'Reid – he's the chairman – said we had several applications, but apparently the majority were from people without the right experience. The ones who *might* have been suitable were asking for payment, which we can't offer. We were providing accommodation and utilities, but I understand why that's not really enough for most people. And a couple of applicants were just taking the Michael from what Reid said.'

Juliette might not have worked in a museum before, but she had an interest in history and had a good head on her shoulders. She wondered why on earth her application had been rejected if the museum was in such dire straits and considered whether she should ask the question. After giving it some thought, albeit briefly, she decided not to mention it. After all, if she had been right for the role, surely they would have interviewed her?

* * *

Once she finished her tea, Juliette decided to head out into the village to explore. The sun was making its descent, but the air was still warm. Glentorrin, an old fishing village, consisted of a narrow inlet of water with a low wall and a wooden barrier. This was surrounded by whitewashed cottages of different shapes and sizes and Juliette smiled to herself as she wandered down the main street. Such a pretty place. There was the convenience store, which was run by Morag's husband, Kenneth, and, in addition to this, there was a café, a bakery and an outdoor gear shop, each building as attractive as the next. It reminded her a little of the location where *Local Hero* was filmed; a movie she and Laurie had watched in their early days as a couple.

At the end of the village was an old slipway that was now closed off with railings, and just in front of it was a white-painted building with sage green shutters and a tiled roof. The hand-painted sign above the left hand door read *Lifeboat Cottage* and a similar but larger sign to the right hand section of the building read *The Lifeboat House Museum*. The two halves were very different, with the left side appearing more homely; presumably it had once provided accommodation to the lifeboat crew when on duty. And whilst the roof line was continuous, the right-side floor of the building sloped away, mirroring the slipway; clearly the part that had once housed the lifeboat itself. There was evidence that windows had been added later, perhaps when it was turned into a museum.

Externally, the updates had been sympathetically done but Juliette wondered what it was like inside. Was the slope still in situ or had it been levelled to accommodate the displays?

For a moment, Juliette stood peering up at the scrolled lettering of the sign, her hand placed over her heart and a wide, teary smile on her face. Her mum had told her of the lifeboat house and the fact that her own grandfather had been a volunteer on the boat many years before. Now it was almost a monument to those who had put their lives at risk to save others.

There was a pretty stained-glass panel in the door that was made up of chunks of sea glass and coloured glass beads which depicted the old lifeboat. Quite an apt and quirky addition to the otherwise plain wood. Only above this was a sign that read 'CLOSED UNTIL FURTHER NOTICE', which saddened her. She would've loved the opportunity to have a glimpse into the past, and of possibly learning more about her ancestry.

As she turned to walk back along towards the pub, Juliette heard someone shout, 'Chewie! No!' and before she could register what was going on, she was knocked off her feet, the air exiting her lungs, and she landed on her back with a *whump* and a groan.

Her face was covered in long wet strokes from a canine tongue and she scrunched up her mouth and eyes, trying her best to avoid the onslaught. 'Get off me! Get off!' she squealed in between licks. A horrid memory of being pounced on by her neighbour's dog when she was twelve sprang to mind, the snarling, bone-shakingly deep bark as Buster, the Rottweiler cross, lurched for her, and then the relief as Shaun, the neighbour's son, had tugged the dog back in the nick of time...

The dog was yanked back by the collar, enabling Juliette to sit up. 'I'm so sorry! I'm so, so sorry, lady! Chewie, you bad boy. Bad boy!' A young boy of around eleven fiddled with the lead in his hand and tugged it over the dog's head. Once secured, he held it with a white-knuckled grip and a look of sheer horror on his face. 'Are you okay? Please, say you're okay.'

Juliette wiped the slobber from her face and scrambled to her feet. The gangly dog lurched forward again, tail wagging frantically and tongue lolling out of its mouth. She stepped back with alarm, not wishing for a repeat of what had just happened. 'I'm fine, no thanks to your dog.' She nodded towards the strip of red corded fabric in the boy's hands. 'Why didn't you have him *on* the lead?'

The boy's cheeks flushed scarlet and he cringed. 'He keeps slipping out of it. He's only a year old and not trained very well yet. I-I'm working on it though!' he insisted.

The dog had shaggy tan-coloured hair and amber eyes. If she were a dog person, she'd think it was cute, but as she *wasn't*, it was simply a drooling menace that evidently couldn't be controlled by its human. 'Well, perhaps you need a different type of lead. It's not good to have him running wild and attacking people.' She swiped at her legs to brush off gravel and grass cuttings.

'I really am sorry. He's not vicious or anything. Just friendly. He loves to meet new people,' said the boy by way of explanation.

Juliette wasn't convinced. Pets were something she'd never had and never wanted, especially one as huge as this dog was but she didn't want to be too hard on the boy. 'It's fine. It was shock more than anything.'

'You can fuss him if you want. I think he likes you,' the dark-haired boy informed her.

She cringed and held up her hands in protest. 'No! Erm, thanks, I'm good.'

The boy pursed his lips. 'You're not a dog fan, are you?'

'Is it that obvious? I can't say I am, no. Bad experience when I was younger.' She cringed as an involuntary shiver shook her.

The boy sighed. 'That's a shame. Dogs are such good friends, you know. They're not all nasty. They don't pick on you. They don't steal your things, unless it's food, of course, and they don't say mean things about you. They just love you.' An air of sadness took over the boy until the dog jumped on him and he giggled. 'Chewie loves me, don't you, boy?' This brought a small smile to Juliette as she witnessed the two of them.

'Okay, but they're smelly and dribbly, and from what I've heard they have a thing about rolling in stinky patches and diving in stagnant water.'

'Not Chewie. He's terrified of water. Aren't you, boy? He's a Hungarian Vizsla and that's a type of hunting dog, so swimming's not really his thing. Ugh, you should see him when we bath him. Nightmare.' The boy rolled his eyes and shook his head.

'What kind of name is Chewie? Does he eat everything?'

The boy laughed. 'Oh no. He's quite good really. He's named after Chewbacca from *Star Wars*.'

Juliette tilted her head and assessed the dog. She could definitely see the resemblance in the size and colour. 'Ah, yes. Good name.'

The boy held out his hand. 'I'm Evin Mackinnon, by the way. I'm eleven, so I don't usually talk to strangers, but seeing as my dog jumped on you, I thought I should tell you.'

She smiled and shook his hand, wondering if he was related to the Mr Mackinnon who rejected her for the job at the museum. 'I'm Juliette. But most people call me Jules.'

'Ooh, like the crown jewels?'

She laughed. 'Not quite. Different spelling. So, do you live in the village?'

'Aye, I do. I live with my dad. And Chewie, of course. Actually, I should get back. Dad will wonder where I am. I had to come looking for this doaty wee creature.'

'I'd hardly call him *wee*.'

'True. Doaty *muckle* creature, eh?' The boy turned and ran away, waving as he went.

Juliette had no clue what he'd just said, so she smiled and waved back, then heaved a deep sigh. In the space of an hour, she'd almost knocked down a pedestrian *and* almost been eaten alive by a space monster masquerading as a dog. She had come to Skye after adventure but it was turning out to be a little more eventful than she'd imagined.

6

Juliette awoke feeling surprisingly refreshed after her first night in the bed and breakfast, but, as she moved to get up, her muscles reminded her of the previous day's events. 'Stupid bloody excitable dog,' she chuntered.

Once showered and dressed, she went down and took her seat at the table set for one in the dining room.

Morag greeted her with a smile. 'Morning, hen. Did you sleep okay?'

'Good morning. Yes, I slept *really* well, thank you,' she replied with a contented sigh.

'I'm so glad. Now, can I get you the full Scottish?'

Juliette's stomach rumbled at the thought of food and she put it down to the fresh Scottish sea air. 'Definitely!'

'Great. I'll take your order through to Kenneth. He cooks a mean tattie scone.' She tapped the side of her nose and left.

Juliette was yet to meet the elusive Kenneth; a multi-talented man, by the sound of it, with this latest discovery that he was also the chef.

Breakfast was a feast for the senses. The thought of haggis had been something that had previously both intrigued and disgusted Juliette in equal measure, but on tasting it, she had to admit it was delicious. And Morag was right; the home-made tattie scones were to die for. Although Juliette knew she'd need to gain willpower from somewhere, as eating like that every day for the foreseeable future would mean she would go home *twice* the person she currently was. Not that a *little* weight gain would hurt.

After breakfast, she resolved that further exploration was on the cards and set out in the warm golden hues of the morning sun to see what other delights the village of Glentorrin held. Her first stop was the bakery at the other side of the inlet.

Caitlin's Cakes and Bakes was another whitewashed building with coloured bunting hanging above the windows. It really was a picture-postcard setting. She walked into the shop and admired the displays of sweet and savoury confections, her mouth watered despite the humongous breakfast she'd consumed mere moments before.

'Hi there, what can I get you?' a woman with fiery red hair asked as she appeared through a beaded curtain at the right-hand side of the shop.

'Oh hi, I'm just trying to decide. It all looks so scrumptious. I'm heading out for a stroll and thought I'd take something for a snack, although I can feel the calories piling on just looking at these displays.'

The woman tilted her head. 'Well, I'm guessing you're on holiday, so the calories don't count.' She gave a wink and giggled.

'Ah well, in that case I'll take some shortbread rounds and a bottle of water, please.'

'Coming right up.' As the woman packaged up the shortbread, she asked, 'That sounds like a north-east England accent, am I right?'

Juliette nodded. 'Spot on, I'm originally from Durham, although I live in the Cotswolds these days.'

'Wow, that's quite a trek you've made. Are you here with your family?'

The question that always seemed to pop up didn't seem to sting as much today. 'No, just me. A bit of time away to recharge the old batteries.'

'Ah, good for you. Are you staying locally?'

'Yes, I'm staying at Thistle House.'

The friendly woman's smile widened. 'You'll have met Morag then. Such a lovely woman. Kenneth's a great guy too.'

'Yes, everyone seems so nice around here. Very welcoming.' With the exception of the grumpy pedestrian she'd encountered when she'd first arrived, Juliette thought.

The red-haired woman grinned. 'Aye, we're not a bad bunch. There are a few sour apples in the barrel, but for the most part we're quite welcoming. My name's Caitlin, by the way.'

With a wide smile, Juliette replied, 'I'm Jules.'

'Well, Jules, I hope you enjoy your stay in Glentorrin. You know where to come if you need to replenish some of the calories you walk off while you're exploring.'

Juliette laughed. 'I think it might be a case of walking off the calories I've eaten if I'm not careful!'

Caitlin laughed along. 'Well, you'd better get walking then, eh?'

'Bye for now, and thanks.' Juliette waved as she left the bakery and set out past the outdoor clothing shop with its window display of brightly coloured wellingtons and fishing gear, then along the road away from the village. The sun cast a rich, balmy glow on the purple heather and hills that surrounded her, and she felt the tension in her neck and arms begin to dissipate.

She was just thinking how quiet the road was as she walked along its curving sweep when a car approached, its female driver seemed to glare at her from behind the wheel. As the car reached her, Juliette could've sworn the driver swerved a little towards her.

She yelped and dived into the banking to avoid being clipped by the wing mirror. 'Bloody hell! Get a bit closer next time and do the job properly!' Juliette shouted at the car's retreating form as it headed towards the village. She stood, brushed the grass and seeds from her legs – an action she'd carried out once too often already – and took a deep breath.

Once calm, she carried on following the vague directions that her mum had provided and eventually found the location of a little croft off the main road. From the descriptions and stories, she was almost certain it was the place her mum used to live with her parents before leaving for the mainland, seeing as there was nothing else around for quite a distance. It was nothing but a ruin now, but Juliette could imagine her mother, as a young girl, playing in the fields that surrounded the now run-down building. What a shame there was so little left to show for the once loved family home.

She snapped a photo of the pretty setting and took a few more shots of the small wood that would have once provided shade to the animals. She had often wondered why her mother had never returned to visit, but seeing the little house in such a state of disrepair she decided it was maybe a good thing. Perhaps she'd send the photos to Dexter and see if he thought Mum would want to see them.

* * *

Later, when she returned to Thistle House, Morag was waiting for her. Gone was the smiley countenance that usually greeted her. It was replaced by one of concern and her fidgeting hands told Juliette that something disagreeable had happened, or was *about* to. 'Oh, hello, Jules. Could I possibly have a wee word in your ear?'

Morag's expression caused worry to niggle at her. 'Sure, is everything okay?'

The older woman waved a dismissive hand, but her narrowed eyes didn't correlate. 'Och yes. Come on through to the kitchen and I'll make a fresh pot of tea.'

Once they were seated, Morag folded her hands on the table in front of her.

She sighed deeply before she began. 'I've been talking to Reid MacKinnon today.'

'Oh yes.'

Another sigh told of her discomfort. 'He made a bit of a complaint, I'm afraid.'

Juliette scrunched her brow. 'Complaint? About what?' What on earth could he have to complain about?

Morag cringed and chewed her lip for a moment. 'I feel ridiculous even mentioning this, so please forgive me. How does the saying go about shooting the messenger? After the incident the other day, he's asked if you could move your car from where you've parked it. He says you're causing an obstruction. I think he's being a pedantic pain in the arse, to be honest.'

Confused, Juliette held up her hand. 'I'm sorry, Morag, but I don't have the foggiest clue what you're talking about. I've only spoken to Mr MacKinnon on the phone and I was very civil, given the circumstances. I've never actually *met* him face to face. So, I'm not sure what incident you're referring to.'

Morag scratched her head, clearly she was equally befuddled. 'Oh. But... Well, he says you almost ran him over. He must be mistaken.'

The penny dropped and Juliette felt the colour drain from her face. With wide eyes, she said, 'Oh! *That* was Mr MacKinnon? He didn't actually introduce himself, just gave me a mouthful. Shit!' She lifted her hand to her mouth. 'Oh, excuse my language. I'm so sorry.'

Morag shook her head. 'It's okay. He's been such a grumpy sod lately, honestly. He rarely smiles these days, and he has such a handsome face when he does. But he seems to have forgotten how. I'm presuming he's blowing this all out of proportion. But he cycles down to the village from his house and he says your car is creating a blind spot which, he says, isn't safe for his son, Evin, either. I'm so sorry. You can always pull into the yard at the back.'

Juliette nodded, her suspicions about the boy's connection to Mackinnon proved correct. 'Absolutely. Of course. No problem.'

Morag went silent for a few moments. 'When you say you spoke to him on the phone, what do you mean?'

With a vengeance, the colour returned to Juliette's cheeks. 'Oh, erm, actually, I applied for the museum job a short while ago. He rang and told me I wasn't suitable as I lived too far away.'

Morag's brow crumpled. 'But now you're here?'

Juliette held out her hands and smiled nervously. 'Now I'm here.'

'And how long were you planning on staying on Skye?'

Juliette shrugged. 'I've taken a sabbatical which is due to end just before the next term begins.'

Morag tilted her head. 'Term? What is it you do for a job?'

'I'm a university librarian. And I'm passionate about history too, which I told him. I know it's not the right type of experience really, but—'

Morag threw up her hands in exasperation. 'But you'd have been perfect! I don't believe this. He said there were no suitable candidates. And here you are, a personable woman with intelligence and a desire to do the job. Ugh.' She pursed her lips. 'I feel like he's chopped off his nose to spite his face, silly bugger. And I'm guessing it's because you're English.'

Juliette gasped. 'What has he got against the English?' The changing colour palette of Juliette's face was now cerise with anger. How *dare* he reject her because of her nationality? There were laws against that kind of discrimination.

Morag backpedalled. 'Oh, no, it's not the English, *per se*. It's... Oh dear, I fear whatever I say will make matters worse. But it's suffice to say his ex-wife is English. She broke his heart and now he has trust issues.'

Morag's admission fuelled the simmering fire in Juliette's belly. 'So, I'm guilty by association of my sex *and* nationality? Perhaps I need to go and have words with this Mr MacKinnon.' She huffily folded her arms across her chest.

Morag waved a hand. 'No, no. Let me talk to him. He's a funny man. Well, he has been since... well, you know. He used to be the life and soul of the party. *Her* shenanigans changed that.'

Juliette seethed for a few moments, her nostrils flared, and her heart thumped at her ribcage. But the truth was that she could do little to improve things, especially if she went off half-cocked at the ignorant arse. So, although she was pretty peeved about the whole situation, she willed herself calm. After all, she didn't want to make herself even more unpopular than she already had.

She sighed. 'No, don't bother. If I'm not good enough for the job, I'll find something else. Please, don't worry about it, Morag. But thank you for being honest with me. Oh, and... if you know of anywhere I could rent for a few months, please tell me. Obviously, the house with the museum would have been ideal, but hey ho...'

It was worry that now creased Morag's brow. 'Och, dear, I don't want you to feel unwelcome. I shouldn't have said anything. I just felt it would be better coming from me.'

Juliette smiled in what she hoped was a reassuring way. 'No, it's fine, honestly. I'm just tired. I think I'll go for a lie-down.'

'Okay, dear. And I'll get my thinking cap on about rental properties. I bet Kenneth will know somewhere. In the meantime, you can stay here as long as you need. I have a spare room in our living quarters, so you can always stay there. Although I've had a cancellation, so there's no need for you to move out of your room at the moment. It's all thanks to the talk of this wretched storm that's supposedly approaching, So much for summer, eh?'

Juliette smiled. 'Oh, thank you so much. I really do appreciate that.'

She stood from the table and made her way up to her room.

Once safely ensconced inside her four walls, she furiously hit dial on Millie's number. After they had got their greetings out of the way, Juliette launched into a monologue about Reid MacKinnon and his ridiculous attitude.

'Well, it sounds to me like you've dodged a bullet. Who wants someone like that breathing down their neck?' Millie said once Juliette had finished telling her what she had discovered.

'I know.' She huffed. 'Although, the job sounded lovely. It would've sorted my accommodation for the trip and I really liked the idea of working there. I'm really annoyed that someone can get away with discriminating in that way just because he's had a shitty experience. He doesn't know me, so how can he judge?'

'I know, honey. It's utterly absurd that he should have such stupid reasoning. He's a bloody adult, for goodness sake. But I'm sure something else will come up, sweetie.'

'Well, if it doesn't, I can always move on, I suppose. I could tour the Highlands or something.'

'Exactly. It'll all work out fine. I just know it.' Millie was always so positive. So optimistic. She'd always been the same. She was just the tonic that Juliette needed.

7

The days of her first week seemed to be whizzing by and Juliette had taken a couple to explore the beautiful isle of her family's origins. She drove the winding roads and round every turn was a stunning vista that took her breath away, to the point where she became perturbed at her grandparents' willingness to turn their backs on the place. Although she knew, deep down, they'd had good reason. Employment had been scarce, and this had been the main issue. But these days Skye was thriving with tourism, fishing and crofting. And, regardless of her lack of a tangible, recent connection to the place, it was definitely getting under her skin.

The residents of Glentorrin were beginning to wave at her and shout out their greetings as they went about their daily routines. Certain faces were becoming as familiar to her as she evidently was to them. And, although the contact from her parents, Dexter and Millie was almost daily, now she was experiencing that initial sense of acceptance in the little coastal village.

The weather took a slight turn, although Juliette didn't let this deter her from exploring. She decided that a waterproof coat was needed and, with a borrowed umbrella from Morag, she set off to the outdoor wear shop in pursuit of one.

'Good afternoon. Jules, isn't it?' said the man seated on a stool beside the wooden counter, as she entered and shook off the rain. He was dressed in khaki, multi-pocketed utility trousers and a checked shirt with a band T-shirt underneath. His dark hair was peppered with many strands of grey.

Juliette cringed. 'Oh dear, does that mean my reputation precedes me?'

The man laughed heartily, his eyes crinkling with mirth, and he held up his hands. 'Only the one about your penchant for short-bread, honestly.'

She wagged a finger. 'Ah, you've been talking to Caitlin.' She laughed. The bakery and its owner were now firmly ensconced in her daily routine, seeing as that elusive willpower was yet to be located.

'Guilty. Honestly, no relationship in this place is sacred.' He laughed and placed a theatrical hand at his forehead. 'Gone are the halcyon days when a woman could confide in her baker.'

He was funny and Juliette immediately warmed to him. With a wide smile still in place, she replied, 'Such a terrible, heartbreaking truth.'

The man stepped toward her from his resting spot. 'I'm Archie, by the way. What can I do for you on this *fine* day?' He rolled his eyes as he glanced out through the rain-smeared glass.

'Luckily for you, I'm on the hunt for a waterproof coat.'

'Well, luckily for *you*, you've come to the right place.' He held out his hands and gestured at their surroundings. 'Actually, you've come to the *only* place.'

'Ah, captive audience.' She grinned. 'Right, well, I'm intending to be here for a while, so can you recommend me something I can pack away easily?'

'And get out at a moment's notice? Absolutely. You'll need that here. Apparently, we're in for the tail end of a hurricane that's been causing a ruckus in the US.' That sounded awful but as Archie had said, she certainly seemed to be in the right place.

After twenty minutes, Juliette left the shop with a foldaway coat in a cheery red and a pair of wellington boots complete with a ladybird print. They were the kind of things she wouldn't look twice at back home, but their sense of fun appealed to her, so she thought, why not? Even if she did now have the look of a five-foot-six toddler. And she wasn't at work now so she could afford to wear something a little more *out there*.

From there, she bypassed the bakery, for once, and headed into the café a little way along the road. *Tea for Two* was a pretty-looking establishment with gingham tablecloths and local artwork for sale displayed on the walls. She took a seat at a table by the window and picked up a menu.

'Oh, hello,' came a disinterested, almost annoyed female voice from beside her. 'What do you want?'

Juliette resisted the urge to comment on the charming greeting. After everyone had been so outwardly warm and friendly, it seemed *this* woman was one of the *sour apples* Caitlin had mentioned.

In spite of it all, she gave a warm smile, deciding that the waitress may be having a particularly bad day. 'Hi there, could I have an Earl Grey and a fruit scone please?'

The woman, a tall, slim blonde with a pretty face – or so Juliette imagined it would be when not crumpled as if a bad smell had taken up residence under its nose – simply turned and walked away without further comment.

When the woman brought the pot of tea and scone and placed it before her, Juliette tried again. 'This is a lovely little place you have here.'

The waitress folded her arms defensively across her chest and cocked her hip. 'It is, yes. I manage it for the owner, Reid.'

'Reid MacKinnon? Oh, I didn't realise he owned it.'

'Well, he does.' The reply was unnecessarily terse. 'But *I* run it on a day-to-day basis. You could say I'm the *driving* force behind things.' She gave a sickly-sweet, disingenuous smile and turned to leave once again.

When the word *driving* was mentioned with such emphasis, a shiver traversed Juliette's spine and she was assaulted by the memory of her experience earlier that week. She eyed the woman with unfounded suspicion. Could this have been the person who had sped past her on the road, almost catapulting her into the hedgerow?

No, that's ridiculous, you're being so paranoid! She had no reason to do such a thing! Did she?

Juliette watched the woman and couldn't help but wonder; after all, she was very offhand. Perhaps she was somehow marking her territory where Mr MacKinnon was concerned? Well, she needn't bother. Reid MacKinnon was firmly on her shit list and she would be avoiding him at all costs.

Despite the frosty welcome, Juliette sat there, leisurely eating her scone – which she presumed was baked by Caitlin anyway – and enjoyed the fact that the rain outside was now bouncing inches up off the pavement where it landed, and thunder rumbled over-head, and *she* wasn't out there in it.

She glanced around at the beautiful artwork adorning the walls. The scenery, all local views that she recognised from her walks, was incredibly lifelike, and she initially thought the pictures were photographs. She spotted one of the tumble-down croft she had visited and was shocked by how well the artist had captured the place. She was considering taking one home as a gift, either for her parents or perhaps even for herself, so she stood to take a closer look and see if she could identify the artist.

As she stepped away from her table, she caught sight of a bright streak of blue outside, in her peripheral vision. Evin was playing in the rain with Chewie. The wind had whipped up now and the water was crashing up the walls in the small harbour. The smile on his face was one of such delight as the boy jumped in puddles and the soggy dog barked and bounded, shaking his whole body intermittently to try and rid himself of the rain soaking his fur.

She wondered if Evin's dad knew he was playing in this weather without a coat. She grabbed her brolly and dashed round the inlet to speak to him. 'Evin, where's your coat? You must be frozen!' she shouted.

The boy shook his head. 'Nah, I'm fine, honest! Chewie loves the rain. Won't go near the sea and hates baths too, so this is a good way of getting him clean!'

Juliette laughed. 'You're just missing some shampoo then.'

The boy tapped his hand against his forehead and rolled his eyes. 'Och, I knew there was something.' Chewie was clearly getting fed up with waiting, he barked in a high-pitched voice as if to say *'Come on Evin! Play with me!'*

'Just be careful, okay? I bet your dad doesn't know you're out without a jacket, does he?'

He didn't answer and anyway, she knew it was none of her business. She guessed Reid MacKinnon wouldn't thank her for interfering, so she left the friends to it and headed back into the warmth of the café.

She sat and poured another cup of tea from the pot on her table and turned her attention once again to the stunning artwork on the walls.

Suddenly the café door burst open, almost crashing into the window. Startled, Juliette looked up to see Evin standing before her.

He was more than rain-soaked now and had a wide-eyed, panicked stare and a red claw mark on his cheek.

'Help me! *Please* help me! He'll drown. He's so scared and I can't get him out! I tried, but I had to get out of there,' Evin screamed at her, eyes wide and skin as pale as parchment, apart from several bloody red scratches to his face. He was shaking violently and was drenched, his dark hair plastered to his scalp and his lips almost blue. 'Jules! *Please*! He's in the water!' he yelled again, pointing towards the inlet and she sprang into action.

Without grabbing her coat, she ran for the inlet where she could see the old wooden fencing had given way. Evin was close behind her. The rain was hammering down even harder now, and the sky had darkened significantly.

She grabbed the boy's arms. 'What happened, Evin?'

'We were playing in the puddles and I... I must have had my back to the barrier. Ch-Chewie jumped up at me and I fell backwards, the barrier broke, and I fell in the water. Next thing I knew, Chewie had jumped in after me. Please help him. He's getting tired. I'm so scared. I tried, I really tried, but I couldn't get him out. He was panicking and he scratched my face. I ran to you because you were closest. Please!' he sobbed.

'Okay, run to Archie's shop, tell him to ring your dad. Then go and get Kenneth, okay? Go!' She let go of his arms, but he didn't move.

'But he'll drown. I'll have to jump back in.' He turned to face the water and lurched forward as a crack of thunder sounded overhead and the sky lit up like midday. Juliette grabbed him once more. 'No! Don't you dare! I'm going in, but *please* go and get Archie and Kenneth, okay?' she shouted.

Thankfully, the boy nodded and ran in the direction of the shops.

As the rain pounded on her back, Juliette leaned forward

nervously. She spotted the tan-coloured, shaggy head of Chewie disappearing and reappearing in the waves, pain-filled howls bursting forth in between each ascent and subsequent descent. Without further thought, she jumped into the ice-cold water, grappling for the dog and fighting against the increasing power of the tide as it rushed and crashed into the wall. The wind had picked up and the dog's panic was increasing too, his paws desperately clawing and clambering for purchase but finding none.

The cold from the water seeped into Juliette's bones and her heart raced as she began to wonder what on earth she'd been thinking. But knowing she couldn't let the poor dog die, she managed to grab his collar and yank the flailing creature towards her. 'It's okay, boy, shhh, it's okay, Chewie. I've got you, I've got you,' she whispered into the dog's ear as he gave little high-pitched yelps. His tongue lapped gratefully at her wet face as he tried to climb into her arms and simultaneously keep his head above the water. It became evident where Evin's scratches had come from as the dog clawed at her and she felt the grazes on her skin through her wet clothing. She silently prayed that Archie or Kenneth would arrive soon. She was rapidly losing strength and the glacial water was taking the breath from her lungs. Her arms ached as she trod water to keep herself and the terrified dog afloat.

Chewie seemed to be weakening now, and it felt like she had been in the water so much longer than a mere matter of minutes. With one arm round the ailing dog, Juliette scooped at the water with her other, attempting to draw herself and the soaked animal towards the ladder, beside which a boat was usually moored; she was grateful for its absence today. The weight of her clothes was slowly dragging her downwards and the effort from staying afloat was sapping the energy from her muscles, but with dogged determination, she continued her strokes against the freezing deluge. *Keep going, Jules, you can do this, keep going.*

She had to get to the steps. She just *had* to.

'Hang on, Jules! We'll get you out!' Archie shouted from above. 'Reid was on his way to pick Evin up when I rang, so he'll be here any time. Hold on! I'm coming in!'

Although she was relieved, she feared that it may be too late for the poor dog; he'd exhausted himself. The last thing she wanted was to let Evin down, but the cold was too much. Her arms and legs were almost numb now and a wave of exhaustion washed over her as she struggled to keep hold of the dog.

A huge splash occurred beside her and, seconds later, Archie grabbed her. 'You're okay now. I'm here,' he told her, and she nodded, but all she could think about was Evin's face when he saw poor Chewie.

'Oh my God! What's going on?' yelled a worried male voice from above. She squinted through the saltwater and could just make out Reid MacKinnon dragging the coat from his body and launching himself into the water. 'Are you okay?' he gasped as he grabbed for Juliette and the dog.

She nodded, relieved and grateful for his help as he made pulling Chewie to the ladder a much easier task.

Archie made a grab for Chewie. 'You get Jules, I've got the dog,' he shouted over the noise of more thunder.

The dog was limp, and she could hear Evin screaming from above.

Juliette closed her eyes. *He's gone... The poor boy has lost his best friend... I couldn't save him...* She could hear sobbing but wasn't sure who was making the agonising noise. Her chest burned and her breathing was coming in gasps and she realised the sobbing was coming from her.

'Hey, it's okay... it's okay... I've got you,' a voice reassured her. Other voices joined in and she felt herself being pulled skyward as if being sucked up by a tornado.

Feeling terra firma beneath her, Juliette was enveloped in a warm blanket, her arms rubbed up and down harshly by someone. 'Oh, my word, Jules. Oh, my word, dearie.' Morag's voice shook with alarm.

Other concerned voices, some of which she recognised, asked myriad questions from all angles: Was she okay? Had someone called an ambulance? Could she breathe okay? By this time, however, her eyes had drifted closed as the shock of what had just occurred began to set in.

'Thank you! Thank you so much, you saved him, you saved Chewie,' Evin sobbed as his small arms clung to her.

The poor lad doesn't know the truth, she thought as she felt rainwater trickling down her cheeks. Perhaps it was tears...

She had no energy to reciprocate the hug and only managed a small pat to his arm that she hoped conveyed what she couldn't say – that she was so very, very sorry.

Her heart rate was still elevated, and her limbs were numb. Her body juddered and her teeth clattered against each other; her natural, involuntary responses fighting to protect her from the cold by raising her low temperature.

'I'll take her home, get her warmed up. If someone can call Doc MacT and send him to mine, I'd appreciate it.' Juliette thought this voice sounded familiar, but she felt herself losing consciousness as she was scooped up, her body leaving the floor.

She absently reached for her locket, fearing it was lost to the deluge. But finding it was still round her neck, relief washed over her, and she let go, giving in to the darkness that was intent on sucking her under.

8

Juliette's eyes fluttered open onto unfamiliar surroundings and, as she turned her head, she was greeted by the worried, red-rimmed eyes of a dark-haired boy.

'Dad! She's awake!' he yelled, which caused a pounding to thump at her skull, and she winced. Evin cringed. 'Whoops, I'm sorry,' he whispered. 'How are you feeling?'

Juliette cleared her throat and blinked a few times, assessing her thoughts about the question in hand. She could move her limbs, she could see, her heart no longer felt like it was trying to exit through her chest. So, all in all, she was okay. 'Erm... I think I'm fine now. Where am I?'

'Oh, it's fine, don't worry. You're in our spare room. Dad thought it would be best. He didn't want you to be on your own. Doctor MacT has been and said you needed to rest. That you'd been through a horrible experience and that your body had just shut down for a wee while to repair itself.'

'What time is it?' she asked because the room was illuminated by lamplight and the curtains were closed.

'It's around nine o'clock, I think. You've been asleep for quite a few hours.'

Confusion niggled at Juliette's mind until recent events came flooding back to assault her memory, and she shivered. She grasped at her neck but, thankfully, found her locket was where it should be. She opened it, desperate to make sure the photo was still intact. By some miracle, it was. Her thoughts immediately returned to the poor terrified dog and how he had apparently lost his battle *just* as he was rescued.

'I'm so sorry, Evin... about Chewie...' Her chin trembled and she couldn't finish the sentence, dreading the response. Guilt niggled at her, not only for being unable to save the poor creature, but her for her initial reaction to the dog. He wasn't a bad animal, just lively. She should've given him more of a chance. But the opportunity was gone now. She tried to sit up, but the movement sent the room into a spin, so she gave up.

A look of confusion crumpled Evin's brow. 'Sorry? But why? He's grand. He's loving all the cuddles and being wrapped in a blanket.' He grinned briefly. 'I... I can't say thank you enough,' the boy said with a trembling chin. 'I was so useless. I tried to get him out, but I wasn't strong enough. But *you* were like a superhero. Even though you don't like dogs, you jumped in to save him. He's my best friend in the whole world and I don't know what I would've done if...' He closed his eyes and tears escaped, cascading down his flushed cheeks.

Relief flooded Juliette and she reached out, took his hand and said softly, 'Hey, it's fine. He's okay now. He clearly adores you.'

'I'm teaching him all sorts of tricks. He's really clever but a bit daft at the same time. He didn't mean to knock me into the water. He was just playing. Dad was so angry. He was on his way to the village to tell me off for being out in the rain when he saw all the commotion. It was awful. I was so scared. I've never known the waves there to be so high. If you hadn't jumped in...'

Juliette reached out and squeezed his arm. 'Try to put it out of your mind now. Get back to teaching him those tricks, eh?'

'Thank you. Thank you so much.' He launched himself at her and sobbed into her shoulder.

She stroked his hair and tried her best to soothe him.

'Hey, Evin, you're going to suffocate our guest,' a gruff voice said from over by the doorway.

As Evin got up, he revealed the owner of the voice. 'Sorry, Dad. I was just saying thank you.' He sniffed.

Reid MacKinnon stepped forward, a steaming mug in his hands and shaggy strands of auburn hair falling towards his eyes, which were shielded by his glasses. He had a look of Ryan Reynolds when he wasn't scowling. 'It's okay, son. Now go and cuddle that dog of yours. He's whining down there because I won't let him come up to bother Juliette.' He turned his attention to her. 'I brought you a cup of tea. I wasn't sure how you took it, but I figured all the drama meant you deserved a sweet one.' He smiled sheepishly and placed the mug on the bedside table. Evin hugged her again and left the room. Reid took his place on the edge of the bed. 'How are you feeling?' His manner was completely different to their first encounter and she realised he had a very handsome smile and kind eyes.

She inhaled deeply and replied, 'I think I'm okay.' She suddenly realised her clothes were dry and quickly glanced under the duvet to find herself dressed in things she'd never seen before.

Reid cringed. 'Oh... erm... I hope it's okay, but Caitlin from the bakery got you out of the wet clothes when you were out cold. She brought you some of her things to borrow.' He held up his hands, his eyes suddenly wide. 'I... I left the room when she changed you.'

Relief flooded her. 'Thank you. And thank you for looking after me.'

He shook his head, his cheeks colouring with a flush of pink. 'It's the least I could do. What you did out there... I honestly think you saved my boy's life.' Juliette opened her mouth to argue, but he held up his hand. 'I mean it. If you hadn't jumped in to save Chewie, Evin would've gone in after him again, I just know it. But he's not a strong swimmer, so I'm pretty sure I would've lost him.' His voice broke and he closed his eyes briefly. 'And I can't lose him, too.' He opened his eyes and shook his head. 'And you, a stranger, and, by all accounts, *not* a dog person, you just jumped into that icy water, in the storm without a thought for yourself. You could've died,' he whispered.

She shrugged. 'But I didn't. And I'd do it again if it was necessary.'

Reid cleared his throat and surreptitiously swiped moisture from his eyes before laughing lightly and shaking his head again. 'Bloody hell. Are you some kind of superwoman?'

Juliette widened her eyes. 'Definitely *not*. And, in spite of my protestations, I think I could be quite fond of that slobbering pooch, given half a chance.'

'Well, I can safely say that he's your number one fan. When we brought you back here, we laid you on the sofa and that dog would *not* leave your side. He watched the doctor like a hawk and then he kept licking you and whining as if he was trying to wake you up to thank you. The dog, I mean, not Doctor MacT.' He chuckled. 'Honestly, it was like something off a TV movie, *Lassie* or something.'

Juliette laughed as tears prickled at her eyes, the emotion of what had happened finally taking a hold. 'Bless him. That's really sweet.'

'Evin told me about the first time he met you and how Chewie decided you and he were going to be best friends. I couldn't believe it when I realised it was *you* in the water saving his life. Especially after... Look, I owe you so many apologies, I don't even know where to start.'

Juliette managed to sit upright. 'Oh no, it's fine, honestly.' After what he'd just been through with his son, she felt her anger over the museum paled into insignificance.

Reid closed his eyes and paused a moment with his lips between his teeth. 'No,' he said eventually. 'No, it's really not fine. I've been having a rough time lately and I took it out on you. I hate that I became *that* kind of person. I *hate* that kind of person.'

Juliette reached for her tea, desperate to break the intense eye contact that was taking place between them. 'Well, I suppose that explains your attitude over me applying for the museum job.' She sipped the tea and tried her best not to wince at the sweetness as she felt her teeth zinging.

His eyes widened and the colour drained from his face. 'Oh God. It's you. You're the woman from the Cotswolds, aren't you?'

She cringed as guilt niggled at her. The poor man was already feeling bad. 'Erm... yes.'

He rubbed his hands over his face. 'Could I look any more like a total prat? I'm so sorry. I hadn't realised it—'

Juliette waved a dismissive hand, unwilling and too exhausted to add to his feelings of guilt. 'Oh no, please don't worry. I kind of understand your trepidation. And I'm guessing you must have someone lined up so...'

'Sadly, no.' He held up his hands as if to defend himself. 'Again, I had no idea it was you. I wondered what Morag meant when she said I had judged you too harshly and that your mum came from here. I had no idea of the relevance. She was very cross with me and kept saying I should've given you a chance. And I think maybe she was right.'

She shook her head and sipped more of the treacle-sweet drink.

'Oh, no, no, it's fine. You don't owe me anything.' The last thing she wanted was to be given a job out of guilt.

'It's not a matter of payback, Juliette. No, I have to admit when I'm wrong, or what kind of example would I be setting for Evin? After all, he's nicknamed you *Sparkly Jewels*.' He grinned and his cheeks flushed again. 'He's quite taken with you. After what you did for him and Chewie, you're his new hero. I've been thoroughly ousted from my pedestal.'

She scanned his features for any kind of resentment but thankfully found none. 'He's a lovely boy. You must be very proud of him.'

'Oh, I am. He's my world.' Adoration flashed across his face. 'But, anyway, the museum. What do you think? Are you still up for it?'

Juliette scrunched her brow and pondered the prospect of things falling into place. Although Morag had said she could stay as long as she needed to, she didn't want to take advantage, and it all felt a little too good to be true, and things that felt that way usually were – in her experience – with the exception of Laurie, obviously.

Her lack of comment must have concerned Reid because he spoke again. 'Look, you've had a bit of a traumatic day. And I've been an arse about the whole thing, so please don't think you have to make a decision right now. But maybe think on it for a few days. See what your heart tells you after you've had some time. But now that I understand what Morag was trying to tell me, and believe me, it's not like her to be so indirect, I feel very foolish for not enquiring further about your interest. I'd had so many applicants that were clearly trying to pull a fast one, I think I became blind to what a good candidate was. I'm very sorry for that, Juliette. Very sorry indeed.' There was genuine sincerity shining in his emerald green eyes. 'And I totally understand if you tell me to sod off.'

At his words, Juliette almost spat out her latest mouthful of tea and she giggled at his turn of phrase. 'Believe me, I would *never* say that.'

He smiled again and Juliette put the flutter in her stomach down to hunger, or shock, or whatever else could cause such a bizarre reaction.

'Can I get you anything to eat? You must be starving.'

She shook her head. 'Oh no, I'm fine. My stomach's a bit churny to be honest. Must be a delayed reaction.'

'Aye, maybe so. Anyway, you're very much welcome to stay here this evening, but, alternatively, I can walk you down to Morag's, if you prefer. It's just along the lane.'

'I think I'll be okay to go back to Morag's. I don't want to impose any longer than necessary. And you've got Evin to think of.'

'Honestly, it's no imposition. And Evin will be fine for a few moments with Chewie here to protect him. He's a very sensible boy. And that dog may appear to be a big softy but today has revealed a protective streak. Anyway, I understand that you want your own space. I've put your clothes through a wash and they're in the laundry room to dry off so I can pop them round tomorrow.'

Reid stood back from the bed. 'Right, well, I'll leave you to get sorted. Your coat is on the chair and Caitlin left you a pair of wellingtons and a rain mac. Apparently, you left it beside your table at the café along with your handbag. You were barefoot in the water so you should probably put those on as I'm afraid if you were wearing shoes when you jumped in, they're long gone now.'

Oh great, my favourite pair of flats. 'Thank you, Reid.'

He raised his hand in a wave and left the room.

* * *

The church clock struck eleven as Reid walked Juliette down the dark lane back to Thistle House, their way lit only by the torch on his phone and the glow of the moon. The rain had stopped, and the stars overhead were a spectacle; tiny dots of light scattered across the navy-blue canopy of the sky. Every so often, playful bats swooped down in front of them, their wings caught by the silvery moonlight.

Juliette sighed. 'Glentorrin is such a lovely place. You're very lucky to call it home,' she told Reid as they walked.

'Aye, I've been here all my life and wouldn't leave for the world. It's where I belong; even now my folks are no longer here.' He shrugged.

'I'm sorry to hear that.' Juliette wasn't sure how she'd cope without her own parents.

'My dad's still alive, but he's in a care home just across the bridge now. He insisted after Mum passed away. Didn't want to be a burden.'

'Do you have any siblings?'

'I have my brother.' The bitter tone of his voice didn't go unnoticed. 'He's a big-shot TV star over on the mainland now. We don't see him too often.'

'A TV star? Wow. What's he been in?'

He rolled his eyes. 'Oh, it's all local television, but you'd think he was a movie star with the way he's revered when he visits home.'

'And you're the businessman of the family.'

Reid laughed and stopped for a moment. 'Hardly. I own a café. Doesn't really mark me out as the next Richard Branson. And it's mine by default, really. It was my mum's originally, and I considered selling up after she died, but it was Kate's idea to keep it going. She's my ex and Evin's mother,' he added for clarification, although with a hint of disdain. 'I didn't even want the bloody thing. Too many memories. But then... well... things happened and now I'm kind of stuck with it. Thankfully, I don't have to be there much. Leanna's the boss.'

'Oh yes, *Leanna*.'

He grinned knowingly. 'She's a funny lass, but I rely on her. Known her since my schooldays.'

'So, are you a gentleman of leisure?' she asked, determined not to talk about how *wonderful* the surly blonde was.

'I wish. Far from it. I'm an artist. I work from a wee studio at the back of my house most days.'

'Oh! Are those your pieces in the café?'

He lowered his gaze to the ground. 'They are, yes.'

His current manner was the antithesis of the man she had initially conversed with on the phone and this surprised her. 'I was admiring them earlier today. I was thinking of taking one home as a gift for my mum and dad.'

'Oh, you don't need to do that. It's just nice to know you like them. Thank you.' His response was one of humility and it struck her that he didn't realise quite how talented he was.

They reached the front of Thistle House and stopped. 'Your work is beautiful, Reid,' she told him with a smile.

If the light wasn't so dim, she thought she may have seen him blushing. 'That's very kind of you.' He locked his gaze on her for a moment but quickly frowned and looked away. 'Well, thank you for today. I know I keep saying it, but—'

'It's fine, honestly. No further thanks needed.' She held out her hand, but he leaned forward to kiss her cheek, so she leaned to reciprocate just as he pulled back and held out his hand. They both laughed awkwardly and chose to do neither.

'Goodnight, Juliette,' he said softly.

He had definitely softened from their first encounter and she had begun to believe he might be a nice guy after all. 'Goodnight, Reid. And please, call me Jules, all my friends do.'

With a wide smile, he nodded his agreement and walked towards his home.

Feeling drained, Juliette tiptoed into the house and managed to sneak up to her room without alerting Morag. She felt a twinge of guilt at doing so but desperately wanted to speak to her mum and go to sleep.

Once inside and changed out of Caitlin's clothes, she picked up her phone, replied to texts from Dexter and Millie asking how things were going – she would fill them in tomorrow – and, even though it was ridiculously late and she risked causing panic by calling, she dialled her parents' number.

'Hi, Dad. Boy, have I had a strange day...'

9

At breakfast the following morning, Morag couldn't do enough for Juliette. She fussed around her like she was royalty. Nothing was too much trouble. And she must have asked if she was okay a dozen times at least. Thankfully, her headache was gone, and her appetite had returned, which was just as well, seeing as Morag appeared to be trying to fatten her up.

'You've not been to *The Coxswain* yet, have you? The pub just along the lane?' Morag asked as she cleared away the plates.

'Not yet, no. But I thought I might go this evening, for a change.'

Morag's eyes lit up. 'Aye, you should definitely do that. You should see if Caitlin's busy. It'd be nice for her to have a friend her own age. She spends a lot of time with her wee girl, Grace, eleven years old. But it would be nice for her to have some more adult company.'

Juliette stifled a smile. Morag sounded like a dear old grandma looking out for her granddaughter. 'Thanks, yes, I might just do that.'

She waved her hand and shook her head. 'Och, listen to me; a right old fusspot. It's just that she's got no family here any more, so I suppose I see myself as a mother figure.'

'That's very kind of you,' Juliette reassured her.

'What time might you think of going?' the older lady asked with somewhat forced nonchalance.

Juliette shrugged. 'Oh, I don't know. Seven maybe. I think I'm going to have a walk across the Skye bridge today, seeing as the storm has passed over. I bet the views from up there are lovely.'

'They are indeed. Well, I must get on. I'm covering the shop today. Kenneth is off golfing on the mainland with Donny, Leanna's husband.'

Juliette decided to refrain from commenting further in case her feelings for the frosty Leanna leaked out by accident. 'Right, well, I'm going to go and get ready.'

'You go and have a lovely day,' Morag instructed in a singsong voice.

* * *

The sun seemed to hover, suspended in an almost cloudless sky, as Juliette made her way towards the arched structure that spanned the mouth of Loch Alsh. From the centre, she could see the houses and businesses nestled along the shore at Kyleakin and, on the other side of the bridge, a little white lighthouse sat below at the edge of a rocky outcrop – no doubt a necessary structure considering the number of chunks of boulder jutting out from the silvery blue sea, and her own experience of how the weather was wont to change at the drop of a hat.

Juliette inhaled the fresh, salty air as the breeze whipped her hair about her face, causing it to dance a merry jig before her eyes. She couldn't help smiling as she gazed out to the mountainous horizon, watching the seagulls floating on the therms high above her head.

As she stood there, she mulled over the proposition put to her by Reid. Her only concern was that he had offered out of duty for what she had done, although he had assured her that wasn't the case. Running the museum would certainly give her a focus *and* a purpose for being here, which is what she'd hoped for all along after Dexter had suggested a working holiday all those weeks ago. Simply put, even though the place was wonderful, she feared that she may have too much time to think if she didn't have *some* kind of occupation to fill her mind; too much time hadn't done her any favours in the past. Plus, it may be a way to satisfy her curiosity about her mother's upbringing or at least the place in which she grew up. Two birds, one stone. She made the decision, right then and there, to accept the role and a flip of excitement rolled around her stomach. Finally, she would get to discover the delights that lay within the old Lifeboat House Museum.

As she strolled back towards the village, she caught sight of Caitlin walking a dog that was the complete opposite of Chewie: small, dainty and, most importantly, *dry*.

People really seem to like their dogs in this place, she pondered.

'Oh, hi! This is a serendipitous meeting,' Caitlin said with a warm smile.

'Really? How come?'

'I was going to pop into Morag's while I'm out walking Cleo. I thought you might like to come to the pub with me for dinner tonight. If you're not busy, of course.'

Juliette was touched. 'Oh, how lovely of you. That would be great. I was thinking of going and had actually thought about inviting you.'

'Ah, now that's what you call serendipity indeed! Shall I meet you outside the pub at seven?'

'Perfect. I'll see you there. So, this is Cleo, eh?' she asked, deciding to make more of an effort seeing as the folk in the village were *definitely* dog people.

Caitlin crouched and scratched the ball of fluff behind her ears. 'It sure is. She's a Yorkie Poo. Aren't you, Cweo? Yesh, you are, yesh, you are,' she said as she stroked the dog, who had begun to frantically wag her tail at her silly voice, causing her whole body to wiggle.

'She's cute, and a lot more manageable, size-wise, than Chewie.' Juliette laughed.

Caitlin stood but kept her eyes on the dog for a moment. 'Oh, that's for sure. She's a cuddly wee creature. I love her to bits. But she's Grace's dog really. Although, guess who gets to walk her most of the time?'

Juliette laughed. 'Grace is such a beautiful name.'

'Aye, love of my life that one. I'll have to introduce you.'

'What's she going to be up to tonight?'

'She's at a sleepover, and when the cat's away... Ah, the joys of summer.' She gave an excited grin. 'So, what've you been up to?'

'I've been for a lovely walk up to the bridge and now I'm heading to the shop to grab a few magazines. I think I'm going to chill out a bit this afternoon.'

Caitlin's smile was replaced by a look of concern. 'I think you deserve it. How are you doing now?'

Juliette waved a dismissive hand, unwilling to dwell on yesterday's events for fear of reliving the whole terrifying experience. 'Oh, I'm fine. Good as new. Thank you for your help, by the way. I'll have your clothes washed and bring them over.'

'No rush.' Caitlin cringed and her cheeks flushed pink. 'I hope you didn't mind me changing you. I just thought you needed to be out of the wet clothes. You were ice cold and shivering and you didn't deserve to catch pneumonia after what you'd gone through.

We haven't had such awful weather in ages. The waves in the inlet were terrible.' She shuddered as if the memory conjured up a chill.

'Of course I didn't mind. I really appreciated that you didn't leave the job of undressing me to poor Reid.' She blushed at the thought of him seeing her naked.

'I'm not sure he could've handled it.' Caitlin leaned forward conspiratorially. 'He's actually quite shy underneath the grumpy temperament, despite what he'd have you think,' she whispered.

Shy wasn't a word Juliette would've associated with Reid MacKinnon. But it was interesting to hear someone else's opinion of him.

Caitlin glanced over at the inlet. 'I honestly brushed off the storm as a load of nonsense until it struck. Never seen weather like it here, not in summer. Give me the light nights, midges and showers we normally get at this time of year, any time.'

'Yes, it was certainly a humdinger. Well, I should go. Those mags aren't going to read themselves. See you at seven?'

'See you then.' Caitlin raised her hand in a wave and set off along the lane.

* * *

Juliette arrived a little early and stood outside The Coxswain waiting for Caitlin. She glanced up at the swinging sign. There was a painting of what she presumed was the old lifeboat and in the foreground stood a serious-looking, bearded man wearing a sou'wester and what looked like a life vest made from cork.

Across from the pub was a church, and she resolved to visit and look at the gravestones for any connection to the McLeods, and beside that a huge field she hadn't really taken much notice of until now. A brightly coloured banner was attached to the fence that read 'Glentorrin Games' and an impending date which wasn't too far in the future. Butterflies took flight in Juliette's stomach at the prospect of witnessing her first Highland games. How exciting.

Beyond the field was a small range of purple-hued mountains, highlighted by the burnt sienna touches of the early-evening sun. It really was the most stunning place.

Juliette smiled to herself as she glanced back down the main road towards the museum. The row of houses that skirted the edge of the little inlet each had their own character, an expression of its occupants, no doubt. And each was picture-postcard perfect. Mistford was a pretty village and Juliette had always been won over by its charms, but Glentorrin possessed something of the ethereal about it. Something almost mystical that she couldn't quite put her finger on. It had only been a short amount of time, but the place had already left its mark on her heart, and Juliette hoped Reid might be at the pub tonight so she could tell him she was happy to accept the job.

Juliette spotted Caitlin walking towards her. She looked incredibly pretty in cropped blue jeans and a vivid green top that contrasted beautifully with her red hair, and a pair of gorgeous beaded sandals graced her feet. Juliette glanced down at her own skirt and top and suddenly felt rather dowdy in comparison.

Caitlin greeted Juliette with a friendly hug. 'I don't know about you, but I'm starving. I forgot to break for lunch,' Caitlin told her.

'How can you forget lunch when you're surrounded by food all day?' Juliette laughed, bewildered at the thought.

'I know, crazy, eh? Anyway, you look fab. I love that skirt.'

Her words gave Juliette a much-needed boost. 'Thank you, I was just about to go back and change.'

Caitlin gasped. 'Don't you dare! You look stunning. Anyway, you'll love this place.' She gestured to the building behind them. 'The Coxswain is a great place to see live music too. Mostly Scottish, so you get fiddlers, accordionists, and folk bands, but the craic is great. They do a mean haggis, neeps and tatties too. It's run by Joren and his wife, Stella. They're a lovely couple. I'll introduce you.'

Juliette followed as Caitlin pushed through the door. The moment they stepped inside, the place erupted with applause, and Juliette looked around for the reason behind the spontaneous outburst. When she saw that Caitlin *too* was applauding and that it was directed at *her*, a hot flush raced from her chest to her cheeks and she self-consciously placed a hand on either side of her face. She fought a nervous giggle and wondered if Skye people regularly applauded new people to the village.

A tall, bearded man behind the bar shouted, 'Three cheers for Jules Fairhurst!' and the rest of the crowd followed with the requested three *hip-hip-hoorays*.

'What on earth—?' But before she could obtain answers, the whole place sang out a rendition of 'For She's a Jolly Good Fellow!'

Reid appeared before her with a huge bouquet of flowers and it dawned on her, rather late admittedly, that this was all because she had jumped into the water after Chewie. Wow, these people really did love their dogs. Anyone would think she'd donated an organ or something! He leaned forward and said directly into her ear, 'I heard that Morag had convinced you to come tonight, so I wanted to bring you these to say thank you, again. Oh, and Evin made you a card from him and Chewie.' He handed over the bouquet and an envelope addressed to *Sparkly Jules* and tears prickled at her eyes.

The whole situation was a little overwhelming. The kindness of the strangers around her tugged on her heartstrings.

Reid paused as if he had more to say, but a flash of conflict seemed to pass over his face. He awkwardly leaned forward and placed a quick but gentle kiss on her cheek and her stomach fluttered as she inhaled the scent of his aftershave. The heat in her cheeks stayed in place a little longer than she would've liked.

When Reid pulled away, she couldn't quite look him in the eyes.

It was just as well as he seemed equally uncomfortable and dashed away, making an excuse about calling Evin to make sure he was behaving for his sitter at home.

Once the excitement had died down, Caitlin led her to a table, where she placed her flowers, and they made their way to the bar. As they walked, Juliette had her hand shaken by people she'd never met, who told her what a brave woman she was and how thankful they were that she had jumped in to save Chewie and, by extension, Evin.

Once they finally reached the bar, Caitlin leaned across it towards the bearded man. 'Evening, Joren. We'll have a bottle of Sauvignon Blanc and two glasses, please. Oh, and this is, of course, the woman of the moment, Jules.' She gestured towards Juliette, who felt her face warming once again, and not only because of the number of bodies in the place.

The huge frame of a man leaned over the bar. 'Welcome, Sparkly Jules the superhero. Good to meet you.' He had a very intriguing accent and held out his shovel-sized hand, so Juliette shook it. He reminded her of one of the actors from *Game of Thrones* and was quite handsome, in an older man kind of way. 'Stella's in the back cooking, but I'll get her to come and say hello. Are you staying for the music? We have an old friend of Stella's coming to play for us.'

Juliette beamed. 'Yes, we're eating and staying for the music. I can't wait.'

'Excellent. We have a local duo on first playing some Scottish folk tunes and then Greg. He's a guitarist and singer. If you like contemporary music, you'll love him.' He leaned closer. 'All the ladies love him. I can't see it myself. Scruffy bearded oaf.' He winked and then grinned as he scrubbed his fingers over his own beard, and Juliette couldn't help but warm to him.

He passed the open bottle of wine and two glasses over to them. 'On the house for our new friend,' he informed her.

Caitlin jumped up onto the bar and planted a kiss on his cheek. 'Joren, you're a bloody top bloke. Do you know that?'

He feigned coyness and shrugged. 'It's been said, once or twice.'

Caitlin led the way back to their table that was just big enough for the two petite women to squeeze round. 'You're in for a treat. Greg is fantastic. Easy on the eyes, too.'

Juliette laughed.

'Hey, there's no harm in looking. He's married anyway and *totally* head over heels in love.' She rolled her eyes. 'Ugh. All the best ones are taken or gay. Anyway, he used to work for Stella at the pub she ran. Really nice guy, too. He plays stuff you'll actually have heard of, like Hozier, Ed Sheeran, George Ezra, never mind all the Scottish stuff.'

It was the folk music Juliette was most excited about. 'You don't like the Scottish stuff?'

Caitlin took a big gulp of wine and swallowed before answering. 'Oh, no, it's good, don't get me wrong, but as kids we're all subjected to social dance, which means we get it shoved down our necks from an early age. *Stripping the Willow* and *The Dashing White Sergeant* and all that. It's fine on a fun night out, though. I might even get you up dancing. They usually clear the space in the middle.'

Juliette glanced around her and wondered how on *earth* such a feat could be achieved when so many people were already crammed into the room.

A smiling, middle-aged woman appeared before them and handed them each a menu. 'So, I take it you're the woman everyone is talking about? I'm Stella, Joren's other half. How are you liking it here so far? Not too dramatic, I hope.'

Another friendly face, Juliette thought with a smile. 'Hi. I wouldn't call myself a hero, but, yes, I'm Jules. Great to meet you. And I'm loving it so far. I feel quite at home with the welcome I've had.'

'Och, nonsense. You're a star around here now. And you're in for a treat tonight. Some fantastic performers. Great craic.'

'Yes, so I hear. An old friend of yours, I understand?'

'Greg? Oh aye, he and I go way back. He used to play at a pub I ran by the bridge at Clachan. Anyway, I'll leave you to browse the menu. Just give Joren a shout when you know what you want.'

Juliette handed the menu straight back. 'No need. I'll have the haggis, if that's okay? Caitlin here tells me it's your speciality.'

'Same for me, Stella, please,' Caitlin agreed.

Their host raised her eyebrows and nodded, smiling. 'Oh, right then. Well, that was easy. Coming right up.' Stella retrieved the menus and marched back to the kitchen.

Juliette sighed in contentment. 'I really could get used to this. I don't think I've ever been anywhere where people have taken to me so easily. It's lovely.'

'Aye, well, don't get too used to it. Leanna and Donny McNair have just walked in. Just know that *whatever* she says, it's bull, so take it with a pinch of salt, okay?'

Juliette crumpled her brow. She was aware that Leanna wasn't exactly a friendly and welcoming person, but was she all that bad? 'What makes you say that?'

'Well, she's rather fond of a certain local artist and café owner. She's absolutely batty about him, to be truthful. I'm talking bunny-boiler level of stalker. Any new woman who appears in the village is automatically seen as competition.' She widened her eyes to accentuate her point. 'If ever you want to know where Reid is or what he's doing, just ask *her*. They've known each other forever and she reckons they're going to end up together someday. Although I'm not sure what her hubby, Donny, would say, if he knew.'

Juliette widened her eyes. 'He doesn't know?'

'Na. Poor Donald, he's *totally* oblivious. Thinks the world revolves around his princess. He's a fair bit older than her and acts like he's lucky she's with him. He's from a long line of crofters and isn't short of cash. Gives her everything she wants, whether it's jewellery or surgery. Not the best basis for a marriage, if you ask me, but it's not my place to break the poor wee guy's heart.'

'Blimey.'

Before Juliette had a chance to respond further, the busty blonde from the café appeared before their table. 'Caitlin, you're in here, *again*,' she snidely pointed out in a pseudo-posh accent.

Caitlin smiled sweetly despite the barbed comment. 'Aye, so it would seem. Just like *you*, I guess?'

Leanna ignored Caitlin's retort and turned her attention to Juliette. 'And you're that *dog* lady, aren't you?' She pursed her lips in a fake attempt at a smile and limply held out her hand. 'I'm Leanna, I think we met before your... *adventure*. You left your kiddies wellington boots in my café. Well, I say kiddies, but they were adult-sized, so I'm guessing they were actually yours. You're the talk of the village now and not even because of the boots.' She forced a humourless laugh. 'Don't worry though, they'll all be bored of you soon and onto something *far* more interesting.' Her words were more than slightly acidic, but nonetheless, always willing to give people the benefit of the doubt – sometimes to her own detriment – Juliette reached out her hand in response. However, Leanna's was swiftly withdrawn as Caitlin spoke.

'I wonder what possible gossip there could be to replace that of such a selfless act as Jules's? Ooh, I know, perhaps someone's teenage crush will get out of hand?' Caitlin tapped her chin before fluttering her eyelids and giving Leanna a knowing look.

Leanna sneered and leaned closer and her own accent made an appearance. 'Whatever, Caitlin. Some women are actually *feminine* enough to attract more than one man. Unlike others I could mention, who don't attract *any*, thanks to spending their time eating their business profits and getting fat.'

Ouch. Now I understand what Caitlin meant about sour apples, Juliette thought silently.

But Caitlin wasn't one to be cowed. 'Be careful, Leanna, won't you? The fire by the bar is lit and we wouldn't want you melting your *perfect feminine* figure, would we?'

Juliette surreptitiously eyed the blonde woman's *assets* and silently agreed that the breasts definitely looked fake. There was clearly not an ounce of love lost between the women. Juliette pulled her lips in between her teeth and widened her eyes, waiting with bated breath to dodge the next insult that flew like a dagger across the room.

Instead, Donny appeared and grabbed his wife's arm. 'Come on, darlin'. I'm parched. Let's get a drink and you can come back and talk to your friends later, eh?'

Once they had walked away, Caitlin whispered to Juliette, 'See, oblivious to *everything,* that man. *Friends,* my arse.'

Moments later, Joren placed two steaming plates of food before them and the accompanying aroma was a heavenly mix of pepper, onions, rich meat and spices. This was to be only the second time Juliette had tried haggis and her mouth watered in readiness. 'Mmm. It smells amazing.'

Caitlin had already tucked in and through a mouth full of food, she mumbled, 'Wait 'til you taste the tatties. Creamiest you've ever tried, I guarantee it.' She tilted her head back, closed her eyes and let out an orgasmic moan.

Juliette didn't need telling twice and scooped up a forkful of mashed potato and haggis, closed her eyes and slipped the food into her mouth. There was an explosion of flavours, from the cream in the potatoes to the spices, and a meaty richness to the haggis.

A similar noise to that of Caitlin's emanated from her throat almost involuntarily. 'Ohmygodthat'samazing,' followed in a rush of slurred vowels and consonants.

'Told you!' Caitlin laughed.

Joren's voice rang out over the hidden sound system. 'Ladies and gentlemen, please give a warm Coxswain welcome to The Toilichte Hens.' His announcement was followed by raucous applause and whistles.

Juliette, still enjoying her foray into Scottish cuisine, glanced over to the fireplace, where two young women – one blonde with a fiddle, and one brunette with an accordion – stood ready to entertain.

As the bouncing rhythm of the music kicked in, Caitlin leaned towards her and said, 'In case you're wondering, their name is Gaelic and it translates roughly to *Happy Hens*.'

'What a fantastic name!' Juliette said as she tapped her foot along to a song the blonde-haired fiddle player had called 'Charlie is My Darlin''. The brunette had a sweet voice as she sang the lyrics and not a single person in the pub was still. As the musicians jigged around, their uplifting notes and glissandos vibrating around the space, they seemed to carry everyone along with them. When they reached the chorus, everyone joined in with a rousing effect and once Juliette had got the hang of it, she couldn't help but do the same.

Once Juliette and Caitlin's meals were finished, a group of men lifted the tables and stacked them against the bare stone walls, and the brunette accordionist announced the first dance was to be 'Strip the Willow'. A cheer travelled the room that was now fit to burst with its audience of smiling, clapping people.

'They're not actually going to try and dance in here, are they?' Juliette asked, surprised.

'They won't just *try*, Jules.' Caitlin grinned as Archie from the outdoor shop and another man approached them. Caitlin took the hand of the older man but told Archie, 'Be gentle with Jules, she's never done this before!'

Archie grinned and leaned to speak to Jules over the volume of the music. 'I'll no' steer you wrong, lass. Just stick wi' me.' And before she could respond, she let out a squeal of surprise as she was spun around in time with the music.

Archie knew all the steps, thankfully, and he shouted instructions into her ear as they hopped, skipped and twirled their way around the bar area that appeared to have tripled in size somehow.

Anyone not joining in the dance was clapping along, and even Leanna was nodding her head in time with the music. By the time the song had ended Juliette was out of breath but laughing.

'That was such fun!' she told both Archie and Caitlin as everyone applauded and whistled. She turned and realised that the applause was once again aimed at her. Her cheeks heated to inferno level, but she performed a little curtsey, much to the delight of the gathering.

10

Juliette stood at the bar and clapped along as Caitlin danced with a variety of men, all of differing abilities but all keen to show off their skills, or lack thereof.

Reid appeared beside her. 'You seem to be enjoying yourself,' he said with a wide smile.

'I am. This evening has been such a laugh. Completely different to my usual nights out.'

He tilted his head. 'Oh? And what do they usually consist of?'

She thought for a moment and realised that perhaps she'd had more nights *in* than out in recent months. Unwilling to share the secret of her less than riveting life, she shrugged. 'The theatre or the cinema with my friend, Millie. Or the local pub. Although it's definitely not as lively as this place.'

'Well, as you can see there's never a dull moment here.' He paused. 'So, did you think on what I said about the museum?'

Juliette took a deep breath and smiled. 'I'll do it. If you still want me for the job.'

He grinned. 'Absolutely. Excellent news. I'm so glad. And I think the villagers will be pleased as punch too that the place is open again. It's not a massive museum, but it pulls people in all the same. It used to be an integral part of the village's tourism, but it's declined in recent years due to the co-op not being… Ugh, sorry, I shouldn't be talking shop. I'm just glad it'll be opening again.'

'Great. Well, I'm happy to be taking it on. When do you want me to start?'

'As soon as possible? How about the day after tomorrow? It'll give me a chance to get the house cleaned and get a float for the cash register. I can give you a bit of training too.'

Crikey, talk about striking while the iron's hot. She realised she'd hesitated a little too long. 'Sounds good to me,' she replied, and then those pesky butterflies were at it again, dancing a jig all over her insides.

As if he'd sensed her trepidation, he said, 'I'll tell you what. Why don't you move into the house the day after tomorrow and get settled in, then I can train you up and you can open next week?'

That seemed a little more realistic and a little less like she was being thrown in at the deep end. 'Perfect.' She held out her hand and Reid shook it. 'So, aren't you dancing this evening?' she asked.

He placed his glass back on the bar and fixed his emerald gaze on her. 'Why does that sound like a challenge, Jules?'

She hadn't meant anything of the sort, but she was rather enjoying this amenable and playful side to the man she'd first thought was out to get her. Secure in the knowledge that it was probably the alcohol playing its part, she went along with it.

She shrugged. 'Not a challenge as *such*. I just know that it made me happy when I danced.'

The fiddler announced the next dance as 'The Dashing White Sergeant' and Reid cocked an eyebrow and held out his hand. 'Come on, then.'

She glanced across at Caitlin, who was watching, open-mouthed.

Juliette raised her eyebrows at her, along with a look that she hoped expressed 'WTF?'

When Caitlin's bemused expression didn't change, Juliette turned back to Reid who had speedily removed his jacket, flung it on the bar and rolled up his sleeves, exposing tanned forearms and long, strong fingers. She threw caution to the wind and took the offered hand.

He led her to the dance space again and she was about to tell him that she hadn't a clue what to do when, as if reading her mind *again*, he informed her with a grin and an overexaggerated version of his accent, 'I'll no' steer you wrong either, lassie.' Then, he winked.

He bloody winked!

The music began and everyone on the dance floor linked hands in a circle. They skipped clockwise for eight steps, then back again for eight more and carried Juliette along with them. After this point, however, the wine had well and truly kicked in, and she descended into a fit of giggles as she tripped over her own feet and those belonging to Reid, *and* the other dancers. She couldn't remember the last time she had laughed so much and the lightness she felt was almost alien to her. But, boy, did it feel good.

She *now* understood what Morag had meant about how handsome Reid was when he smiled. His eyes crinkled at the corners and he laughed with abandon, revealing a set of white but crooked teeth as he tried his best to twirl her in the right direction when she insisted on going in the wrong one. The feel of his strong and commanding hand at the small of her back was unfamiliar and strange, and when he locked his gaze on hers, she shivered at the intensity of his viridescent eyes. She hadn't been pressed so close to a man for what may as well have been eons, and something about the way he held her, along with the sensation of his body next to hers, made guilt niggle at the back of her mind.

She was snapped from the moment when she realised most of the spectators were laughing at her ineptitude, but it was all good-natured... almost. In her periphery, she caught sight of Leanna. Her face was pursed into a mask of pure anger and disgust combined as she glared at her. *Blimey, if looks could kill.* But Juliette soon brushed it off and tried to concentrate on the fancy footwork.

'You're a good mover. Light as a feather too, which helps,' Reid said into her ear as they bounded around the room.

'Thank you, I think?' She laughed.

'It's a compliment. I like a woman I can bend to my will.' She widened her eyes, unsure how to take what he'd said. He scowled and continued, 'God, I swear I meant on the dance floor, that's all. I didn't mean... I didn't mean anything else by it.'

His demeanour had changed, but the dance seemed to go on forever, only in silence now, and at the end, the whole place erupted in applause and laughter. Juliette was patted on the back, hugged and congratulated over and over.

She glanced around to find Reid to thank him, but he was already at the bar. He gulped down the remainder of his drink and raised a hand in a kind of awkward half-salute. His handsome smile was now absent, and a distinct look of melancholy had replaced it. He paused briefly as if he was about to change his mind, but then walked out of the pub and into the night. For a moment, Juliette was saddened by his departure and felt an urge to check on him, but Caitlin grabbed her by the hand again and led her to the bar.

Once the impromptu ceilidh was over, the men replaced the tables and Juliette and Caitlin returned to their seats with a fresh bottle of wine that they were informed Reid had kindly paid for before leaving.

Caitlin placed her drink down and nudged Juliette with her shoulder. 'Get you, Jules. You rare creature. Able to make Grumpy-erse-MacKinnon smile... no... no, *laugh* even.'

'Yes, but he soon left. I must have totally embarrassed him with my inept dancing. I think I resembled one of the Teletubbies stomping around out there.'

Caitlin laughed and raised her glass. 'Ah well, let's be thankful for the minor miracle that occurred here tonight.'

Juliette followed suit. 'I'll drink to that! Oh, and I've decided to take the job at the museum.'

Caitlin squealed with delight. 'Brilliant! Double celebration! And more nights out to look forward to!'

Joren's voice came over the sound system again. 'Ladies and gents, it's my pleasure to announce the main act for tonight, all the way from Clachan Seil, Greg McBradden!'

Another wave of enthusiastic applause swept around the room as an incredibly handsome, dark-haired, bearded man took the space where the Ceilidh musicians had been earlier.

'Evenin' all,' he said to the gathered crowd in his broad Scottish accent. 'How yous all doing?' A cheer of appreciation followed. 'Right, well, I'm going to kick off tonight with a wee bit of The Proclaimers.' Another even louder cheer ensued. 'Aye, I thought yous would be happy with that.' He laughed. 'But hey, do me a favour and don't bloody go singing along, eh? Bloody hate it when folks do that.' He was grinning as he spoke, and Juliette guessed it must have been an inside joke as everyone laughed along with him. 'So, this one's called "I'm on My Way".'

He began to play, and Juliette was impressed with the richness of his voice and his deft guitar playing. But she couldn't help giggling when it came to the chorus and almost every single person began to sing along. Greg rolled his eyes and shook his head, but his grin remained in place as he sang.

As she listened, Juliette's thoughts drifted back to her dance with Reid. Why had he left in such a hurry? Was her dancing so bad? He'd smiled down at her as they'd jigged around the floor and she'd been taken aback by the flutter in her stomach. Of course, she put it down to the nerves of dancing in front of all those people; what other possible reason could there have been?

* * *

As the pub emptied, Caitlin hugged Juliette goodbye and left. Juliette collected her coat, bag and bouquet, and bid goodnight to some of the people Caitlin had introduced her to but, embarrassingly, she couldn't remember the names of.

'He's not interested, you know,' came a voice from beside her.

Juliette swung round to find Leanna staring at her with the look of someone suffering from severe phantosmia.

Juliette frowned and straightened up, alcohol providing the bravado she wouldn't normally feel. 'I'm sorry?'

'You should be. It's quite sad, really, watching you throw yourself at him.'

Juliette rolled her eyes, her patience melting away. 'What the hell are you talking about?'

'You think you can come up here with your posh accent and your prissy clothes, and you can act all helpless and then heroic and you'll grab yourself a rich man. Well, it won't work. Reid isn't on the market.'

Juliette made an unladylike snorting sound. 'You really have no clue about anything, do you? I'm not interested in Reid.' She leaned closer and hissed, 'And neither should you be. You're married, *remember*?'

Leanna widened her eyes and opened her mouth to spit forth more venom, but Donny appeared beside her.

'Come on, princess, I'll have to steal you away from your new friend. I'm taking you home to ravish you.' He gave her a slobbery, drunken kiss on her cheek and Leanna flinched, that look of disgust appearing once again.

* * *

The following morning arrived, and along with it came a fuzzy head and a mouth that tasted like Juliette had been licking the floor of a birdcage. Her mind flashed back to her conversation with Reid and the encounter with Leanna. She thought she'd left adolescent bitchiness at Benson High School. Clearly, she was mistaken. Leanna definitely had it bad for Reid and she pitied her a little. After all, it must be awful to be at the mercy of unrequited love, or was it obsession? The way Leanna behaved was rather too scary and possessive. That, in turn, made her feel bad for Reid.

With Reid now on her mind, Juliette wondered if he was okay and if she should contact him to tell him that she hadn't been offended by what he'd said as they'd danced, just a little taken aback. She regretted not making that clearer when the incident happened. She should've made some jokey comment about him throwing her around; it would have saved a lot of wide-awake hours and whirring thoughts throughout the night.

She groaned and scrambled from the bed with a wobble, showered and dressed before making her way down the stairs to the dining room for breakfast. Her mouth was dry, and she craved fruit juice and coffee, *lots* of coffee. There had been so much dancing and the room had been full and incredibly warm, meaning the wine she had drunk must have sucked all the liquid from her brain. Or, at least, that's how it felt.

Her mobile vibrated and she glanced at the screen. Several text messages were waiting. The first was from Caitlin:

There's a wee package for you with Morag. Great hangover cure. Or at least that's the excuse I use. C x

This was followed by a winking emoji and a green-faced emoji. Juliette laughed but the vibration hurt her head, so her amusement was short-lived.

Still feeling worse for wear, she sat down at her usual table and, sure enough, before her was a paper carrier bag with a note from Morag telling her to go back to bed. Inside the bag was a bottle of the famous orange-coloured Scottish pop that the ads say is made from metal beams, and a few pieces of shortbread dusted with sugar that sparkled like glitter in the morning sunlight. Much to Juliette's surprise, her stomach growled in anticipation, and she took her hoard of treasure back up to her room.

As she munched on the melt-in-the-mouth biscuits and guzzled the orange, fizzing liquid, she read the rest of her text messages. The one from Millie made her grab her phone immediately and hit dial.

'Ah, so you haven't forgotten about me then?'

Juliette rolled her eyes. 'I spoke to you yesterday, Millie! Now spill it! Who is he? Tell me everything!'

There was a giggle across the airwaves. 'I thought that'd get your attention. Are you sitting down?' The question she always asked before imparting something exciting.

'Yes!' Juliette replied eagerly. 'Come on!'

'Okay, keep your hair on! So... I went out drinking with Dex on Friday night. Remember him? He's your brother.'

'Funny. Get on with it.'

'So... we went to the King's Head Hotel in Cirencester, and there was this big wedding do on in one of the function rooms. I went out to get some fresh air because it was *so* bloody warm. You remember what summer feels like, don't you, honey?' She giggled. Juliette smiled and shook her head but chose not to respond verbally, so Millie continued, 'Anyway, I was standing out there and this guy: tall, blonde, a bit like a younger version of Paul Bettany, you know? Just my type. Well, he came out too, and we started chatting. He's a financial director for a company in London and it was his brother's wedding. He lives in London. In *Notting Hill*, no less! Anyway, when it was time for his speech and he had to go, he asked if he could have my number and I gave it to him, never expecting anything to happen. But then he called me yesterday and we went out last night!' Millie's words came out in a rush and the pitch of her voice belied her excitement.

'And how was it? Where did you go? Is he nice?'

Millie gave a dreamy sigh. 'He's sooo nice. Really sweet. Brought me a huge bouquet of flowers to the restaurant. We went to Alessandro's. It was so yummy and so was he.'

Juliette was carried along by her best friend's ebullience. 'You haven't told me his name! How old is he? How tall? What car does he drive?'

'His name is Harry Rose and he was born the year after *Prince Harry*. He's thirty-five, so no real age gap. I would say he's around six four. Really tall. Very handsome, but not in the obvious way. And he drives a very nice but *not* brand-new Range Rover. That surprised me, but he really seems quite grounded. He rents an apartment in Notting Hill and told me all about the area as he grew up there too.'

'You sound smitten,' Juliette said.

Millie paused and gasped. 'I do, don't I? Oh heck.'

'Why "*Oh heck*"?'

'What if he's too good to be true, Jules? Men who *appear* to be usually are.'

Juliette sighed and wished she could hug her friend. 'You're not marrying him, Millie, so stop worrying, just take it slow and see how it goes.'

'Yeah... I suppose you're right. I've just been on my own for so long, I've forgotten what it feels like to be adored and spoiled. And he really does seem to be smitten too.' She sighed. 'Watch him turn out to be a lying, unemployed mummy's boy who rented a car for the day and lives in a caravan.'

Juliette laughed out loud. 'That's it, look on the bright side. You daft woman, just enjoy it. And... you know... maybe check his profile online, just to be sure.'

'Ooh, good plan.'

'I have news too.'

'Really? Don't tell me you're buying a house up there.' The joy in Millie's voice had gone.

'Don't be silly. No, I've taken the job at the museum.'

'Oh my word. I'm so glad. I had a feeling you would when you texted to say he had offered it to you. You'll be brilliant, chick. I know it.'

'Thank you. I'm quite excited.'

'I bet. Right, I'm off to search for some dirt on Harry. Let's hope there isn't any. Love you! Bye!'

'Call me later and let me know what you find out. Bye.'

The line went dead, and Juliette decided to freshen herself up. Afterwards, she dressed and as she allowed her hair to dry naturally, she finished the rest of her impromptu breakfast delivery while reminiscing about her first official date with Laurie.

She'd expected to be taken for dinner, but instead he picked her up from home and took her to a local art gallery, where they spent an hour just admiring the paintings and chatting quietly about what they loved and what they didn't. Juliette had been delighted to find out they had just enough in common to agree on *most* things, but that they differed on others, meaning discussions would be interesting. After the gallery, they had eaten at the most wonderful French restaurant in Cheltenham. At the end of the meal, they had walked along the main precinct that was all decked out in Christmas splendour. He had kissed her under a huge sprig of mistletoe, hung from an archway of holly that led into the Christmas market. Laurie had been oblivious to the people walking by, some of whom whistled, some applauded. It had felt like a romantic movie and she hadn't wanted the moment to end—

She was pulled from her daydream by a knock on the room door. When she opened it, she was shocked to find Reid standing there.

'Hi, I hope it's okay that I popped round. I wondered what you were doing today. I thought I could maybe show you around the museum, if you're not busy. Evin has gone to visit his mum, so I'm at a bit of a loose end.' He shrugged and she noticed the tinge of hope in his voice.

'Oh, okay, yes. That would be lovely. I'll just get my shoes on.'

She grabbed a cardigan and checked her reflection in the mirror. She was pale and her eyes were rimmed with dark shadows. It was a good thing she wasn't trying to impress Reid as her *morning after the night before* look wasn't exactly fetching.

11

Reid opened the door and switched on the lights as they stepped inside the old lifeboat house. Juliette stood for a moment, taking it all in. Case upon case stood before her, the full length of the room, which sloped away to a wall she presumed had once been the doors for the lifeboat to go through. Each cabinet was shored up to make it level and filled with multiple artefacts, all with a historical connection to Glentorrin and the surrounding area. The ceiling was high and arched; it reminded her of an upturned boat, and she wondered if that was intentional.

'It's a gorgeous old building. Dates back to around eighteen twenty-five. The lifeboat was launched from the slipway down there to my left, and it was stored in this main building. It was larger than other lifeboats in the area, so there was a lot of upkeep, I suppose. It was operational as a lifeboat station until the sixties. But then they centralised things up at Portree.' There was a hint of sadness to Reid's voice. 'Oh, I forgot to mention, I've got cleaners coming into Lifeboat Cottage today to give the place a once-over. No one has stayed there in a while, so it'll be quite dusty, I imagine,' he told her as she slowly walked along the first row of display cases, perusing each item with intrigue.

'That's great, thank you. Wow, just look at this stuff.' She shook her head in disbelief as she peered through the glass at a display about weddings in the local church. A delicate lace veil sat on a stand; the pearls and jewels that adorned the edge glistened in the artificial spotlight that shone down on it from above, just bright enough to catch every detail but low enough so as not to cause any damage to the aged fabric. Beneath it sat a faded photograph of a couple on their wedding day; the veil appeared in the photograph, worn proudly by the beautiful bride.

'Oh yes, that piece is of particular interest to one of our locals, Hamish Gair. I don't think you'll have met him yet. He's been on the mainland for a wedding. He donated the veil, bless his heart. It belonged to his wife. He comes in regularly just to look at it. He misses her like crazy, poor wee fella.'

Juliette placed her hand over her heart and imagined the bride and groom on that special day. Empathy for the groom caused her throat to tighten as she imagined his sorrow over his loss. She knew just how that felt. 'Poor man,' she whispered.

'Sorry, I didn't mean to bring you down. I suppose they just had that rare and almost non-existent thing called forever love.'

Juliette turned and faced Reid where he stood, hands in pockets, watching her. 'That sounded a tad cynical, Reid. Don't you believe in such things?'

He snorted derisively. 'Hardly. It all just fades away, doesn't it?'

'Not for me,' she replied instinctively.

'Oh, sorry, I didn't mean to compare our relationships. I'm sure yours is a very happy one. Mine... not so much.'

'Mine *was* very happy, yes. Sadly, I didn't get the opportunity for forever.'

'Ah, you're divorced too, eh?' he asked with an air of sympathy.

'Widowed,' she replied with a small, forced smile.

'Shit! I'm so sorry. Me and my big mouth. God, I'm such an idiot.' He rubbed his hands roughly over his face and then held them almost in prayer over his nose as he exhaled through puffed cheeks.

'It's fine. You weren't to know.'

'I just... I presumed you were just single. You know, with you coming up here alone. I didn't even think... I'm so sorry for your loss.'

'Thank you. It's been a couple of years now.' She shrugged as if that made the pain any less. But, of course, it didn't. It just became more manageable.

'Look, I'll leave you to have a look around. Take as long as you like. I'll pop back later to lock up,' he said with a crumpled brow and then made a hasty retreat.

Why did people do that when they found out she was widowed? It was as if they had nothing else to say to her; as if all other conversation topics were now off limits. These were the exact situations she'd been hoping to avoid on this trip. Maybe she should've just kept her mouth shut? Let him believe she was divorced? She heaved a deep sigh and carried on strolling around the museum.

There were displays giving information about the businesses that had been established in the village since the eighteen hundreds: a candle maker, a saddler, a blacksmith, regular fishing expeditions, all long since gone. There was a display about the church and the reverends who had taken the pastoral role since the same century; photographs showed very dour, serious expressions, each man clutching what she presumed to be copies of the Bible.

After over an hour of reading every snippet of information she encountered, devouring it all with relish, Juliette reached a display about crofting and immediately recognised the little white house she'd visited only days before. Standing in front of the building in the photograph, dated 1952, were three people: a man wearing baggy trousers and a jacket; both of which were decidedly dirty from working the land, a kind of flat cap topped off his ensemble. Beside him stood a woman, presumably his wife, in an A-line dress and white apron and, between them, holding one hand of each adult, stood a little, fair-haired girl with a huge grin on her face. There was no information accompanying the photo, other than the words *Crofter's Family*, but as Juliette leaned closer, she realised the face smiling back at her was oh-so familiar.

'Well, hello there, Mum,' she said as her eyes filled with tears. For some reason, it filled her heart with joy to be in the place where her mother grew up. She immediately took out her phone and snapped a shot of the image to send on later.

One of the biggest displays was almost a memorial to the lives lost in a fishing boat disaster off the coast of the island in the early 1900s. The lifeboat had been instrumental in saving the lives of those who were able to cling on to the wreckage of their boat, but tears stung Juliette's eyes as she read about the men who had perished; the families who had lost fathers, husbands and sons. There was a beautiful sculpture in the case dedicated to the lifeboat men depicting the boat at sea and women standing on the shore. She gasped when she read the inscription: *Created by Reid MacKinnon and donated to the museum in 2009*.

'Wow,' she whispered.

'Oh, yes, I should've warned you there was a self-indulgent section.' The voice made her jump and she spun round. She'd been so engrossed in what she was reading she hadn't heard Reid return.

'Oh gosh, no, not self-indulgent at all. Just beautiful. Are there no end to your talents?' she asked, but as she turned, she realised he was bent looking into the case too and when she faced him, she could feel his breath on her cheek. Her stomach leapt.

He immediately stepped back with wide eyes and held up his

hands. 'Whoops, sorry. I didn't mean to crowd you. I... I don't often look at the sculpture myself. I think I'd forgotten what it looked like.'

'No, no, it's fine,' she replied, smoothing down her hair and trying to hide the fact that her cheeks were almost at the point of spontaneous combustion. 'As I said before, you're very talented.'

He scratched his head, clearly uncomfortable at the compliment. 'So, what do you think? Could you stand to work here for the summer?'

'Absolutely. I can't wait to start. Oh, and I found a photo of my mum and my grandparents. I never really knew Granny and Grandpa and probably wouldn't have recognised them without Mum being there. I couldn't believe it. I was hoping to find something, but I think deep down I didn't *expect* to,' she said as she walked towards the photo to show Reid.

He bent to view the image. 'Oh wow. So that's your mum. Is she still a cutie?' he asked, and then his cheeks flared as bright as hers had moments earlier. 'God, that sounded so creepy.'

Juliette couldn't help letting a laugh escape. He was quite sweet really. His ability to put his foot in his mouth was kind of endearing. 'It's fine, and yes, she still has that cheeky grin even now she's in her seventies.'

'Lovely,' he replied. 'Right, well, let me show you the cash register, eh?' He was a master of changing the subject and she followed him to the reception desk. He went over the souvenirs for sale and the list of codes for each item, where the change was kept, where the figures were completed at the end of the day and what to do if the till stopped working – she laughed but hoped he was kidding about that part. 'When customers come in, just chat to them as you would back at your library and when it's quiet, you can read if you have something with you. If not, Morag has a selection of books at the B and B that you can have a look through. I... I hope you won't be bored.' He cringed.

'Not at all. I have my laptop too, so I can have a look at the local area and familiarise myself with places I can visit, perhaps. It'll be good for me to gain a little more local knowledge to share with visitors.'

'Excellent. For sure. And you'll get all ages and all nationalities visiting. It's surprising really. But I'm sure you'll settle right in.'

'I'm sure I will too. I'm looking forward to opening it up.'

'Yes, and the next three days until then will no doubt fly by.'

She smiled. 'They invariably do.'

He nodded and settled a somewhat wistful gaze on her before shaking his head as if coming out of a trance. 'Okay, well, I'll get locked up if you've seen enough for today. I've been and checked and the cleaner is almost done next door. You can move your stuff in tomorrow. You should have everything you need, but, if not, just let me or Morag know, and we'll see what we can do. Obviously, the house is rent-free with you working here, but you'll need some provisions. Anyway, I'll pop the keys around later tonight. I'll drop them with Morag, so I don't disturb you again.'

'Thank you. I'm looking forward to seeing the place.'

'It's nothing fancy, but I'm told it's comfortable enough.'

Juliette walked to the door with Reid and said her goodbyes as he locked up the building and then she made her way back to the bed and breakfast.

Once back in her room, she called Millie, Dexter and her parents to fill them in on the news of the museum and the photograph she had discovered. Of course, her mum cried when she saw the photo that Juliette sent via message, meaning Juliette quickly followed suit. The pair of them laughed through their tears at how soft they both were.

'Like mother, like daughter!' her dad shouted down the line.

* * *

At breakfast the following morning, Morag hurried over, jangling a set of keys from her fingertips. 'Look what I've got for you!' she said giddily.

'Oooh, fab!' Juliette clapped her hands before taking the proffered keyring. 'I can't wait to see the place.'

'It's a lovely wee place. I think you'll really settle in. And I'm so glad Reid saw sense. He's a funny one.' She shook her head.

After seeing a different side to the man, Juliette was both intrigued *and* unwilling to judge him. 'I suppose if he's been through a tricky divorce he won't easily trust again.'

'You got that right. Honestly, since Kate left, we've all been walking on eggshells. He worried me at one point. I thought he was a little more than just angry and upset, if you know what I mean. I feared for his mental health. He just wasn't himself for so long. Still isn't really. But, thankfully, he has that beautiful, kind-hearted boy to keep him on his toes. I don't know what would become of him if he didn't.'

'Evin's great. Such a sweet lad.'

'Aye, he is. So, what did you think of the museum now you've finally seen it?'

Juliette went on to tell Morag about the photograph of her mum and how much she loved the place and couldn't wait to start working there. The museum would be totally different, in many ways, to the job she was used to back home in the university library, it maybe had more in common with her volunteering job at the charity shop. But she was looking forward to chatting to people and learning more about the local area. And, as they say, a change is as good as a rest!

* * *

Juliette's stomach was aflutter as she stepped over the threshold of Lifeboat Cottage adjoining the museum. It had once been a kind of dormitory for the lifeboat crew seeing as they couldn't fit in the station house with the boat itself. It had been expanded and renovated over the years to include an inside bathroom; a fact Juliette was most grateful about. She placed her bags down in the hallway, deciding she'd have a proper look around before unpacking. The hallway was small but clean and very bright; black and white tiles covered the floor and pale cream paint the walls. A small sign on a locked door simply said *Museum Access*, which meant she didn't need to leave the house to get into the place. *Good, if the rain comes again.*

There was a framed photograph that she guessed was dated around the nineteen twenties, which showed a line of men in full waterproof regalia and oilskin sou'wester hats, proudly standing before their small lifeboat. Behind the men was the building to the right of the cottage – the old boathouse. It looked vastly different today, with its additional windows and fancy glazed front door, but the size certainly lent itself to an interior crammed with historical artefacts.

On a shelf under a rather ornate mirror that hung beside the photograph sat a little locally produced book. Inside were some accounts of rescues and a list of the brave men who'd taken part. It seemed the team was small but mighty in the number of lives they had been involved in saving. She spotted the MacKinnon name and assumed this was the reason why Reid still had a connection to the place.

There was a staircase that led up from the hallway and a small table by the door with a large well-kept plant sitting atop it in a mosaic pot. There was a little folded card beside the pot which read: *GUESTS PLEASE READ.*

Obediently, Juliette lifted the card and opened it.

Dear Guest,

I'm Florence the Philodendron and I've lived here for many years. I like to be kept quite dry and in low light, hence my location. Please do not water me more than once a week and do not be tempted to move me to another location within the house or shop. Follow these instructions and I will stay around for many years to come.

Thank you,

Florence

Foliage with a human name was something completely new to Juliette and she couldn't help the giggle that escaped at the prospect of being bossed around by a pot plant.

'Hello there, Florence, or can I call you Flo? I'll take your silence as a yes. Anyway, Flo, I'm Jules and I'm here to look after you for a few months. I promise to behave and leave you where you are.' She nodded at the inanimate object and then rolled her eyes. 'Well, talking to plants is supposed to be good,' she outwardly informed the half of her brain that was screaming at her that she was being ridiculous. She huffed. 'Hey, if it's good enough for Prince Charles, then it's good enough for me.'

The kitchen was a good size and featured all the mod cons she would need. There was a small table to one side and a range of rustic oak units to the other. The living room was painted a deep red, which wasn't a colour she would've chosen for such a small space, but it somehow worked. There was a log burner in a large brick fireplace, and she knew she would be making plenty of use of it during her stay. There was a portable radio, a small flat-screen TV and DVD player with a selection of old movies just like most *holiday let* houses.

The rear bedroom was small and only housed a single bed. Juliette smiled when she imagined Dexter trying to fold himself into it if he did come to visit. The bedroom at the front was the bigger of the two and had the best views. It reminded her a little of her room at home. The ceiling was quite low – although not too low for Juliette's five feet six frame – and the walls were painted a rich cream. There were beautiful watercolour Highland scenes framed on the walls, each with the signature she now recognised as Reid's; just the kind of paintings she loved. The large oak wardrobe held plenty of storage for her things and there was even a matching dressing table.

The window overlooked the inlet to the front, and she stood for a few moments taking in the view. A small fishing boat bobbed up and down on the water as the skipper prepared nets and another man swept the deck. Beside the boat something was splashing around and playing in the water. She couldn't quite make out what it was but wondered if it was an otter like the one that had inspired the author, Gavin Maxwell.

Her heart skipped and a wave of happiness washed over her, taking her somewhat by surprise. This felt right; like the tonic she needed. She even managed to quell the niggle of guilt playing on her subconscious.

No, Laurie would want me to be happy. He'd fully support my being here. I'm doing exactly what he told me to do.

Elsewhere, there were more landscape paintings adorning the walls. They depicted sea views and mountains vistas and were displayed in an array of frame styles. It was like walking into a gallery dedicated to Reid MacKinnon's work.

After she had unpacked her belongings, Juliette made a drink with the tea bags and milk that had been left in a welcome basket for her and she munched on a piece of Caitlin's melt-in-the-mouth shortbread from the cling-wrapped plate that had been left too. There was a little note that read:

Dear Juliette,

We, the *Lifeboat House Museum Co-operative*, sincerely hope you enjoy your stay at our wee museum. If there are any problems, please do not hesitate to contact myself, Reid MacKinnon, on the number below, or Morag McDougal at Thistle House, and we will be happy to assist you.

We wish you a very pleasant stay.

How lovely of them, she thought as she placed the note back down beside the plate of shortbread.

She carried her tea back through to the museum with the intention of getting to grips with the place before the grand opening. It wouldn't be a grand opening for anyone but her, nevertheless her excitement vibrated through every bone and nerve ending.

Standing in the centre of the museum, Juliette inhaled a deep calming breath and a wide smile played on her lips. She had the urge to bounce around on the spot and fist-bump the air as she could already tell this was going to be the most incredible experience, and she couldn't wait to get to work when the place opened the following week.

12

Juliette had become a regular at the village shop, which was a similar building to the cottage that accompanied the lifeboat station, only set out the opposite way round.

Kenneth was always very pleasant, and they chatted easily as she paid for her shopping that she had collected in a little wicker basket. There was a selection of wines by the cash register and she decided to treat herself with a nice bottle of Shiraz.

Reid walked in wearing scruffy, paint-spattered clothes again and his hair was back to the appearance of having been dragged backwards through a hedge. Juliette doubted any other man could carry off such a wild look, but on Reid it somehow worked. And even in this unshaven, unkempt state there was no hiding his attractiveness.

Juliette stifled a gasp at her inner thoughts, feeling her cheeks warming and that twinge of guilt niggled at her mind. 'Hi, Reid. I just wanted to let you know I'm unpacked, and I've been having another look around the museum. Getting to grips with everything.' She beamed.

He stopped just a little further down the first aisle and turned to face her. 'Hmm. Well, I trust everything is in order.' He was back to the stern-faced persona she had first encountered. No warning. Just a terse manner and an unsmiling face. 'Obviously, you have our contact details should any issues arise, but if you want my advice, make Mrs McDougal your first port of call. She's easier to get hold of. Anyway, must go. Dinner to make.' He gave a swift nod and marched off to the back of the shop.

Juliette cringed, why was he so mercurial? So sweet and pleasant when they were alone but almost standoffish when anyone else was around. Was he trying to keep up the reputation he had acquired and if so, why? After all, people had commented on his grumpiness, but she only ever saw it when they were around others. He really was baffling.

Her disquiet must have been evident in her features as Kenneth leaned forward and patted her hand. 'Pay no mind to him, the wee dafty. He's auld before his time, that one,' he whispered and glanced over to where Reid was collecting groceries and then continued in his quiet voice, 'Far too serious, if you ask me. Heart o' gold beneath the dour exterior though, right enough.' He chuckled and shook his head.

Juliette relaxed a little and lowered her own voice conspiratorially. 'That's good to know. I thought we'd turned a corner, but maybe I was wrong, I feel like I'm back to annoying him.'

Kenneth waved a dismissive hand and leaned closer once more. 'Och, no. I think the very presence of *everyone* annoys him at some point.' With another quick glance to make sure the coast was clear, he said, 'It's all since his English wife left him. But that's not my story to tell. Anyway, pay no heed. You've a big day coming up. I should imagine you're champing at the bit to get started.'

Glad of the focus being back on her new role, Juliette smiled. 'Oh, yes. I can't wait.'

Reid appeared beside her again and she gave him a nervous smile that *wasn't* returned.

Kenneth said, 'Well, Jules, go and enjoy your wee tipple. And I can sincerely say on behalf of the *whole* co-op that I hope you enjoy your time at the museum.' There was a sideways, disapproving glance towards Reid and then a sly wink at Juliette.

Juliette hesitated, unwilling to cause trouble but also unwilling to be seen as a pushover. 'Thank you, Kenneth. I appreciate that very much. It's nice to be made so welcome.' And without a backwards glance, she left the shop, letting the door jangle closed behind her.

* * *

Juliette rose early on opening day and padded downstairs to the kitchen to make her first cup of tea of the morning. She eyed the bread she had purchased the night before but wasn't sure she had room in her stomach for food; apparently a kaleidoscope of butterflies had taken up residence in there. She glanced up at the clock on the kitchen wall as she waited for the kettle to boil and drummed her fingertips on the work surface. It was only six thirty and the museum opening hours were ten until four, Tuesday to Saturday. But sleep had evaded her, thanks to excitement, and so here she was, hours from opening and no appetite.

She flicked on the radio, tuned it to Radio Skye, tucked it under her arm and opened the back door. She carried her tea out on to the little stone patio that formed part of a small, enclosed cottage garden. There was a chill to the air, and she pulled her dressing gown closer around her shoulders and checked the metal chair to make sure it was dry before sitting down. Fleetwood Mac sang about a 'Gypsy'; the unmistakable voice of Stevie Nicks brought back memories of slow-dancing with Laurie in their lounge as they celebrated one of their anniversaries. If she closed her eyes, she could almost smell his aftershave as he'd held her close and she'd nuzzled his chest…

Eventually, Juliette decided to go through to the museum to do some final checks, but before unlocking the door, she stood in the empty building. There was something quite magical about being surrounded by nothing but history and silence. She left the shutters closed for a while and let the Tiffany lampshades cast their warm glowing rainbows over the tiny slivers of the past in the cases before her.

There was a knock on the museum door and, when she peered through the stained glass, she recognised Morag's outline standing there.

She opened the front door and was greeted with a very smiley face and a cloth-covered plate being held towards her. 'Good morning, Jules, and sorry for the intrusion. I thought you might like a wee sweet treat before your big day begins,' she said.

'Oh, Morag, that's so kind of you. Thank you. Come on in.' She stepped aside to let Morag through the door. 'So, what's under the cloth?' she asked eagerly as her mouth watered.

'I know how much you like my Scotch pancakes and I'm missing seeing you at breakfast, so I brought you some.' She lifted the cloth and an aroma of delicate sweetness wafted through the air from the plate.

Juliette's stomach rumbled loudly in anticipation and the two new acquaintances laughed. She covered her tummy and felt the heat of embarrassment flush her cheeks. 'Well, if I wasn't hungry before, I certainly am now. Can I offer you a cup of tea or coffee?'

Morag glanced at her watch. 'Oh, I don't want to keep you, hen. I know you must have plenty to do.'

Juliette cringed. 'Don't think me sad, but I've been up and at 'em since six thirty and now, with an hour to go before I open the doors,

I'm all prepared. To be honest, a bit of company might help calm my opening-day nerves.'

Morag smiled. 'Well, in that case, coffee with milk please, lead the way.'

They went back through to the cottage kitchen and Juliette flicked on the kettle as Morag sat at the table. 'I never asked before as I was afraid to pry, but... forgive a nosey old woman, what brought you all the way up here? I know you said your mum grew up here, but are there other reasons?' she asked as Juliette made the drinks.

She wondered how much to say but went with something that wasn't exactly a lie, it just wasn't the whole truth. 'I just wanted to get away for a break. Work has been quite hectic and, of course, I know about the village, thanks to my mum. It seemed the perfect escape.'

'Well, I hope you get to do some sightseeing. We don't want to work you too hard. Now, you get stuck into those pancakes. My Kenneth was none too pleased that I hadn't made them for him.' She laughed, the skin around her bright eyes crinkling at the corners.

Juliette grinned as she took a big bite and rolled her eyes upwards as the confection melted on her tongue. 'Oh dear. I was going to say I don't want to make an enemy of Kenneth, but now that I've remembered how good these are, I think I'd be prepared to fight him.'

Morag laughed. 'That's more like it.'

They chatted briefly about Juliette's job back home and sipped on their coffee. Everything felt easy and relaxed and Juliette's nerves abated.

Eventually, Morag stood. 'Now, I'll be away and leave you to it. If you have any problems at all, you know where to find me.' She turned to leave but stopped. 'Kenneth mentioned you'd had a run-

in with Reid at the shop.' She shook her head and sighed. 'I just
wanted to say, don't bother with old grumpy-erse MacKinnon.' She
winked and tapped her nose. 'What he doesn't know, he cannae
complain about. Although I can just tell you're going to be fine.'
Juliette made to stand too, but Morag held up her hand. 'Oh no,
you don't. You've more pancakes to eat, I'm determined to put some
flesh on your bones, missy. I know my way out. Have a wonderful
day, Jules. Or, should I say, Sparkly?' She laughed. 'Wee Evin's
quite fond of you, you know? His nickname for you makes me
smile.'

Juliette smiled again. 'He's such a sweet boy.'

'Aye, he's grand. Well, bye just now,' she called as she disappeared down the hallway and out of the door.

Juliette tucked into her second pancake, her heart a little lighter
and her excitement rising once more.

* * *

Just before ten, Juliette stood at the door, one hand poised to open
the latch and one poised to turn round the 'Open' sign. She had
opened the shutters on to a bright sunny day, the sunlight dancing
on the water opposite and people were already out and about in the
village. She counted the seconds down in her mind. Five... four...
three... two... one. The sign was flipped, and the latch released.

This is it!

Within minutes, Evin appeared with Chewie. The dog was
bright-eyed, and his tongue lolled out of the side of his mouth. It
was good to see him looking so happy.

Evin looked down at him. 'So, you've to stay here. Don't go bothering anyone if they walk by, okay, Chewie? This is a museum, so
you're not allowed in.'

The dog tilted his head as if taking in every syllable and Juliette couldn't help smiling. She was definitely warming to the idea of a canine friend and the thought surprised her.

Evin walked through the door. 'Good morning, Sparkly Jules. How are you today?'

She grinned at his name for her. 'Good morning to you too, Evin, I'm good, thanks. And you? And how's Chewie doing?'

The boy glanced over his shoulder through the open door and then back to Juliette, his eyes shining with happiness. 'I'm great and the muckle dafty's back to his usual self, thanks to you.'

'I'm so glad to hear that. You were right about his dislike of swimming though.'

'Aye, alls Chewie seems to do is eat, sleep and poop in between wanting to be on your lap.' He grinned.

Juliette laughed as a mental image formed of the huge, slob-bering dog, dwarfing anyone whose lap he decided to favour. 'Ah, well, I suppose he doesn't realise quite how big he is. How did you end up with such a big dog anyway?'

'A man over on the mainland had a dog who had pups. My dad knows him and took me to see them. The man said Chewie was the runt of the litter and no one was wanting him, so I begged my dad. And I begged and begged. And then I came home from school one day and there he was. It was the best day of my whole life,' he beamed.

'Well, I bet he's glad you wanted him. So, young sir, what can I do for you today?' Then concern settled over her. 'Shouldn't you be at school?'

'No, it's the summer holidays, thank goodness. I hate school.' He grumbled.

Realising that the holidays would be different up in the north of Scotland than back in England, Juliette was relieved to know she wasn't aiding and abetting in a skiving ploy. 'Oh dear. That's a shame. Some say it's the best time of your life.'

Evin huffed. 'Aye, well only doaty dobbers would say that.'

Juliette pursed her lips, keen to not alienate her first visitor. This place was an education, that was one thing she was loving. All these new phrases and sayings she was committing to her memory bank would give her something funny and sweet to look back on. 'Okay, well, maybe being here is the best thing for you, eh? Have you been before?'

He nodded. 'Loads. I like the old-fashioned toys display. It makes me laugh that kids used to play at catching a wooden ball in a cup, but now they all sit and stare at a screen. My dad banned me from my Xbox today because I left a pile of dirty dishes in my room, so I thought I would come and see the toys. So... I'm here.' He held his arms out as if to prove a point.

'Here you are indeed. You can be my helper if you like. Now... let's get some water for Chewie, eh? It's a warm one today.'

13

Juliette smiled a warm welcome as a few more people entered the museum. Since Evin had arrived, it had become quite busy. Some of the visitors were people she recognised from the local area as she had walked around, meaning they were here to suss her out. She didn't mind. It must've been quite strange for the villagers, having an interloper running one of the local businesses.

Evin helped put some new leaflets in the tourist display that had been dropped off by the postman. They chatted in between customers and he divulged his love of all things fantasy and prehistoric. He could name many of the dinosaur species which impressed Juliette, and he clearly had a passion for dragons and other mythical creatures. Eventually he asked the time and when Juliette told him it was after one, he gasped.

'Yikes! I should go home and eat lunch. Dad will be thinking I'm not hungry and I'm *always* hungry!' He left, collecting his obedient dog on the way. Thankfully, Chewie hadn't slipped his lead this time and had stayed where he was, tethered to a hook on the wall outside.

Later, Juliette was sitting, thumbing through one of the display books about the local area, and another visitor entered. She lifted her head to see the smiling eyes of an elderly gentleman.

He shook his head. 'Well, I never. Fancy seeing you again. I was right when I said this island was small, eh?'

Her eyes widened as she recognised the kind man from breakfast at Gretna. 'Oh, my goodness. Hello. How lovely to see you again. Did the wedding go okay?'

The man smiled wistfully. 'Aye, it was grand. A really good wee break. My grandson and his new husband are happy and that's all that matters.'

'I'm so glad to hear that. So, what brings you to the museum?'

The man glanced at the floor and waved his hand. 'Och, it's a silly thing. I come in quite often as I only live in the next village. I like to visit to see my wife. Well, a photo of her in her wedding frock. You must think me a silly old fool.' He shook his head, his cheeks tinged with pink.

'Ah, then you must be Mr Gair. I think it's very romantic that you still come here.'

'Why, thank you, dearie. Please, call me Hamish.'

Juliette held out her hand. 'And I'm Jules.'

He shook her hand. 'Jules? Oh, now, would you happen to be the young lady who jumped into the water to save that wee boy's dog?'

Juliette's cheeks tinged pink now. 'Goodness me, news does travel in this place.'

His eyes twinkled and he gave her a warm smile. 'It certainly does, even from one village to another.' He laughed. 'I'm so very glad our paths have crossed again. I look forward to seeing you around and about the place. Now, I'll leave you to your book and I'll go and visit my darling Mary Ann.'

'Please do. Lovely to see you again.' Juliette's heart melted as she watched the elderly man make his way through the display cases to the place his wife's veil and photograph were. She had only been missing Laurie for two years and it already felt like a lifetime, but this poor man had been without his true love for decades. *His heartache must be overwhelming.* Her eyes began to sting, and she had the urge to see Laurie's face. She opened the silver locket that sat around her neck and gazed at the handsome man captured in the photograph. 'I miss you so much,' she whispered.

* * *

Juliette closed the shop for a half-hour lunch break at two and was eating a ham and cheese sandwich at the garden table, while, on the radio, KT Tunstall sang about being 'On the Other Side of the World', and she was swept away by the melancholy for a brief moment as she listened to the sadness of the lyrics. Determined to stop her mood from descending on such an important day, she switched off the radio and decided to listen to birdsong instead.

Later, as she was serving one of her many customers with souvenir postcards and pens, she caught sight in her peripheral vision of someone standing outside peering in. Once the sale was complete, she turned to see Reid watching her, a stern, almost annoyed expression fixed in place, hands on narrow hips.

She raised a hand. 'Oh, hi, Reid!' He waved and walked in as the customer left. 'I had Evin in here earlier. He seems to like this place.'

'Yes, yes, he's fascinated...' he said distractedly, avoiding eye contact. 'Listen I wanted to say... I mean... I'm not exactly...' He sighed. 'It's been brought to my attention that I upset you, in the shop. So, I wanted to pop by and say it wasn't my intention. I seem to have a knack of putting my foot in it.'

Juliette shook her head, trying to think of what to say. She didn't want to let him off too easily. It wasn't exactly an apology but more of an explanation, however, she didn't want to drag the negativity out either. 'Oh, it's fine,' was all she managed to utter.

He rubbed his hand roughly over his messy hair and briefly lifted his chin to lock his gaze on hers. It was a split-second exchange and his cheeks were aflame. 'Okay. Good... great. Anyway, that's what I wanted to say... so...' This time, he lifted his chin and fixed her with what she presumed to be an apologetic smile. Her stomach fluttered a little and she absentmindedly placed a hand over it. Reid stepped forward and opened his mouth as if to speak again but instead immediately stepped back. 'Right, well, bye for now.'

Before she had a chance to respond further, he walked out of the museum and left her sitting there, open-mouthed yet again. It wasn't exactly an apology; more of an acknowledgment of the fact he'd been an arse. It was something, she supposed.

In a lull during the afternoon, Juliette stood at the door, looking out onto the inlet. It was a warm day with a slight breeze coming in off the water. The sky was a cerulean blue, dotted with little fluffs of slow-moving white cloud. Seagulls were taking turns at sitting on the railings that skirted the water while their friends performed aerobatics, crying out as they swooped down to the small fishing boat where the skipper, who she now knew to be a man called Gus, was readying to set sail again. Tourists stood at the other side of the inlet, right at the edge, taking photos of the view reaching into the inner sound. The bunting that stretched along the whitewashed cottages opposite fluttered in the gentle breeze and the sun cast its glow on the rocks rising up behind the buildings.

The temporary nature of her stay popped, unwelcomed, into her mind and she turned and stepped back inside. She knew she must make every minute count.

* * *

Just before closing time, Morag appeared, a warm smile fixed in place as always. 'Hi, Jules. How's your first day been?'

Juliette beamed. 'It's been amazing. I've met some of the locals and some of the people travelling through on holiday too. It's been surprisingly busy. The takings are good too.'

'Grand. It's a popular wee place. But you've enjoyed it?'

'Absolutely loved it more like. Although...'

Morag frowned. 'What's wrong, hen? Is something troubling you?'

Juliette cringed and waved a dismissive hand. 'Oh, it's nothing. Ignore me.'

'No, no, if there's something awry, I'd rather know.'

'It's just that... Reid was here earlier. He walked in and I tried to engage him in a conversation. Just to tell him Evin had been in. But he was acting a bit odd and he blurted out an awkward monologue about upsetting me in your shop and putting his foot in it. It was a bit confusing. I know he and I didn't get off to the best start, but after the whole Chewie thing, I thought we'd turned a corner. I hope he doesn't think I've been telling tales like some sulky schoolgirl.'

Morag rolled her eyes. 'Ah... I might be at fault there. Kenneth told me how abrupt Reid was with you in the shop, so I may have told him he owes you an apology. He's not the best at explaining how he feels. He's a grumpy erse and can be stubborn with it, but there's no real harm in him. I'm sorry about my interference, hen. Look, why don't you pop round once you're closed up, and I'll make us a pot of tea? I've been to Caitlin's and nabbed the last of her shortbread rounds. If that doesn't tempt you, nothing will.'

Whilst the thought of the Scottish confection was so tempting, Juliette didn't want to create the wrong impression. 'Honestly, it's fine. I wish I hadn't said anything. I must sound like a real busybody.'

'Not at all. And I insist. Kenneth will be there too.'

'Ooh, well, I hope he's forgiven me for the pancakes.' Juliette laughed.

Morag grinned. 'We'll soon find out, eh? See you in a wee while.'

'See you soon!'

Juliette stood for a moment looking out at the view. She pondered Morag's comment about Reid being unable to express himself and hoped that was all it was. She didn't want to appear to be a gossip. But one thing was clear, conversation seemed to be something he preferred to avoid. She glanced up at the clock and couldn't quite believe how fast the day had gone.

Once she had run the end-of-day reports and completed the logbook with the figures, she locked up the shop and headed along the road.

She knocked on the back door at Thistle House and Morag greeted her, wiping her hands on a pristine white and blue gingham tea towel. 'Ah, you made it. Come away in.'

Juliette cringed as she glanced at her own empty hands. 'Thank you. I'm afraid I haven't brought anything.'

'That's just as well. You didn't need to. Come on to the kitchen. Kenneth has got the kettle on the stove.'

'Afternoon, Jules. Good first day?' he asked when they both sat at the table.

'Great, Kenneth, thanks. Can't wait to do it all again tomorrow.'

'Grand.' He leaned in and lowered his voice. 'Although let's have no more of my pancakes going missing, eh?' He winked.

Juliette scrunched her face and shook her head. 'Oh dear, I'm afraid I won't make a promise I can't keep.'

Kenneth burst out laughing and wagged a finger at her as he glanced at his wife. 'Oh, I like this one. She's feisty, just like you, darlin', eh?'

Morag whacked him playfully. 'And don't you forget it, *darlin'*.'

'I see we've some of Caitlin's shortbread,' Kenneth said as he eyed the sugar covered rounds. 'You do know that with my wife's baking and Caitlin's cakes you've no chance of staying so slim, Jules.'

'Och, away and boil your heid, you dafty,' Morag laughed.

Juliette loved the banter between the married couple. There was such affection between them, and she wondered if perhaps she might get a second chance at love someday.

* * *

Juliette chatted to Morag and Kenneth for around half an hour before Kenneth announced that he was going to watch his favourite quiz show.

Once he had gone, Morag squeezed her arm. 'Are you okay now, hen?'

'I'm fine, honestly. I shouldn't have taken Reid's behaviour so personally.' She tried to shrug it off.

'Aye, but he shouldn't feel it's okay to be so damned crabbit the whole time. He's been like it for so long now that I think he's forgotten how to smile.'

'What was it that happened? I mean, obviously I don't want to gossip, but maybe it would help me to understand.'

'Well... His ex-wife was... *is* an English lassie, from the Midlands somewhere. He met her when they were teenagers and her folks brought her to Skye on holiday. He followed her back there and they were married. They moved up here when the wean was a bairn. Evin, you know?' Morag's mouth took a downward turn. 'He didn't deserve that one for a mother. She had an affair with a chap who used to come up on holiday on his motorbike. He used to go into her café, you see. The one across the way. Reid owns it, and his mother before him. He moved back here to take over when his mother passed away. Anyway, that's beside the point. So, his wife, Kate, had this affair and then one day upped and left on the back of the man's motorbike. Left Evin behind too. He was only three at the time, the poor wee lamb. She divorced Reid and married the biker man. She comes up to see the laddie every few months, but it's not natural. She cannae have had any maternal instinct in her. Dipping in and out of his life whenever she sees fit.' Morag scoffed. 'And Reid has never got over it. He's a wonderful father, but he's built up walls, you see. So much so that he can't even see fit to make friends or make time for the ones he already has.'

Juliette blew out air from puffed cheeks. 'Wow... I suppose there's no wonder he's so distant sometimes.' Thoughts of the poor boy caught in the middle of it all tugged at her heart and she couldn't understand any mother abandoning her child. For someone who desperately wanted to be a parent, it seemed so cruel and unfair. She knew she could never do such a thing and that Evin deserved a mother who put him first, as did all children. She shook her head to dislodge the sadness creeping in. 'So, she used to run the café?'

It was a rhetorical question, but Morag rolled her eyes. 'Aye. These days he has Leanna for that. She's lived here forever. They grew up together and were very close when they were younger. But then he went off to England to follow Kate, and Leanna was broken-hearted. She married Donny eventually, but she still holds a candle for Reid. She just gave up and married the first man who doted on her. I guess you could say she settled for second best. It's a sad state of affairs, if you pardon the pun.'

It certainly explained a lot and confirmed Caitlin's thoughts too. 'Does Reid know how Leanna feels about him?'

Morag sighed. 'To be quite honest, hen, I don't think he'd know someone fancied him if they danced a naked jig on his doorstep.'

Juliette giggled at the imagery. 'Surely, he's not *that* dense.'

'No, he's not dense. Just oblivious. Although, I reckon it's self-inflicted ignorance. I think he's trained his sel' not to acknowledge the attentions of the fairer sex. Coping mechanism.' She shrugged.

Juliette felt a twinge of pity for the poor man. 'He must live an extremely lonely life if he treats all women as if they're a potential hazard.'

'Not *all* women. Just young, attractive ones. He daren't say a wrong word to me.' She laughed heartily. 'And he seems to think he doesn't need anyone but Evin. He has his brother too. He's a TV personality and lives on the mainland near Glasgow. Kendric is quite the opposite of Reid. Outgoing, friendly, sweet. Single too, for some strange reason. Their mother passed away, as I said, and their father is in a residential care home across the bridge. Dementia, poor wee soul.'

Juliette let the new information sink in. 'It's strange really, Reid and I have a little in common. We've both suffered loss. Although, my husband didn't run away with someone...'

Morag tilted her head. 'So, there *are* other reasons for you being here? I'd guessed as much. I have a sixth sense for these things,' she said with a sad smile.

Juliette lowered her gaze. 'You got me. I'm not running away though. Not as such.'

'You'll get no judgement from me, hen. And you don't have to tell me a thing. Although... sometimes it helps to tell someone who isn't directly involved.'

Juliette sighed and stared at her mug. 'It's quite a long story, so I'll give you the concise version. My lovely husband, Laurie, passed away two years ago, and I feel like people back home still don't know how to treat me even after all this time. To be honest, I'm sick of people looking at me with pity in their eyes. I know they mean well but... I wanted a chance to get away and, I suppose, to prove to them all that I'm fine. That they don't have to constantly check up on me. I'm devastated, obviously, but we had time, Laurie and I, to deal with things, to talk things through and I promised him that I'd live my life to the fullest. I didn't really fulfil that promise to begin with. I struggled with depression after his death, you see, but I finally feel like I'm ready to start living again.' Juliette suddenly felt exhausted from her outpouring. This was the first time she'd really told anyone how she felt, and whilst it was cathartic, she also felt her energy drain away.

Morag sat in silence, listening to Juliette tell her story, and when she had finished and handed over a mug of steaming, fresh coffee, her new friend smiled and shook her head. 'My goodness. It's like listening to myself twenty-five years ago.'

'Really?' Juliette asked.

'Aye. My first husband, Duncan, he passed away when I was forty. The kids were at high school. Everyone thought I was going to fall apart and, truth be told, I almost did. But I was determined to carry on. It was what he would've wanted. Duncan was a wonderful man.' Her eyes shone with fondness. 'The best father. I think at first I was too worried I'd not be able to cope but... you find the strength. You carry on. You have to.' She shrugged.

Juliette reached out and placed her hand on Morag's arm. 'I'm so sorry to hear about Duncan,' she whispered, finding her own grief bubbling to the surface.

Morag placed a hand on top of Juliette's. 'And I'm sorry about Laurie, hen.' She reached and took a sip of her coffee. 'So, you've no weans?'

Juliette smiled at her accent. 'Children? Sadly no. We were planning to, but... it never happened.'

'Och, I'm sorry, lass. That's a shame.'

A lump tightened Juliette's throat and her vision blurred. 'It is. He would've made such a brilliant dad. He was great fun, and so intelligent. To see him holding his own newborn baby would've been a dream come true, but... Ugh, sorry, I didn't mean to get all weepy.' She dabbed at the escaped tears as they trickled down her cheeks.

Morag reached across the table. 'Never apologise for feeling, hen. The older I've got, the more I've realised that what other people think is *their* issue. And if someone judges you for missing your man... well, they're not worth a second's thought. And we're not all crabbit folk around here, I promise. Some of us have a great sense of humour.'

Juliette smiled. 'Don't worry, I can certainly tell that's true. Well, I should be going. I have a museum to open in the morning.' She stood to leave. 'Thank you for your hospitality.'

Morag stood and walked her to the door and Kenneth shouted goodbye as they passed the living room. Once Morag had hugged her goodbye, she told her, 'Just try not to pay any mind to Reid. He's not intentionally obtuse. Not really. I just think he's very misunderstood.'

'Thank you. I'll bear that in mind.'

'Now, have another good day tomorrow. And shout if you need anything.' She reached out and placed her hand on Juliette's arm. 'And... I know we don't know each other all that well just yet, but... I really hope you find peace of mind here after all you've been through.'

Juliette smiled. 'That's very kind of you. Thank you.'

'Oh, and I forgot to mention that you'll be here for the village games. You can close the museum for the day and attend. That's what usually happens.'

'Ooh, village games, yes, I saw the banner. What's that all about then?'

'It's away round on the church field. There's caber tossing, Highland dancing, stalls and a talent show, to name but a few things. It's good craic. Lots of giggles. Caitlin and the staff from Reid's café run the refreshments in the main marquee. You might even see Reid MacKinnon smile.' She nudged her lightly. 'Although don't hold your breath, eh?'

The prospect of witnessing something so inherently Scottish sent shivers of excitement down her back. 'That sounds perfect. When is it?'

'First weekend in August.'

'Well, I'll look forward to that. If I can help at all just let me know, okay?'

Morag laughed. 'Whoops, you've done it now. You'll be roped into all sorts. We've a meeting tomorrow evening, so I'll let everyone know you're a willing participant.'

'Fantastic. I've never been to a Highland games before. I'm quite excited.'

As Juliette left the bed and breakfast, she walked over to the railings overlooking the inlet. She had lost track of time whilst at Morag's and the evening sun was making a slow descent behind the houses, the sky a glowing palette of orange, cerise and indigo. She inhaled a deep breath and a serene smile spread across her face. The village and the people she had met were already firmly ensconced in her heart, and whilst her stay on Skye was temporary, she wouldn't allow melancholy to take a proper hold. Choosing instead to embrace the time she did have and to make every moment count: every sunrise, every sunset, every conversation. Then, slowly but surely, she knew she would return to her happy-go-lucky former self. Obviously, she would never forget Laurie. He was the love of her life. But one of their final conversations meant that she had promised to carry on. To live life. And even though she had been grieving for longer than she promised – Laurie insisted she not be sad for more than six months, but he must have known it was unrealistic – she knew the time was right to start the *living* part. The time already spent in Glentorrin had highlighted that.

She'd witnessed three extremes since her arrival: Morag, widowed many years before but finding new love and happiness with Kenneth; Hamish, also widowed but choosing to stay alone with only his memories to keep him company; and, of course, Reid, a bitter divorce had left him with apparent trust issues and the impenetrable wall he'd constructed around himself. Juliette thought perhaps there had been a shift after the incident with Chewie and that maybe they could be friends, but after today's encounter and her chat with Morag, she'd realised there may not be much chance of that, after all. The thought saddened her. At his house, she'd seen something in his eyes that screamed of loneliness but also hope. But it was as if he'd realised he'd let his guard down and had quickly repaired the ramparts with reinforced concrete.

14

Waking before her alarm wasn't an issue Juliette had ever had before, but it seemed to be becoming a habit. She took her mug of tea out to the back patio to drink it and enjoy the early-morning sun. She had dreamed of Laurie again, which was nothing new. But what *was* new was the way he looked in the dream and how this affected her on waking up. Instead of the shaven head and sunken eyes of when he was sick, Laurie was back to being his usual handsome, bright-eyed self. Just as he was when they had first fallen in love. And for once, she wasn't sad or angry... just calm. Morag's words about finding peace of mind rang around her head again. Was that what was happening? Was she finding peace?

She closed her eyes and let the sun warm her skin as she remembered sitting in their own garden the summer he was seriously ill, and they had been told he wouldn't recover. He sat in the blue and white striped deckchair under the umbrella and covered with the quilted throw from the spare room. They held hands and sat in a loving, companionable silence, enjoying the chatter of birdsong and watching the sparrows fighting off the pigeons from the feeding table.

'I know I've said it before, but I could definitely see you travelling, you know. When I'm gone,' Laurie had said, completely out of the blue.

She had stopped fighting him now when he said such things. They had been told it was inevitable, a matter of time, so she had promised herself that she wouldn't altercate needlessly. Instead, she smiled. 'You could?' She'd glanced over at him and her heart had squeezed in her chest. How the hell could she imagine *any* such thing in the future, when she was so desperate to hang on to the very last threads of the present?

He'd nodded and smiled. 'Oh, I can. Zipping off to all the places we didn't have a chance to see. Finding your way into people's hearts and making friends all over the place. Cajoling them into reading all your favourite books.' He'd chuckled. 'I remember how insistent you were for me to read *The Goldfinch*. You wouldn't leave me alone until I agreed. Badgered me senseless.'

'Charming. You loved it in the end though, didn't you? Admit it.'

Laurie had perked up and said playfully, 'Maybe I did.' He grinned. 'Why not leave the library and buy a motorhome or campervan? You could write a book about your travels. Put your creative writing degree to use. How much fun would that be?'

She'd grinned and squeezed his hand. 'I don't think there are enough hours in a day for such a frivolous plan. As appealing as it might be.' It was her way of stopping the conversation she knew was coming. Laurie needed to know she was going to be secure without him. It evidently preyed on his mind.

His expression had turned serious and he'd fixed her with stern eyes. 'I'm making sure you'll be comfortable, you know. I won't leave you unless I know you're going to be okay. I can't,' he'd told her as if he had a choice in the matter. 'When I'm gone, I want you to go ahead and make something wonderful of your life, Jules. *Please* don't sit around missing me and grieving for me. Where's the joy in that? And you deserve so much joy. You've brought *me* so much joy and I'm so grateful that I met you. That you love me.' He'd punctuated his words with a squeeze of her hand and his eyes welled with tears. 'I hate the fact that after us being so happy together, after I *promised* in our wedding vows I'd never hurt you *or* leave you, that I'm going to be the reason your heart breaks, and that there's nothing I can do about it. All I can do is ask you to promise me you'll do something that *will* make you smile. Something that will fill the void I leave behind. Don't sit around thinking about me. Move on. Live your life. Be damn well happy.' His voice broke and he'd closed his eyes for a moment. 'I know you'd make the most wonderful mother and I'm just so very sorry we didn't have the chance to make a baby of our own. I know how much that would have meant to you. I feel I let you down so badly there. And it would've made things easier to bear probably. I'm so sorry—'

Juliette's throat had constricted, and she'd turned in her seat to face him. 'Laurie, *please* stop apologising. You have nothing to be sorry for. Nothing at all. I wouldn't have changed a single second of our precious time, apart from taking this bloody, wretched illness away. And *please* don't ask me not to grieve for you. At this point in time, I can't even begin to think about how I'll cope without you. So *please* don't ask me to make promises I can't keep. Nothing will make this easier. Nothing.' By now, tears were cascading down her face and she had fallen to her knees before him, her head in his lap as he stroked her hair and tried to soothe her as best he could.

* * *

The museum got busier as the days went on and Juliette greeted every customer with the same enthusiasm and positivity. Sharing her love of the place was in no way difficult. It was a pleasure rather than a chore. And every visitor that walked away from the

Lifeboat House Museum did so smiling and holding, in their memory and their heart, a little snippet of the history of the beautiful village and the fascinating people who made it so special.

After lunch, she was dusting the display cases with a brightly coloured, feathery contraption on the end of a long stick that reached high enough to clean the light shades, when her very first visitor returned.

'Hi, Sparkly Jules!' Evin said brightly as he walked in through the door.

'Oh, hi, Evin. How are you?' she asked as she glanced outside to where Chewie sat, tied to the hook and obediently waiting for his master, tongue lolling out of the side of his mouth as usual.

'Brilliant!' he announced proudly, in a singsong voice.

'Really? Well, I'm very glad to hear that.' Juliette grinned.

'Yep. This morning, me and Chewie sat in the garden while dad was feeding the chickens and we learned a new trick. It's awesome! I reckon I'll be a good dog trainer when I grow up.'

'I bet you will too. You could work with police dogs or maybe on movie sets.' She smiled, his enthusiasm was contagious.

Evin rubbed his chin. 'Ooh yes. I'll maybe do something like that.'

'Well, I'm glad you've got something you enjoy doing with your best pal.'

Evin's cheeks coloured a bright pink. 'Thank you. Are you having fun running the museum?'

'Oh, I am, Evin. I absolutely love it. It's funny, I never imagined doing something like this, but it's like it was what I was always meant to do.'

'You should buy it! You could move in forever and then you could come and see Chewie do his tricks now that you like dogs!'

Juliette laughed. She loved how children thought life was so simple. 'Yes, that would be amazing. But, sadly, the museum isn't for sale. And I have to go home after the summer.'

Evin's brow crumpled. 'But I heard dad saying...' Clearly, he thought better of sharing whatever it was and instead sighed and turned towards the exit. 'Maybe I should go and show my dad Chewie's new tricks anyway. It might cheer him up.'

Juliette's interest was piqued. 'Is he sad?'

Evin shrugged. 'Sometimes. But he's grumpy a *lot*. My grandad is really poorly, and my uncle is always going away on trips for TV, so he doesn't visit much. I think my dad wishes he had some friends, but he won't admit it. My mum says he's as stubborn as an ox.'

'Ah.' Juliette decided not to pry further in case news of her nosiness reached Reid. She wasn't entirely sure where she stood with him, so the last thing she needed was to provide him with reasons for disliking her. 'Are you not playing with your friends now it's summer?'

Evin crumpled his nose and shook his head slowly. 'I don't really have any.'

Her heart sank at his confession. 'Oh, but you're such a friendly boy.'

He shrugged. 'I'm not popular. I got bullied a bit, but it's okay now. They just ignore me. I think they think I'm boring.'

Juliette scoffed. 'Pfft! You're the *least* boring person I've met here. You're great fun.' Her heart went out to the poor, disheartened child.

He grinned. 'Do you think so?'

Memories of her own experience of bullying at school came flooding back. The cruelty of those so young could have a dire effect and she wanted to help him. 'I *know* so. Anyway, it's their loss. And what you must remember is that bullies are usually quite insecure people. They bully others because they think it makes them look big and cool. But it doesn't. It's quite sad, really.'

He pursed his lips and nodded. 'I've never thought of it like that. It makes lots of sense.'

'Anyway, take it from me, you don't want fake friends in your life. One day, you'll meet someone who loves the same things that you love. So, try not to worry.'

Evin's eyes brightened. 'Thank you. See, you *are* Sparkly Jules. You make everything seem bright.'

Touched by his words, Juliette struggled to find any more of her own. Her throat tightened a little. Ever since that day she helped pull Chewie from the water, there had been this affinity between them. In spite of what he'd no doubt been taught about strangers, he clearly trusted her and, even though it probably shouldn't, the fact made her heart swell. She thought that if she ever had a little boy, she would love for him to be just like Evin.

'Well, I'd better get going. I'm supposed to call for bread and milk. Ooh, I nearly forgot, are you coming to the games? There's a talent show and all sorts of other fun stuff.'

'Talent show, eh? Are you entering?'

Evin cringed. 'I don't have any talents.'

Juliette placed down the duster. 'I'm sure that's not true.'

He looked at his feet. 'I can't sing, or dance, or play a guitar, or do rapping, or—'

'How about you focus on what you *can* do? Talent isn't just about music, you know. I distinctly remember moments ago you saying you had trained Chewie to do tricks. That's a talent. And you'd get to do the show with your best friend. Sounds perfect to me.'

Evin's eyes brightened as he lifted his face. 'Do you think people would think I was talented if I did that? I mean, is it the kind of thing you *do* in a talent show?'

'Absolutely. There was a TV talent show where a girl and her dog did tricks. She went on to have her own movie.'

His eyes widened. 'Coooool! That's it then. You *have* to come to the games to see me and Chewie do tricks!'

She held out her hand. 'Deal.'

He shook it and beamed. 'Deal.'

15

Later, Caitlin called round at the cottage with a gift of her home-made lemon cake. Juliette filled the kettle and put it on to boil. 'It's funny, I wasn't expecting to be so welcome, with me only being here for the summer. I never expected to be treated as part of the village,' she confessed.

'Aye, well, go jumping into ice-cold water to save a dog and your reputation spreads like wildfire. Things have a way of happening like that around here,' Caitlin informed her.

Juliette wasn't sure whether she should be worried at being so high on a pedestal. 'I can assure you it's not something I generally make a habit of. Freezing my bum off out there isn't something I plan on repeating.'

'Aye, well, the fact you did it at all has tongues wagging. Although certain tongues need bloody chopping off,' she sneered.

This startled Juliette a little and her stomach knotted. 'Oh? Has something *bad* been said about me?'

Caitlin huffed. 'Nothing that anyone is listening to, so don't worry. It's just *darling* Leanna sharpening her claws.'

Juliette rolled her eyes. 'Oh God, what's she been saying now?'

Caitlin laughed. 'Just that you almost mowed Reid down on your arrival in the village and then planned the whole dramatic rescue to try and get back in his good books.' She laughed as she spoke. 'Bloody delusional, I'm not kidding.'

Juliette's cheeks flamed with heat and she covered her face. 'Good grief. If people believe her, they'll think I'm some kind of nutcase.'

Caitlin waved a dismissive hand. 'Don't be daft. Like I said, no one takes her seriously these days. And as for Reid, his head's up his erse. Miserable pig that he is. Honestly, if you *had* mowed him down, it might have knocked some personality back into him.'

'Caitlin!' Juliette gasped but laughed along.

'Well... Honestly, ever since Kate left, he's forgotten how to be kind. He's changed so much. And some weeks it feels like he's disappeared off the face of the earth. You don't see him for ages and then, when you do, he jumps down your throat or blatantly ignores you. Sometimes he looks like he's been dragged through a hedge backwards and I have no idea why, he's a stay-at-home dad, for goodness sake. I mean, yes, he paints when Evin is at school so it's not like he's sitting around, but... he used to be so well put together. Handsome, smart, toned. Now he makes no effort most of the time. And he acts like he thinks *everyone* is out to get him. Like he thought we all knew what she was up to.'

A twinge of pity tugged at Juliette's insides and she thought back to the similarities of her depression and how Reid was behaving. He didn't strike Juliette as a wallowing kind of man. Terse and mercurial yes, but not one who indulged in self-pity. She wondered if there may be more to his situation. 'But *no one* knew? About Kate, I mean.'

Caitlin shook her head. 'Na. Not a thing. It was a huge shock when she upped and left with that biker.'

'What was he like... you know... before?' Caitlin's story made a lot of sense, although Juliette wondered why he'd chosen to be so up and down with her. She could've received whiplash from his sudden changes in mood.

Caitlin rested her chin on her hand and her elbow on the table. 'Oh, he was the life and soul.' Juliette's disbelief must have been evident in her expression as Caitlin continued, 'Seriously! He was the first to suggest fancy-dress parties and anything that involved laughter. He used to play the guitar and would always get up on stage at the talent show as the compère, and he'd sing a few songs too. And I'm telling you he has the most handsome smile you've ever bloody seen. And his body...' She widened her eyes and proceeded to fan herself. 'He always used to set up the marquees for the event and he used to do it shirtless. There wasn't a woman who could keep her tongue in her mouth! These days, he might as well wear a sack cloth and a sign that says, "Females need not approach".'

'Blimey, so he really *has* changed then?'

'Sadly, aye. Such a bloody waste of a good man. I doubt he'll ever trust another woman as long as there's breath in his squidgy body.' She grinned. 'His loss though, eh? We're not all cheating bitches.'

Juliette shook her head as she sat opposite Caitlin at the kitchen table. 'No, we're certainly not.'

'So, what's your story? I see a wedding band but no man in tow.'

Juliette glanced at the white gold band set with diamonds on her ring finger. 'My husband died two years ago. I've had my shot at love, so I'm happy to be single these days. I don't need a man in my life. Well, not one that isn't Laurie, anyway. It may sound corny but he was my soulmate.'

'Oh, you're preaching to the choir, sister. I've yet to meet a man worthy of commitment myself.' Caitlin reached across the table and squeezed her arm. 'It must've been hard for you, though. I can't begin to imagine what it must be like to meet your soulmate, let alone to lose him too.'

'Thank you.'

'So, what made you come up here then? People trying to match you up on blind dates?'

'There was a bit of that, yes. All good-natured though. I had a bit of a disastrous date and that's what triggered this trip. It turned out he was almost a carbon copy of Laurie and I'd been oblivious to the fact until I sat across from him in a restaurant. I had a kind of panic attack and made a hasty retreat.'

'Shit! How awful. You poor lass.'

'Hmm. It wasn't my finest moment. But also it's the pitiful looks and the *"Are you sure you're okay by yourself, Jules?"* that I'm asked over and over. I know people mean well. And my best friend and my brother haven't been deliberately like that, but others have.'

'So, you've come up here to prove to them, and to yourself, that your life can go on?'

Juliette smiled. 'Something like that.'

'Well, I say bloody good on you. And I think you're very brave coming here.'

Juliette crumpled her brow. 'Brave?'

'Oh aye. We're all as mad as a bucket of squirrels, we are. Have you not noticed already?' Her theatrical wink showed she was kidding. Although, from what Juliette had experienced of Leanna and Reid, she wondered if there was some truth to it all. Caitlin giggled. 'Honestly, you must think I'm such a busybody. I don't usually go around spreading gossip. Ugh, who am I kidding? Of course you'll think that.' She shook her head. 'You won't have met Kendric yet. Reid's brother. Although I'm sure you've heard about him. He's a celebrity.'

'Oh yes, Morag did mention him. And, come to think of it, so did Reid.'

'Yeah, he travels a lot. He's a TV presenter on the mainland.' She held up her hands, palms facing Juliette. 'And oh. My. Word he is *gorgeous*. He's like the sexier, more amenable version of Reid.'

'Intriguing,' Juliette said, although she had never been one to swoon over stars or be wowed by fame and fortune.

Caitlin leaned forward conspiratorially. 'There's a *rumour* that he's coming home for the games. Might even be bringing a film crew to do a piece on his home village. So you might get to meet him. I'll be sure to introduce you. Oh, and to top it off, he's *really* sweet too.' She stood and placed her mug in the sink. 'Well, I should be going. Grace will be home soon from yet another sleep-over. I'm telling you; her social life is way better than mine.'

'So, I might get to meet her too, at some point.'

'Absolutely. She's incredible. I know I'm biased, but... well, she is. She's my world.'

'You're very lucky. Both of you.'

'Hmm, not everyone is as accepting of my life choices where she's concerned.' Juliette's confusion must have been evident as Caitlin explained, 'You see, I chose to have Grace *without* a man. I used a donor. It's not a common thing around here, and there are those who think I've played God by doing so. But I've stopped caring what people think.'

Juliette held up her hands. 'I don't blame you. And you'll get no judgment from me.'

Caitlin smiled widely. 'I had a feeling from early on that you'd have that attitude.' She hugged Juliette quickly and then winced. 'Sorry, I'm a hugger. I should've warned you. Well, I suppose I kind of *did* with the whole *"bucket of squirrels"* thing, but... Ugh, I should go before I say anything else that makes you pack up and head back home, eh?'

Juliette's smile was firmly fixed in place now. 'That's okay. I'm a hugger too.'

When they reached the door, Caitlin paused and turned to face her. 'I was wondering... feel free to say no, but... well, I have a stall at the games, and I wondered if you might fancy helping me on it?'

Juliette's stomach fluttered. She was honoured to be asked, again loving the feeling of belonging it extended her. 'That would be wonderful. I'd love to.'

Caitlin grinned. 'Brilliant! We can spend the day blethering and eating my profits.'

'Can't wait!'

Caitlin fumbled around in her handbag and produced a little pink card. 'Almost forgot to give you my number. Or you could just pop across to the bakery. I live behind and above it. The little white door to the side is the entrance to my wee place, if you fancy some company or a glass of wine and a chat. Believe it or not, I *am* a good listener, as well as a good bletherer.' She stepped forward to leave but paused again and shook her head. 'You know, Morag was right. You'd fit in so well around here. It's a shame you're not staying longer.'

And with those final words, Caitlin left Juliette on the doorstep feeling a bizarre combination of happy and sad all rolled together, forming a knot in her stomach.

16

On a Sunday at the end of her first hectic month on Skye, Juliette woke to bright sunshine creeping in through the sides of the window where the blinds didn't quite meet the wall, and the happy knowledge that she had a free day ahead. Her head was fuzzy thanks to fitful sleep, so she decided fresh air might be the best medicine.

After showering and dressing in a cheery, floaty yellow summer frock, she pinned up her wavy blonde locks and slipped on a pair of green ballet pumps, then took to the streets of Glentorrin, inhaling lungfuls of the sea breeze that danced along the little village. She was going to sit and watch the world go by for a while before considering what to do with the rest of her day. As she reached the other end of the inlet, she spotted a figure sitting on a bench with the unmistakeable furball, Chewie, beside him.

'Oh, hi, Reid,' she said as she approached, realising too late that she had forgotten she was supposed to be avoiding him after his former rudeness. 'You look a little lost. No Evin today?'

Reid shook his head and blankly stared out at the water. 'At his mother's for a few days.'

Juliette hesitated but lowered herself gingerly to the bench beside him and scratched Chewie's head. The canine seemed to love the attention. Reid, on the other hand, looked quite despondent.

She pondered Evin's worries about his dad's loneliness. 'Ah. I bet you miss him when he's away.'

He nodded. 'Aye, I do. Although I get the feeling the lad misses Chewie more than he misses me.' There was a slight wobble to his voice and, even though he smiled, it was half-hearted, and it appeared he almost believed what he was saying.

She smiled in encouragement. 'Oh, I know that's not true. He cares a lot for you.'

Reid turned his head and looked right at her; his gaze filled with hope. 'Has he said so?'

'He always speaks fondly of you when he comes into the museum.'

'Thanks. That's good to know.'

'He seems to be quite excited about the games. I hope it's okay, but I encouraged him to enter the talent contest with Chewie. He wasn't going to enter at all; said he didn't have any talents to speak of, but I assured him his dog-training skills are just the kind of thing people love to see. And it's quite different to the usual singing and dancing you get.' Reid said nothing, so she stupidly filled the silence: 'I get the impression he feels a little misunderstood by his schoolmates and feels a little out on the periphery.'

Reid's expression suddenly hardened; gone was the hope and pride, and in its place was a look of disdain as he turned to face her. 'You make him sound like he's got no friends or something. And you're telling me you've convinced him to get up on a stage to do *tricks*? You think that'll help, do you? You think his schoolmates will suddenly think he's *cool* if he can make a dog roll over? You've met him a few times and, okay, you saved his dog's life, but that doesn't give you the right to interfere in *anything* else. I mean, honestly, how would *you* know *anything* about him, *or* us?'

Juliette's cheeks flamed and she opened and closed her mouth, unsure how to respond to the vitriol. She hadn't meant any offence.

Reid's brow creased, and he paused as if he was waiting for an explanation. When none came, he said, 'Don't forget your job here is temporary, Juliette. You're running a museum, *not* a mental health clinic. Not that my lad needs any such help. And if he *did*, *I* would know. Okay?' He stood to leave.

Affronted and confused at his attitude, Juliette stood too, straightened her spine and fixed him with a glare. 'Actually, we've chatted at length, Evin and I. So, I *know* he worries about you. I know he feels bad when you're unhappy, which is quite frequently from what he tells me. I know he's being bullied at school because he's not one of the *popular* kids, and that he *isn't* surrounded by friends, which makes him incredibly sad. All of which you *should* probably know, but I'm guessing you don't, seeing as you're so wrapped up in yourself and your own negativity and self-pity.' She stopped and clamped her mouth shut, very much aware she had overstepped a line in the sand between museum guardian and co-op chairperson. He could very well insist that she packed up and left immediately. She held her breath, awaiting the impending fall out.

Reid frowned and stared out at the water for a moment, seemingly absorbing her harsh words, and she was suddenly wracked with guilt. He was displaying so many of the symptoms connected to depression that she wanted to tell him he needed help. She wanted to offer help even, but she'd just burned that bridge.

She watched his expression closely and held her breath. But instead of anger, she recognised in him a sense of defeat. She'd felt that same defeat herself when she was on the slippery slope to darkness and wanted to kick herself for how she'd just spoken to him.

Without making eye contact, he cleared his throat. 'Things have been... *difficult* lately. I've been dealing with a lot. But, believe me, I don't feel a single ounce of self-pity. Yes, my wife betrayed me in the worst possible way – I'm sure you've heard all the gory details, and so, yes, I've been a little distracted. But I *know* I'm totally to blame, Juliette. I'm under no illusions there.' He paused, and she fought for the right words to make things better. She didn't want this, but he spoke before she could. 'Anyway, this has been very informative, thank you. I feel thoroughly reprimanded.'

He turned to walk away, and Juliette inwardly cursed herself. It had been totally out of character for her to speak to someone in that way and she regretted it immensely. And how could he think that his wife's infidelity was *his* fault? He didn't force her into the arms of another man.

A lump of emotion tightened her throat and she quickly reached out to touch his arm. 'I'm so sorry, Reid. I've spoken completely out of turn.'

He stared down at where her hand rested, then raised his gaze to meet hers. His was heavy and clouded with deep sadness. 'No, Juliette, perhaps you're right. There are things I should know but don't. I should pay more attention, so I don't lose my son, too.'

Oh shit, the pain in his eyes. She'd truly hurt the man. Her stomach knotted, and she felt physically sick. 'Reid, I really am incredibly sorry. There was no call for me to—'

'Really, it's fine. I should get going. I need to go and...' A variety of emotions rapidly flashed across his face, as if he was trying to fabricate an excuse to vacate her presence. 'I should... check in on the café.' He almost physically shrank before her eyes. His shoulders hunched and his head bowed as he walked away.

For a split second, she considered dashing after him, trying to undo the damage, but she thought better of it, knowing she would possibly make things even worse. Instead, she flopped back down onto the bench and watched helplessly. The weight of her guilt pushed her down until she feared she may disappear into the cobbles beneath her feet.

She was the last person to dole out advice on *anything*, let alone raising children. What did *she* know? And after complaining so much about people offering *her* unwanted help, she'd just done exactly that to a man who was, to all intents and purposes, a stranger.

After Laurie's death, she had hit a downward spiral that had morphed from grief into a dark hole of depression and she feared she may never resurface. The inability to converse. The lack of motivation to get up. The feeling of utter helplessness. The need to remind herself to breathe in and out. The ache of regret for doing and saying, or *not* doing and saying things. There had been a point where she had almost completely given up, and if it hadn't been for her family and Millie insisting she went to see her GP, she may have done just that. When she thought about it, there was no wonder they had wrapped her in cotton wool.

Getting the feeling that this was something Reid was possibly struggling with or on the verge of facing made her angry at herself for not spotting the signs sooner. His wife had left him, so he was grieving the loss of his marriage. It wasn't a death, but it was still life-changing and traumatic. It was still a loss.

She could see it now. His brusque manner was a way of keeping people at a distance in order to protect himself. Or perhaps a method which helped him to deter people from taking the time to ask questions. And as soon as he realised he had let his guard down, even slightly, he did everything he could to build it up again, just as he had with her. She wondered if he had anyone to really talk to. Although, there was no doubt, she would be the last person he would speak to now. He seemed determined to suffer in silence, and alone; something she was aware many men tended to do. Perhaps they saw it as a weakness if they admitted they needed help? She suddenly wanted to shout from the rooftops that it didn't matter your gender, your age, your sexual preference, your race, et cetera, it was okay to not be okay.

She thought back to her sessions with her therapist, Michael, a man in his late fifties who'd gone into counselling after his own experiences had taken him to the darkest of places and he too had been pushed to take action... Juliette had sat, curled up in a ball on a comfy beige couch, wearing tattered old jogging bottoms and a faded Cambridge hoodie that had belonged to Laurie. Her hair was scraped back into an unbrushed ponytail and she had seen just how pale and gaunt her face looked as she'd caught sight of her reflection on the way in.

Michael had sat opposite in an armchair. His grey hair and beard both neatly trimmed. His legs crossed and his attention fully focused on her. 'So, tell me, Jules, what have you done this week? I know how much you love reading, have you read anything new?'

'I can't...' She'd sighed. 'I can't seem to focus on anything. My attention span is just...' She'd stared out of the window.

He'd left a long silence before asking, 'And how are you sleeping?'

She'd turned her attention back to Michael, her brow crumpled, her voice almost monotone. 'I doze mainly. I'm exhausted, but... it's like my brain won't switch off. I keep replaying things that Laurie and I did together. Replaying times when we were so in love. So happy. And then I remind myself that I'm probably never going to be that happy again.' She'd gritted her teeth and clenched her fists in her lap. 'That if I'd *made* him go and see his doctor sooner, if I'd *insisted* he got checked out... Then maybe I'd still have him. And then...' Her chin had trembled. 'And then I start thinking that there's no point trying to sleep. That if I wasn't alive any more, none of this would even matter.'

'But you're still here, Jules,' Michael had said with a warm smile. 'You *want* to be here. Why do you think that is? And I'm not being glib when I ask. I genuinely want to know what keeps you going on. What makes you fight this?'

She had lifted her chin and tears had spilled over onto her cheeks. 'Because deep down I know I'm loved. I know I have people around me who care for me and I don't want to hurt them.'

'Okay, that's good. But let's just consider what you said before. You're feeling as though Laurie's death was somehow your fault, would that be right?'

Juliette had closed her eyes and nodded as a sob left her chest. It had only been a matter of months, but the pain was still as raw as if it happened a matter of hours before. She couldn't form words. She couldn't lift her chin. The guilt she was carrying weighed her down like lead resting on her shoulders. She wanted the ground to open and absorb her. She wanted to just fade into nothing.

But then, what about Mum... Dad... Dex... Millie...?

She heard Michael shuffle in his chair. When she'd opened her eyes, she found he was leaning forward, his elbows on his knees. 'Jules, Laurie's illness was not your fault. You know this deep down. Nothing you could've done would have made any difference. What *did* make a difference was how you loved him, how you looked after him, how happy you made him. *Those* are the things you did. What you *didn't* do is cause his cancer. And you couldn't have pushed him to see a doctor earlier because the symptoms weren't there until the illness was at a critical stage. But you *did* make his life worth living. And you know he survived longer than the prognosis and that was down to *you*. You gave him hope. You gave him something to fight for. And he did fight. But he knew he wouldn't get well again. He knew it was only a matter of time. He told you he'd accepted that, didn't he?'

'Yes.'

'Did he ever once appear to blame you? Did he ever, even in anger, tell you that any of this was your fault?'

'No. He... he didn't get angry.' She'd smiled. 'He just wanted to love me right until the end.'

'So, the only person who appears to blame you...'

'Is me.'

'Now, turn the tables. Take a different perspective, as if you were a bystander and you were looking in on this situation. Would you blame the person in your shoes?'

Silence.

'As an outsider looking in on this situation, what would you say to the person in your shoes? Be completely honest, this is a safe place, remember.'

She'd thought about things for a moment and tried to step out of her own shoes into those of someone watching this situation unfold as he had suggested. She lifted her chin. 'If I was observing... I'd say... you didn't do this. You did all you could, but you couldn't have changed the ending. So, don't feel guilty and don't let it weigh you down. Think of the happy times. Because there were so, *so* many happy times.' More tears had spilled over and trickled down her damp cheeks. 'Think of the love you shared and how special it was to have known him. To have been loved by him.'

Michael had sat up straight once more. 'Can you turn that outward dialogue inwards, Jules? I don't mean right this second. But can you try, until we next meet, to remind yourself of what you've just told that person you were addressing just then?'

'I... I can try.'

'Take as long as you need. But keep saying it. Make it your mantra. And keep focusing on the things he did that made you laugh. Things you did that made him laugh. All the things that made you fall in love with each other in the first place. Those are the things to cling to.'

Looking back now, she was grateful that this experience had helped her to deal with her grief and to release herself from the shackles of the guilt she'd been carrying around since Laurie's passing. But she hated that she hadn't had that foresight to recognise the symptoms in Reid.

Luckily for Juliette, when she had stopped eating, stopped washing and was barely functioning, she'd had people around her who insisted she sought help; when she had, it was as if a light had been switched on. She wasn't one to pour her heart out to people, except for Laurie, but having a therapist just listen to her was the beginning of climbing out of the darkest place she had ever been. She hoped that Reid was on the cusp of a similar breakthrough and she vowed that, whilst she was here, at least, she would do whatever she could to help.

'Good morning, hen. How are you? Enjoying your day off?' Juliette turned to meet Morag's warm expression, but hers clearly didn't shine in return as Morag sat down quickly. 'Whatever's the matter, Jules? You look like you're on the verge of tears.'

Juliette sniffed and dabbed at her eyes with her free hand. 'Oh, I've just been putting my foot in it. I seem to be a bloody expert these days. Especially where Reid MacKinnon is concerned.'

'Fancy coming for a cuppa and you can tell me all about it?'

Juliette shook her head. 'Oh, goodness no, I'll be fine, honestly. I'm not going to keep you on *your* day off.'

Morag stood and waved a dismissive hand. 'Och, pish. Come on. Kenneth's in the shop today, so I'm free as a bird. And it looks like you might need a friendly ear.'

Despite her words to the contrary, Juliette was relieved to have some company. And as Morag linked her arm, she felt a wave of affection for the woman who had made her so welcome.

Once they were seated at the kitchen table with a fresh pot of Earl Grey before them, Morag spoke. 'Out with it. What's he done now?'

Juliette cringed. 'It's not what Reid has done. This one's all on me. He was his usual self and I took offence and told him some home truths. Now I feel sick and wish I was at home in Mistford.'

'Oh, it cannae be that bad, hen. Tell me all about it.'

Juliette relayed the way she had advised Evin about the talent show and how she had commented to Reid about his worries, and how Reid had, quite rightly, told her she was interfering in things she knew nothing about.

Once she was finished, she rested her head in her hands as tears pricked at her eyes, guilt eating away at her. She wished she could turn back the clock and start this whole thing all over again. From day one and her first encounter with him. Sticking her nose in other people's business wasn't something she'd *ever* done before, so why now? Why Reid? The night they had danced together, she had felt so alive, so giddy. She couldn't deny she had enjoyed it; enjoyed *him*. But then, why had she been so harsh today? It was clear he was in pain and the last thing she would ever deliberately do is hurt someone. In addition, she wasn't a single parent, so had no right to judge *or* to speak ill of someone who was. Her heart squeezed when she thought about the expression on Reid's face after her series of unnecessary and cruel words.

Morag sighed. 'I think you're being too harsh on yoursel', dear. I think you reacted just how I would have, if I'm honest. I know he's been through a lot, but you don't know all the details, no one does, because he won't talk about it. And you cannae help what you don't know.'

'Promise me you won't breathe a word of this to anyone, Morag. I don't want to add gossip to the list of reasons he hates me.'

Morag held up both hands. 'I give you my word. And you're not gossiping. That infers you're making things up for the drama, and clearly this has affected you. But I think perhaps he could use a friend right now. And I think perhaps *you* might be the perfect candidate.'

Juliette shook her head. 'There's no way he would want that now. I've blown it.'

'Oh, I think you may be wrong there. I know the Reid MacKinnon from before Kate happened to him. He was such a caring man. He'd give the food from his plate if he thought someone was going hungry. And that boy is his life now. Give it a day or so and see what happens. But I think he may see the error of his own ways.'

'It was me who was in the wrong, Morag. I take full responsibility.'

'If you want my opinion, I think Reid has a lot to answer for too. But from what you've said about your own experiences, I think he will come to that conclusion himself. But, whatever you do, don't go running back to Mistford, eh? You'd be missed.'

Juliette smiled. 'Thank you. I won't... not yet anyway.'

17

A few days passed and Juliette got the feeling that Reid was avoiding coming down to the village. With Evin away, she wondered if he had maybe lost his anchor. It seemed the child was the only thing keeping him going on some days. She hadn't seen him, even from a distance, but how could she blame him? She had been weighing up the pros and cons of going to see him. Perhaps she *could* help? From her own experiences, there were so many books she could recommend.

During the evenings, she spent time researching the best books on mental health that were specifically aimed at men, seeing as it was a fairly taboo subject for many. It sounded as if Reid subscribed to the "shut up and get on with it" mentality which helped no one. She dreamed of a day when such matters were discussed as casually and easily as chickenpox or the flu.

Eventually, she narrowed her book choices down to two. She hovered her finger over the purchase button several times and chickened out at the last minute. He already thought she was an interfering busybody and she wasn't going to help her situation at all by adding fuel to that particular fire.

She questioned her reasons for caring so much. As he had pointed out, she was only going to be here temporarily, so it didn't really affect her, going forward. Except she knew, deep down, that, for some strange reason, it did. Just knowing a tiny part of what he might be going through made her desperate to help him. She wouldn't wish that cloud of darkness and the accompanying feeling of despair on her worst enemy. It was like being at the bottom of a well, unable to see daylight and having no energy to climb out. If she could help him avoid going there, she had a duty to do so.

When she had been going through depression, she had lost count of the number of people who had told her to *cheer up* or *look on the bright side*. She had rapidly realised some sad truths at the time: first and foremost, that what many people don't seem to understand about depression is that it isn't a life choice. You can't simply *snap out of it* or just decide one day to be happy. You can't just *cheer up* and *look on the bright side*, because when you're in the depths of hopelessness there *is* no bright side. When you're looking around and wondering if the world would be a better place without you in it, you *can't* count your blessings and be glad to be alive. If only it *was* that easy.

If Reid was anywhere close to feeling as low as she once had, she knew he needed help before it was too late.

* * *

Juliette's role at the Lifeboat House Museum continued to be an education. Each spare moment she had was spent reading the displays and getting to know all about the place her mother spent her childhood. With each visitor to the museum came a different personal story and reason for them being there, whether it was pure intrigue, a family connection or just passing through. She was loving it for the most part. But she wondered how Reid was and what he was up to. Was he painting perhaps? She hoped so. After seeing his work, she would hate to think of such a talent being stifled by sadness and loneliness. She was still trying to pluck up the courage to make the first step and visit him. But her behaviour the last time she had spoken to him was still in the forefront of her mind. What if he told her to get lost?

Wednesday evening was warm and, once the museum was closed, she ate a quick dinner and decided to go for another walk. It was becoming a routine for her after her nightly phone calls home. She walked towards the little church beside the field and found a peaceful memorial garden at the opposite side. An abundance of wildflowers surrounded stones and plaques and the constant droning of bees merrily carrying on with their work resonated around her. She wandered around reading the gravestones, looking for hints of her mother's family name and found a couple of McLeods buried there. It was a balmy evening and she was grateful for the large trees that afforded a little shade. There was a wrought-iron bench placed against the wall for contemplation. She took a seat and sat in silence for a while.

'Oh, Laurie, I wish you were here. There are so many things I've needed to talk to you about since I arrived in Glentorrin. Funny stories mostly. But there are other things too... I'm terrified of betraying your memory, you see. I miss you so much, but I know I have to move on, and I think that's the scariest part. I... I felt things for Reid when we danced, you see. Please, forgive me. It's been so long since I've felt a man's arms around me, and it felt good. But that makes me hate myself. Maybe that's why I was so quick to snap at him? I don't know. But I regret it so much. I want to help him, but after how I've behaved, I'm worried he'll just turn me away. You were always my voice of reason. You always had solutions. But this is one thing you can't help me with. If you were here, I wouldn't even be thinking like this. But you're not here. You never will be.

However hard it is, Laurie, I have to accept that you're gone, and that I don't want to be alone.' She sighed deeply and closed her eyes for a moment, listening to the birdsong and letting the warm rays of the sun warm her skin through the gaps in the leaves. 'Anyway, you'd love this place, Laurie. I think it's just how you expected Skye to be. Beautiful, peaceful, healing. I know I'm going to miss it when it's time to go home.'

'Jules? Are you okay?' She jumped and turned to see Evin and Chewie standing further along the wall in the shade of the trees.

'Oh, Evin, you're back from your mum's!' She beamed at her young friend.

He glanced around her in search of something. 'Who were you talking to? A ghost?'

She laughed lightly. 'Not really. I was just talking to Laurie. My husband.'

Evin's eyes widened and he looked around eagerly. 'Oh! Where is he?'

She cringed, this was something that hadn't come up before and she wasn't sure how to explain. 'Oh, no, erm... he's... he died.'

Evin crumpled his brow. 'So, you *were* talking to a ghost?'

She shook her head and smiled. 'No. Just to his memory, I suppose.'

Evin walked towards her and Chewie followed obediently. 'But he can't answer you, can he?' The look in his eyes was a combination of fear and intrigue.

'Sadly, no. But I find it helps to talk to him sometimes. Even though he can't talk back.' She shrugged in search of a fitting explanation. 'It makes me feel closer to him.'

Evin pondered her words. 'Oh. I didn't know you were supposed to do that when people died.' He fell silent and tilted his face up to the sun. After a few moments, he returned his attention to her. 'Sometimes I miss my grandma, and I wish I could talk to her. Especially when something bad *or* good *or* funny has happened. Dad doesn't always have the time to listen to me going on and on.' He rolled his eyes and grinned to make light of his comment, but Juliette felt for the boy.

'Well, then you should find a quiet place to sit and talk to her.'

'Can I sit with you for a minute?' he asked politely.

'Of course.'

He lowered himself to the bench and they sat in silence for a while, enjoying the peacefulness of the location. 'Do you think you'll get married again one day?' he asked out of the blue, as children were wont to do.

'Oh, gosh.' She laughed, taken aback by his directness. 'It's not something I've thought much about, but honestly? I... I really don't know.'

He turned to face her with pleading in his eyes. 'People *do* get married again though, don't they, after divorces and things? They do get to be happy again, don't they? I mean, my mum did, but that was... *different*, I suppose.'

Juliette nodded, wondering how much the boy really knew about the circumstances of his parents' split. 'Lots of people do, yes. But it's a very personal thing, Evin. There are no rules or guidelines. Every person has a different experience. You just have to follow your heart.'

Evin nodded and absorbed her words again. 'I... I suppose it's hard though. I mean... I've heard Uncle Kendric telling Dad to forget my mum and move on, but I don't think he wants to. Although he doesn't seem happy as he is either. Grown-ups are so confusing.'

She smiled again, this time at his innocent take on things. 'That's just it though, Evin. People don't always *want* to move on. Moving on almost makes it seem like you're forgetting.'

'But... if you keep remembering the past, won't you be lonely for the rest of your life?' There was an edge of desperation to his voice as he spoke. 'That's what worries me about my dad. I can see he's lonely now, and so sad. And I *want* him to move on. And I *do* want him to forget about what happened with my mum. But he won't.' He sighed and stared at the ground. 'I can sometimes hear him crying. And when I go into his room, he pretends it was the TV or something. He turns his back so I can't see his face. But I'm not daft. I always know it was him. And... I feel bad for still loving my mum even though she hurt him.'

Juliette's heart ached for the boy. No child should have to choose between their parents, but it was clear Evin was feeling he did. She reached out and squeezed his hand. 'No, no, you mustn't feel bad, sweetheart. She's still your mum. And your dad wouldn't want you to stop loving her. Believe me when I say that.'

He shook his head. 'I just wish things were back to how they used to be. Not with Mum there or anything. But... I really wish Dad could forget. You know, like how one of those mind-wiping things works in *Men in Black*? Only for him to just forget the sad bits. And I wish he was happy again.'

Juliette softened her voice, wishing she could do more to help him. 'I know you do. I can't speak for your dad, and I know our situations are very different. But I know that in *my* situation I don't want to forget. Laurie is part of who I am. He's part of what made me who I am today. And I'm guessing that's how your dad feels about your mum. Just because she hurt him doesn't mean he wants to forget. And he doesn't want to forget because your mum is part of *you* too. And you are a *very* special thing that came from them being together. So, to forget your mum would be to forget the happy times they had, and that includes you coming into the world.'

'But I don't know what to do to make him happy. I used to make him laugh, but I think he's forgotten how.'

'Hey, none of this is your fault, okay? It may take your dad a while to heal from the sad things that happened, but some day he'll be able to look back and just see the happy things. That's what I'm trying to do. But it's difficult. Grown-ups don't always let themselves ask for help, and they don't always know how to tell people how they feel. Just give your dad time. And if you do need to talk to someone who can answer you, you know where I am.'

Evin turned, and with bright eyes, he said, 'Maybe he'll see me at the talent show and that'll make him happy!'

She thought back to Reid's words about the talent show and hoped he was just lashing out, that he would support his son and be proud. With a lump of emotion tightening her throat, Juliette slipped her arm around his shoulder and squeezed him to her side. 'Absolutely. I think he'll love it. You'll make him so proud.' She only hoped she was right.

18

Aside from being busy in the museum with the tourists passing through, preparations for the games were on everyone's minds. Juliette was getting to meet more of the locals as she attended various meetings to finalise who was doing what on the day. Thanks to lots of local publicity, a huge crowd was anticipated, and the village was buzzing. As each day passed and the event loomed closer, more decorations appeared around the place, adding to the festivities. Each house was dressed to impress. The flowers in every window box and garden pot seemed to be blooming too, and Juliette hadn't seen a sight as pretty for a long time. Everyone was out in force, ready to make these games the best ones yet.

A huge marquee was erected on the field and inside it was a temporary stage, tables and chairs. It was a bright space and Juliette was surprised at the size. Surely, it wouldn't be filled?

Father McAllen, the local vicar, had been away on sabbatical but had returned in time to help with the preparations and had wasted no time in introducing himself. He had come into the museum midweek.

'Ah, you must be Mrs Fairhurst. You're quite the talk of the town,' he'd said as he held out his hand.

She shook it and said, 'And you must be Father McAllen. It's lovely to finally meet you.' He was roughly mid-fifties with grey hair, a beard and, overall, he bore a striking resemblance to Father Christmas. She had made a mental note not to call him this.

'And you. And please call me Geoff, or Father Geoff, if you must.'

Don't call him Father Christmas, don't call him Father Christmas. 'Father Geoff it is,' she'd replied, relieved that the right name popped out.

They had chatted at length about local history and had even got onto classic novels and his love of Walter Scott's writings. Laurie had been a fan of *Ivanhoe*, but his particular favourite by Scott was *Marmion*. Juliette remembered, above everything else, the quote about tangled webs and deception and smiled at the memory of Sunday mornings in the garden, her head in Laurie's lap, long before his illness took hold, as he read aloud to her.

That thought led to more reminiscing and she remembered a haunting conversation they'd had on one such day when his illness had been hitherto undetected. They were sitting in their cottage garden on a spring morning as he read to her from her favourite Brontë classic, *Wuthering Heights*. They had reached the part of the story where Heathcliff demands that Cathy haunt him, that she can't leave him alone. It always tugged at Juliette's heart and, as she'd wiped away the tears, Laurie had placed the book down and said, 'Would you want me to come and haunt you? You know, if I died?'

She had sat up straight and laughed. 'Erm, probably not keen on that idea, as much as I love you. And why the talk of death all of a sudden?'

He'd shrugged. 'Well, I'm ten years older than you; stands to reason I'll go first.'

She had shaken her head. 'Maybe we should read something a bit more light-hearted next time, eh? I don't particularly want to talk about you being dead, Laurie.'

He'd held up his hand, a mischievous grin playing on his lips. 'No, no, come on, humour me for a moment. So, you wouldn't want me to communicate with you if I could?'

She'd cupped his face and planted a kiss on his luscious mouth. 'I'm not exactly sure how I'd feel about some floaty, transparent version of you hovering at the end of the bed. It's a little bit too *A Christmas Carol*-esque for me.'

'Okay, so maybe not a ghost then. How about if I visit you as something else? Like a... like a... I don't know, a *bird* or something?'

She'd shaken her head and smiled, playing along for a little longer. 'But there are a *gazillion* birds in the UK, so how would I know it was you?' She'd stood to pour some more tea.

He'd thought for a moment, then said, 'I'll come back as a robin or something, but at the wrong time of year. When you wouldn't expect to see one. That way you'll know it's me. I'll make sure it's at a significant point though, not just because it's a Tuesday or something silly like that. I'll wait until... I don't know... a time when you're needing support, or to know you're on the right track.'

'But robins are here all year,' she had told him with a smile as she stroked his cheek, thinking of a hundred things she'd rather be doing with him right then than talking about the aviculture of the UK.

He'd pulled her into his lap, which was far more to her liking, but, much to her chagrin, he'd continued, 'Yes, but you don't *see* them in the summer usually. Food is plentiful so they stay out of sight. That's why they're a Christmas card symbol, because they're much more visible in winter.'

'Okay, deal, so if I need you, you'll come back as a robin. If it's ever necessary, I'll look out for you,' she'd told him, keen to get off the rather morbid but fantastical subject. 'Now, are you going to take me to bed or what?'

With that, he had scooped her up in his arms, causing her to squeal in delight, and carried her upstairs.

A week later, he had presented her with a silver locket – the same locket that had adorned her neck since he had passed – a friendly robin engraved on its front side and a photo of him on the inside.

* * *

It was Thursday evening and the final meeting was taking place in the church. Caitlin was seated beside Juliette and Morag flanked her other side. The atmosphere was tense with excitement and anticipation. Reid was nowhere to be seen and, in fact, had been noticeably absent for most of the preparations, which was, she was told, rather odd. She still hadn't plucked up the courage to visit him and, as she looked around the people in the pews, a sense of guilt niggled at her insides. She had seen Evin walking with Chewie a couple of times, but when she had enquired after his father, he had been somewhat evasive. She vowed that she would go to see them straight after the meeting.

Kenneth stood at the front of the church near the altar and brought the meeting to order. 'Now, ladies and gentlemen, we know that there will be quite a crowd here on Saturday. There are plenty of holidaymakers who've never witnessed a Highland event before, so we need to make this extra special. The Scouts have agreed to be on litter patrol and we really appreciate them doing this as I'm sure most, if not all, of them, would rather be having fun at the gala. So, they'll be working in shifts to give them a chance to enjoy the day too. Caitlin has done just about enough baking to sink the MPV Jura.' A rumble of laughter travelled around the gathering. 'And, of course, this year she will be ably assisted by everyone's favourite dog whisperer, our current museum guardian, Jules.' A rumble of laughter traversed the church.

These people really weren't willing to forget her crazy act of heroics. Her cheeks heated with the attention.

'There's the tombola, which is around twice as big as last year, the bouncy castle, which I'll be keeping well away from... bloody deathtraps, those things.' More laughter. 'And we have the Fire Service here with one of their engines for the wee 'uns to climb on and look at. The usual flower stalls, craft stalls, coconut shy and dunk the teacher will all be set up by the end of Friday evening in readiness. The Highland games events and other games will be at the west end of the field where there are no houses... *Bobby Duncan...*' Kenneth glared, but then winked at someone on the front row and a roar of laughter and jeers aimed at the poor victim almost raised the roof.

Caitlin leaned towards Juliette. 'Quoits. A bit too much enthusiasm, a broken window and lots of embarrassment, you get the picture.' She rolled her eyes and grinned with a shake of her head. Juliette giggled at the mental image.

When the laughter had subsided, Kenneth continued, 'And we're very fortunate to have guest prize giver, Gregor Edmunds, with us on Saturday. For those of you who don't know, shame on you because he was the 2007 Highland Games Champion and he's a top bloke too.'

A cheer erupted, followed by raucous applause and whistles. Clearly this Gregor chap was a firm favourite.

'So, we'll be at the field from seven in the morning and the event starts at eleven. We have plenty of time to get set up. The Toilichte Hens will be playing music in the main tent throughout the day. We have a caller for the dances, but all those who already know the steps get yourselves in there and show our visitors how it's done, eh? We've agreed on five pounds as the standard entry charge, but people are welcome to donate more, if they wish. And let's hope they wish. The police have already put cones along the roads where parking isn't permitted, so let's be vigilant about that, folks. We have to keep the way clear for the emergency services should they need to get through. Now, obviously I haven't gone through every single stall and event, as you all know the score, and for those that don't, it'll be a nice surprise on the day. So, that's it, folks. Have a fantastic Highland games!'

A final applause vibrated through the pews and people began to leave.

Caitlin linked arms with Juliette. 'So, are we off to The Coxswain for a cheeky glass of vino?'

Juliette cringed. 'Oh, no, do you mind if I don't? There's something I need to do.'

Caitlin frowned. 'Ooh, Mrs Fairhurst, that sounds fairly cloak and dagger. Is everything okay?'

Juliette's face warmed, but she forced a laugh. 'Of course. Everything's fine. I just have some last-minute stuff to do, you know, before the gala.'

Caitlin shrugged. 'Okay, well, if you change your mind, I'll be in there. I think Archie is going for a pint, so I won't be too lonely. See you soon!'

The friends parted company at the junction and Juliette waited for Caitlin to disappear out of sight before she headed to Reid's. She didn't want to set tongues wagging, after all.

As she walked up the lane, she thought about the last time she had been there. With the starlit sky above, it could've been quite romantic on that night. Sadness tugged at her insides again, but this was soon replaced by a twinge of guilt. Why on earth was she thinking about romance, for goodness sake?

She arrived at the detached stone cottage and admired the pretty exterior she hadn't seen the last time. It looked a little tired and in need of TLC, but the bones of the building showed its true character and age. There was no sign of Reid, but Evin was outside with Chewie practising tricks in the overgrown garden. He approached as she walked up the front path to the door.

'Hi, Sparkly Jules, w-what are you doing here?'

'Hi, Evin. I just thought I'd stop by and see your dad... about...' *Dammit, I haven't thought this through.* '... the gala. Yes, the stalls and other bits and bobs.' She shook her head and waved her hands around, hoping she sounded genuine.

His eyes widened. 'Oh, erm, he's not feeling too well today. I... I think it's the flu or something, but it's probably best that you don't go in. You don't want to catch it.' His insistence worried her.

'Oh, I'm sure it'll be fine. I've had my flu jab. Maybe I can make him some soup.'

Evin gave a weak smile and stood in front of the door. 'Oh... I don't think he really wants any. I don't think he's hungry. You know, it's just the flu. Like I said.'

Juliette folded her arms across her chest and cocked her head to the side. 'Evin, what's the matter? You're being very cagey.'

Another forced smile. 'No, I'm not, honest. He's just... snotty and coughing and looks a bit disgusting, that's all. No one wants to see that, believe me.' He pulled out his tongue and feigned vomiting to add to his dramatic performance.

She stepped closer to the door. 'Well, in that case I won't stay long. I just need to have a quick chat to—'

Evin blocked her path. 'Please, Jules! Could you just come back another day? I'll tell him you stopped by, I *promise*.'

She sighed deeply and reached out to touch his arm. 'Evin,

you're really worrying me now. Is he okay? I mean, *really* okay? Can I do anything? Do *you* need any help with anything?'

Tears welled in the boy's eyes and his lower lip trembled. 'I'm looking after him, I really am. I'm doing really well. I've cooked his dinner and everything. And I'm making my own food, too. And I hoovered and tidied up all the rubbish from the living room.' His eyes widened. 'Not that there was loads of rubbish or anything. He's really tidy, you know, when he's not all snotty.'

His emotional reaction and the way he protested wasn't lost on her and she knew something was seriously amiss. She decided to go and speak to Morag. Surely, she'd know what to do.

She softened her voice and smiled kindly. 'Okay. I believe that you're looking after him, Evin. You're a good son. But please, *please* call me at the museum or the house, or...' She scrabbled around in her bag for a scrap of paper and a pen and quickly scrawled down her mobile number. She thrust the paper at him. 'You can get me on my mobile if you need *anything*. Anything at all. Okay?'

His smile widened and he swiped at his eyes. 'Ugh, hay fever. But at least it's not the flu like Dad. I'm fine, honest. Dad will be fine too. *Honest*. But I need to practise my tricks with Chewie now.'

Juliette took all the 'honests' with a pinch of salt and the not-so-subtle hint that he was done talking. She resisted the urge to hug the boy. 'Right, well, I'll see you soon, okay?'

He nodded vigorously, but, as she walked away, she knew she couldn't leave things alone.

She arrived at Morag's and knocked at the door.

Kenneth opened it. 'Oh, hi, hen. If you're after my better half, you'll find her in the shop. I'm going to join her in a few minutes as there's been a huge delivery ready for Saturday.'

'Okay, thanks, Kenneth. I'll pop there now.'

* * *

Morag frowned and shook her head. 'Oh dear. I think you did the right thing walking away, hen. But you're also right that something must have happened. I know Evin's just come home from his mother's and things can be quite tough when he's been there, so I wonder what's been said. That poor boy's caught in the middle. Reid cannae be coping. I think I need to contact his brother.' She rubbed her chin and chewed on her lip as worry creased her brow. 'I get the feeling Reid needs help. I just can't see him accepting it from the likes of you and me. So, I think his brother is the only one who's likely to get through to him at this point.'

Juliette's stomach knotted and she paced the canned goods aisle as Morag paused from stacking the shelves. Along with the knot in her stomach came a feeling of nausea. She twisted her hands in front of her body. 'Oh god, Morag, I feel like I've opened Pandora's box. I'm so worried now. I don't want to be the reason authorities intervene or anything like that. I'd never forgive myself.' She could hear the strain of panic in her own voice.

Morag turned and fixed her with a determined, yet kind gaze. 'Look, love, you're concerned, as am I. And, believe me, it won't come to that. There's no need for the authorities to get involved. Evin isn't neglected, that much is obvious. But he is stuck between a rock and a hard place. And I think maybe Reid's trying to deal with everything by himself. Whether that's pride, fear, or denial, I don't know, but he can't carry on. He needs his family.'

Morag went off to make the phone call to Kendric and in a bid to keep herself occupied, Juliette took up the old-fashioned pricing gun and carried on where her friend had left off.

19

After phone calls to check in with her parents, Millie and Dexter, on the day of the Highland games, Juliette made her way across to help with the set-up. The sun was already scorching when she carried the last of the trays to the table in the marquee, as Caitlin popped up some pretty little lace cake covers to keep the wasps at bay. Strangely, and unlike previous years, so she'd been told, Leanna had set her stall up at the opposite end of the marquee. Juliette wondered if this was her way of making one of her badly thought out points but decided she was being utterly paranoid and put the thought out of her mind.

A pretty red-haired girl arrived holding Cleo on a lead, and Caitlin hugged her. 'Jules, this is the love of my life, Grace. Gracie, this is my new friend, Jules.'

'Are you the lady who saved Evin's dog?' the little girl asked, shyly, her head tilted inquisitively.

'That's me. It's lovely to meet you, at last.'

The girl's eyes widened, and she gave a broad smile. 'It's nice to meet you too. Anyone who loves dogs as much as I do is fine with me,' Grace said with a wide smile.

Juliette inwardly cringed, knowing full well that she hadn't really *loved* dogs before her encounter with Chewie. But she had to admit that after getting to know the huge slobbery canine, and after meeting Cleo, she was definitely feeling happier around them.

The atmosphere, like the weather, was heating up and there was a merry buzz about the place. The games arena had been pegged out with a 'no-go' zone to keep people, and windows, safe. Juliette had watched one of the men tossing a caber as a dry run and was surprised at how far it had travelled. It was clear why the cordon was needed.

The Toilichte Hens had arrived early and were making themselves useful wherever they could. It was so lovely how everyone was getting stuck in, and there was a real sense of community to the place. It warmed her heart to see the smiles on each and every face as nothing seemed too much trouble. It was a little like Christmas, only in the summer. All tiffs put aside for the interests of the greater good.

Morag had been in touch earlier to say that Kendric wasn't in when she had called again. There had been three attempts to contact him since Juliette went round after seeing Evin and his mobile was going straight to voicemail. She figured he must be away for work. Or, and more hopefully, he was already on his way to Glentorrin. Juliette couldn't help but wonder where, and how, Reid was. Evin hadn't arrived yet and, thanks to her feeling of responsibility, she was having to fight her conscience on the matter of heading up there once more to check on him. Morag had been and taken some food, but she'd had to leave it at the door with the boy, who'd once again been reluctant to allow entrance to his home. But, at least, she knew he was going to eat something wholesome, instead of whatever poor Evin had been able to provide.

'Penny for 'em?' Caitlin asked.

Juliette smiled and shook her head. 'Oh, nothing. Just in my own little world today.'

'*Check... one... two... one... two... check,*' said a voice over the PA system.

'Give us a wee song, Archie!' Caitlin hollered across the marquee.

Archie laughed loudly over the mic and almost deafened everyone. He cringed. 'Whoops, sorry, folks! My bad! I think I'll leave the singing to the professionals, Caitlin,' he replied as the two women from The Toilichte Hens took their positions on stage for a soundcheck.

Even though it was just a quick run-through, Juliette couldn't help stomping her foot along to the tune they played on the fiddle and the accordion.

Suddenly Caitlin grabbed her hand, tugged her into the middle of the room and swung her. Juliette almost lost her footing but was overtaken with giggles as her crazy friend twirled her round and round in time with the music. The gathered crowd took a break from setting up and clapped along as Caitlin shouted instructions at Juliette and, at the end, cheers and whistles joined applause and laughter.

'I'll make a Highland dancer out of you yet, Jules!' Caitlin told her and they staggered back, arm in arm, to their stall.

As the sun beat down, Juliette was thoroughly grateful that she was undercover and she guzzled on water from the bottle she'd brought.

'Well, this is all looking marvellous, ladies,' Morag told them when she arrived at the stall.

'Thank you. I just hope we manage to save some to sell. Grace has already eaten three fairy cakes.' Caitlin laughed.

'Well, it looks grand. I reckon you'll have a busy day. And I'll come and look after things for you later so you can have a wander around.'

'Thanks, Morag, that's lovely, but won't you need to be at the shop?'

Morag laughed. 'Not on your nelly, Jules! Kenneth and I will be here all day. We've a casual worker who runs the shop on gala day and holidays and such. That's why we needed to make sure everything was priced up. Makes life easier for her. So, I'll be glad to give you a wee break when you're ready. The event will be opening in ten minutes, so I'll be off just now.' She backed away and waggled her fingers. 'Toodle-oo!'

Juliette waved at Morag's retreating form. 'Thank you! See you later.'

'Have you seen Reid this week?' Caitlin asked once Morag was out of earshot.

Juliette spun round and frowned at her. 'Me? Why should have I seen him? What do you mean? And no, I haven't, anyway.' Had someone said something? Was news of Evin's predicament spreading around the village? Shit, what would happen if it was?

Caitlin's eyes widened and she laughed. 'I wasn't interrogating you, honestly. I was just a bit concerned. He's usually at the forefront of organising this thing. You could say he's a control freak.' She rolled her eyes. 'Anyway, I heard he's bad with the flu. Strange though, as illness doesn't usually stop him from being a bossy beggar.'

Juliette feigned tidying a pile of biscuits. 'He must be quite poorly then.'

'Aye. I might take him some baking. It usually cheers him up.'

Juliette felt a change of subject was urgently needed. 'So, where's your gorgeous daughter gone? I thought she was helping.'

'Oh, aye, she is. But she's mad keen on gardening, so she's gone to check out Archie's plant stall before, and I quote: "all the good *specimens* have gone". Bless her. She's a wee green-fingered wonder is my Grace. She's all about the environment. No clue where it comes from. I can kill *fake* plants myself.'

Juliette snorted with laughter.

A voice she recognised as Kenneth's came over the other sound system. 'The event is now open, ladies and gents. I repeat, the event is now open! Have a wonderful day!'

A loud cheer followed and suddenly his voice was replaced by Big Country's 'In a Big Country', the perfect soundtrack to get everyone smiling.

* * *

By half twelve, Juliette couldn't quite believe how popular the little cake stall had been. She glanced over their rapidly depleting stock and cringed at Caitlin.

'Worry not. I've some more on the go back at the shop.' Caitlin tapped her nose.

Once again, Juliette had been in her element, chatting to the visitors, and, if it was clear they were holidaymakers, she made sure to tell them to visit the museum too, after the weekend.

Morag appeared at one thirty so that Juliette could have a spot of lunch and a wander around the other stalls and attractions. Grace had arrived to help Morag and Caitlin had gone back to the bakery to check on the ovens. Juliette wasn't exactly hungry as she'd already munched on tiffin that Caitlin and Grace had made especially for the day, but the chance to have a walk around was welcome.

'Ladies and gentlemen, the children's talent contest will take place in the main marquee at three o'clock. You don't want to miss it,' Kenneth announced over the sound system as she walked towards Archie's stall to look at the flowers.

'Ah, Miss Jules. You won't have met Kendric MacKinnon, will you?' Archie said as she approached.

A tall, broad-shouldered man, wearing jeans and a pale blue shirt, stood with his back towards her. He turned round as Archie mentioned him by name, and when she was greeted by the full view of him, Juliette half expected Barry White music to play and for the sun to glint off his perfect white teeth.

He smiled warmly. 'Jules? The dog saver?'

She scrunched her brow as she wondered how he knew this already and if everyone on Skye was as obsessed with their canine companions as they were here. She nodded and he continued.

'Good to meet you. I'm Kendric, I've been told you're quite the hero to my nephew, Evin.' He had the most lilting accent, more subtle than Reid's, and very smiley eyes. He held out his long, tanned hand. She could immediately see what Caitlin had meant about his striking good looks. He was definitely movie-star material, although there was no movie star, *or* famous man for that matter, to whom she could compare him. All she knew was that he was probably the best-looking man she'd ever laid eyes on – she sent up a quick apology to Laurie, who she knew would simply laugh at her goggle-eyed stare and tell her to stop catching flies.

'Is the sun getting to you too, Jules?' Archie asked, snapping her back to reality.

She touched her hair, then her forehead as her cheeks almost spontaneously combusted through embarrassment. 'Oh, good grief, yes, I think it must be. I'm so sorry. Jules Fairhurst. Lovely to meet you too, Kendric.' She shook his hand. He had a very firm grasp and smooth skin.

Bloody hell, get a grip, will you?

'There's no wonder. It's such a scorcher today.'

'It is.' She glanced around. 'Is Reid not with you?'

Kendric frowned and cleared his throat. 'Ah, no, he's... erm...'

'Still down with the flu?' she interjected, not wishing to force him to explain things.

He nodded. 'Yes, that's right. Poor guy. He might make it down a little later.'

'Ah, good. So, have you brought your camera crew?'

He glanced around him as if expecting to see them behind him, then he laughed. 'Oh no. Not this time. I was considering doing a piece on the games, but I figured what the heck, all work and no play, et cetera. So, I'm going to spend some quality time with Evin and keep Reid stocked up on flu meds.' He laughed awkwardly.

'Well, I'm glad you're here for him. And it's nice to meet you.'

'Likewise. See you later, maybe.'

'See you later,' Juliette replied as she turned and wandered off to look at the other stalls. When she glanced back, she saw that a small crowd had gathered around Reid's brother, but, strangely, his eyes were fixed on her. She immediately turned away.

She made her way to a row of portacabin toilets and waited in line, tapping her foot to the music before one became free. Once inside, she locked the door and heard loud whispers.

'Do you think she wants him back, then?' a female voice asked.

'Pfft. Well, she can swivel if she does. Although, I'll say one thing, Evin should definitely go and live with her. It's where he belongs. And if it was up to me, that's what would happen.'

Leanna.

'So, you'd get him all to yourself, you mean?' the first woman giggled.

Juliette held her breath and strained to hear.

'Erm, I'm a married woman, Celia. What do you take me for?'

'I take you for someone who's obsessed with a man she can't fecking have, that's what.'

'I think you'll find that if I made it *known* that I want him, I'd damn well *have* him,' Leanna scoffed.

'So, what's stopping you? Apart from the obvious, of course.'

'If I wanted to have an affair, Donny couldn't stop me. But, anyway, that dog snogging bitch is trying to get her claws into him. Have you seen how she swoons over him? It's pathetic.'

'Oh, that Janet woman? What do you mean dog snogging?'

'She probably gave Chewie the kiss of life to impress Reid.'

'Oh yeah! Probably. It's pathetic.'

Juliette opened her mouth in a silent growl, her brow creased, and her fists clenched. *Janet? My name's Juliette, you cow. And I didn't snog Chewie!*

Leanna continued, 'I mean, who does she think she is? Just because she can swim. It's ridiculous how people keep going on about it too. But she keeps on lapping up the attention. I feel sorry for her.'

'Totally ridiculous how she's lapping it up. Totally,' Celia repeated.

'Anyway, I'm off back to the tea stall. But, whatever you do, if you hear anything about Reid, let me know, okay, Celia? He wouldn't see me when I went up last night. And that's not like him.'

'Totally not like him, no.'

Juliette wasn't sure whether to scream at what she'd overheard or to laugh at the pathetic schoolgirl-type bitching she'd been privy to. She waited for the adjacent cubicle to become silent, then left her own.

20

'I hear you met the delightfully scrummy Kendric,' Caitlin announced as Juliette arrived back at the stall.

Juliette rolled her eyes. 'Good grief, Caitlin, have you got eyes everywhere, or do you employ spies?'

Her friend tapped her nose. 'That, my dear, would be telling. So, come on then, what did you think?'

'He seems really sweet.'

'And...?'

Juliette shrugged, fully aware of what Caitlin was getting at. 'And genuine. Not what I expected for a TV star.'

Tugging on her arm, Caitlin continued, 'Annnnnd...?'

She wagged her finger. 'Tall. He must be six two, maybe taller.'

'Ugh! You're bloody insufferable, Fairhurst. You know exactly what I mean.'

Juliette smirked. 'Yes, I do. And yes, he is very good-looking. Let's leave it at that, eh?'

Caitlin nudged her shoulder. 'Did he ask you out?'

Juliette gasped. 'What? No! Of course he didn't ask me out! I spoke to him for all of two minutes.'

'But you wish he had, don't you?'

Juliette felt her cheeks warming for the millionth time – she would really have to get a handle on that. 'No! I'm not interested in anything like that. You know I'm not.'

'Excuse me?' To Juliette's relief their banter was interrupted. 'Do you have any more shortbread? The plate is empty.'

* * *

'Ladies and gents, I'm delighted to welcome to the stage the first of our youngsters for the talent contest. Euan Dalgetty, who'll be playing "Flower of Scotland" on the bagpipes. He's been having lessons for around six months now, so give him a huge warm Glentorrin welcome!'

The marquee erupted in applause as a nervous, kilted young man – whom Juliette recognised from around the village – took to the centre of the stage. He began to squeeze the bag under his arm whilst blowing on the pipe jutting out of the top. When he got in to the full swing of the tune, Juliette couldn't help thinking that a choir of tone-deaf cats might have sounded more appealing, but the lad had guts to stand up there before a room full of people, strangers and jeering peers alike, and play his heart out.

Once he was finished, clapping ensued and the red-faced boy took a stiff bow before tripping over his own feet as he exited stage left. Next was a teenage girl with braces who performed a Highland sword dance. She was incredibly light on her feet and the audience clapped along to the music that came from a CD player on a small table beside her. Her costume was a pretty tartan kilt in lilac and green, complete with matching sash and a white blouse with billowy sleeves. Her curled hair bounced as she jigged, and the whole scene put a huge grin on Juliette's face from where she stood behind the stall in the corner. This was the epitome of all things Scottish.

Following singers, magicians and comedians, eventually it was Evin's turn, and Juliette held her breath as he took to the stage with Chewie. She was almost dreading this moment. If it all went horribly wrong, she would cry for him and Reid would be proved right, meaning she'd be totally responsible for encouraging him. She just had to believe that everything Evin had gone through lately would be forgotten momentarily, as he showed the crowd that he *did* have talent. That he *was* special, contrary to his perception of their feelings.

Caitlin nudged her. 'Go on, get over there. I can see you're dying to. I can keep an eye on things here.'

Juliette gave her a quick hug and made her way through the throng to stand just out of sight so as not to distract the performers. She watched in awe as Evin gave short commands to Chewie and the huge ball of fur followed every single one. From giving his paw and rolling over, to dancing like a show pony, the pair of them did an amusing, if a little clumsy and comical, variation of the conga, and all in time with the track 'Heroes' by David Bowie. A wonderful choice, she felt. Evin beamed and Chewie's tongue lolled out as his tail wagged frantically – evidently, he was thoroughly enjoying the game.

Pride surged up inside Juliette as the canine and his human even bowed in synchronicity at the end of their performance. She'd never seen anything like it. She didn't care who heard or saw, and as applause erupted around the marquee, Juliette whooped and cheered louder than everyone.

Evin spotted her and gave her a double thumbs up as his grin widened.

Someone appeared beside her and she looked up to see Kendric banging his hands together above his head. He whistled and then bent to speak to Juliette. 'I hear this is all thanks to you. It's clear you've made a massive impression on the lad in the short space of time you've been here.' She turned to smile at him but found his expression quite serious as he continued, 'It's nice that he's taken to you, but I'm worried about what will happen when you leave. Just be careful, eh?'

Tears pricked her eyes as she watched the boy leaving the stage to countless pats on the back and scratches behind Chewie's ears. If this hadn't boosted his confidence and popularity, then nothing would. But she totally understood Kendric's concerns, her own heart would suffer too when it was time to leave the boy behind. She had become very fond of him.

'Look at that boy's face,' Kendric said, and Juliette was about to reply when she realised he wasn't addressing her. Much to her relief, she saw Reid, pale-faced and unshaven, looking more unkempt than normal, applauding proudly beside his brother. He glanced at her briefly and a ghost of a smile played on his lips before his concentration returned to his son.

* * *

Once the talent show was over, all the acts were asked to return to the stage for the announcement of the winner to be made. Caitlin, Grace, Morag and Reid and Kendric were now standing beside Juliette as they anxiously waited for the results.

'Now, the panel have had a very tricky job, as you can imagine. Choosing a single winner from twelve incredible acts was nigh on impossible,' Kenneth told the crowd. 'And we had to have a deciding vote due to a tie between two of the contenders, so I'd like to thank Gregor Edmunds for doing the honours. So, in third place... we have wee Esther Douglas with her angelic performance of "Blooming Heather".'

The audience applauded and Kenneth handed the young girl a white envelope.

'In second place... and you must understand how difficult this decision was, folks, with so many talented youngsters here today... anyway, as I was saying, in second place we have Evin MacKinnon and his amazing dog, Chewie!'

Cheers and whistles filled the room as Kenneth handed the ruddy-faced boy a white envelope. Evin searched the crowd with his gaze. When he found his dad, his face brightened and his grin spoke a thousand words without him needing to make a sound. Loud whistles pierced the air from where Reid stood, and Juliette was so happy to see the man radiating admiration and love.

'And finally, the winner of the Glentorrin talent contest this year, I have to say it was a wonderful performance, considering this is all new to him and I think that's what gave it the edge. So, our winner is... Euan Dalgetty on his bagpipes!'

Juliette applauded along with everyone else but equally fought the urge to shout, 'Fix!'

As the contestants left the stage, Juliette watched once again as Evin was surrounded by people congratulating him. He wasn't in the least bit disappointed to have not come first. And she was delighted to see that Grace had joined him too. Some of the boys from Evin's school year were fussing over the dog and chatting animatedly about how Evin managed to train him to do such brilliant tricks.

She glanced to the side and caught Reid watching her. She smiled and he nodded at her, as if admitting she'd been right, at least about this one small thing. The shared moment was fleeting, and his attention once again returned to Evin, who, she hoped, could bask in his newfound glory for as long as possible.

* * *

The stalls were all packed away, and the cash counted in readiness for the evening's entertainment. But first it was the turn of the main event of the day.

The Highland games!

Caitlin took the cash to put in her safe at the bakery and, when she returned, she brought a couple of deckchairs, which she unfolded for herself and Juliette; a rug was laid at their feet for Grace, Evin and Chewie. Many people had the same idea, and as Kenneth announced the first event, more people gathered.

Hamish arrived and placed his chair beside her. 'Now then, Jules, how are you enjoying your stay?'

'Hamish! Lovely to see you. I'm having a great time. I haven't seen you in the museum lately.'

'No, I went to visit my daughter for a few days. And my grandson and his new husband have arrived to stay as part of their honeymoon.'

'Be sure to bring him to the museum to say hello,' she said.

He smiled. 'Don't you worry, lassie, it's on my list of priorities.'

Once again, there was no sign of Reid and Juliette couldn't stop thinking about him. But her attention was pulled back by a nudge from Caitlin.

Huge, muscular, kilted men waved as they marched into the cordoned-off arena to Kenneth's call of their names, and each audience member cheered for their favourite. The caber toss was up first, and it turned out that the hulking men were able to lob the giant piece of tree trunk a lot further than Juliette ever anticipated. She watched in awe as the hefty poles were tossed into the air, landing metres away, with a vibrating thud. She wondered how on earth someone came up with the idea for the event. Were a bunch of lumberjacks, perhaps, standing around one lunch time trying to keep warm, when one suddenly chimed in, 'I know, let's see which one of us can throw a sawn tree trunk the farthest!'? It was bewildering but great fun to watch. The crowd were enraptured, and the volume of cheers rose exponentially as each toss was completed.

In between the caber toss and the hammer throw, there was a musical interlude. A pipe band from a neighbouring village marched into the arena; the spectacle was wonderful and so vibrantly colourful. Tartan kilts and sashes were worn by each band member, along with a little black hat adorned with feathers at one side. The vividly coloured socks matched the smart waistcoats and each band member had a sporran attached to a chain belt around their waist. 'The little wooden blowpipes are called Chanters,' Caitlin had told her when she'd asked, and each piper looked a little like a hamster storing food as they blew.

The marching stopped and a lone piper played the opening bars to 'Amazing Grace'. A lump of emotion lodged itself in Juliette's throat. It had been Laurie's favourite hymn, and Judy Collins' version had been played at his funeral. She closed her eyes briefly as she let the memory swirl around her mind.

'Hey, are you okay?' Caitlin asked with a squeeze of her hand.

Juliette opened her eyes and nodded through a fog of tears. 'I am. I just have such mixed emotions about this song as it reminds me of Laurie.'

Caitlin rubbed her arm. 'It has the same effect on me, for obvious reasons.' She nodded towards her daughter, Grace, where she sat and gave a warm smile just as the gathered crowd spontaneously began to sing the hymn. Shivers travelled Juliette's spine at the sound of myriad people singing a song that was so special to her, even though they were completely unaware. But that was it for her; tears fell unabashedly down her cheeks, although she smiled through them and joined in as best she could. Caitlin gripped her hand and her eyes welled too as she leaned her head on Juliette's shoulder in a show of support for her new friend.

Once the song was over, the applause and cheers were almost

deafening, and Juliette's spirit was strangely lifted. It was as if Laurie had arranged the whole thing especially for her, to let her know he was still with her. Through this clarity and with the momentary absence of the guilt she'd been carrying, she thought about Reid and silently asked if she should try once again to make amends with the man.

At that moment, a movement caught her peripheral vision and she glanced up at the cordon around the field. She gasped and her heart leapt. There, on the rope before her, sat a little red-breasted robin, a halo of light surrounded him where the summer sun shone down. He seemed to watch her for a split second before fluffing out his chest, fluttering his wings and taking off towards the trees as Juliette covered her mouth with her hand and let more tears freely trickle down her cheeks.

21

The games continued and the atmosphere at the gala buzzed with excitement. After seeing the robin, Juliette had resolved to have a conversation with Reid. Perhaps she could iron out the creases of their friendship? She could only try. She decided she would make an effort to visit him, or perhaps phone if nerves got the better of her.

Expecting some kind of wooden mallet to be launched by each of the burly men, Juliette was shocked to discover that the 'hammer' in the hammer throw was, in fact, a kind of metal ball attached to a strip of steel ribbon. It was flung rather like a discus, in that the thrower spun in circles to gather momentum before letting go of the perilous object, which then flew at a surprising velocity through the air and landed with a dull thump on the grass.

Caitlin was like a woman possessed as she whistled for one of the competitors, a rather handsome dark-haired, bearded man with arms almost as thick as the cabers being tossed earlier in the day. Juliette found her reaction hilarious and almost expected her eyes to pop out of her head and her tongue to hit the floor.

'You've got to admit, Jules, there's nothing sexier than a man in a kilt, except for a *huge*, *muscular*, *bearded* man in a kilt!'

After admiring the athletic prowess of these men, Juliette was coming around to the idea.

* * *

With the day's main events over and the prizes awarded, Juliette and Caitlin made their way, arm in arm, back to the main tent for the evening's entertainment. Already a dab hand at ceilidh dancing – Juliette guffawed at this description of herself by Caitlin – it took no time to get her on the dance floor as The Toilichte Hens took to the stage, and Kenneth did the honours of calling the steps.

She wasn't sure who suggested that she tried the Skye single malt, but Juliette knew she was going to regret agreeing to it; the realisation occurring right about the time she was being swung around, in time with the music, by various adept partners. The earthy liquid warmed its way to her stomach, creating a false sense of contentment that she knew would feel rather different come morning. Wine and whisky? Possibly not a wise decision, but she couldn't help being carried along on the wonderful, positive vibe of the day. Her very first Highland games had been an incredible experience that left Juliette on a high, and not only from the alcohol. It felt good to laugh again.

Once the Toilichte Hens had finished their set to a raucous applause, it was the turn of the DJ, none other than bitchy Leanna's oblivious husband, Donny.

'Evening all! So, I was asked to bring my karaoke stuff th'night instead of a straight-up disco, so come and get your name down if you want to sing some'hin'!' he announced.

'Jules! Are you going to sing?' Grace asked as she flopped down beside her mother.

'Oh yes! You should definitely get up and sing,' Evin said. 'I bet you're a brilliant singer, don't you, Grace?' His friend nodded eagerly.

She waved her hand. 'Oh, good grief, no chance!' She laughed at the thought. 'And anyway, why aren't you kids in bed?'

Grace grinned. 'Mum lets me stay up until the end when it's the games.'

'And if she's allowed then I don't see why I'm not. Uncle Kendric says he'll come and get me when it's time to go. You have to sing before that.' Evin tried his best to encourage her.

Juliette shook her head. 'Absolutely not. I hate karaoke. In fact, I think that might be my cue to leave,' she informed Caitlin and Morag as the first 'singer' took to the stage.

'Oh, come on, Jules, you can't leave now, it's just getting good!' Morag laughed.

Caitlin raised her glass. 'I agree. It'll be a laugh. Just another thirty minutes and, if you're *really* hating it, we can head home.'

Feeling everyone's gaze fixed on her, Juliette rolled her eyes and reluctantly replied, 'Thirty minutes and that's it! And don't think for a *second* that I'm getting up there.'

Grace and Evin went off to dance and lark around in front of the stage. Archie delivered a passable rendition of 'Sweet Caroline', much to the delight of the audience, who were now verging on worse for wear. And the three women giggled as Caitlin made a joke about throwing her knickers at him.

A variety of songs followed; some fairly tuneful, others downright murdered on stage by their performers. Morag and Juliette tried to convince Caitlin to get up to sing, but their appeals fell on deaf and highly reluctant ears.

'But you were the one who insisted we stay!' Juliette whined.

'Aye, but I want to sit here and enjoy the music, not clear the room with my caterwauling!'

Archie finished his second song, 'Crackling Rose', and once the applause had died down, everyone in the marquee began to filter out to make their way home.

'And a good night was had by all,' Caitlin slurred.

Evin and Grace returned, along with Kendric, and Caitlin fell silent as she unabashedly made eyes at the man. 'So, you ladies have had a good day, I take it?' he asked with a grin.

'It's been brilliant,' Juliette replied, trying her best to sound sober.

'I'm glad to hear it. Anyway, Jules, I was wondering if I might have a chat with you tomorrow, if you're free? Just a wee idea I've had that I want to run past you.'

She frowned. 'Oh... erm... yeah, sure.' She wondered what on earth he could be talking about and what idea he could possibly need to run past *her*, someone he had literally just met.

'Great, see you tomorrow. Here's my card, just drop me a text when you're ready.' He turned to his nephew. 'Come on, champ, let's get you home to bed, eh?' Evin grumbled but his words became lost in a huge yawn. Kendric turned back to Juliette. 'I could pick you up and take you for lunch or something?'

She wanted to say that lunch wasn't necessary. That they could chat at the pub or somewhere else less... *date*-like. But she didn't get a chance as he had already turned and left.

Once he had left, Caitlin whispered loudly, 'Ahhh, he fancies you. I knew it. So obleous. I mean obvelous... urgh, you know what I mean.' She waved a hand in Juliette's face.

'Muuuum!' Grace moaned, clearly embarrassed.

'I think you need to get home, Caitlin, you're oot yer tree.' Morag laughed. 'Come on, I'll walk you both over. Night, Jules.'

'Night, Morag. Night, Caitlin. Night, Grace.'

She turned and almost walked slap bang into Leanna. Before the woman even spoke, Juliette groaned and rolled her eyes.

'Not satisfied going after just *one* brother then, eh? Hedging your bets. Probably not a bad idea for someone like you.' Leanna said, arms folded across her chest, lips pursed in that sour way she had.

'Leanna, believe me when I say I'm not after *either* of the MacKinnon brothers. Regardless of what you and your toilet buddies were talking about. Just drop it, please. Do us both a favour, eh? Go home with your husband and be happy.'

Initially, Leanna's eyes widened and it was clear she was embarrassed at being caught in her gossiping, but then she huffed and changed her stance from leaning on her left leg to leaning on her right. 'You'd love that, wouldn't you? If I was out of the way.'

Juliette sighed deeply, suddenly feeling drained. 'I don't *know* you and I have no clue why you have such a strong opinion of me. You know nothing about my life, about why I'm here. But you seem hell-bent on making me feel unwelcome. And, to be honest, that says a lot more about *you* than it does about me.' She felt quite proud of herself for not turning into a shrinking violet during the confrontation. 'Anyway, I don't have the energy to argue with you, Leanna. Or the inclination. You're seeing something that simply isn't there. But, really, it would be absolutely none of your business, if there was. I'm single, Reid is single. And, to top it off, Kendric is single too. You're the one making assumptions and pining for a man that's not your husband. Seriously, take a long hard look in the mirror. See if you like the person looking back. Now, goodnight, I'm going home.' She turned and headed towards Lifeboat Cottage.

'Home? *Home*?' Leanna almost shrieked. 'It's not *your* home though, is it? It's *my* home. It's *Reid's* home. You're only here for the summer. And *I'll* still be here long after you've gone. So will Reid!' she shouted.

Juliette couldn't be bothered to respond and so continued to walk without looking back. She'd never met anyone so vindictive and unpleasant. Poor Donny. What had he done in a previous life to deserve such a woman as a wife?

As Juliette reached the inlet, she spotted a rather bedraggled-looking Reid sitting on the bench where they'd had their altercation. With a little trepidation, she made her way towards him and sat down warily. 'Reid? Are you okay?' It was a stupid question, she realised, as soon as the words had fallen from her lips.

He jumped and sat up straight, wiping at his face. He cleared his throat. 'Oh, hi. I'm... I'm fine.'

In the tiny dots of light from the strings strewn around the inlet, she could see his assertion was far from truthful. 'Look, I know I'm probably the last person you want to speak to after... well, you know... but... I'd really like to help, if I can. I'm a good listener.' She shrugged.

'Shall we add that to your ever-growing list of talents?' he asked snidely and immediately closed his eyes. 'Shit, sorry, that was totally uncalled for.'

'It's okay. It's clear to me that something's not right. I hate to see anyone looking as despondent as you do right now.'

'Despondent?' He laughed humourlessly. 'That's putting it mildly. Honestly, I wouldn't even know where to start.'

'Well, I have nowhere else to be. And it's a lovely evening. We could just sit for a while maybe. Enjoy the stars,' she said, glancing up at the clear navy-blue blanket overhead, its twinkling adornments putting on their own light show.

'You want to rescue everyone, don't you?' he said, turning towards her. 'But who's rescuing you?' That question had been one she'd considered and dismissed, telling herself she didn't need rescuing. She couldn't think of a reply and Reid took her silence as an invitation to continue. 'It seems to be your life's mission. I've never met anyone quite like you.'

She wasn't sure if this was a compliment or another gripe at her newfound talent for sticking her nose where it didn't belong. 'I guess I've learned from my own experiences of despondency and I just want to help others to get through it like I did. I think it can be misconstrued though, so I know I need to curb my enthusiasm.'

He nudged her with his shoulder. 'No, don't do that. It wasn't a dig. I think it's really sweet. I think *you're* really sweet if the truth be told.' He smiled and she felt her face warming as butterflies set to dancing in her stomach and the alcohol clouded her thought processes. He laughed. 'That sounded a lot less cheesy in my head.'

They sat there in silence for a few moments, but she could feel his gaze on her.

Eventually he sighed. 'I know there's been a lot of talk about me today. And it's not the first time. In fact, there's been a lot of talk about me ever since Kate left.'

'I think people just care for you, and for Evin. They don't want to see you suffering when there's help available.'

He gave that humourless snort again. 'Well, unfortunately, it's not going to stop any time soon.' He clenched his jaw and closed his eyes, lowering his head.

Concern nagged her. 'What is it? What's happened?'

'Well, apparently, I'm a *crap* father.' He lifted his chin and fixed his gaze on her.

She swallowed hard. 'I never said—'

'Not you. *Kate*.' Disdain dripped from his tongue. 'I have it on good authority that I'm the crappiest of the crap.'

Juliette felt affronted on his behalf. 'You know that's not true, don't you?'

He shrugged. 'Do I?'

'You should. Don't let someone else's bitter, spiteful words make you think otherwise.'

'That's not the worst of it.'

She waited for him to speak, worrying that if she pushed too hard, he would clam up and leave. She didn't want that.

Eventually, and to her relief, he spoke again. 'Apparently, I'm a womaniser now. And I'm trying to replace Evin's mother. Apparently, it's okay for her to cheat on me, but if I go on dates...' He laughed again, this time he seemed genuinely amused by the thought. 'Chance would be a fine thing.'

'Who's filling her head with this nonsense?' Juliette asked.

Reid raised his shoulders and dropped them heavily. 'Not a damn clue. The sick thing out of all this is Kate doesn't want me, didn't want either of us, yet the moment she gets wind that I'm happy with someone new, even if it's a blatant lie, she wants to swoop in and remind me of *us*. Earlier, when she phoned, she was trying to be all sweet and saying things like, "Remember when we used to take Evin to that theme park on the mainland and we'd stand there holding hands watching him play? How cute were we as a family?"' His tone was mocking. 'Then, at the end of the conversation, she announced she's thinking of suing for full custody. We have joint custody at the moment, with him living with me for the majority of the time and just visiting her for some holidays and some weekends. But now she's decided that isn't enough. Wants things to change. Apparently, she can't get pregnant with her current husband, so she thinks she can just take *my* kid. I don't know what she thinks she's playing at.'

Juliette's heart sank. 'Oh no. Reid, that's awful, I'm so sorry.'

'She does this, but then, on the other hand, hints, not-so-subtly, that she wants us to get back together so we can bring Evin up together.' He shook his head.

'Maybe she's realising what she's lost?' Juliette offered.

He turned to her and smiled. 'That's kind of you.' He sounded surprised. 'But I don't think that's it. She enjoys being in control, like I'm her puppet and she's the bloody master. But, ultimately, I think she actually enjoys me being alone and unhappy.'

Juliette reached out and placed a hand on his arm and grinned mischievously. 'Well then, you need to be happier than ever just to piss her off.'

He laughed and his whole face lit up. Then, without warning, he leaned close and kissed her gently on the lips. It was unexpected, sweet and soft, and she closed her eyes and allowed it to happen, until she remembered they were outside where anyone could see and pulled away swiftly. She brought her fingers to her lips and fought for something to say, but no words would come.

Seeing her reaction, Reid stood. 'Shit, I'm so sorry. That was... I didn't mean—'

'No, no, it's okay. You took me by surprise. But—'

'Look, I should get going. Kendric is watching Evin and no doubt he'll be letting him eat too much sugar before he goes to bed. I'm sorry. I don't know what came over me. I'll blame the single malt.' He smiled nervously, cleared his throat and raised his hand. 'Well, goodnight Juliette.' And there was that formal use of her name again, closing down the barriers between them once more.

'Any time, Reid. I *mean* that. I'd like to think we could be friends,' she told him, hoping he would know she meant that's *all* they could be. Even if there were conflicting thoughts going on inside her.

22

As she fluttered her eyelids open, Juliette already knew she'd need painkillers. It hadn't helped that she'd hardly slept a wink through worrying about Reid and that kiss. She hadn't been kissed on the lips by a man in so long that reliving it both excited and scared her. It was something she would never have anticipated. Up to that point she had presumed he didn't like her; that he tolerated her for Evin's sake. Could she have been wrong or was it the alcohol, like he'd said?

She wondered who on earth could be so vindictive as to pass on false stories to Reid's ex-wife when they knew that there was potential for terrible repercussions. Who would want to hurt Reid and why? Clearly, *someone* enjoyed meddling rather too much. Her mind wandered to Leanna, but surely she wouldn't do such an evil thing to the man she supposedly adored?

After her third cup of tea and a couple of paracetamol, Juliette took some dry toast out into the garden and sat quietly, letting the morning rays of sun warm her skin. At least the museum was closed today so she didn't have to face anyone looking as she did, which, from a quick glance in the hall mirror, was grey with a slight tinge of green.

She returned inside and was standing at the bottom of the stairs, contemplating returning to the comfort of her bed, when the landline phone rang. She picked up the portable handset and walked carefully through to the kitchen, each step on the tiled floor vibrating through her tender skull.

'Hello?'

'Hi Jules, it's Kendric, Reid's brother. I know I said I'd wait to hear from you, but something has come up and I wanted to let you know I'm not free today, after all. I'm so sorry.' Relief flooded her veins. She had felt uneasy about meeting with him after what Leanna had insinuated. The last thing she needed was to be accused of playing the brothers off against each other, even if she'd been doing no such thing. She had only just met Kendric, for goodness sake.

'That's fine. I hope everything's okay.'

'I wish it was. But sadly no. I won't go into details, but let's just say Reid's ex-wife has a lot to answer for.'

Concern sent a shiver of unease down Juliette's spine and she chewed her lip. 'Is Reid okay?'

'Far from it. Look, I need to get going. I'll be in touch soon.'

She wanted to say that he shouldn't, unless it was to update her on Reid, but politeness stopped the words from forming and, instead, she simply replied, 'Okay, no problem. Bye.'

She hung up and sat in one of the dining chairs, wondering what on earth had befallen poor Reid now at the hands of his ex-wife.

* * *

'Oh my God! He *kissed* you!' Millie's squeal almost deafened Juliette, and she was glad they were on video rather than voice call. Her eardrum wouldn't have survived. 'How was it? How do you feel? Are you okay? Did you *want* him to do it?' As usual, and in true Millie style, a barrage of questions landed one after the other without giving her time to respond.

Juliette rolled her eyes and took a deep breath. 'I felt... *guilty* at first.' She cringed and waited for the inevitable telling-off.

Pity filled Millie's expression. 'Oh, honey, no. You've nothing to feel guilty for.'

She sighed at Millie's unexpectedly soft reply. 'But... to answer your other question... it was... it was lovely. It was a shock but... a nice shock if that makes sense? Well, until I ruined it.'

'Ruined it how?'

Juliette curled her lip and gritted her teeth. 'I pulled away as if he'd slapped me with a kipper.'

Millie closed her eyes for a second. 'Oh, Jules. What did he do?'

'What *could* he do? He apologised profusely and left. I felt awful. I wanted to... I wanted to...'

Millie leaned closer to the screen. 'You wanted to...?'

'Urgh! I wanted to shout him back and say, "Look, can we just try that again now that I'm prepared?" but of course I didn't, and he left and now I feel like crap. And then this morning Kendric called and said that Reid's ex-wife Kate has struck again, and I have no idea what that means, or if I should go round to see if I can help, or if he'll just shut the door in my face and tell me to sod off, although he'd tell me that first, then slam the door in my face, obviously.' Her words rushed from her mouth, taking every ounce of breath with them, and Juliette felt light-headed when she stopped talking.

Millie was alarmingly wide-eyed and silent for what felt like an age. Eventually she said, 'Bloody hell, Jules. I think you might have it bad for this guy. You should totally go round there.'

Juliette snorted. 'I don't have *anything* bad for *anybody*. I'm just... I'm so confused, Millie,' she whined. 'I don't want to like the fact that he kissed me. I don't want to feel anything like that. But then again...'

Millie gave her a knowing look. 'I don't think you're as confused as you say you are. Take a step back here. Do you find him attractive?'

Juliette pictured Reid's unshaven face, his scruffy, wayward hair and his paint-spattered clothes and a slight smile appeared on her lips. He was almost the antithesis of Laurie. 'Yes,' she replied in a small voice.

'Did his lips feel nice on yours?'

Again, the lightning-quick memory of the tender kiss flashed into her mind. 'They did.'

'Will you regret it if you don't go round and check up on him, at least as a *friend*?'

'I think so. Maybe. Yes.'

Millie smiled. 'You have your answer, honey. Go and see him. And if he *is* cold with you, it'll probably be embarrassment, so don't take it personally. Men have their pride, remember.'

Juliette grinned now. 'Listen to you, an expert in the field now you have Harry, eh?'

Millie laughed and held up her thumb and index finger. 'Just a lil' bit.'

'Anyway, enough about me, how *are* things with Mr Harry Dreamboat?'

Millie gave a loved-up sigh and her cheeks coloured slightly. 'Oh, it's all going so well, Jules. He's wonderful. He gets on really well with Dex too, which is a bonus seeing as *he's* my surrogate *you* just now. Harry's just... everything. I think... I think I'm falling for him... or I've fallen... I don't know how to tell. It's all so weird. But I go to sleep thinking about him, and I wake up thinking about him.

And sometimes I wake up thinking about him and he's actually *there*, which is incredible.'

Juliette raised her eyebrows. 'Oh! So, things have moved pretty quickly then?'

Millie giggled. 'You could say that. I'm going to stay at his place in London this coming weekend.'

'I'm so happy for you, sweetie. I can't wait to meet him.'

'Well, hopefully that will be sooner rather than later. I miss you.'

'I miss you too.'

'So, how was the gala event thingy?'

Juliette smiled. 'The *Highland games* event was incredible. Such fun. Exhausting too, but worth it. I saw caber tossing, hammer throwing, Scottish dancing, a pipe band.'

'Lots of men in kilts?' Millie asked with a twinkle in her eye.

Juliette laughed. 'Lots!'

'Lucky beggar.'

* * *

'Right, that's it, I'm coming up. You've made it sound so bloody amazing. I should have come up earlier, but things have been a bit manic at the garage. Anyway, I've got to come and see why this place has its hooks in you, Jettie,' Dexter insisted when they video-called later as Juliette was trying to pluck up the courage to go and see Reid.

'Come for a visit. It'll be lovely to see you. But I *will* be working, so don't expect me to be taking off on day trips on the back of your bike, okay?'

'Spoilsport,' Dexter replied, his bottom lip sticking out as it had when he sulked as a child. But, then again, she wasn't sure he'd ever really grown up in the true sense. That's what made him such a fun big brother. 'Although I'm sure I can entertain myself. From what I've seen on the internet, Skye is my kind of place.' He grinned.

Juliette laughed at his enthusiasm. 'Well, I'll look forward to introducing you to everyone.'

'Great! That gives me something to look forward to that *doesn't* involve my ex badgering me every five minutes.'

She was relieved that he seemed so cheerful and that he didn't flinch when he mentioned Brid. 'Hmm. The break will probably do you both good.'

'It'll definitely do *me* good, that's for sure. I'll head up the long way and call and see Mum and Dad too. I hear you've been in regular contact. I think they appreciate that.'

'I'm trying to ring every other day at least. Mum was asking if I got photos of the men in kilts.' She laughed.

'Really? She's a dark horse.' He paused. 'I think they're missing you more than they're willing to admit, you know?'

Juliette sighed as guilt niggled at her again. 'I know. But you know what they're like. They won't say anything if they think it'll spoil things for us.' Juliette smiled as she remembered her latest conversation with her dad. He wasn't the most talkative person to chat to on the phone. But they had covered the weather, the scenery *and* the whisky.

'Bless 'em. Well, I'll give them a hug from you. I'm guessing Mills has filled you in about Harry?'

Juliette grinned. 'She's got it bad, she has.'

He rolled his eyes. 'You're telling me. He's a top bloke though. I'm chuffed to bits for her.'

'Yes, she said you got on well with him.'

Dexter nodded. 'We've had a few laughs and we're going out at the weekend.' He checked his watch. 'Right, best be off. Out for beers with the guys tonight. Need to wash my hair.' He laughed and she joined in.

'Love you a squillion, Dex.'

'Love you a squillion. Bye.'

* * *

It was early evening and Juliette had achieved virtually nothing. Several phone calls but little in the way of food, exercise or leisure. She glanced out of the window at the fluffy white clouds as they silently sailed overhead.

'A walk. That's what I need.' She grabbed her keys, slipped on her shoes and left the house.

Before she could think about where she was heading, she found herself at the front door of Reid's cottage. There was no sign of Evin or Chewie and Kendric's car was absent. Hesitantly, she lifted her hand and knocked on the door.

A few moments later, the door creaked open. 'Oh, it's you.' Even though Reid's words seemed unwelcoming, his expression told her he was more surprised to see her than disappointed. 'Do you want to come in?'

She cleared her throat and felt heat rising to her cheeks. 'If... if that's okay?'

He frowned and hesitated. But eventually he stepped aside and gestured for her to enter. 'Can I get you a drink? I have tea and coffee, I think, although I can't guarantee it's decent stuff as I sent Evin to Morag's for provisions. I have the distinct feeling he was quite frugal with the money, if the baked beans he bought are anything to go by. Talk about bullets on toast.' His laugh was forced, and a feeling of sorrow washed over Juliette.

'Tea would be nice. But here, let me make it. You sit down.'

Reid huffed and rubbed both hands over his face. 'I'm not an invalid, you know. I *am* still able to function... despite how it may seem.'

She smiled and guessed that he'd been handled with kid gloves by everyone he'd encountered in the months since the divorce, and she knew what that was like. 'Honestly, I'm very picky about my tea. Let me.'

He rolled his eyes. It was clear he knew what she was doing. But he chose not to argue further on this occasion. He walked through the hallway towards the kitchen which was situated at the back of the house and she followed, taking in her surroundings. It was a pretty home, quite plain, but she noticed plenty of photos of Reid and Evin dotted around the walls. One of them on a beach beside a huge sandcastle; one on a ride at a theme park where they both look terrified; one of them with Chewie in the middle of a group hug. Each image depicting a father and son with a great deal of love for one another.

The kitchen was a typical farmhouse style, with wooden units and granite worktops. To her surprise, Juliette found the place clean and fairly tidy. Although she wondered how much of this was Reid's doing and how much was Morag's, seeing as she had been visiting too.

'So... to what do I owe the pleasure? And don't tell me it's a social call,' Reid said as he sat at the old beaten-up kitchen table and gestured to where the kettle was.

Ouch. She set about gathering cups, a spoon, and she clicked the kettle on to boil. 'Actually, it's *just* that. I wanted to see how you're doing. Kendric mentioned that something had happened.'

He sighed. 'Oh, *did* he now? It's nice to know you're both discussing me.'

Juliette turned to find him frowning at her. 'It wasn't like that. He said he wanted to put an idea past me when I saw him at the games. I have no clue what it's all about. But then he phoned me to say something had come up, that Kate had struck again. So, I was worried about you.'

Reid held up his hands. 'Hey, you don't need to explain yourself to me. We're just friends, remember?' There was a hint of bitterness, but Millie's words rang around her head, reminding Juliette about his pride.

They went through to the living room and Reid gestured for her to take a seat on the sofa. He sat beside her, but far enough away that another person could easily take the spot between them.

'So, what's happened, Reid?'

He sighed heavily. 'Kate's on another mission. But this one really takes the biscuit,' he said through gritted teeth.

Juliette remained silent, waiting for him to say more.

'That boy is my life,' he hissed. 'He means everything to me. Everything.' He shook his head. 'I've struggled since she left. I admit it. But only because it was all such a shock. It broke me. But at least I had Evin, you know?'

'You *still* have, Evin,' she assured him.

Reid grimaced, his physical pain almost palpable. 'Not for long, if *she* has anything to do with it. Apparently, I was seen kissing yet *another* woman last night and she's heard *all* about it.'

Immediately, the hairs stood up on the back of Juliette's neck. *She* had been the woman he'd kissed. Someone had witnessed their brief exchange and had gone running to Kate with the details. Her stomach roiled. 'Reid, I'm so sorry, I—'

'I kissed *you*, remember? And, anyway, *she's* married. It's fucking ridiculous!' The colour drained from his face and he held up his hand. 'Sorry, I don't usually swear, not with Evin being...'

She wanted to reach out and comfort him but knew that it would only make matters worse, so she clenched her hands in her lap.

'Anyway, the upshot is...' He inhaled a shaking breath. 'She's definitely suing for full custody now.'

Juliette gasped. 'What? How can she do that? On what grounds?'

He closed his eyes. 'Oh, it's a doozy. Knocked me for six, I can tell you.' His eyes welled with tears and panic washed over Juliette.

'What has she said?'

He lifted his face, clutched his shirt over his heart, and with a trembling chin, he whispered, 'She's told me Evin's not my son.'

Juliette's blood ran cold. She lifted one hand to her mouth and placed the other over her own heart. '*What*? But why *now*? After all this time?'

He shook his head, his expression bereft of all hope. 'Maybe it's because she can't get pregnant again and she's hurting, so wants me to hurt too. Maybe she thinks she can make up for lost time with him? Maybe she's finally realising she made a massive mistake? I don't know. I can't believe it. I *won't* believe it. Because *he's* all that matters to me.' He pointed to the empty space before him. 'That boy is my life. How the hell can he *not* be my son? After everything else, now this?' He rubbed a hand over his messy, uncombed hair. 'In spite of whatever lies some bastard has been telling Kate, *he* comes first. *Always*. And he's the one whose opinion of me matters. Not hers, not anyone else's. Just his.' He gave a morose laugh and swiped moisture from his eyes, but his action was futile as more tears escaped and trickled down his unshaven face. 'I told you it was a doozy.'

Horrified, Juliette's voice came out in an angry whisper. 'You can't take her word for this, Reid. You can't.'

'I know, I know. Kendric has gone rushing off to the mainland to talk to a friend of his who's a doctor of genetics. I wanted to go, but he said I should stay here.'

'Well, that's good. At least Kendric can find out what the next step is.'

He clenched his eyes shut. 'I want it to be another lie. Even if that makes her the biggest, most evil bitch in the world, I want her to be just being cruel. It'll break my heart if it's true, Jules. But no matter what anyone says or where *he* goes in this world, he will always... *always* be *my* baby boy. Mine. I raised him. *Me*. I've loved him.' He opened his eyes and fixed her with a determined expression. 'I've been there since he was born. I maybe haven't been the best husband, and I hate myself for that. But I've *always* been a good dad. I hate that I couldn't stop my marriage from breaking down. I hate that I wasn't good enough back then. People can fire off comments to Kate and spread their gossip, because *nothing* those people can say will hurt me any more than I've hurt myself. Believe me. I beat myself up every single hour of every single day. And I wonder *every* day why I wasn't good enough for my wife. What could I have done better? How could I have been different? What could I have done to make her love me... love *us* enough to stay? It destroyed me for a while when she left. I'm still broken, I mean, just look at me.' He laughed, short and humourless. 'But you know what? Now, I'm actually *glad* she's gone, for the first time since this whole thing started. If it does turn out to be true, she's known this all along. She's kept this from me *and* Evin. What kind of mother *does* that? And if it is a lie... well, that just proves I'm better off without her.' He balled his fists in his lap and clenched his jaw. 'And even if it does turn out that she's telling the truth and Evin isn't mine, I will fight her tooth and nail. Because blood doesn't make him mine, it goes way deeper than that. I won't let her take the one good thing I have left in my life. And if she's playing dirty, I will use *everything* I can to fight this.'

23

Reid's revelation left Juliette reeling. As someone who would love to be a mother, she couldn't contemplate behaving the way Kate was. Using a child to get some kind of misguided revenge on an ex was plain wrong and completely inexcusable. She hoped desperately that the woman was lying. But as Reid had said, if it was all a ploy, it made her *the* most reprehensible person.

They were onto their second pot of tea when Reid said, 'You know, your words, that day at the inlet, were the kick up the arse I needed. Things can't continue like this. I think... I think I do need help. I mean more than the general help I've been getting from Morag, Leanna and Evin.' He broke eye contact and rubbed at a spot of ink on the leg of his jeans. 'You were harsh, true. But what you said made me sit up and think. I haven't really laid any of this stuff to rest. There's been no closure. I'm not normally one to open my heart and let my feelings spew out, in spite of what I've just done. But... there *are* things I need help to address. And I've finally realised I can't do that alone. I've... I've been slipping away, emotionally. Shutting myself off from things. Perhaps this wall I've constructed is a little higher than I'd intended. So... I have an appointment with my GP tomorrow. I'm going to ask if I can be referred for counselling.'

Juliette smiled. 'That's such a positive step.' She paused. 'But I really do regret the things I said. You must believe me when I say I'm *not* a cruel person.'

He lowered his gaze. 'Despite my first greetings to you, neither am I. I probably should explain my initial animosity towards you.'

She cringed. 'I presumed it was because I almost mowed you down on my arrival.'

Reid scrunched his face. 'Aye, I think I overreacted there. You can't have been going above five miles an hour. No, it was something else entirely.' He took a deep breath and she could see the distinct blush to his cheeks which was a stark contrast to the pallor he'd had when he opened the door. 'When Morag mentioned your name, my initial thought was that perhaps you were here to spy on me. I thought that maybe Kate had somehow sent you. That *you* were here to watch me, and feed more lies back. Give her more ammunition. She told me that's what she was going to do, you see? That she was going to be watching me. Not personally, but *remotely* as she put it. Then you turned up and... Well, two and two made nine, as it turned out.'

Juliette straightened up in her seat. 'You thought I was Kate's spy?'

He laughed and rubbed the back of his neck. 'It sounds crazy, paranoid even, I know. I mean, I'd never even met you. But you applied for the job just after I'd had that conversation with Kate and alarm bells rang. I thought... you know... why would a single woman from down south want to be coming all this way to run a museum on Skye? To my scrambled mind, it didn't seem to add up. Look, I'm sorry.' He shook his head and his shoulders hunched.

Juliette raised her eyebrows and huffed out the air from her cheeks. 'Well, it certainly explains a lot. I knew you'd taken an instant dislike to me, but I'd put it down to your disgust at my reckless driving. I can assure you though—'

He held up his hands. 'You're not a spy. I know, I know. God, I'm such an idiot. But... she's been chipping away at me for so long, I think I'm suspicious of everyone I meet now. I've even been reticent about having Morag here. It's ridiculous. But when someone tells you you're a crap excuse for a father and husband, over and over, and that they're going to do whatever they can to take your child away, you begin to believe it, and then, when they hint that they want you back... well, you can imagine how bloody confused I was.'

Trying to hide how appalled she felt at his ex-wife's behaviour, Juliette waved a dismissive hand. 'Oh hell, there's no wonder. I'm so sorry you're going through all this. I can't imagine the amount of stress that's put you under.'

'It's not been fun, that's for sure. I've kind of... spiralled lately. It's all got too much, but...' He clenched his jaw and his brow furrowed. 'I feel pathetic admitting that. That's why I haven't wanted to. I feel...' He sighed deeply. 'I see other single parents making everything look easy, you know? And Evin is such a *good* kid. He's the best, so I have no reason to feel so under pressure all the time. Leanna pretty much runs the café, so I have little to do other than be a father and produce paintings to sell, which is why I feel like... like such a damned failure.' His jaw tensed and he lowered his gaze.

'Oh, Reid, you really have it wrong. You're not a failure. Not in the slightest. You're just grieving for the loss of your marriage. This is *grief*. I know, I've been there. I still am. This... this is not you failing at life. This is you trying to make sense of a world that's changed beyond recognition. A world where you had a partner in everything to one where you have to be so much more than just a dad.'

He lifted his chin and locked his eyes on her. He opened his mouth as if to speak and then closed it again. She knew there was more he wanted to say so she remained silent and, sure enough, he spoke again.

'I don't know, but maybe, I *was* heading for some sort of breakdown. Everyone's been so scared to say the wrong thing around me, but you... *you* told me exactly what you thought. It shook me. But it woke me up. And, in some ways, I'm actually grateful.'

Juliette cringed; it wasn't the way things should have happened. But she figured now he was talking, she could share a little about her own struggles. 'After Laurie, my husband, died, I had it all. From one extreme to the other. People on the one hand telling me to just get on with life, pull myself together as it's *what Laurie would've wanted,* and then there was the whole wrapping me in cotton wool, "don't upset her, she might jump off a bridge" thing too. I think that's the trouble, people don't know *how* to deal with someone in that kind of situation. We all need to be told that it's okay to not be okay. Anxiety, depression, whatever it is, it doesn't make us lesser people. And it doesn't mean we won't be well again one day. It just means that we're dealing with things in our own way, but it's not a fault. It's not something to be used as ammunition. It really makes me angry that people are so willing to attach a stigma to issues like this. And we *all* need someone to talk to. There's no shame in that. People need people.'

Reid sighed and paused before he spoke again. 'To be honest, I was shocked when I admitted as much as I did to you. Saying things hadn't been easy was a vast understatement, but the fact that I said it in the first place was a turning point for me. I think I'd been in denial until then. I certainly hadn't said it out loud to anyone else, even though I knew things weren't getting any better. And... on top of that, I didn't want to admit defeat. To admit that I couldn't just *get on with it.*'

Juliette understood completely. He was going through the

thoughts and feelings she too had experienced. She hoped it would help to know he wasn't alone. And she hoped he believed her when she told him he wasn't a failure.

Reid continued, 'My dad, bless him, was of the school of thought that a man should just get on with things. Men had to be strong and be the providers. Be the ones who held everyone else up. But that's utter bull. I love my dad, don't get me wrong, but now I'm stuck with the feeling that I'm some kind of weak, pathetic excuse of a man. And I'd convinced myself when Kate left that everything was *my* doing. That I'd somehow forced her into the arms of another man because I hadn't been the best version of myself. I'd spent so long trying to be who *she* wanted, instead of being me, that I lost sight of who I really was. So, when she left, I managed to convince myself that I could actually understand why. And then I started to lose interest in myself.' He stopped talking, deep in thought for a while and they sat in companionable silence. Then, he turned to face her. 'Can I ask you something?'

'Of course.'

Reid opened his mouth and then closed it for a moment. Then he leaned closer as if he didn't want the risk of anyone overhearing, even though the house was empty. 'When you were... you know... depressed... Did you ever feel like you were totally overwhelmed with everything but that at the same time you didn't know how to *feel*? Like you were sort of... numb? And as though sleep was the best escape you had?'

Juliette nodded slowly. 'I did. I used to get up and immediately begin watching the clock, waiting for it to be bedtime again.'

'God, that's just how I've been feeling,' he whispered.

'I used to feel so scared to be alone, but at the same time I didn't want to be around anyone. I was terrified they'd realise I wasn't worth the bother, so I was better off by myself. I didn't want to talk, but I hated the silence... too much time to think, too much time in my head wasn't a good place to be. It's an illness of painful contradictions. But it *is* an illness, Reid. It's not simply being sad and down in the dumps. It's so much deeper than that.'

'Yes! I get that now. I really do. Sometimes... when Evin is away, I can't even get out of bed. It's as if I have nothing to get up for, you know? And I'll get hungry, but I don't want to eat because it would take up too much energy. And I've *wanted* to talk to someone. For someone to tell me I'm not losing my mind, but that would've meant giving more ammunition to Kate. She'd have a field day with all of this.'

Juliette pleaded at him with her eyes. 'You can't think about her now. You can't let her stop you from getting to the bottom of this. I'm no doctor, but I really think you've made the right decision to see your GP. You've recognised the symptoms and you've acted, and I so wish I'd done the same thing.'

'But you were the one who made me realise, Jules. If it hadn't been for you, I think I would've carried on as I was, in denial. Waiting for someone to pass me a ladder to climb out of the hole I was in, when *I* was the one with the bloody ladder. I'm so grateful to you. And I'm so sorry for the times I've been less than pleasant. You don't deserve that. Not one bit.' He reached out and took her hand in his and fixed his gaze on her.

She couldn't look away, she was caught; the connection between them now more meaningful. They had common ground which was deeper than just a flutter of attraction. Her heart rate increased, and she waited for what she hoped might come next...

'Hey, Dad! I'm home! Hi, Sparkly Jules! You're here! Chewie has a new girlfriend!' Evin blurted his rush of words as he burst through the door with a wide grin on his face, closely followed by his huge ball of fluff.

Reid almost leapt across the room away from Juliette. 'Really? A girlfriend, eh? Lucky Chewie.'

'Yes, me and Grace think he loves Cleo. They were playing and running together. Caitlin says they remind her of Lady and the Tramp.'

Reid laughed, the love for the boy he'd always known as his son evident in his eyes as he ruffled Evin's hair. 'You'll be feeding them spaghetti next.'

Juliette stood. 'Well, I think I should be going.'

'I'll walk you to the door,' Reid told her.

'Bye, Jules!' Evin bounded over and hugged her.

'Bye, Evin. I'm glad you had fun with Grace.'

'She's awesome. I think we're best friends now.' He beamed. 'It's funny because we've been going to the same school for ages, but I didn't think being friends with a girl would be good. But Grace isn't like a girl... I mean she is a girl, but she's...' He looked to the ceiling. 'She's just Grace.' He shrugged as if it made perfect sense.

Juliette's throat constricted with emotion. Evin was so happy, and she'd had a small part in that. 'Well, that's fantastic. And you treat Cleo well,' she told Chewie, which made Evin howl with laughter.

When they reached the door, Reid shoved his hands in his pockets as if he didn't want to risk them acting alone. 'Thanks for today. I can't tell you how much it's meant to me.' He seemed shy now, reserved.

Juliette smiled warmly. 'I think you just did.'

'Aye. Well, I've a long way to go, I know that. And I know I have demons to face. Mainly the one named Kate.' He smiled and raised his eyebrows. 'But I have to make some changes. For Evin.'

'And for *you*,' she pointed out.

He glanced towards the living room door and lowered his voice. 'Aye... and for me. Although my main concern *must* be Evin. And keeping him here. I can't let *her* take him away.' He sighed and closed his eyes briefly. 'Sorry, the last thing you need is me waffling on and on about my rubbish.'

She shook her head. 'No, don't do that. Please don't apologise. Remember I've been there, different circumstances, I know, but I suppose it makes it easier for me to understand. And... if you do want to talk to someone who isn't directly connected, then... well, as I've said before, I'm a good listener. And I'm not here forever so you don't need to worry about seeing me at every turn once my time at the museum is finished.' Her heart sank as she heard the words fall from her lips.

A sad smile appeared on Reid's face. 'It's a shame really, you've settled in so well.'

His words made her stomach twist. 'Yes, I have, and I love it here so much, but my life is down in Mistford, so after the summer, I—'

'You'll go home, I know. But we're all grateful for what you're doing. Keeping the museum open one last season is all we want.'

Juliette frowned. 'One *last* season?'

He shook his head. 'Oh... erm... Never mind all that. It's nothing for you to worry about. Just co-op politics.'

She wasn't convinced at all by his assertion but chose not to press him further in the light of their recent conversation. 'Okay. If you're sure. Well, I'd better go; I need to go to the shop for dinner.'

'Thank you again for coming. I really do appreciate your visit. And thank you for listening. You're right... you're very good at that.' His cheeks reddened a little, and Juliette's stomach flipped *again*.

She nodded and tucked her hair behind her ear like a teenager with a crush. 'It's been really good to talk.'

'It has. Well, I'm guessing Kendric will be calling on you when he gets back. You know? To talk about whatever it was.' He shrugged as if it was obvious. 'My guess is he's quite smitten.' This time, his smile was fleeting and far from genuine.

Juliette felt the urge to explain herself. 'Oh, I doubt it's anything like that at all. It didn't sound like that kind of thing. And, I mean, I've met him for all of five minutes.' She laughed.

'Time has nothing to do with it. Haven't you ever heard of love at first sight?' he asked, an intense gaze fixed on her.

'I... erm... I...'

He forced a laugh, as if realising he'd overstepped another invisible line in the sand. 'I'm messing with you. Sorry. Terrible sense of humour. But... honestly, don't be surprised if my darling brother asks you out.'

Feeling flustered, Juliette was lost for words. 'Well... bye. And take care of yourself, Reid.'

He took her left hand in his right and gently shook it as if sealing some peace deal. 'Thank you, Jules, sincerely.'

His thumb grazed the skin on the back of her hand and she shivered. However, unhappy with her reaction in the light of his comments about Kendric, she turned and dashed away from the cottage as fast as she could and didn't even turn back to wave.

24

Juliette stared at the records on her laptop screen. So, her grandfather had been a lifeboat volunteer? And her grandmother, along with other wives, used to cook for the lifeboat crew when they had returned from their missions. Her connection to Glentorrin strengthened still at that discovery. Now that she looked closer at some of the lifeboat crew photos, she could pick out her grandfather, standing proudly with his colleagues. She texted her mother to let her know the details.

Sunshine blazed in through the glass in the front window of the museum. As the rays were caught by the Tiffany-style lampshades, little shards of colour were cast across the wooden floor like a multifaceted mosaic. Everything about the place was beautiful.

A wave of sadness washed over Juliette as she thought about Reid's obscure 'last season' comment, and then imagined it being turned into something utterly prosaic like a tacky gift shop, or, worse still, having it be swallowed up as a minor cog in a well-known corporate machine.

'Ah, hello there, young lady.'

Juliette was pulled from her daydream to find Hamish Gair

standing before her. Seeing his smiling eyes always cheered her up. 'Hello, Hamish. How are you today?'

He handed her a bunch of the most beautiful flowers. 'Oh, I'm grand. I brought you these from my garden. I thought they'd cheer up your counter. They were my wife's favourites. She did love her garden.'

Touched by his kindness, Juliette accepted the bouquet that was tied with twine. 'Thank you, these are so beautiful.'

'You're welcome, my dear. Is everything okay? You looked a little lost when I arrived.'

Juliette was surprised how observant the elderly gentleman was. 'Did I? Oh, it's nothing. Just feeling a little melancholy, I suppose. Not sure why.' She shrugged.

'I have those days too. But that's why I'm glad I have my garden and my museum to visit.'

'You do. And it's always a pleasure to see you, Hamish.'

'And you, my dear Jules.'

'How's your grandson enjoying his stay?'

'Oh, grand. He and his Michael have gone to the mainland for a wee bit of sightseeing. I thought I'd pop along here whilst they're out.' He smiled warmly.

'Ah, lovely. Well, I'll let you get on with your visit.'

He nodded and made his way to the same spot in the museum that he always visited.

Her heart sank a little as she watched him, knowing that there was a possibility of the place being closed for good at the end of the season. What would poor Hamish do if the museum closed? Would his wife's belongings simply go back into a cupboard at his home? At least he could see them on display here and know they were being enjoyed by others. She knew that gave him so much joy. Juliette vowed that she would chat to Morag. Perhaps she could come up with a strategy, a rota, or something that would mean the place could remain open long after she'd gone?

* * *

A group of chatty Americans came in during the afternoon and she talked to them about the area, surprising herself with how much she was able to tell them from memory. Pride gave her a boost, and for the rest of the afternoon she found herself singing as she tidied the children's discovery area and restocked the shelves of souvenirs.

That is until an unwelcome visitor arrived.

Leanna walked in around an hour before closing.

Juliette was determined to be civil despite their last meeting. 'Oh, hi, Leanna, do you have the day off today?' she asked with a friendly smile.

Leanna surveyed her with undisguised disdain. 'Reid is a very understanding boss.' The way this was delivered was as if Juliette had insinuated otherwise.

'Well, that's good to hear.'

The woman glanced around at the display cases with those same pursed lips as if a putrid smell had taken up residence under her nose. 'I've heard that you've been handing out all manner of advice to people. It's not what you're here for and it's not welcome around here, you know. You should also know there have been complaints already,' she said with a sneer.

Juliette frowned. 'Advice? I don't know who's said that, but they've got it totally wrong. I've been chatting to the visitors about the area, that's about it. There's nothing wrong with recommending places to see and eat, is there?' She tilted her head.

Blatantly ignoring what Juliette had said, Leanna mirrored her tilted head and looked her up and down again. 'Also, I hear you've been visiting Reid. Trying to be all sharing and caring, like he needs a bloody counsellor or something. Well, I can assure you, he's *not mental*. And he doesn't need the likes of *you* swanning in here with your new-age hippy shit, your mind-trickery and your know-it-all attitude. You know *nothing* about him *or* his struggles. You don't have a clue what's best for him. *I* on the other hand *do*. I've known him my whole life. He doesn't need advice from a miss goody two shoes like you. He has enough friends. I suggest you leave him alone.'

Juliette's nostrils flared. 'I can assure you I have never once considered Reid to be mental. That's an obscene word to use. And, as an adult, I think it's up to Reid to decide who he would like to be friends with, don't you? And, quite honestly, I have no idea why you have such a problem with me. You haven't taken the time to get to know me so how can you even begin to judge me?'

Leanna gritted her teeth and glared at her. 'Oh, I know you, right enough. Got no man in your life, no one down south is interested in you, so you've come up here looking to find someone to replace your dead husband with. And you might think you can play two brothers off against each other, but we all know your game.' Her words were spat and laced with venom.

Juliette had never witnessed such uncalled-for animosity from another woman, and it sickened her. Leanna clearly wanted Reid for herself, so was it her who was responsible for feeding lies back to Kate? She certainly had the motive.

Leanna stepped closer and leaned over the counter. 'Look, yous are not local. You don't belong here. You dinnae know any of us. Even though you act like you're *in* with everyone. I can't believe they even encouraged you to stay by letting you run this old place. They must be desperate is alls I'm thinking. It might be okay where you're from to be all *in your face* about stuff, but here we keep our private shit private. And we don't need someone from down south coming in to try and make us all hippies, running around naked and talking about our *feelings*.'

Her tone was mocking, and Juliette had to really bite her tongue. But she let the woman rant, unwilling to get into a verbal sparring match. Trying to be the bigger person.

'It seems to me that you're just an interfering, smart-arsed bitch who needs to go back down south where that kind of mumbo-jumbo is accepted. But no worries, eh?' Her expression turned to one of smugness and Juliette had a sudden urge to slap her. Leanna, oblivious to Juliette's inner dialogue, continued, 'My guess is that the museum will be sold in no time, so you'll be away before the month is up and it'll be bye bye smart-arsed *Janet*.' She waggled her fingers. 'In the meantime, stay away from Reid and keep your well-being and mental crap to yourself. It's not wanted, *nor* needed around here.' And with that, she flung her blonde curly hair over her shoulders with a swipe of her hand – reminiscent of Miss Piggy – and stormed out of the museum.

Juliette stared after her in utter bewilderment. 'It's *Juliette* by the way! If you're going to insult me, you could at least get my name right!' she hollered at the empty doorway.

Her heart was hammering at her ribs. So, Leanna knew about whatever was going on with the museum. Was there no end to this woman's finagling of information? Now, she was struck with another thought: should she tell Reid of her suspicions about the gossip getting back to Kate? Would he believe her? He'd known Leanna for so long, perhaps he'd be angry hearing such an awful thing from a virtual stranger? And anyway, if Leanna loved Reid, why would she be so desperate to sabotage his life like that? No... it couldn't be her... could it?

Juliette shook her head to dislodge the ridiculous notion. *But then again, love does make people do crazy things.* She had learned her lesson as far as getting involved in other people's business though, so decided it was probably in her best interests to remain silent on the matter.

A few moments later Evin arrived, no Chewie but a brown paper bag in hand. 'Hi Sparkly Jules. What was up with Leannna? She looked raging when she just walked by me.'

'Oh, nothing, she's just having a bad day, I think,' Juliette replied, determined not to discuss what had actually happened.

Evin made a snorting noise. 'Aye, well, don't be upset by her. Every day's a bad day wi' her.' He glanced around and leaned in conspiratorially. 'She's a mean and grumpy radge.'

Juliette hadn't a clue what a *radge* was but from his turned up nose and crumpled brow it can't have been pleasant. She tried not to smile at his turn of phrase but couldn't help it. 'You're not a fan, then?'

His eyes widened. 'Nah! No way. She always complains about Chewie pooping outside the café but it's not him. I've telt her, I don't know how many times, that I clean up after him. I'm a very responsible dog owner.' He straightened his back and Juliette's affinity with the boy strengthened knowing they had a dislike of Leanna in common.

'You certainly are. Now what can I do for you? Where is Chewie?'

'He's at home. I wanted to bring you a snack as I thought it might be busy today and I wasn't sure if you'd have time for lunch.' He held the brown bag towards her.

Such a thoughtful boy, her throat tightened and she had to clear her throat before she could speak. 'Oh Evin, that's so kind.' She opened the bag and found a cheese and tomato sandwich inside. 'Ooh yum, my favourite.'

Evin's cheeks coloured. 'I just thought it might be nice for someone to look after you, seeing as you're always looking after other folks. That's what my dad says anyway. I know you've looked after him.' He lowered his gaze. 'And I wanted to say thank you.'

Juliette chewed the inside of her cheek and walked around the counter to where Evin stood. 'Would it be ok if I give you a hug?' she asked.

He didn't reply, instead he flung his arms around her. She gave him a squeeze. He pulled away and looked up at her. 'I think you should be a mum one day. I think you'd be brilliant at it.' And with those words he dashed out of the shop and out of sight.

Juliette was grateful that the museum was empty at that moment as a small sob escaped her as she clutched the sandwich to her chest.

* * *

After work, she phoned Morag and asked if they could meet for a chat. Morag suggested The Coxswain and they agreed to meet at seven. When Juliette arrived, Morag was already waiting at a corner table with a chilled bottle of white wine.

'Evening, hen. Pull up a pew and I'll pour you a glass.'

Juliette sighed. 'Thank you. It's been quite a day.'

'Oh dear, that sounds ominous.'

Juliette glanced around them to make sure there was no sign of Leanna, and then with a little hesitation, she said, 'Morag, I know this is absolutely none of my business, but can I ask you about the sale of the museum?'

Morag's smile faded. 'Ah, yes, I was going to chat with you about it out of courtesy. I'm afraid the co-operative is going to be selling it at the end of the season. People feel the upkeep of the building is just too much. Too time-consuming. It's an old building and it's listed, so every repair costs crazy amounts. It's such a shame. In fact, there's now talk of it being put on the market sooner than the end of the season. *Certain* members of the co-operative are pushing things forward a bit faster.' She raised her eyebrows and Juliette wondered if Leanna was actually on the board.

Juliette thought of Hamish Gair, her mum's photo and all the fishermen to whom the place was dedicated. 'But that's such a shame. Why now?'

Morag shrugged. 'It's just a timing thing. We all have our own lives. Our own businesses. I'm afraid it's time to let the village move forward. There's been some interest from a couple of chains on the mainland. It's a prime tourist spot. The investment would be good for the place. And I think the difficulties we had in finding someone to run it compounded things really.'

Juliette's heart plummeted. She'd become so very fond of the place and the thought of it being swallowed up by a corporate entity made her sad beyond words.

Once Morag had left, Juliette sat nursing a drink she hadn't touched. Her thoughts a mixture of the museum, Leanna and Reid and Evin.

'Penny for them?'

She lifted her chin and found Kendric smiling down at her. 'Oh, hi. Sorry, I was miles away.'

'Can I join you?' he asked, pointing to the chair opposite.

She glanced around, a little uneasy to be seen with him after Leanna's accusations. 'Oh, I was actually just about to go home. I've had enough to drink.'

'Just stay for a little while.' He nodded at her full glass. 'It doesn't look like you're in the mood for wine. I'll grab us a coffee.' He smiled that million-dollar smile that made Caitlin swoon but didn't have the same effect on Juliette.

'Okay, just one coffee. Then I really must go and phone my folks.'

He nodded and disappeared to the bar, returning soon after

with the coffees he promised. 'I wanted to chat to you about something.'

A little nervous twinge tugged at her insides. 'So you said. What, exactly?'

'I'm compiling a piece about local heroes. I've a man who saved his neighbours from a house fire, even after they'd been feuding for years. I have a family who rallied to help out a refugee who was going to be deported. And after what you did for Chewie, jumping into ice-cold, thrashing waves to save an animal that wasn't even yours, *and* in the light of the fact that you're not from here, I think it would be very interesting for our audience. A great addition to the show and a real personal-interest piece. It would be done on camera and you'd need to come to Glasgow with me to shoot it. We'd get your hair and make-up done and the interview would be somewhere swish, a nice hotel, maybe.'

Juliette twisted her fingers in her lap and scrunched her brow. 'Oh... I don't think... I mean, it's not something people will be bothered about, surely. It's not really heroic. And I'm not sure I want to be on TV.'

The door to the pub swung open and in walked Leanna and her husband, Donny. As if trained like a homing missile, Leanna's gaze fell immediately on Juliette. She glanced at Kendric and then back at Juliette and shook her head, her lip curled into a sneer.

Great, this is all I need.

'Did you hear me, Jules? You drifted off there.'

She tore her attention from her nemesis and shook her head. 'I'm so sorry. What did you say?'

'I was just saying that I feel like your story is an interesting one. People love stories about animals that have happy endings. And, let's be honest, you're an incredibly attractive woman. Very photogenic, I bet. I'm sure the camera would just love you. Plus, I've discovered you're connected to Skye too. It's all stuff that gets viewers. I really think it would be a great piece. Would you at least think about it?' He pleaded with his eyes.

Leanna continued to glare over at Juliette and she swallowed hard. She couldn't talk about this. Not now. Not here. Not with the eyes of Leanna boring into her. No prizes for guessing how quickly Reid would find out about her apparent rendezvous with his brother.

Realising that Kendric was still waiting for a response, Juliette stared into her coffee. She watched the tracks of steam rising and disappearing into the air. She wasn't one to search out the limelight. She didn't consider herself a hero. There were almost certainly better people he could interview. Eventually, after considering her words carefully, Juliette said, 'Thank you, but... I really don't think I'm your person. I'm sorry. Look, I have to go now.' She stood, grabbed her bag and jacket and left the pub as quickly as her legs would carry her.

25

Morag informed Juliette that the museum was to be closed on Friday so that an estate agent could come and take photos for the sales brochure. The sorrow that descended at this news was quite overwhelming and she wondered how on earth they could bear to let the place go. So many memories of lives lived and lost were contained within the walls, within the very fabric of the building, and the fact that *she* felt this after such a short amount of time led her to believe that hearts would break when it eventually closed.

But everything was arranged for the visit of the estate agent and Juliette was relieved to have been given the day off; the thought of being there to witness the beginning of the end was something she simply couldn't face.

Knowing she was at a loose end, Caitlin offered to take her on a shopping trip to Inverness. Her Saturday assistant was available to cover a day early so the pair planned to head off first thing.

There was a golden glow atop the mountains across Loch a' Chuilinn as they made the journey across the country. The water was millpond still, apart from the odd bird diving in for breakfast. Juliette was surprised by how quiet even the main roads were; a car every few miles passed them going in the opposite direction, but it was hardly the gridlock of southern cities that she was used to. She smiled serenely as the scenery floated by.

At around ten o'clock, Caitlin pulled her car into a space in a small multistorey. 'Right, I don't know about you, but I think coffee and a croissant should be our first port of call!'

'Music to my ears,' Juliette agreed as her tummy rumbled its approval.

Caitlin led the way to a small French coffee shop, and they sat at a table by the window. Once the waitress had been and they had placed their order, Caitlin said, 'So, are you going to go for it?' Wondering what *it* was, Juliette frowned, so Caitlin continued, 'Kendric MacKinnon, silly.'

Juliette fiddled with her napkin and felt the heat of embarrassment rise in her cheeks. 'He and I hardly know each other, and besides, I'm not really looking for anything—'

Caitlin held up her hands and narrowed her eyes. 'Whoa, I meant the TV show. He mentioned it to me when he called into the bakery. What did you think I meant?'

Juliette stared, open-mouthed for a moment. 'Oh! Right! Yes, of course.' She shook her head. 'I don't think it's really me. I'm not the type to appear on TV. I think I'm too awkward and I'd probably trip over my own words or, worse still, sit there frozen and unable to speak.'

Caitlin shrugged. 'I know what you mean. I'd probably be the same to be honest. But it might be fun? Something to take you out of your comfort zone. A real challenge for the new Juliette?'

She had thought of that but still had rendered the same conclusion. 'Yes, but... it's not something I really feel ready for. Maybe it's a challenge too far, you know?'

Caitlin nodded. 'I get you.' She chewed on her lip for a moment and then leaned closer. 'Look... can I tell you something? I don't want to upset you... but there's something you probably should know.'

Juliette's heart leapt. No positive conversation began with *that* sentence. 'What? What is it?'

Caitlin huffed. 'There's a rumour. Well, it's not a rumour as such... more of a case of *someone has told someone who shut it down*. But the fact it was said—'

Frustration bubbled up within Juliette. 'Caitlin, just tell me, will you?'

'Okay... so, *someone* has been saying that you're making a play for *both* MacKinnon brothers and that you're trying to get Evin out of the way by passing things on to Reid's ex.'

Juliette rolled her eyes and let her head loll back. 'Not this. For goodness' sake. I bet I can guess who's been churning the bloody rumour mill,' she hissed.

Caitlin cringed. Her brow crumpled with concern. 'And you'd probably be right. Look, *I* know it's all bull. And I said so right away. But Reid has a tendency to believe Leanna. He thinks she has his best interests at heart. Although you and I both know the only interests in *her* heart are her own. In fact, I'm not even sure she *has* a bloody heart. But... I'm just concerned because... I get the feeling Reid really likes you, and I would hate to see either of you get hurt. You've both been through some awful things and in a strange way I think you could be good for each other.' Juliette's glaring expression was clearly not missed as Caitlin held up her hands. 'But, having said that, I know you're not looking for a relationship and I get that. But if there's any chance you might be feeling anything for Reid, you should be careful.'

'Careful how?'

Caitlin pulled her lips between her teeth as if to stop some secret escaping. 'You should know, you were seen at the pub with Kendric. It's a small village, remember. Leanna put two and two together and obviously made five. I'm guessing she will have told Reid already, or she'll at least make sure he finds out, and that it's all twisted into some clandestine thing. She's a shit-stirrer. She sees you as a threat to her and Reid's future, even though she's already married. But she's delusional. Honestly, I think he's only ever seen her as a sister figure. It's quite sad, really. And, before you say anything, I know this has nothing to do with me, but I'd like to think you and I are friends now, and I look out for my friends.' She appeared to scrutinise Juliette's expression. 'Shit, I hope I've done the right thing by telling you this.'

'You have. I'm glad you've told me. But… I think maybe Reid has had second thoughts about things between he and I. When we last talked, he seemed to think that Kendric was going to ask me out. Why would he mention that if he wanted to be with me?'

Caitlin pondered for a moment. 'Did you ever think that perhaps Reid's scared too? It's possibly a defence mechanism. You've both been through so much when it comes to love and my guess is he's scared to overstep the mark in case he's read your signals wrong. If he pushes you towards his brother and you go, his pride remains intact. If you don't, maybe he'll realise you actually do like him.'

Juliette hadn't quite looked at it that way. But she knew that she'd felt hesitant, and still did if she was honest with herself, so she could definitely understand that. 'I don't want Kendric to ask me out. It's all too complicated. But it's all pretty moot anyway, I suppose. I can't offer Reid anything, or Kendric for that matter. I can't even begin to think… I mean… Laurie…' She sighed deeply, unable to form a coherent sentence that would explain her mixed emotions. 'Leanna's made it patently clear that I'm not welcome here and that I should keep away from Reid. She's like a bloody Rottweiler.' She laughed without humour, unwilling to share her true feelings just yet.

'I think the only time Leanna would be happy is if she and Reid were on a deserted island together.'

Juliette laughed. 'I think you may be right.'

'So, I bet your friends are missing you, eh?'

Juliette was relieved at the sudden change of direction. 'Oh yes. Millie texts me every five minutes. Or so it seems. And Dex, my brother, keeps promising to turn up here, but then life gets in the way...'

'Is Millie married?'

'No, but she'd like to be. Although she's met this super-hot Paul Bettany lookalike and things seem to be going really well with them, so you never know.'

'And your brother?'

'Oh god, no. I'm not sure he'll ever marry. He's such a lovely guy, but women seem to use and dump him. I think he's swearing off relationships for a while. You'll get to meet him when he comes to stay.'

'Does he, by any chance, look like Tom Hopper?' Caitlin asked with a hopeful grin.

'Erm... not in the slightest. He's like a cute and cuddly, motor-bike-riding bear. Think Seth Rogan, only not quite as funny.'

Caitlin huffed. 'Totally *not* my type then. Shame.'

'I thought you'd sworn off men?' Juliette laughed.

'Meh... I have... kind of... But I still like looking, you know, just in case.'

* * *

Following their breakfast, Caitlin showed Juliette the sights of Inverness, the most northern city in Scotland and, much to her delight, one of those sights was a huge bookshop in some kind of converted church building with arched windows. It was bizarrely called Leaky's and apparently it was the largest second-hand book-shop in Scotland. Juliette walked through the doors and stood open-mouthed, just staring at the thousands of books surrounding her. The smell of old paper, the log fire, the myriad possibilities, all contributed to a heady feeling of euphoria.

'Oh. My. God. I've died and gone to heaven,' she eventually said and hugged her friend tightly.

Caitlin laughed. 'I had a feeling you'd love this old place. Now, I'm giving you an hour, okay? I need to hit more charity shops and I'm taking you drinking and dancing tonight.'

Juliette nodded slowly. 'An hour. Right. I'll try my best to stick to that.'

* * *

The evening air was balmy as they walked along the road to The Coxswain. When they pushed through the doors, they found it already busy with familiar faces. They made their way to the bar and were greeted by Kendric MacKinnon.

'Hi, ladies. It's good to see you. Can I get you a drink?'

'Oh no, it's—' Juliette began.

Caitlin nudged her and said, 'That's really kind of you. We'll have a bottle of Sauvignon Blanc to share please, Kendric.'

'Absolutely. Joren, can I have a bottle of your finest Sauvignon Blanc for the ladies? Make sure it's nice and chilled.' He winked at Joren, who rolled his eyes in response.

'So, what have you been up to today?' Kendric enquired. 'I understand you weren't around when the estate agents came.' His expression was unreadable.

Juliette found herself bumbling a little around him. He was the complete opposite of his brother and she found it a little intimidating. 'We just had a girls' day in Inverness. Bit of lunch and some shopping.'

'Buy anything nice?' he enquired with a genuine smile.

She shrugged. 'A few books, some clothes...'

He eyed her outfit. 'Did you buy that?'

Juliette self-consciously smoothed down her skirt. 'I did, yes.'

Kendric nodded his appreciation as he appraised her. 'Great choice. You look lovely. Very summery,' he said with a smile.

She wasn't sure what to say. She didn't want to encourage him and give more power to the rumour mill. 'Thank you,' she said in a small voice.

Silence fell between them and the general hum of conversation in the pub filled the void for a while. 'I hope you're going to do me the honour of dancing with me this evening, Jules,' Kendric said eventually.

Caitlin interjected. 'Oh yes, she's getting good at the *The Dashing White Sergeant*.'

Juliette felt that familiar and unwelcome blush rising under her skin. 'Oh no. That's absolutely not true.' She laughed. 'Don't listen to Caitlin.'

He leaned closer. 'Well, I think we should dance anyway, and I'll be the judge.'

'Kendric's a great dancer too. He was always the lad the lassies wanted to dance with at school, weren't you?' Caitlin nudged him.

He too, seemed to turn pink in the cheeks. 'Oh, I wouldn't say that. Anyway, Jules, how about saving a dance for me?'

She glared at Caitlin, hoping she'd rescue her, but when Caitlin chose to stay quiet for a change, she had to think on her feet. 'We'll see. I'm quite tired from our shopping trip.'

A flash of disappointment crossed his face but was gone in the blink of an eye and he shrugged. 'Ah well. I'll ask again later maybe.' He glanced at Caitlin as if unsure how much to say in front of her. 'Reid said you'd been to see him.'

Someone caught Caitlin's attention. 'Back in a sec, guys.'

Once Caitlin was out of earshot, Juliette turned back to Kendric. 'Yes.' She lowered her voice. 'Do you know how he got on at the GP at all? I was going to phone him when I got home, but time has run away with me. I did send a text, but he hasn't replied.' Reid had popped into her mind on several occasions throughout the day and she hoped he had followed through with his appointment.

Kendric nodded. 'Yeah, good, from what he said. I'm sure he'd appreciate a call though. Knowing Reid, he probably forgot to charge his phone, so I'd give him another try and he can tell you all about it himself. Probably not my place, really.'

'Oh yes, of course. Sorry, I didn't mean to pry,' Juliette said just as Caitlin returned.

A wide smile spread across Kendric's handsome, clean-shaven face. 'Hey, please don't apologise. I think it's really sweet that you're concerned for him, he needs all the friends he can get. And I'm sure you'd brighten his day if you called round.' He glanced at his watch. 'Well, I'll leave you lovely ladies to it for a while. I think I'll go and mingle. Catch up on the gossip.' He gave another of his heart-stopping smiles and then made his way through the other patrons to the opposite side of the pub.

Once he'd gone, Juliette turned to her friend. 'Shit. I think he's trying to sweet-talk me into doing this interview.'

'Oh, come on, it's more than that. He clearly has the hots for you. He couldn't take his eyes off you, for goodness sake. I thought he was going to trip over his own tongue. Poor Reid.'

'Why poor Reid?'

Caitlin sighed and leaned closer. 'There's always been this rivalry between them. Reid was a grade-A student, but it was Kendric that got into the best university. Reid was the artistic one, but Kendric is the one who got famous. I'm not sure the rivalry stopped there, to be honest.'

It explained some of the disdain Reid showed when talking about his brother. Juliette raised her eyebrows. 'Oh, right.' The last thing she wanted was to become some kind of perceived third wheel between the brothers.

Caitlin nodded and pursed her lips. 'Yeah, that's why I wanted you to be careful, you know? Small-village mentality.' Her eyes widened. 'Not that you've done anything wrong, of course.'

'Like I said, I'm not in the market. I've had my match made in heaven and now he's back up there.' She touched the locket that remained eternally round her neck and glanced heavenwards.

Caitlin clamped her mouth shut, then grappled her into a hug. 'Me and my huge, gigantic gob. I'm such a tube. Please, forgive me for my constant talk about men.'

Determined not to bring the tone of the evening down, Juliette nudged her. 'Oh god, let's not get all morbid. My fault.' She waved her hand and took a big gulp of wine. 'Let's have a brilliant night, eh?'

'Deal,' Caitlin replied with a grin.

* * *

Back at the cottage later that evening, Juliette unlocked the joining door that led to the museum. She stepped inside and flicked on the lights and the radio. The sounds of a beautiful ballad called 'Caledonia' danced through the room and the warm glow of the lamps filled the space. It looked magical. It *was* magical. There was no other way to describe it. The place had once stored a vessel that saved lives and now it contained so many memories, so much local knowledge and so many wonderful stories that, even after all this time, it was *still* helping to change lives. The song faded and the announcer talked about local news.

She wandered down to the wedding photo of Hamish and his beautiful bride and her heart ached for him. The thought of seeing the poor man's face when he found out that his beloved museum was being sold caused her stomach to clench and her eyes to sting.

Turning her back on the picture and the veil, she let herself slip to the floor and rested her head back on the glass display case. Snow Patrol's 'Run' came on the radio and the lyrics hit a little too close to home. A lump formed in her throat as images of Laurie played in her mind and she allowed tears to flow freely. He had begged her to live life to the full, but how could she let herself? At first, she had been the same with Laurie as Hamish was with his wife's memory. But, lately, Reid was taking up too much space in her head, meaning guilt was constantly tugging at her insides too. If she allowed the thoughts about Reid to continue, would this mean memories of Laurie would completely fade? She knew she had to move on, but she wasn't ready to let go of him. Not yet.

She closed her eyes, inhaled a shaking breath and allowed her consciousness to wander. 'Oh Laurie. I wish I could hold you one last time. I wish I could feel your arms around me and your heart beating against mine.' Tears continued to escape and slip silently down her face.

Laurie's voice could be heard from somewhere off in the distance, like an echo of a time gone by. *'I know, my love. But you can't live in the past forever. This is who you are now. And you need to embrace it. Maybe not here but somewhere. This is what you need to do. To be in your element. And in the happy moments know that I'm there with you...'*

Sometime later, Juliette awoke with a start and glanced around, startled as the memory of Laurie's voice returned. But, of course, the place was empty. The dream had been so vivid and her heart filled with a heaviness that wouldn't seem to lift.

She clutched at her locket and allowed herself a few more tears. She tried to cling on to the sound of his voice before it evaporated into the ether, as dreams inevitably do when you wake from slumber.

She checked her watch. Four thirty in the morning. She had a few hours left before she needed to be in the museum again, so she took herself off to bed, hoping she might jump back into that same dream again...

26

After a busy day at the museum Juliette decided to walk along to Reid's. The trees rustled and waved in the warm breeze, letting shards of light dance and fall about the path before her. Birdsong floated sweetly from the lofty branches overhead, and every so often a brave little winged creature would swoop down to pick up a treat from the ground close by. It was such a peaceful location, the perfect setting for an artist.

Evin came to the door. 'Sparkly Jules! It's so good to see you!' he said as he launched himself at her with open arms.

She staggered but managed to keep her footing, hugged him tight and giggled. 'It's good to see you too, Evin. How have you been?'

'Great! Uncle Kendric took me to the cinema to see a film called *How to Train Your Dragon: The Hidden World*. It was incredible!'

'That sounds like fun. A bit different to training Chewie, I guess?' She grinned.

Evin frowned. 'Oh yeah, totally! Imagine if Chewie could fly. I'd never be able to keep up!'

She laughed. 'Oh wow! Now, that would be something. Is your dad in?'

'Yeah, he's in the kitchen. Uncle Kendric is out for the day, I think. You can go through to see Dad. I'm off out to play fetch with Chewie. He's waiting on me round the back.'

'Okay, fab. See you later then.'

He waved and ran off to dash out of the back door, shouting, 'Dad! Sparkly Jules is here to see you!' as he went.

Juliette made her way to the kitchen and found Reid standing at the sink washing up dishes. Radio Skye played 'High Hopes' by Panic! at the Disco in the background and Juliette smiled as she watched him bobbing along in time with the music and mumbling the lyrics too. He certainly had rhythm.

She cleared her throat. 'Hi, Reid. I thought I'd pop in and see how you're doing.'

He turned and smiled brightly over his shoulder. 'Hey, Jules. Can I get you a cup of tea? Coffee?' He reached over to turn the music down. It was so good to see that he was dressed, and his eyes seemed less sunken.

'Tea would be lovely, thank you. I'll even allow you to make it today,' she teased.

'Haha, thanks. Take a seat.'

Once he had made tea, he sat opposite her at the table and his mouth tilted upwards somewhat shyly.

'It's really good to see you.'

She lost herself, momentarily, in his smiling eyes and lilting Scottish accent. 'You too. You look so much better. How did it go with your GP?'

He heaved a sigh, but the smile remained. 'He was great. So reassuring. I have a long way to go, but, to be honest, I feel like a weight has been lifted already and that's before I even see the counsellor, just knowing I'm dealing with things is a big step. I have some medication which he says will take a while to kick in, but I'm booked to see a counsellor too.'

Juliette's heart skipped in her chest. It was so good to see Reid upbeat and to hear him being so positive. 'That's wonderful.' She beamed.

'Yeah, I was completely honest about how things have been, which wasn't exactly easy, but I figured if he was going to help me, he'd need to know everything. It was such a relief to tell someone. To get some of my feelings out there. Although it was a bit uncomfortable at first and I felt a bit daft but... after a while, it all just poured out.' He cringed. 'I broke down too, which I, of course, apologised for, I mean, he's the GP, so it's not really his job to counsel me, but he didn't seem fazed at all. Just told me to take my time. I mean... like I said, I know I have a long, *long* way to go, but I feel like I've made a positive start.'

She reached over and squeezed his arm. 'You really have and I'm so happy for you.'

His cheeks coloured a little. 'Thank you. Ugh, sorry, now I'm waffling at you.' He smiled. 'It's like a bloody floodgate has opened.' He shook his head and his cheeks flushed.

'No, don't apologise. It's absolutely fine.'

'Yeah, but no one likes a crybaby, eh?' He laughed and Juliette had to fight the urge to hug him and tell him she didn't think that.

He fell silent for a few moments and stared at his shoes, so Juliette gave him time, in case he wanted to say anything else. She wanted him to know that his feelings were valid and that she was happy to listen too.

Eventually, he spoke again. 'He warned me that I'll possibly still have bad days. I might even have days where I can't function as well as others, but now I've asked for help and I know it's going to be forthcoming, it's okay. It *will* be okay.' He covered her hand with his. 'Jules, I want you to know I'm *so* grateful to you. I know you were angry at yourself for how you handled things, but regardless of that fact, *I'm* glad you said the things you did.'

The feel of his warm hand covering hers was a sensation she tried *not* to enjoy. 'I'm pleased to see things are looking up for you.'

He removed his hand and straightened up. 'Aye, me too. But I still need to get to the bottom of who's been spreading lies to Kate. And as for the other stuff about paternity, I need to prepare to fight my corner there. I can't let Evin go. That would break me in two.' His voice wobbled and he cleared his throat before reaching for his tea and taking a sip.

Juliette immediately wished she had an excuse to touch his hand again. 'Has she insinuated further about the paternity issue?'

'If you mean, has she told me who the "*real*" father is.' He made air quotes and sneered. 'No. She says it doesn't matter. Can you believe her?' His nostrils flared. 'I'm not sure the bloke in question would agree, if he even exists, or if she even knows who he is. I know how much this is tearing me apart. But still, I'm not sure I *want* to know.'

'That's understandable.'

'Anyway, enough of that. How are you? I'm guessing the games were a bit of an eye-opener?' He grinned.

Her smile mirrored his. 'It was great fun. The atmosphere, the kilts, the pure... *Scottishness* of it all.'

He laughed. 'Really? You see, when you've grown up with it, I suppose you take it for granted. It's like bagpipe music, I've seen people cry at how emotional it makes them. But for me, I'm only reminded of when Kendric had lessons when we were kids, so it's just lots of high-pitched squeaks that would be much better replaced by a bit of Jimi Hendrix.' He played air guitar and made a silly noise that sounded worse still.

She joined in his mirth and held up her hands. 'Oh, I'm *so* guilty of the crying. I sat there and blubbed like a baby. Don't laugh! It really got me. Especially when the pipers played 'Amazing Grace'. That was Laurie's favourite. And then, to top it off, I saw a little robin on the fence and I...' She lowered her face and her words drifted off; she hadn't meant to say that part out loud.

'A robin?' When she lifted her chin, Reid's head was tilted, and a confused expression had replaced his smile.

She shook her head. 'Ugh, sorry, talking to myself there.'

Reid didn't move; evidently, he was waiting for her explanation, so she reluctantly obliged, feeling her cheeks, ears and chest warming as she continued.

'It's a silly thing, really... Laurie once said, and this was a long time ago, before he was even ill, that if *he* happened to pass away before me, and I needed his reassurance about something, he'd come back and visit me. But not as a ghost, because I told him that would freak me out.' She cringed, unable to believe she was actually sharing this story. 'So, he said he'd come back as a robin in the summer, so I'd know it was him.' She lowered her gaze and feigned a detailed inspection of her fingernails.

He nodded enthusiastically. 'Ah yes. I get it. Because food's abundant in the summer so they can merrily skulk around without being seen, meaning they're more synonymous with colder weather and Christmas. You see one in the summer and you know there's a reason. Clever bloke.'

Juliette gasped and lifted her face to meet his gaze, amazed that she hadn't needed to explain the significance. 'Yes, exactly that,' she whispered.

'And you saw a robin at the games?' His smile was warm, his eyes crinkled at the corners. He wasn't in any way mocking her and she swallowed hard as her heart tumbled over itself in her chest.

'I did. It was beautiful. Such a bright red breast.' She swallowed and willed her eyes to stop stinging.

His face softened and he leaned across the table to touch her hand again. 'If you were needing reassurance about something and he gave it, that's wonderful.' A strange silence fell between them, an understanding, almost. Until he spoke again, breaking the spell. 'So, how's the museum going? Sorry I haven't been down in a while. But I see that the gift shop takings have shot up since you took over.'

'It's absolutely fine. I'm loving it, even more now that I know my grandparents were connected to it.'

'You know what? I bet our grandparents knew each other. They had to. My grandpa was a lifeboat volunteer too. That's why I'm so passionate about the place.'

Juliette's eyes widened at the prospect that they too, had a historical connection. Then sadness washed over her. 'But... the sales particulars are being drawn up as we speak.'

'Ah. Yes.' He rubbed the back of his neck and shook his head. 'Want to buy it?' he blurted.

'I'm sorry?'

Reid stood up, hope and enthusiasm seemed to ooze from him as he paced the kitchen floor. 'You could buy it. I mean, it's clear how much you love the place. You just fit it. It's like you *belong* there. And I think... I think maybe you belong here too, in Glentorrin.' She opened her mouth to speak, but he held up his hand. 'Before you say anything, I know it's only been a short amount of time, but I've seen your face when you're in there. You light up, Jules. In fact, you light the whole place up.' His eyes were fixed on her and the gravel in his voice caught her off guard.

Her stomach fluttered, but she straightened up in the hope it would stop. 'That's really sweet of you, Reid. I do love the place. I love the fact that I feel connected to it. It's wonderful but... This was only ever supposed to be temporary. So, sadly, I can't.'

'Can't? Or won't?' he asked quietly.

She shrugged. 'Both, I suppose. I don't have enough money to buy the place, unfortunately, and my life is down in Mistford. I belong *there*.'

He nodded, but his expression was tainted with sadness. 'I understand. There are a lot of memories there. And your friends. I'm sorry if I got a little ahead of myself. It just seemed like a perfect solution.'

'No, no, it's absolutely fine. I know it would be easier if you could sell to someone you know would love the place as much as you do—'

He flopped onto his chair again. 'You think I mentioned it for convenience?' His brow crumpled; he looked hurt.

'No,' she insisted. 'I didn't mean that. I just mean... I know you don't want to see it become something that would spoil the legacy. And I understand that, completely. And if things were different...'

At that point, the front door was flung open. 'Hi, honey, I'm home!' Kendric called from the hallway.

'We're in the kitchen, Ric,' Reid called dryly, and Juliette noted his clouded expression.

Kendric appeared and made straight for Juliette. 'Hey, Jules. What a wonderful surprise. How are you today?'

'Hi, Kendric, I'm fine, thanks, you?'

'All the better for seeing you.'

Reid rolled his eyes as he said, 'I must apologise for my brother. He's an eternal flirt.'

Kendric laughed. 'Aw, brother dear, don't be so tetchy.'

Noting the sudden tension in the room, Juliette stood. 'Well, I really should be going.'

Reid smiled warmly. 'Thank you for coming. It was really lovely to see you,' he replied as he made to stand.

'Don't get up, bro, I'll walk our guest out,' Kendric insisted, placing a hand gently on Juliette's back.

Lowering himself again, Reid scowled. 'Fine, whatever. Bye, Jules. Hope to see you again soon.'

'Bye, Reid.' She walked to the front door but couldn't help feeling there were things left unsaid.

After opening the door, Kendric said, 'So, how about I take you for lunch. See if I can convince you to change your mind about the TV piece.'

She shook her head. 'Oh, no, sorry, but I don't have the time, really.'

'Okay, maybe next week then.' And before she could think of an excuse, he said, 'I won't give up. I think you'd be perfect for the show.' He leaned and kissed her cheek, lingering a little too long. 'And I really would love to take you to lunch anyway.'

Juliette stepped back slightly and shivered involuntarily. 'Right, I should be going.'

He smiled warmly. 'Well, it was lovely to see you. I wish I'd arrived home a little earlier.'

She nervously tucked her hair behind her ears and peered up at his painfully handsome smile. 'Th-thank you. Bye, Kendric.'

'Bye. Hope to see you again soon.'

She raised her hand and walked away. How on earth did two brothers get to be so different but so attractive, each in their own individual way?

27

Hours and days were being rapidly chipped away from Juliette's time remaining on Skye. The end of August had arrived, and she wondered why things seemed to move so fast when you hit adulthood. When she was a child, days had felt like weeks, and weeks like months. Now, though, each day seemed to whiz by her at a rate of knots. The air was chillier too and the leaves were beginning to turn.

One of the things her counsellor had always encouraged her to do was get out in the fresh air. 'Exercise,' he told her, 'is good not only for the body, but for the mind, too.' So, lately, her evenings had consisted of after-dinner walks with Morag, if she was free, or with Caitlin, Grace and Cleo, if they were up for the outdoors. And when it rained, she stayed indoors and read from the wonderful array of stories she'd brought with her. She revisited some of her favourite classics and discovered new authors; along with whom came new stories and writing styles.

Each evening, she saw a different part of the village and beyond. Caitlin told her stories of growing up on Skye and Morag did the same, only their experiences were completely different. The one thing that rang true for both, however, was that the island was an amazing place to live. Grace delighted them with the story of how, thanks to Juliette, she had become friends with Evin MacKinnon. And that he was really cool... for a boy. Now that they were back at school, they were hanging out there, too. And they had started to take Chewie to the big field at the weekends and try to teach him new tricks. Juliette's heart was so full.

'And he's not like other boys,' Grace informed her. 'He doesn't think chasing girls with worms is funny. He actually talks about things that aren't silly. He wants to help animals when he grows up. And I think that's totally great because I want to do that too. He's so mature.'

Juliette exchanged amused glances with Morag and Caitlin, and Caitlin mouthed the words *proud mummy* and clutched her hands at her heart.

* * *

On one of the warmer evenings, Juliette did as she had promised herself at the beginning of her trip: she drove alone to the Skye bridge and parked up to walk across. Armed with her digital SLR camera, she stopped at the midpoint and snapped photos of the evening sunlight dancing upon the water, and of the little village of Kyleakin overlooking Loch Alsh. Across the other side of the road bridge, she could see beyond the island of Eilean Mòr, and in the distance, thanks to the clear sky, she could see the edges of Raasay stretching like a long stony finger up the middle of the Inner Sound.

She inhaled the fresh sea air and closed her eyes. There was a serene peace all around her. The water lapped on the rocks below and gulls cried overhead; sounds she would miss and long for when she returned to her landlocked home.

'Well, fancy seeing you here,' a voice beside her said, making her jump.

She turned to see Reid smiling, and even though he was still unshaven, his eyes sparkled.

'Oh, hi, Reid. It's a lovely evening for a walk, isn't it?'

'Aye. I met with my counsellor for the first time today and she said that fresh air and exercise would help, so...' He shrugged. 'Here I am. I've even brought a flask. Thought I'd find a bench with a view and sit for a while. Care to join me?'

'That'd be lovely, if you don't mind sharing.' She was not only relieved but delighted to hear that Reid had met his counsellor and even more so on discovering he was already putting her advice into practice. He may have a long way to go to his recovery but these were incredible starting points.

'Not at all, and there's a wee bench down the way there. You get a nice view of Kyleakin and Loch Alsh.'

'That sounds perfect.' And it really did. Around every corner was another spectacular view offering up more memories for her to take away.

They walked along the road bridge and, sure enough, not far from where Juliette had parked, was a wooden bench overlooking the water. They sat and Reid opened the flask. He poured out coffee into the cup that came with it and some into the little plastic lid. He handed the larger of the two to Juliette.

'It's not quite champagne, but here's to positive steps, eh?'

'Positive steps,' she repeated and clunked her cup into his. 'So, how did it go with your counsellor? I'm surprised you got in so quick.'

'Aye, not as surprised as me, I can tell you that. It went well though. Having the appointment come so quick meant I didn't have the time to talk myself out of going. Anyway, she seems nice. She just let me haver on at her and she made a few notes, but mainly, she listened.'

'How did you feel afterwards?' she asked, taking a sip of her drink and relishing the earthy flavour of the coffee on her taste buds.

He huffed. 'Bloody exhausted. I never knew all this emotional stuff could be so draining. But then, after I got home and had a wee grampa nap.' He rolled his eyes and grinned. 'I felt... I don't know... lighter? Does that sound daft?'

She smiled. 'Not in the slightest. I totally understand. And I'm glad things went so well.' She nudged him with her shoulder.

'So, are you looking forward to your date with my brother?' he asked, without looking at her.

Her stomach plummeted. 'Sorry? Date? We're not going on a date.' In spite of Kendric's texts of encouragement, Juliette had managed to hold off.

Reid smiled but kept his gaze locked on the view. 'Methinks the lady doth protest too much. He's a good-looking fella, my Ric. He has 'em bloody swooning at his feet wherever he goes.'

'Yes, he's handsome, I'll give you that,' she replied, not knowing what to say. *But I don't fancy him in the slightest* felt a little harsh, so she kept that to herself.

He turned to her and smiled. 'You could do a lot worse.' Why didn't he sound convinced?

'Yes, but I'm not really looking... I mean, I don't really want... I'm happy with the way things are,' she finally admitted.

'Really? Don't you get lonely?' he asked.

She thought about his question for a few moments. 'Sometimes. But I have my best friend, Millie, and, of course, my family.'

He nodded and frowned. 'Well, that's good.' He fell silent for a while. 'Obviously, *I* don't get lonely, you know, I have Evin. He's great company. And Chewie, of course.' He sounded as though he was trying to convince himself.

'I don't like night-times.' She was almost shocked that the words fell from her mouth instead of remaining as thought like she had planned.

He nodded. 'Aye. I get that. Too much time in the wee small hours for thinking.'

'Yes, far too much.'

A silence fell between them, but it didn't feel uncomfortable, or like she needed to fill it with inane small talk – a habit she'd picked up in her youth when her confidence wasn't quite there. Laurie had helped on that score. He was always so interested in what she had to say, but, on the flip side of that, he made her realise that companionable silences were quite acceptable too.

Eventually, Reid spoke. 'So, what will you do when you go back down south?'

She shrugged. 'Get back to normal life, I suppose. Back to the university library during term time.'

He smiled and nudged her with shoulder this time. 'Ah, that's right, you're a bibliophile.'

She laughed lightly. 'I guess you could say that, yes. Books are my life. So many stories to dive into. You're never lonely when you've got a book. I think I might have pinched that line from someone, but you get the point.'

Reid nodded his head. 'I do. I used to love reading. Used to read to Evin every night when he was wee. Such special times. These days, I can't seem to concentrate for long. Same with the painting, sadly.'

'I'm sure it'll come back, the inspiration, I mean. The attention span will definitely improve. I found it did. And then books became my escape. Beats getting drunk or staying in bed all day sleeping.'

'Very true.'

They sat in silence for a while, admiring the view and sipping on their coffee. 'Kate's coming to take Evin for a week's holiday and I'm dreading it,' Reid offered out of the blue.

'Oh? How come? What about school?'

He shrugged. 'She takes him every so often. Special dispensation with us living so far apart. He has a tutor when he's there. It's part of the legal custody agreement. I can't really stop her. I haven't told her about what's going on with me and I won't be doing so. I don't want to give her anything else she can use against me. I'm just scared of what will happen. If she'll not let him come home.'

'Reid, she can't stop him from coming home if it's gone through the courts. Your name is on his birth certificate so you're his dad until it's proven otherwise. And Kate would be foolish if she let him know what's going on before it's dealt with properly. He'd end up hating her, so I'm sure she won't risk that.'

He lowered his gaze and kicked at the dirt beneath his feet. 'I wouldn't put anything past her now. Not after everything she's done.' He shook his head. 'I wonder what I saw in her, you know? Was I so blind?'

'Love makes you see things that are sometimes not there, and vice versa.'

'She was fun, back then. So carefree. And I have to admit she was beautiful. But it's amazing how ugly someone can become when they show their true colours.'

'Did she change a lot?'

He nodded. 'Completely. I'm loath to admit that I suspected her of having an affair before we got pregnant. But I ignored it. I loved her so much, I swept it under the proverbial rug and carried on. I wasn't willing to risk losing her. She made me so happy. Or so I thought. But when I look back, I can see that she was manipulative. She used every trick in the book to make sure she got her own way. Right down to keeping the café. It was all about status symbols and money. Stuff like that's never interested me.' He tilted his face skyward and sighed a deep, weighty exhale. 'I feel like an idiot. So bloody gullible. But my dad always said that you shouldn't give up on marriage. If it's not working, you *make* it work. Simple as that.'

Juliette knew it was never so simple and clear-cut. The black and white areas were always muddied with grey. 'What's happened about the paternity test?'

'It's taken care of. I just have to wait for the results. Kate doesn't know I've done it.'

She reached over and grabbed his hand. 'You must be so worried. How long will it be?'

He glanced at her; his expression pained. 'It could be weeks. We tried to expedite it, but...'

'I'll keep everything crossed for you. And if I can do anything at all... If you need a distraction when Evin's away...'

Reid nodded; his smile was tinged with sadness. 'Thank you. I appreciate the offer.'

For a brief moment, she surreptitiously gazed at their hands. The sight of them sitting there, fingers entwined, felt somehow right. But as soon as she allowed the thought to surface, she released her hold on him.

'Is it me or is time flying by?' he asked.

'It's definitely flying by.'

'It's good that you're here for another month.' He smiled and a pink flush spread across his cheeks. 'It'll be so strange when you've gone though. I didn't exactly make a great first impression thanks to all the shit I was... *am* going through and I'm relieved to have had a chance to make things right. I'm glad... I'm glad we're friends.'

Her smile widened and something warm bubbled up from deep

within, wrapping itself around her heart, slotting more pieces back in place. 'I'm glad too. Very much.'

And with that, they went back to a companionable silence as the sun began its descent over the horizon, marking the end of another day filled with progress and promise.

28

An open day had been arranged at the museum for potential buyers, so, once again, the place was closed to the public. Juliette spent the morning in a fractured state of concentration. She tried to read, she tried to watch TV and she tried to listen to music. Nothing was able to keep her focused.

At around eleven, there was a knock on the door, and she almost skipped to answer it, looking forward to seeing either Caitlin or Reid. Instead, she opened it to find Kendric standing there, holding out a huge bouquet of fragrant, colourful flowers.

He pointed to the bottom of the bouquet. 'They have their own little water bulb, so you don't even need to worry about putting them in a vase,' he told her proudly.

It was an unexpected visit and she was aware her greeting was less than enthusiastic. 'Oh, err, that's really kind of you. Thank you, but you shouldn't have.'

He took a step closer to the door. 'I get the feeling you've been avoiding me and I felt really guilty about that. I spoke to Caitlin and she told me about your husband. I could kick myself. I'm so sorry. I must have come across like such a giant arse. I felt like I should apologise for being so pushy, so I took the liberty of buying some tasty things from the deli in Kyleakin, some treats from Caitlin's and I thought we could eat here. Less formal.' He cringed and closed his eyes. 'Or is that even more pushy?' He lowered his gaze to his shoes. 'Shit, I didn't think this through, did I?'

Juliette took a deep breath before she spoke. 'Kendric, this is very kind of you, but, yes, a little pushy too, if I'm honest. And I'm sorry, but you've had a wasted journey. I've told you I don't want to do the TV interview. I still don't. I *can't*. I'm sorry.' She began to push the door closed, but he stopped its movement.

'Hey, this isn't about the TV interview. This is just about me hoping to get to know you a little better. My brother speaks very highly of you and considers you a good friend, and I really like that about you. You've helped him so much.' He shrugged. 'Look, I know I come across as a bit over the top, and I apologise for that. I blame my career. I'm expected to be this larger-than-life person on screen, and I think I forget how to drop that in my everyday life. If you give me a chance, you'll see I'm actually a nice guy.' There was a pleading look in his eyes. 'Please?'

Reid considers me a good friend... Against her better judgement, Juliette stepped aside and gestured for him to enter.

Kendric grinned. 'I brought a bottle of Prosecco,' he announced as he entered the kitchen. It irked her how he was making himself so at home.

'Look, Kendric, I think we need to talk.'

He pushed on the plastic cork and it flew off with a loud pop. 'We do?'

'Like I said, this is all very kind of you, but I need to be honest with you. I don't wish to lead you on.'

He sighed and lowered his head. 'I know what you're going to say. You're not interested in me, are you?'

Heat flushed her face and she twisted her hands in front of her as she shook her head. 'No. I'm sorry, I'm not.'

He nodded. 'Don't be sorry. It's fine. I had a feeling your heart might be already taken, but then I found out about your husband and it fell into place. Can't blame me for trying, eh?'

'No, no. My heart isn't...' *My heart is so bloody confused it doesn't know which way is up.* 'I'm just not really looking for a relationship.' *Well, not with you, I'm afraid.* 'I hope you can understand.'

'It's fine. I was too pushy. It's what I do when I set my mind to something, or some*one*, I like.' He frowned and scratched his chin. 'I'm sorry if I made you feel uncomfortable, Jules. It wasn't my intention.'

She held up her hands. 'No, it's fine, honestly. I was just a bit taken aback. I mean... you're clearly a popular man, and I can see why most women are falling at your feet.' She smiled. 'But—'

'But you're not most women?' It was said with a smile. 'You see, the annoying thing is *that's* why I like you. But, hey, friendship is good. You can never have too many friends, or so they say.'

Relief flooded her and she sighed. 'Very true.'

'Look, I've brought all this stuff, oatcakes, pâté, shortbread... Could we maybe just enjoy it as *friends*?'

Juliette pulled out a dining chair. 'That would be lovely.'

They sat munching on the picnic Kendric had provided and chatted about his career and Juliette finally felt able to relax in his presence. The elephant had been evicted from the room and it felt so much better. He imparted some hilarious stories about the people he'd encountered since beginning his rollercoaster life as a TV star. He'd had stalkers, threats, marriage proposals from both women *and* men, and everything in between.

'I wouldn't mind, but one guy warned me off his wife even though I'd never even met the woman!'

Juliette almost choked on her glass of fizz. 'Oh, my word. That's ridiculous.'

He laughed and took a sip of his drink. 'Seriously, there are some crazy people out there. This is why it's nice to come home every so often and witness the *normal* side of life for a wee while.'

'I can imagine.'

'Anyway, enough about me. You seem to have found your way into the hearts of the locals, from what I can see. Saving dogs, helping at the games, cheering up my brother.'

'Hmm, not everyone's being so accepting,' she mumbled.

Kendric frowned and tilted his head. 'Who *hasn't* taken to you?' He seemed genuinely surprised.

She waved a dismissive hand. 'Oh, it's nothing, really. Just a friend being very protective over Reid.'

Without prompting, Kendric rolled his eyes. 'Leanna, by any chance? Why, what's *she* said?'

Juliette giggled nervously. 'She came to give me a friendly warning to keep away from Reid. Oh, and to tell me my *mind-trickery* and *hippy shit* isn't welcome here.'

Kendric burst into laughter. 'Mind-trickery? Hippy shit? So, that's what they're calling friendship these days, is it? Bloody hell, what century is she from? She'll be demanding you're burned as a witch next.' His eyes were watering as he laughed. 'Seriously, you need to ignore that one. She could do with some bloody mind-trickery.'

Juliette shrugged, feeling a little guilty for poking fun at the woman. 'She just cares deeply about him, seeing as they've known each other for so long.'

He raised his eyebrows. 'Hmm, I think it's more than that.' He leaned forward. 'She's obsessed with him,' he told her with a twinkle of delight in his eyes. He seemed to be relishing the fact that, for once, such a story wasn't about him. 'Always has been.

They were almost an item at high school, but I think he got the measure of her. They were good friends though. Quite inseparable until the *summer of Kate*.' He waved his fingers around dramatically and imitated a horror-film announcer's voice, causing Juliette to laugh, the tension she'd felt around him before had now dissipated and she was enjoying his company.

'Ah yes, when she came on holiday with her parents.'

He nodded as he chewed. 'He was totally besotted with Kate from the moment he set eyes on her. My folks thought she was the bee's knees. Me too, at first. I suppose I was a little jealous though. Reid was my big brother after all, and suddenly he wasn't interested in me because he had this incredible, beautiful woman and they were always together. As time went on though... I wasn't so keen, but that's by the by. Anyway, so he started spending all his time with Kate, and Leanna pretended to be friends with her while secretly seething. I have to admit I felt a little sorry for Leanna as Reid really did drop her like a hot brick. When Kate went home, they wrote to each other, phoned each other every night. Honestly, it was vomit-inducing.' He crumpled his nose and shivered.

'He talked about her nonstop, which drove Leanna mad, and eventually he went off and followed Kate to England, where they got married. Leanna went to the wedding and took *Donny* as her date. Everyone was so shocked at that. He's not her usual type. Much older than her in age *and* attitude. But I think she clung to the first man who showed an interest. It's quite sad, really. I think she genuinely wanted to be loved and Donny worships the ground beneath her manicured feet. He's not short of cash either, and so he lavished her with gifts, bought her affection, if you will, and she was sucked in. He made a better prospect than being on her own. But ever since Mum died and Reid came home, she's tried to take things up from where they left off in high school. It's a good job Donny appears to be oblivious to it all. Then, when Kate cheated and ran off, you'd have thought it was bloody Mardi Gras. Leanna has hung around him like a fly around a turd.'

She gasped in mock outrage. 'Kendric! You can't liken Reid to poop.'

He laughed. 'Sorry, but you know what I mean. I don't think anything he does would *ever* put her off. And I know for a fact she'd have her cake and eat it if only Reid was willing.'

'Do you really think Donny is oblivious?'

Kendric widened his eyes. 'He must be. Honestly, the way she fawns over Reid. She's always popping round, always finding an excuse to hug him and tell him she's there for him. And then she goes and warns *you* off just for turning up here and being a nice person. Bunny boiler. I'm telling you. I'm talking *Fatal Attraction* territory, no doubt.'

'Well, I'd already decided to avoid her, but I think you've confirmed my decision, that's for sure.'

Kendric poured more bubbles into their glasses. 'I think that's the best plan where she's concerned. I've never known such a bitter person. You'd think if she cared about him, she'd want him to have friends and be happy.' He paused, deep in thought for a few seconds. 'Although my darling brother seems to have a track record with nutty women. Take Kate, for example. I shouldn't speak out of turn about my nephew's mother, but she's a true piece of work.' He shook his head and swirled his drink around the glass, a look of bitter disdain on his face. 'Flirts with everyone. Sleeps with *anyone*...' He let his words trail off and he appeared a little lost in his own head again for a few moments before he shrugged his shoulders. 'Ugh, ignore me. Sorry. I just... I can't stand that woman. I don't think I've ever really *hated* anyone before, but her... it comes pretty close, I can tell you. The things she's done. The things she's made other people do. Manipulative... spiteful...' He stared at an empty spot on the table.

Juliette watched his expression and heard the acidic tone of his voice, and a niggle of worry played around at the back of her mind. One particular thought wouldn't leave her alone. And she hoped it was a case of two and two making five. Because it was a thought that was too horrible to even consider. She wanted to eradicate it. For it to disappear. In fact, she wanted more than anything for it to have never materialised at all. Because the thought that Kendric could've betrayed his brother and potentially fathered Evin made Juliette feel sick to the stomach.

29

Juliette lay in bed listening to the rain pounding on the windows. It was quite hypnotic, but sadly not enough to send her back to the land of Nod. She wasn't due to be up for a couple of hours but had been plagued by dreams; although this time they weren't about Laurie. Instead, she was playing detective and was on a mission to discover the deceitful one who had been spreading lies about Reid. But, of course, round every corner she turned in the haze of her subconscious, there was Leanna warning her off, blocking her path. If she wasn't convinced of Leanna's involvement before, she certainly was now.

Juliette had eventually walked into a kitchen she didn't recognise, and there, on the steel stove, was a huge boiling pot; its lid lifting and rattling as steam escaped and water spluttered, spilling over the sides. She was stretching out her arm, about to lift the lid, when she somehow realised she was dreaming and had forced herself awake with a start.

She immediately blamed Kendric.

All that blooming talk of Fatal Attraction *and bunnies...*

Dexter had messaged the night before to say he'd finally got around to arranging some time off and would be arriving soon for his visit, which suited her fine. She reached across to check her phone and noticed a string of texts from Millie.

Hey, honey, are you up? I know it's early but I have news xx

Jules, message me when you get this!

Ugh! Why are you sleeping in when I'm so excited and want to share news?

And finally, Don't message when you read these, just call me, okay?

Juliette immediately hit dial, avoiding the video call button on account of her lack of sleep, and before the phone even had a chance to ring at the other end, she heard Millie's breathless voice. 'At last! Good grief, I thought you'd switched your phone off, which is totally unlike you!'

'Hey, Millie, is everything okay? It's five in the morning. What couldn't wait?'

'Are you sitting down?'

Juliette glanced at the ceiling from her recumbent position on the bed. 'Not exactly *sitting* but go ahead.'

'He's asked me to move to London!' This was followed by a high-pitched scream, which forced Jules to yank the phone away from her ear.

She shook her head, feeling sure she'd heard wrong. 'What?'

'Harry has asked me to move to London to live with him!'

'Bloody hell, Millie, that's... that's *wonderful*!' She forced moderation on her initial reaction.

Millie missed nothing and sighed. 'I know you were going to say it's fast. And you're right. I know it is. But when you know, you just know. He's the one, Jules. I'm finally in love. *Real* love.'

'But you hardly know him, lovely. It's been a couple of months. I just don't want you to get hurt.'

'I know that. And I appreciate it. I really do. But I've met his family and friends a few times now and I really think I want to say yes.'

Juliette was experiencing conflicting emotions; some of them leaning towards downright selfishness. If Millie moved away, what would she do? They had been in each other's lives for so long, she wasn't sure she would cope. Of course, she didn't utter a word of this out loud. 'Well, if he makes you happy, sweetie, then I'm over the moon for you. I can't wait to meet him.'

'So... you think I should say yes?'

Juliette sat up straight now. 'Wait, you haven't said yes already?'

'No, I haven't given him an answer yet because I wanted to tell you first.'

'Millie, you didn't need to do that. I'm not in charge of your life.'

Millie sighed again. 'No, I know that. It's just... You've needed me these past few years and the last thing I want is to abandon you. I mean, obviously it's only a couple of hours' drive, so I can be there if you need me. I can run my business from there quite easily. And—'

Juliette immediately stamped on her selfish feelings. She wanted Millie to be happy. Of course she did. Especially after everything she had done for her. 'Millie, stop. Please, say yes to Harry. You can't spend your life hanging around in case *I* need you. I love you for caring so deeply, but the last thing *I* want is for you to pass up a chance at happiness because of me. I'll be fine. I *am* fine. Go and be happy, honey, okay?' Her voice broke. Millie had been holding her up for so long she'd evidently forgotten how to make a decision that didn't consider her first. Guilt and love fought for supremacy in Juliette's heart.

'Thank you, Jules. Thank you *so* much. You'll love him. I just know you will.'

Juliette smiled. 'If you love him, then there's no doubt in my mind that I will. Now please, go and call him and tell him to clear you some space in his wardrobe for your ginormous designer shoe collection, for goodness sake!' She giggled.

'I'm on it like a car bonnet! I love you so much, Jules. I mean that with all my heart, and if you ever need me...'

'I know, Millie. And I love you too.'

When the call was over, Juliette walked over to the window and pulled back the curtains. The sky that had been vibrant blue most days up to now was grey and filled with heavy clouds, almost mirroring the way she felt. Her heart ached at the thought that her friend had been putting off her own future to ensure she was okay.

She thought back to the times Millie had visited when she was in the depths of her depression and unable or unwilling to leave the house. How she didn't expect conversation or to go anywhere, instead she would simply sit beside her, silently. There was nothing she could do to make things better *physically*, but her emotional presence and support had meant the world: a simple hand on her arm, a hug, a smile of reassurance, a cup of tea, a shoulder to cry on. Millie had known just what to do when nothing *could* be done. And for that, Juliette would always be grateful. But Millie deserved to have what she had experienced with Laurie. And now was her time. There was no way Juliette was going to stand in the way of her best friend's happiness.

* * *

After work, Juliette tidied the children's discovery area and eventually locked the museum door behind her. A text pinged through from Dexter to say he would be arriving the following day and a jitter of excitement sparked in her stomach. Thankful that the rain had abated, she made her way across to Caitlin's shop to collect something nice for after tea and something to greet Dexter with too.

'Hey, you. How's it been today?' Caitlin asked with a wide smile as she walked in.

Juliette couldn't help but enthuse. 'Incredibly busy. Hamish was in again today, bless him. I want to adopt him as my grandad. He's so sweet. A few more of the locals came in today too. I thought, at first, they were coming to spy on me for Leanna, but they all seemed far too nice. Remember when Leanna said that people had been complaining about me? I'm thinking she made it up.'

Caitlin laughed. 'And you doubted that because...?'

'Okay, fair point. Can I have a lemon cake please?' she asked, glancing at the empty space where it should have been. 'Or have you sold out?'

Caitlin cringed. 'All gone, I'm afraid. The campsite down the road is full and I think Archie has been telling everyone to come here.'

'He runs the campsite too?'

'He doesn't just run it, he owns it.'

Juliette shook her head. 'Wow, he is a busy man. Okay, what have you got then?'

'I've a couple of tray bakes left. Just don't tell Evin you took the last ones. He's rather fond of the caramel and white chocolate ones, a fact I discovered seeing as Grace keeps stealing them for him.' She rolled her eyes.

'Aww, it's so sweet how they've become such good friends.'

Caitlin smiled. 'Hmm, not great for my profit margins.'

'No, I can imagine. How does Evin seem? I haven't seen him for a couple of days.'

'Ah, yes, he's been at his mum's. He's as bright as a button though. Still constantly talks about you. I think you have your own fan club there.'

Juliette grinned. 'Oh, he's just such a sweet boy. I'm glad he's doing well.'

'Aye. Grace might have something to with it too. So, is a tray bake okay?'

'Sounds good to me. Pop a couple of melting moments in too,' Juliette said as she eyed the mouth-watering confections.

'Are we on for a drink at the pub later or are you wanting a night at home?' Caitlin asked as she placed the cakes in paper bags.

'Oh, I'm definitely up for some company, but do you fancy coming to me and I'll stick a pizza in the oven? I don't feel like going to the pub tonight. My brother is arriving for a visit tomorrow and also... you know... Leanna...'

'That's fine by me, but don't go letting her stop you from enjoying yourself. If you ask me, the hard-nosed bint needs to stop being so possessive over what she has absolutely no claim to.'

Juliette giggled at Caitlin's harsh choice of words. 'I know, I know. But come to me anyway. Oh, and bring wine.'

Caitlin shook her head. 'As if I'd even consider coming without!'

* * *

As Juliette walked towards Lifeboat Cottage, she spotted Reid leaving Morag's shop. He was in his paint-spattered clothing, which she took as a positive sign.

He greeted her with a wide smile. 'Hi, Jules. How are you?'

'I'm fine, thanks.' She nodded at his clothing with a grin. 'I see you've been painting.'

He cringed. 'Yes, I think I'm wearing more than I put on the canvas. Just popped down for some milk.' As the breeze ruffled his tatty old shirt, she caught the masculine fragranced body spray he wore. She was momentarily caught off guard; it was nothing like Laurie would've worn, but she had to admit he smelled divine.

She glanced down at his long, paint-mottled fingers. 'That's good. What are you working on?'

He shrugged. 'Oh, nothing much. Just messing really. Where are you off to?'

She nodded towards the house. 'Just back home to devour some sweet treats and a good book before dinner with Caitlin. Anyway, how are you?'

His eyes seemed to twinkle in the early-evening sunlight. 'I'm...' He stopped to consider his words and his smile faded. 'I'm not really sure *how* I am, to be honest. Today has been strange. I've had a call from Social Care.' He lowered his gaze and dragged his hand through his hair. 'Kate's been on to them telling them she wants to sue for full custody, and they want to come and speak to me and Evin tomorrow. I just... I can't imagine him being dragged away from his home, and his school. Being thrust into a new life, all thanks to her selfishness.' He rubbed the back of his neck and scowled. 'I need to chat to Evin, so he understands what's going on, but that worries me. I don't know how he'll react. And if they interview Evin... well, he'll tell the truth about me, just as he's been brought up to do, but what if that raises more questions than it answers? I just don't know. I hate to think of him being put in a position where he feels like he has to choose. I know they won't ask him to do that, but that's how he'll feel. I just know it.'

Juliette wanted to be able to say something reassuring but knew nothing of these types of situations. 'They'll see that Evin is well cared for. And they'll know you're getting help. The last thing they will want to do is move Evin out of a stable environment. It's always a last resort. And it has to be about what's best for him. *You* didn't leave him behind. Kate did. Try not to worry. And if I can help... well, you know where I am.'

He lifted his chin and, as their eyes connected, his shoulders seemed to relax. 'Thank you.' He didn't need to say anything else. His earnest expression told her of the gratitude he felt, although she wasn't sure what help she'd really been.

'Hey, I have tray bake and melting moments,' she said, to lighten the mood. 'Care to join me for a cuppa?'

'Melting moments? How can I refuse?'

They walked back to Lifeboat Cottage and, once inside, Juliette made a pot of tea and they sat at the kitchen table.

'Has Kendric gone home?' she asked tentatively, the horrible thoughts of a brother's betrayal rearing their ugly heads again.

'No, no, he's taken Evin shopping. He needs new school shoes as he's already ruined the ones I got him in the holidays. And apparently Ric knows the *trendiest* places to shop.' He laughed. 'I get the feeling my lad sees me as a boring old fart.'

'I'm sure he just enjoys spending time with his uncle.'

'Aye, and he knows he'll get spoiled rotten too.'

'Are things okay with you and your brother?' There was no hint that a conversation had taken place, so she didn't want to push too hard on the matter.

'Aye, things are great. Although he was all cagey after he returned from lunch at yours. I think he's really taken with you. Which is a wee shame...' He placed his cup down and froze, visually tensing. After a brief pause, he continued, 'I mean, you know, with you not being here for very long. Distance and all that.' He flashed a rapid smile before reaching for a cake.

Juliette took a piece of gooey, caramel tray bake and, without looking up, said, 'As I said before, he and I are just friends... acquaintances even.'

'Aye, I know you did. Sorry. I don't mean to pry or push. I know you're not looking for a relationship. Especially with you heading home in a few weeks. But... do me a favour... let him down gently, eh? If he chooses to make his feelings known.'

Unable to speak her mind or tell Reid what she was thinking, she simply nodded and swallowed down the cake that suddenly felt dry in her throat. '*If* he chooses to say something along those lines. But I honestly don't think it's an issue. Anyway, enough about all that...'

Thankfully, he took the hint. 'So, tell me about Mistford. I've always fancied visiting the Cotswolds. Is it as beautiful as it looks on TV?'

For the next half an hour or so, they chatted about the village Juliette called home and the place in the North East of England where she grew up. Then, Reid regaled her with tales of his own upbringing, meaning she got the other side of the stories Kendric had told her. The time flew by and they laughed together, which felt good. Seeing Reid smiling more and more lifted her spirits too.

'Well, I really should be going,' Reid said as he placed his cup on the table.

'Okay. Caitlin is coming round for pizza and wine, except I haven't actually bought the pizza yet.' Juliette cringed and added, 'Whoops!'

Reid's crinkled eyes and wide smile were wonderful to see and when he laughed, deep and vibrating, she found herself a little captivated.

'Aye, well, you'd better get to Morag's pretty quick, eh? I know what Caitlin's like when she's hungry. The Hulk's got nothing on her.' He growled and flexed his muscles, making her laugh.

They stood and made their way to the front door, where a strange silence fell upon them. 'It's been good to see you looking so well. And happy,' Juliette eventually told him.

Reid nodded slowly, keeping his gaze fixed on her. 'And I've you to thank for that.'

She tucked her hair behind her ears and shook her head. 'I haven't done anything.'

'You have. You've been here for me. You hardly know me, yet you've not given up on me, even when I've been a crabbit arse. And I've appreciated everything.' His voice had lowered, and he seemed closer. 'You're such a special person, Jules. Warm and giving.'

She lifted her chin slightly and noticed the distance between them had reduced again. Her heart hammered at her chest and, for the first time in so long, she felt something akin to desire begin to warm her insides. 'I've just been a...' she swallowed as he parted his lips, 'a... *friend*,' she stuttered.

He reached up and gently touched her cheek. 'You have. And I'm grateful to know you,' he whispered as he leaned and touched his lips to her cheek, his warm breath feathering lightly over her skin, causing a shiver to travel her spine. She closed her eyes and waited for his lips to move to hers, but when they didn't, she opened them and cleared her throat, breaking the spell he'd cast.

'Well... bye for now, Jules. Take care.' He yanked the door open and sped off down the path.

When he was comfortably out of sight, she made her way to Kenneth and Morag's shop, having berated herself a hundred times for her reaction to the man she absolutely did *not* want to want. Her sense of betrayal and guilt weighed heavy on her and she almost made a detour to cancel her plans with Caitlin.

Her friend, however, appeared from the direction of Lifeboat Cottage. 'There you are! I thought you'd stood me up.'

Gathering her thoughts and plastering on a smile, Juliette replied, 'Oh no, not at all. I just realised I'd forgotten the pizza.'

30

The next morning, Juliette was once again wide awake far too early. Not only was she nursing a hangover from the wine she'd consumed with Caitlin, but her stomach insisted on roiling every time she replayed what she now called 'kiss-gate' with Reid. Twice, this situation had arisen. Once, when he'd *actually* kissed her and taken her completely by surprise, and once, when she'd *wanted* him to kiss her, but he hadn't. She could close her eyes and be back by her front door, the sensation of his lips so close to hers, the heat radiating from his body, the smell of him, tantalising and new. Then, she'd recall the way she felt when Laurie had first kissed her. Shy and sweet. How she'd fallen for him long before that even happened. How could she even *consider* kissing another man? It was ridiculous and selfish and wrong.

But she *had* wanted Reid to kiss her, nonetheless. And she hated herself for that.

There was a hammering on the front door, which startled her into action. It was a familiar sequence of knocks that she knew so well. She grabbed her robe and dashed down the stairs to see a huge figure looming at her through the stained glass.

Dex!

She flung open the door and launched herself into his arms. All the emotions she'd battled with over the last day or so bubbled to the surface and, feeling her brother's arms around her, they spilled over in the form of tears.

'Dex, I've missed you so much,' she sobbed.

Concern crumpled his smiling face. 'Hey, Jettie, what's wrong? Why are you crying?' he asked as he led her inside with his arm around her shoulder, slamming the door behind him. Once inside, he crouched to meet her gaze. 'Come on, tell me what's happened. Who do I need to have words with?'

She swiped at her eyes and waved her hands dismissively. 'Oh, nothing, no one. Ignore me. I'm just happy to see you, that's all.'

He stared at her; head tilted and with suspicion evident in his eyes. 'Hmm. Not sure I believe you, but you'll tell me in your own time, I suppose. Now, point me to my room and I'll get my leathers off. Stick the kettle on, eh? I could murder a cuppa.'

'Top of the stairs and to the left,' she told him with a genuine grin replacing what was there before.

Dexter made his way up the stairs two at a time, his rucksack bouncing against his jacket. 'Back in a sec!'

Juliette went to the kitchen and filled the kettle before getting out the fresh almond croissants she'd bought when she'd called for pizzas the night before. A few moments later, as promised, Dexter appeared in jeans and a T-shirt, his frame filled the doorway like a cuddly brown bear and his familiar smile warmed Juliette's heart.

'Ooh, croissants. Great. I'm bloody starving.' He grabbed one and almost stuffed the whole thing in his mouth. 'Delicious,' he said, regardless of the crumbs he sprayed.

'Disgusting!' Juliette chastised with a smile and an eye roll. 'Anyway, how come you're here at seven in the morning? It's a bit early isn't it?'

He pulled out a chair and plonked himself down on it. 'I stopped at one of the hotel chains on the motorway on the way and when I woke up early, I figured I'd get an early start. Quiet roads.' He shrugged. 'Anyway, how are you? I mean, how are you *really*? What were the tears for?'

'Honestly, it's nothing, I'm fine,' she insisted. 'I'm just a wee bit hung-over, that's all.'

'Listen to you, all Scottish. *Wee bit*,' he repeated in a terrible Scottish accent that made her giggle.

'Don't go talking like that around here, will you? You're likely to get nobbled! Anyway, how was your ride up?'

He curled his lip. 'Wet. Although, it's good to see the sun's shining here. Did you order the weather in especially?' He grinned.

'Well, of course I did. Only the best for my big brother. Look, I'm due to open the museum soon, so what are you going to do all day?'

He shrugged and stuffed in another croissant. 'I'll come and see the amazing museum that's stolen your heart, then I might go for a wander. You could point me in the direction of that old croft of Mum's.'

'Great. Although don't go being a nuisance. Remember, I'm here for a while longer yet.' She was teasing.

He pouted and placed his hand over his heart. 'Little old me? A nuisance? How very dare you?'

'Hmm, butter wouldn't melt, eh? Help yourself to more tea while I shower and get ready. There's bread in the crock if you fancy some toast. Toaster's by the kettle.' She headed upstairs, showered quickly and dressed. Excitement danced in her belly at showing her big brother the museum. She knew he'd get it; he'd understand why she'd fallen in love with the place so quickly.

* * *

Half an hour later, they stood in the museum. Dexter gazed around his new surroundings and whistled. 'Flippin' heck. It's incredible.'

She showed him the photo of their mother as a child, and the one of their grandfather by the lifeboat, and she could've sworn she saw tears in his eyes.

He cleared his throat as he gazed at the photo of his mum and shook his head. 'Look at that cute face. Now I see where I got *my* cuteness from. You must take after Dad.' She whacked him playfully and he guffawed loudly. 'Seriously though, Jettie, this place is *awesome*. The history, the family connection... And Glentorrin is so... *you*. You fit right in. There's no wonder you don't want to come home.'

She nudged him with her shoulder. 'Oi! I never said I don't want to come home.' She paused as she pondered her feelings. 'I just don't want to leave here either.' She crumpled her top lip. 'I wish I could afford to buy it. Although it's not a realistic option, is it? Anyway, my home is Mistford.' She shrugged.

'Who are you trying to convince? Look, you have the money that Laurie left. And the house is paid off. You could sell that or maybe rent it out and get a small mortgage to make up the difference.' He made it sound so easy, but she doubted she would get a mortgage, let alone the fact that she didn't really want one.

She dismissed his comments. 'There's no time for all that. It'll go long before the house sells. It'll be some chain coffee shop or something.'

He stepped in front of her and placed a hand on each shoulder. 'Isn't it worth trying though? If you love it here so much. Laurie told you to go for your dream, and *this* is clearly your dream even if you didn't know it before.'

Ugh! Not him as well.

She shook her head and laughed. 'No, it's a silly *pipe* dream, that's what it is. Anyway, I have my job at the uni, I have *you* down there too, and Millie.'

'But you know Millie's moving to London, Jettie. And you don't need to stay down south for me. To be honest, I'm thinking of moving back to Mum and Dad's, anyway.'

Juliette gasped. 'What? Why?'

'I need a fresh start. I need to leave Brid and all her crap behind.' He walked away and began browsing the displays, or at least pretending to. 'I've had enough. I want to be somewhere where *she* isn't.'

'I get that, but you can't let her force you from the place you call home,' Juliette insisted.

He turned and smiled sadly. 'I don't think of the Cotswolds as home any more. Not since Brid cheated. My best pal is gone, Millie's moving away, you're getting thoughts to move too, admit it. It all makes me feel like I want to start over. I can stay at Mum and Dad's until I decide what to do with myself.'

Juliette sighed. Laurie's death had affected Dexter badly. They'd not only been best friends but like brothers. She understood fully how he felt about the Cotswolds too, because in the depths of her heart she knew she felt the same. The prospect of going 'home' to a place where she had no one to go home *to* filled her with a deep sadness. But she knew full well she hadn't got the capital to buy the museum, and even if she *had* the money, she was seriously lacking the courage to make such a massive change in her life all over again. So, the sooner she got used to the fact she'd be returning to Mistford, the better.

* * *

After work, Juliette linked her arm through Dexter's as they walked around Glentorrin. The early-evening sun was pleasantly warm as they headed towards The Coxswain. She had waxed lyrical about the haggis, neeps and tatties, and Dexter was eager to try them. As they walked, she pointed out Caitlin's bakery, Morag and Kenneth's shop, Archie's outdoor gear place and her brother grinned at her.

'Why are you looking at me like that?' she asked.

'Because you're talking about these people as if you've known them forever. As if you belong here. As if you're settled.'

She felt a little defensive by what he was insinuating. 'No, like I've said, home is Mistford. I wouldn't want to leave my memories of Laurie behind.'

Dexter stopped and turned to her. 'Hey, look, I'm not having a go. I think it's brilliant that you're so happy here. You deserve happiness after what you've been through. And remember, sis, memories live in your mind and your heart. Places are just reminders. But you take your memories with you wherever you go.'

He was right, of course, but she wasn't ready to admit the fact, so she didn't want to pursue the conversation. Luckily, she spotted Reid and Chewie off in the distance. 'I'll have to introduce you,' she told her brother and she waved to catch Reid's attention.

He seemed to stare right through her. He looked a little dishevelled and she wondered if he was having a bad day or if perhaps it was something worse. Kendric's comments about Kate sprang to mind again and she shivered.

As they got closer, Reid turned and called to Chewie, despite her calling out to him.

'Hmm. He can't have seen me,' she said as she watched him hurrying towards his home. 'We can call round tomorrow, maybe.'

Dexter pursed his lips and frowned. 'Erm, sorry, sis, but I think he *did* see you. It looked to me like he was hell-bent on avoiding you.'

Juliette laughed nervously. 'No, that won't be it. I'm sure he was just in a rush to get home. He's had... erm... *visitors* today; important ones.' She remembered he'd had his meeting with Social Care and hoped it hadn't gone badly. She had to stop herself from running after him.

As if sensing a problem, Dexter tugged on her arm. 'Well, leave him be just now. He looks like he's in a rush. We'll go see him tomorrow, but right now I'm bloody starving, so let's go and eat, eh?'

She nodded and smiled but kept her gaze trained on Reid's retreating form. 'Yes.' She shook her head. 'Sorry, yes, let's.'

They pushed through the doors into the pub and Juliette spotted Caitlin at the bar. She dragged her brother along behind her.

'Caitlin! I'm glad you're here. I'd like to introduce you to my brother, Dexter. Dex, this is my lovely friend, Caitlin.'

'So, you're the big teddy bear I've heard about, are you?' Caitlin asked with a wide smile.

Dexter grinned. 'Is that what she calls me these days? It's been worse, I can tell you. Lots worse.'

The two began chatting easily and Juliette saw a sparkle in her brother's eye as he spoke to Caitlin like an old friend that he hadn't seen in a long while. Sadly, the same sparkle was completely absent from Caitlin's eyes. Such a shame, but she'd already said that cuddly men weren't her type.

Poor Dex.

* * *

When they left the pub, the sky was navy blue overhead and a crescent moon hung amongst dotted stars. The street lanterns gave an amber glow that danced on the rippling water of the inlet.

Dexter patted his belly as they walked back to Lifeboat Cottage. 'I could definitely get used to eating like that.'

Juliette laughed. 'You're a haggis convert then?'

'Oh yes. Consider me a fully paid-up member of the *I love haggis* club. I need to make sure to get some to take home with me. Maybe take some for Mum too. A taste of the old country.' He grinned.

'I think we can arrange that.'

'I was a bit shocked when everyone moved the tables and started dancing though. Not a great idea on a full stomach.' He huffed out through puffed cheeks. 'Does that happen a lot?'

Juliette laughed, the memory of her brother being flung around by Caitlin would be one she would revisit frequently to cheer her up. 'It appears to be a regular occurrence, yes.'

'That Caitlin can move though,' he said wistfully.

Juliette's mind was elsewhere. 'Hmm. Look, do you mind if I give you the key and meet you back at the cottage later? There's something I really want to do. I'll not sleep otherwise.'

He frowned. 'You're wanting to check up on that Reid guy, aren't you? What's the deal there?'

'Deal? There isn't a deal. We're just friends,' she snapped rather too harshly and then cringed. 'Sorry. He's been going through some stuff and I've been trying to help. Although, to be honest, I think I maybe hinder more than anything.'

'Do you want me to come with you?'

'No, honestly, it's fine. Go and chill out for a bit. I won't be long.'

'If you're not back in an hour, I'll come looking for you,' he warned her.

She scoffed. 'I'll be absolutely fine. Get a bottle of red open, will you? It can breathe until I get back.'

She handed over the cottage keys and headed up the road towards Reid's place. The lane was dark, and after tripping a couple of times, she took out her phone and switched on the torch. Once she arrived at his house, she knocked on the door.

Kendric opened it. 'Oh, hi. What are you doing here?'

She was a little taken aback by his attitude. 'I just wanted to check in and see how things went today. See how Reid is.'

He quickly glanced over his shoulder. 'Oh, right, yes. Well, he's fine. Well... not exactly *fine*, but... Look, to be honest, he's not having a great day. It's probably best you leave things just now.'

Her worry deepened. 'Did things go badly with Social Care?'

'He's locked himself in his studio, insisting he can't be disturbed because he's in the midst of a very important piece. When I tried to talk to him, he spouted off something about never trusting women again. That all they do is ruin his life. I'm guessing part of that was connected to the two women from Social Care, but he won't confirm anything now as he won't come out of his room. I think he needs to be left alone for a while.'

'Oh no, that doesn't sound at all good. Can I do anything? Anything at all?'

Kendric sighed and shook his head. 'In all honesty, I think the only thing that would help him now would be for Kate to see sense, or for the person that's been filling her head with lies to come clean and admit what they've been doing. But, as neither is likely, I'm at a total loss.'

Juliette's heart skipped and flipped in her chest. She scrambled through her mind, trying to think of some of the things her counsellor had told her when she hit rock bottom. 'Can I just talk to him? Even if it's through the door?'

Kendric closed his eyes and pulled his lips between his teeth. 'You can *try*. But please don't be upset if he doesn't respond. Or if he responds negatively.' He stepped back and let her through.

'Where's Evin?' she asked, worried that he was witnessing his father's struggles.

'He's at Caitlin's for a sleepover with Grace. They're camping in the garden, apparently.'

'Great. Can you point me to Reid's studio?'

Once she was outside his door, Juliette knocked lightly.

'Reid. Hi... it's me, Jules. I called to see how things have gone today, but I gather that maybe they didn't go quite how you'd hoped.' Silence. 'I just want you to know that you don't have to talk. Not if you don't want to. I understand. I can only imagine how hard this whole thing is for you. And it's okay to have days like this. No one is blaming you. I want you to know that there are people here who believe in you. You're not alone, okay?' Silence. 'I won't stay because I know that sometimes being on your own is what's needed to make sense of everything. But please, Reid, remember that you can call on me, on Kendric, Caitlin, Morag and countless other people, if you need us. I know I'm not a permanent fixture here, but I'm your friend too. And I care.' Her voice wavered and she paused to gather herself. 'I've been where you are. The circumstances are different, I know, but I want you to know that you *can* get through this. You can fight it. And we'll all help you as much as we can. Don't forget that. Keep fighting for Evin. For *your* son. He adores you. And he will always adore you, no matter what.'

The door clicked open and, much to her surprise, Reid appeared. His face was pale and drawn. His hair a mess and his eyes puffy and red. 'Why are you here, Jules? Haven't you got a *biker* to entertain?' His tone was harsh and he scowled at her. 'I was walking Chewie early this morning. I saw you launch yourself at him on your doorstep.'

Suddenly the penny dropped as to why he had avoided her earlier. 'Reid, that *biker* you saw me with—'

'What is it about men who ride motorcycles, eh? Why do women go for that? Is it the thrill? God, the way you looked at him when he arrived. It was clear how happy you were to see him. And I wasn't spying, in case you're wondering. I hadn't slept and I thought fresh air might help perk me up. Why didn't you say you had a boyfriend? I kissed you and you said nothing about him. I wanted to kiss you again the other night, but I thought you weren't ready to be with someone. Then I realise you've been with someone all along. I've been... I've been *feeling* things for you, Jules. Letting my guard down. I feel such an idiot. I don't see why you didn't just mention him. Or was it the biker thing? Because of Kate? Look, it doesn't matter, I can do without the drama just now. I've enough on my plate, so just go, okay?'

He made an attempt to close the door and she wedged her foot in it, angry at his assumptions. 'Reid MacKinnon, just stop and listen, will you?' she snapped through clenched teeth. 'You've jumped to the wrong conclusion about this whole thing. That *biker* – not that it's any of your business – is my big *brother*. He's come for a visit. I've missed him. And I can't be held responsible for *your* feelings. They belong to you. All I've ever offered is friendship. It's not my fault if you've misinterpreted that.' She knew deep down she was hiding the fact that she'd been feeling things too but was certainly not going to admit it; it was too painful.

She turned away but he reached out and grabbed her arm. 'Oh god, Jules, I'm sorry. Please, forgive me. I'm just so confused and angry and upset about *everything*. I don't know how to act any more. Who to trust. What to think.'

She turned to face him again and his pleading gaze tugged at her heart. Her voice softened. 'I know. And that's why I'm here. That's why I continue to show up. You can trust *me*, Reid. All I've ever wanted to do is help.'

His chin trembled and he opened his mouth to speak but couldn't seem to form the necessary words. She gave him the space and, eventually, he said, 'They came... today. I asked if they were taking him away, but they wouldn't tell me. They wouldn't say anything. But they didn't have to. I just know it. I know they're taking him, Jules. I can't put him through it all. I can't make him feel like he's choosing between us, so I'm going to step back. She's won.

I've made the decision for him,' he sobbed before slumping into the door frame.

Juliette enveloped him in an embrace and sank to the floor, holding the broken man in her arms. He had made the most selfless decision any parent could make and once again had put Evin's needs first. His whole world was falling apart around him, so Juliette did the only thing she could do: she held him as he cried.

31

There was a strange atmosphere around Glentorrin for the few days that followed. On the last day of his visit, Dexter went out on his bike to explore the island and buy gifts. On his return, he informed Juliette that a *For Sale* sign had appeared at the café.

Reid's café.

So, either Reid had been right, and Kate *was* automatically getting full custody of Evin – which she doubted – or Reid had folded and given in to her like he'd said he would, unwilling to put Evin through the stress of a custody battle. That thought angered her. She presumed Reid was selling up to head down south to be nearer to him, just as she'd expected him to. Things didn't feel right. There was something niggling at the back of her mind. It was all too fast and convenient. She wished she could hunt down the peddler of the lies and stop this horrific situation in its tracks, but she was powerless.

Dexter left to go back home, and the place felt strange without him there. He'd taken Caitlin out on the back of his bike a couple of times and she'd raved about how *cool* he was. Dexter had tried to wheedle information out of Juliette about her, but she'd had to be clear that he was barking up the wrong tree. The daft oaf hadn't been deterred, however. He'd promised to visit again 'as friends' and Caitlin had said he'd be more than welcome. The trouble was, she'd later told Juliette how wonderful it was to have a male *friend* who was just that: a *friend,* with no extra expectations, no pressure, no sexual attraction to ruin things. Little did Caitlin know...

Reid descended further into the depths of despair, but along with Morag, Kenneth and Caitlin, Juliette made a point of calling round regularly, texting and phoning to check in on him. When she visited, she just sat beside him most of the time. Like Millie had done for her. Just to be there.

Her heart ached for him and although she told herself it was because of similarities in her past situation and his present one, she was beginning to admit to herself that there was more to it. Much more. She wished she could do something – anything – to change things. But the fact was that her tenure at the museum was slipping away and therefore so was her time to tell him how she felt. This simply wasn't the right time. Despite this, he was on her mind when she went to sleep and again when she awoke. Seeing him in so much emotional pain made her angry and sad simultaneously. He didn't deserve this. He deserved to be loved and to be allowed to get on with a life with his son.

There had been a few interested parties to visit the museum, but, as no offers had been forthcoming, she presumed that two businesses for sale in the same small village was making potential buyers wonder what was wrong with the place.

Sitting in her pyjamas with a bottle of wine open and Lewis Capaldi singing sad songs in the background, Juliette read the same page of her book over and over again. She figured she might as well go to bed and, as she blew out the candles, someone hammered at the door.

Nervously, she walked towards the pounding to see a slumped

figure through the glass. She couldn't make out if it was Reid or his brother, but she opened the door tentatively to find a swaying Kendric, red-eyed and pale, bottle in hand.

He raised a hand. 'Hey... I didn't know who to... I had nowhere to go,' he slurred.

'Kendric, you're pissed. What the hell are you doing here in this state?' she snapped.

'I have to tell him, Jules. He'll find out eventually. Then he'll hate me. But he'll hate me even more if *she* tells him.' His eyes were narrow due to the copious amounts of alcohol he'd apparently consumed, and he wobbled on the spot. 'It's all ruined. Everything.' He held up his arms and let them flop down to his sides, the bottle of amber liquid he held sloshing in the process.

'For goodness sake, come in.' She angrily tugged on his jacket.

He staggered into the doorway and ended up in a crumpled heap on the floor.

She didn't offer to help him up and instead growled, 'Go and sit in the lounge, Kendric. I'm making you some strong coffee.'

Once she'd made a pot of fresh coffee, she walked back to the living room to find Kendric slumped on the sofa.

She thrust a mug in his direction, angry at what she was being dragged into. 'Drink this.'

He took the drink. 'I had no one else in the village to turn to,' he told her by way of explanation. 'Everyone thinks of me as an outsider since I left. And those who don't think that are too star-struck by me to want to listen to the fact I have issues too. But you... you're an outsider too.'

'You hardly know me. I don't know why you felt it was okay to come here.'

He scowled up at her where she stood, arms folded defensively across her chest. He opened his mouth and gawped for a moment. 'Wait, why are you mad? You don't even know—'

'That you slept with your brother's wife and may be Evin's father? Let's say I had a hunch.'

His eyes widened and he covered his mouth with one hand. 'Shit! How did you...? When did you...?'

'I saw how you talked about her, about *Kate*. The insults you doled out about her. It didn't take a genius, Kendric.' Anger spiked within her and she clenched her fists. 'I just don't know how the hell you could do something like that to your own brother!'

Suddenly, he seemed sober and lucid. He stared at the rug, a look of desolation in his eyes. 'I wanted him to know what she was *really* like. How she was using him and manipulating him, cheating on him with anyone and everyone.'

'So, you slept with your own brother's bloody wife? Oh yeah, you showed him all right! Good for you!' she shouted; her whole body shook with fury as she paced up and down.

He put his mug down and sighed deeply, rubbing his hands over his face as his eyes welled with unshed tears. 'I know how it makes me look.'

'Like a total bastard? Like a man who shags his brother's wife to prove a point?'

'Jules! Please!' he shouted. 'I didn't do it out of malice. I had no feelings for her. I never meant to hurt him. You have to believe me when I say that. I *love* him. I'd never hurt him intentionally.'

Her nostrils flared and she clenched her jaw. 'But you never told him. So how did you prove anything?'

'I couldn't. I was ashamed when I realised how stupid I'd been. So, I took the coward's way out and moved away.'

'What a waste of a brother's trust. Was it worth it?'

'Of course not. I was drunk when it happened. We were at a party, but Reid had gone home early due to a migraine. I promised to get Kate back safely. In my own twisted, alcohol-addled brain, I was helping. I know that sounds crazy. But I knew she wasn't right for him. I wanted him to realise. But I screwed up. I've never been able to tell him and then... Then, she started talking about paternity... I thought he'd just know. But he doesn't have a clue.' A sob escaped his chest. 'I know I have to tell him. I just don't know how.'

Juliette sighed and ran her fingers through her already messed up hair. 'You do know you'll lose him, don't you?'

He nodded and his chin trembled. 'I know. And I know I don't deserve him.'

'And if Evin turns out to be yours?'

Kendric lifted his chin; tears escaped his pained eyes. 'I have no idea.'

* * *

Juliette's head was pounding from all the unwanted information she had acquired the night before. The aspirin hadn't kicked in yet and she was already checking the clock for when she could take the next dose. She wondered what was going on back in Mistford, where life had been so simple; where she wasn't dragged into family dramas that were nothing at all to do with her.

The museum was as busy as usual, and Hamish's latest visit had made her want to cry. 'I can't believe it's closing,' he'd said, the heartbreak evident in his eyes. 'I can't believe my darling will be forgotten.' His voice had broken, and she'd had to swallow the lump of emotion in her throat before she could speak.

She'd reached across the countertop and taken his hand. 'She won't be forgotten, Hamish. She'll always be in your heart.'

He'd smiled, but his words had pierced her heart. 'But *I* won't be here forever. Then, who'll remember her? She deserves to be remembered. Just as your Laurie deserves to be remembered.' Once he'd gone, Juliette had closed the museum temporarily and returned to the house to compose herself.

Just after lunch, Caitlin burst into the museum, panting, out of breath. 'You'll never believe what's happened!'

'Good grief, Caitlin, are you okay?'

Caitlin waved both hands dismissively. 'Yes, yes, I'm fine but... the café. It's *sold*,' she said as she bent double, resting her hands on her knees.

Juliette raised her eyebrows. 'Sold? That's happened quickly.'

'Yes, but it's *who's* bought it that's the big news!'

'Why? Who's bought it?'

'Bloody Donny McNair!'

Juliette scowled in disbelief. '*Leanna's* Donny? What the hell does *he* want with a café?'

'*Bought it for his princess*,' Caitlin replied in a mocking tone.

'Oh, right.'

'There's something fishy going on. Have you seen Reid lately? He's not answering my messages or calls. Is he okay?'

Juliette sighed as the weight of his reality pressed her down. 'I've not seen much of him, no. I think I'll head round again tonight to check on him.' Kendric's admission rattled around her head and made her stomach knot. She wasn't sure if she wanted to walk into the firing line.

'Good idea. He needs all the friends he can get just now. He shouldn't be leaving. None of this should be happening.' Caitlin was right, even if she didn't know the half of it.

* * *

Juliette ate dinner quickly and picked up her phone to video-call her parents. Safe in the knowledge that they were well, and that Dexter had arrived with them, she said her goodbyes and ended the call. Her mind was filled with mixed feelings about Reid. She'd started simply wanting to help him in his time of need – the commonality of depression drawing her to him in her desire to stop anyone from going what she went through after losing Laurie. But things had changed. What had once been simply a kinship had, for her, become more. She didn't want to feel that way. There were so many reasons why she shouldn't. Laurie being the main one. But spending time with Reid had meant she'd grown closer to him. His smile warmed her, and his laugh – as infrequently as it happened – was music to her ears. She never expected to feel this way, especially so soon after losing Laurie. But she couldn't seem to stop the way her stomach flipped when they made eye contact. Or the way she smiled when she thought about him.

Then, there was the news about Kendric and Kate and the fact that she'd been almost made complicit in their dark deeds. Juliette couldn't tell Reid, but she couldn't expect him to understand if he found out that she knew. She was utterly conflicted and hated that Kendric had put her in this position. The only saving grace was that she would be returning home soon and Reid would be moving on with his life too; although that fact didn't fill her with the relief she expected.

Right now, Juliette needed to hear the voice of reason – well, actually, she simply needed to see Millie's face.

'Hey, honey! So good to see you,' Millie beamed into the camera. 'How are things on the wild isle of Skye?'

Juliette let out a sigh of relief at the familiarity of her friend's smile and happy tone. 'The place is wonderful, and I feel... I feel at home here in a strange way. I know it's silly and I'm heading home soon, but I really will be sad to leave.' Knowing Reid was leaving, however, did mean the place wouldn't be quite the same if she were, in fact, staying.

'Aww, sweetie. When you get back, me and Harry are coming up to take you out and cheer you up. How is that hunky chap with all the crap going on?'

'Reid? He's dealing with such a lot. And it's only getting worse,' she mumbled. 'I'm trying to spend time with him to encourage him. Like you did for me, when... you know.'

'Well, he's a very lucky man. But... You seem a little bit down. What's wrong?'

Juliette wanted to tell her everything she was feeling and everything that was going on but was scared to admit it all out loud. 'I'm just... I don't know... Reid is... I feel... Ugh!'

There was a pause before Millie spoke. 'Right... so I'm going to read between those incomplete sentences and interpret what I *think* you want to tell me, okay? Correct me if I'm wrong.' Another pause. 'You like him. But you like him more than a simple friendship. You're attracted to him and you're scared that people will judge you for that, seeing as Laurie was the love of your life and he's only been gone two years. Am I close?'

Juliette's eyes pricked with tears. 'Scarily so.'

Millie's expression softened as did her voice. 'I had a feeling this was going to happen. As soon as you told me about him, something in your voice told me it was more than just you helping someone in need. Oh, honey. I wish I could hug you.'

'What do I do, Millie? I'm leaving soon and I'm guessing I'll never see him again unless I do something about this. I don't know how I feel about that. I get the feeling he likes me too. But... he's going through so much, and things just keep happening to make his situation worse. I don't want to make a colossal mistake or end up being one for him. This is the last thing either of us need. And the guilt... I feel like such a traitor. I never expected to be attracted to anyone ever again. Especially not so soon. It's such a betrayal of Laurie's memory.'

Millie frowned. 'Hey, stop that. Remember what Laurie said? Remember how he said you had to move on and let yourself love again? Well, he meant every word. He wouldn't want you to go through life alone.'

'I know he said those things, but I never expected I'd need to think about them. And what if... what if this is just a lust thing? What if it's just curiosity and some deep-seated need to feel wanted again? How can I drag someone else down that path? Especially someone who's been hurt so much.'

'Look, honey, all you can do is go with the flow. Don't push things, but don't fight them off either. If it isn't meant to be, you'll both get over it. But don't avoid the possibility of being happy.'

Juliette managed to smile. 'Spoken like a woman in love.'

'Absolutely. I never expected to meet Harry when I did. And I certainly never expected things to go the way they have as quickly as they have, but I'm happy, Jules. So happy. And I want the same for you. It's what you deserve.'

'I'm so glad you're happy, my lovely. It's about time.'

'It bloody is!' She laughed. 'Now, chill out and enjoy the last few days you have there. Let the breeze take you where it will.'

32

Later that evening, Juliette sat beside Reid on his sofa tapping her foot to 'Payphone' by Maroon 5 playing in the background, Millie's encouraging words ringing in her mind. Kendric was nowhere to be seen and, judging by Reid's state of mind, nothing had been said. Reid had showered, eaten and looked a little brighter. His whole demeanour was more positive, and it was encouraging to see. A few days earlier, she'd taken him a couple of books to read – comedies that had made her laugh out loud and that she felt perhaps he might like too. She'd been right.

'That one about the doctor, good grief, I almost needed stitches I laughed so much. It felt really good.'

She loved to see him smiling. 'I'm so glad you liked it. I know some parts were a bit gory, but the laughs outweigh the yukky stuff.'

'Oh, absolutely. It really cheered me up.' He nudged her with his shoulder. 'You have a real talent for that too, cheering me up.'

She picked at an invisible thread on her sleeve and shrugged. She also had a *talent* for keeping secrets that would crush him. 'Oh, I wouldn't call it that. I just know books worked for me.'

'It *is* a talent though, Jules. You read people so well. You read *me* so well.'

His comments gave her a warm and fuzzy feeling; a feeling she hadn't felt in too long. He was quite chatty and was evidently having a much better day despite the café being sold. Although she did wonder if that's *why* he was so relaxed. Perhaps it was because he could now close that chapter of his life and move on.

'Why do you keep coming round? I'm not exactly scintillating company,' Reid asked as they sat drinking tea.

'Because knowing you're not alone is a huge thing during the low times. I found that people just being there for me was a great help. So, I suppose I'm trying to be that for you.'

He smiled but shook his head. 'But... *why*? I mean... you're going home soon. I don't get it. And you could be spending time with Caitlin, Morag, anyone else. Instead, you're here with old crabbit pants, drinking tea when you could be out dancing at The Coxswain, drinking wine and enjoying yourself.'

She turned in her seat. 'I *am* enjoying myself. Because, believe it or not, I want to spend time with *you*.' She realised the weight of her words and quickly added, 'It's what friends do. And I understand what you're going through.'

'Well, I hope you know how much I appreciate your friendship.' He smiled and glanced down, his flushed cheeks a clear sign of embarrassment as he reached for her hand.

She tried not to acknowledge how nice his hand felt around hers again and how much she'd missed it since the last time. 'I can't believe how fast my time here has gone.'

'I know. And to think I almost spoiled the chances of you running the museum when you're a natural. You've fitted right in. I just wish...' He shook his head as if stopping himself. 'Well, I'm so glad it all worked out in the end.'

As Juliette contemplated his words, she wanted to say, *This doesn't have to be the end*, but she couldn't bring herself to let the words form.

The opening bars of 'Someone You Loved' by Lewis Capaldi began in the background and he went on to sing about heartbreak and the pain of loss.

She inhaled a shaky breath as she met Reid's intense gaze. 'I'm glad it worked out too.'

The powerful lyrics of the song seemed fitting somehow, and she tried to block them out as Reid brushed the hair from her cheek. 'It's a shame that the timing isn't better really, isn't it?' He paused and contemplated his next words. 'You see... I was drawn to you early on when you arrived, after I'd got over myself.' He smiled. 'I didn't like the fact that I was attracted to you, obviously. The last thing I wanted was to risk being hurt again. But you're different. And, of course, Ric is so damned good-looking, so when he turned up, I resigned myself to the fact that you wouldn't be interested in me, anyway. But now... I see how you are with him and I know that, unlike other women, you're unimpressed by all the glamour.' He paused and smoothed his thumb across the skin on the back of her hand and she wondered if his self-deprecation was another result of his ex-wife's treatment of him. 'But... I guess me and you... well, it's just not meant to be, eh? Regardless of the paternity test results, I'm going to be moving away to be nearer to Evin – he's still my boy, no matter what – and you're going home.'

She opened her mouth to speak, but he held up his hand.

'You don't need to say anything; I know you don't want a relationship with *anyone* just now... But what gets to me is who knows what might have been? If the timing had been different... If our stars had been aligned. If I hadn't been such a huge mess of a man.' He smiled, but the sadness behind his eyes was clear and her throat tightened.

He glanced at her lips with longing and she wanted to give in. He'd got it so wrong. She *was* attracted to him. Had been for a while. But there were so many things stopping her. Mostly guilt. And then, there was the fear of letting someone get close to her again. But hearing him say how *he* felt made her want to admit her own feelings. Although he'd already said the timing was wrong. And he was right about that.

She reached up and touched his cheek. 'You're not a mess of a man, Reid. Far from it. You're passionate, loyal, kind... incredibly handsome.' She smiled as his eyes lit up. 'I've been so scared to let go, and even more afraid of betraying Laurie. But how I feel about you is changing things. You should know that I—'

There was a loud crash as the door bashed into the wall when it was flung open. 'Dad, I've *had* to come home.' Evin was out of breath, his voice high-pitched, showing his distress. 'I saw Leanna outside Grace's. I know what's going on. I know about it *all*. I know you've sold Grandma's café too! How could you *do* that? Why haven't you told me anything?' His attention snapped to Juliette and he flung himself at her. 'Has my dad told you that they're making me move away? Has he? Has he told you that I don't want to go and live with Mum? It's not fair. I don't want to go and leave my friends behind. Not when I've only just got them. And she won't let me take Chewie. She says he's messy and smelly, but he's not. She's *wrong*. He's lovely and he's my best friend and I *hate* her! I've told Leanna I hate her too and I'll run away. I won't go with Mum and that doaty bawbag man. I won't!' The young boy was distraught and sobbing. It broke Juliette's heart to see him like that.

Reid reached out and pulled Evin into his arms. 'Come here, son. Don't cry, eh? Please, don't cry. I'm sorry I've let you down. I'm so, *so* sorry.'

Juliette watched as Reid tried his best to console his boy. It was a heart-breaking scene to behold. After everything they'd both been through, this seemed like the ultimate cruelty. She stood and mouthed the words, 'I'll go.'

Reid nodded and gave her a pained smile before closing his eyes and burying his face in his son's mop of dark hair.

33

Juliette hadn't heard from Reid for a couple of days and she tried to convince herself it was a good thing. That way, she could pretend that she wasn't feeling anything for him. That he wasn't a continuous thought rumbling in the back of her mind. That it didn't feel like a missed chance for something. There was news that an offer had come in for the museum, so that too was the end of her dream. Not that it was ever something she knew she wanted, nor even was it an attainable thing – not really. She found herself daydreaming in between visitors. Pretending it *was* hers and that this was now her home. Then she remembered she would be going back to her real home very soon and the ache in her chest worsened.

She wandered around gazing at the exhibitions , but her mind was too distracted and she ended up looking online for a gift for Evin to take away with him to his mum's and remind him of Chewie. She found a cute little ornament of a Hungarian Vizsla that was stocked locally just across in the mainland. She thought it was probably the type of thing old ladies collected, but she felt sure Evin would love it regardless. She paid extra for next-day delivery and hoped it would reach her in time.

At the end of the day, she made her way up towards Morag's shop to find something for dinner, even though her appetite was pretty much non-existent. As she walked, inhaling the salty air and admiring the vivid blue of the sky, Juliette spotted Reid by the bench that overlooked the inlet – the place of their first argument. He was staring out at the water, watching Gus the fisherman preparing his boat. He looked a little lost and she was almost taken over by the urge to talk to him; to comfort him. She was fighting it but knew she was losing miserably.

Acquiescing to her inner voice, she began to walk towards Reid but stopped in her tracks when Leanna appeared from the direction of the café. She couldn't hear what was being said, but she could see the woman was upset; her flailing arms were a dead give-away, and she was clinging to Reid's coat as he tried to walk away from her.

Juliette looked on; the vignette was like something from a silent movie, all that was missing was the hurried and overly dramatic piano music. Reid tried to pull away again, but Leanna was clearly begging him not to. He tried in vain to release her hand from his coat, she screamed at him to stop. It was pitiful. Ridiculously theatrical and clearly in emotional overdrive, Leanna launched herself at Reid and tried to kiss him.

Juliette gasped, held her breath and covered her mouth with her hand. She was rigidly glued to the spot. If she moved, they'd notice her, so she was frozen in place, statue-like, trying to be invisible; it all felt voyeuristic and wrong. She waited for Reid's reaction, which seemed to happen in slow motion. He jerked his head away and held her at arm's length and Juliette could've sworn she heard him yell, 'What the hell are you doing?'

Suddenly, Donny appeared out of nowhere and grabbed Leanna. She screamed as he flung her out of the way, and she dramatically fell against the sea wall. Donny's fist flew at Reid's face, connecting with a force that caused the victim's head to ricochet backwards. Reid staggered and tripped, causing Leanna to scream again, only this time it was a bloodcurdling cry, akin to something from a horror movie.

Juliette couldn't stand by any longer. She had to do something, although she had no idea what. As if fuelled by adrenaline alone, she ran towards the fracas. 'No! Stop! Donny, *stop*!' she screamed at the top of her voice.

Donny ignored her and continued to pummel his fists into Reid's body, spitting out expletives as he did so.

Reid held up his own fists to guard his face. 'You've got it wrong, Donny! You know you have. She kissed me and I pushed her away!' But Donny, enraged and unwilling to listen to reason, was undeterred.

Thankfully, Archie and Kenneth appeared and made a grab for Donny and managed to manhandle him away.

Donny growled in anger, with an edge of violence Juliette had never witnessed before. 'You bastard! She's *my* wife! You can't just leave her alone, can you? You fucking bastard! And then, people wonder why your boy's being taken! I'm so fucking glad you got what you deserved there. I'm glad I told Kate. She needed to know what a liar you are. Maybe now you'll keep your hands off my fucking wife!'

Juliette grabbed the angry man's coat. 'Donny, stop it! That's enough!' she yelled and tugged at him without considering the consequences.

He turned his wide, manic eyes to her. 'What's it got to do with you, eh? Still can't make your mind up which one of the brothers you want, is that it?' Saliva foamed at the corners of his mouth, giving him the appearance of a rabid dog, and in that moment, she realised she was out of her depth.

Reid scrambled forward, blood dripping from his nose and a cut above his eye. He was clutching his body around his ribs, yet he grabbed Donny by the shirt collar. 'Leave her out of this, Don, it's me you're angry with,' he said breathlessly. 'And what do you mean you're glad you told Kate? Told her *what*?' he shouted through gritted teeth.

Donny grinned maliciously. 'I told her *everything*! About you and your drinking and you neglecting that boy, leaving him outside in all weather. Him nearly drowning and you being nowhere around. And all the women. Oh, she knows it *all*, pal. Every last little bit. She knows how you were cheating on her with my fucking wife! And I'm glad I told her! You don't deserve that lad!' He lunged forward again, forcing Archie and Kenneth to tighten their grip.

Reid's brow crumpled in confusion. 'Donny, what the hell are you talking about? None of that's true. You *know* it's not true. Why would you do that?' Desperation caused his voice to break.

Leanna scrambled to Reid's side. 'I swear I didn't know, Reid. I swear,' she sobbed. 'Donny, stop it! Please, just stop.'

'You should go on home, Donny,' Archie told him. 'Go and sober up, eh?'

The crazed man's grin remained in place as he strained against his captors. 'Nah, nah, not yet. I'm not finished. I also found out something else from Kate that's quite interesting.'

Juliette instinctively knew what he was going to say, and she closed her eyes for a moment. Should she risk interfering again or let things unfold? She took a deep breath and stood firm. 'Donny, don't do this here. Please. It's not the time or place. Listen to your wife,' she pleaded with him, but he glared at her with disdain.

'Evin's not even your kid, is he? So, you've no claim over him, anyway. Unlike your brother, eh?' He laughed again, a sickly, possessed sound.

Reid gripped at the short strands of hair on his own scalp and his face contorted into what seemed like a million different emotions – none of them positive. 'What do you mean by that?' He glanced at Leanna. 'What does he mean, Leanna?'

Leanna sobbed into her hands. 'Donny, no! He doesn't deserve this. Please!'

'Donny?' Reid asked, his chest heaving. 'You've lied to my wife and now you're making up lies about my boy too? I don't know what your problem is.' He walked up to Donny and pointed in his face. Lowering his voice, he said, 'The stuff Kate has said about Evin's paternity has *nothing* to do with Kendric. I'm sorting it out. *Me.*'

Donny laughed. 'Really? Not thought about how much Evin looks like your dear brother? Ask your wee English girlfriend what she knows, eh? They've been talking all about it.'

Reid turned briefly to look at Juliette. She covered her mouth, unable to find any words of explanation when she saw an expression of utter confusion in his eyes. When she didn't speak he turned back to Donny, his nostrils flared and he snapped his fist back.

Juliette grabbed his arm. 'Reid, No!'

Instead of hitting Donny, Reid let out a bloodcurdling, guttural growl. 'What did I ever do to you? You're basing all this on a bloody fantasy! I never slept with Leanna. She's like a sister to me! So what possible reason could you have to want to ruin my life, eh, Donny? We were mates.'

'Mates?' Donny spat. '*Mates*? My wife only has eyes for *you*. It's always been the same. How do you think that makes me feel, eh? Playing second fiddle to someone like *you*? I have money, a big house, a fancy bloody car. I offered her *everything* she ever wanted, but it turns out it was *you* she wanted all along! So, I want you gone by any means possible. I want every trace of you removed from Glentorrin. I want *everything* you touch to fail. It's what you deserve. She'll never love me right while you're around. Never have my baby if there's a chance she can have yours. Aaargh! I'd *kill* you, but you're not worth the fucking prison time!' He strained forward again, almost dragging his sentries along the cobbled road. Luckily, between them they had the strength and determination to hold him firm.

'Whoa, whoa, Donny, knock it off, lad. That's enough now,' a red-faced Kenneth said, trying to calm the situation.

By now, there was a crowd gathered around them. Spectators all disbelieving what they were seeing from Donny, the mild-mannered, oblivious man. *Not so oblivious, after all*. Juliette was shocked to the core at the lengths Donny had apparently gone to, to ensure his wife was free of the temptation of Reid's presence.

Two police cars with blue lights flashing turned the corner and stopped beside the crowd. Four uniformed men leapt, two from each vehicle, and took over from Archie and Kenneth.

'Move along, folks. Let us do our job. Away you go now,' one of the officers said as he held his arms out towards the gathered throng. It didn't help, the people were too invested in what happened next.

Ignoring the presence of the police, Reid shook his head. 'Donny, I never *loved* Leanna,' he told him helplessly. 'Not like *that*. You had no competition from me. None at all.' He pointed a finger at Donny's chest. 'You've ruined my life for a fantasy you created in your head. Didn't you think to speak to me? My God, Donny, my *son* is being taken away, I'm being branded an alcoholic and a woman-iser. I've lost my business, all because you thought I was after your wife?' He threw his arms up in the air in utter exasperation. 'Jeez man, Leanna and I grew up together. We were friends. *Were* being the operative word.' He glanced at Leanna where she stood in a shaking, sobbing heap, his gaze filled with disdain at her recent behaviour. 'I've *never* thought about her as anything other than a friend. If she felt more for me, then that's not my fault. I've never led her on. I've *never* encouraged her, Donny. I can assure you of that. I adored my wife. *She* was all I wanted. I would *never* have cheated on her. I *didn't* cheat on her. She cheated on me. She abandoned me and Evin and now you've given her the ammunition to march in and take everything from me! And, to top it off, you drag my brother into this too?'

Wide-eyed, Donny struggled to release himself from the grasp of the officers. 'But I saw you. I saw you just then! You were kissing! In bloody public, brazen as you like. I'm not blind!'

Reid laughed, a harsh, humourless sound that erupted from his chest. 'Well, apparently you *are*. She tried to kiss me. I stopped her.'

'It's true, Donny, I saw it happen,' Juliette pitched in.

Reid continued, 'She'd come to tell me not to go away. That she didn't want the damn café you've bought for her. That she only worked there to be close to me. It was news to me, I can tell you that with a hundred percent honesty. I was shocked and horrified, if you want to know the truth. But you... you jumped at the chance to get rid of me. You were so damn quick to buy the café, weren't you, Donny? Without even knowing the truth or bothering to find out, you were quick to make sure you got rid of me from Glentorrin. And it's not enough that you do all that, but you try and drive a wedge between me and Kendric too?'

Morag appeared beside Juliette and put a reassuring arm around her shoulder. Soon after, Caitlin joined them. 'Are you okay, hen? What the hell is going on?'

'You wouldn't believe it if I told you,' Juliette managed to utter.

Donny's nostrils flared, his anger unabated. 'She only ever wanted *you* even though *I* married her, and I'd had enough. I knew that if Evin was gone, you'd sell up and piss off too. And I couldn't bloody wait. So, *yes,* I bought your shitty business. And I'm not lying about Kendric. Kate told me. They slept together.' He was seething, but there was a sick look of pride in his expression. His face was beet red and his chest heaved as aggression continued to emanate from him.

Morag gasped. 'Hang on. What's this about Kate and Kendric?'

Before anyone could reply, the police officers dragged Donny to one of the waiting squad cars, handcuffed him and shoved him into the back seat. Then, it was Reid's turn to be bundled towards a car.

Juliette dashed forward. 'Wait! He did nothing wrong. I witnessed this whole thing. He's the victim here. You can't take him away!'

'Sorry, madam, they're both coming to the station at Kyle of Lochalsh. Let us do our job, eh? He'll be allowed to call home once we've got to the bottom of all this. Go on home.'

'But—'

'Jules, it's fine. I'll be okay,' Reid said with a small smile of reassurance. 'Can you just make sure Evin is all right?'

She was taken aback by his lack of anger towards her. 'Of course. Absolutely,' she told him with a shaking voice.

Reid nodded his thanks before ducking his head to climb into the car willingly.

As the vehicles pulled away towards the bridge and the crowd dispersed, Morag heaved a deep sigh. 'Come on, ladies, back to mine. I think we all need a stiff drink after that. Jules, you can call Kendric from my house and let him know what's going on. Make sure he's got Evin with him.'

Juliette was still quite stunned by what she'd witnessed, and when she glanced down at her hands, she realised she was shaking. Suddenly, the prospect of alcohol appealed to her. 'Th-thank you, Morag.' She peered over to where Leanna stood, still sobbing violently.

As if she sensed that she was being watched, she raised her chin, and when she locked eyes on Juliette, she glared at her before turning to stomp away, back towards *her* café.

'I hope she's okay,' Juliette whispered.

Morag tutted. 'Oh, just leave her be. Daft wee mare. She has no clue what she's done. She'll soon be playing the victim again, no doubt.'

* * *

Back at Morag and Kenneth's, Juliette called Kendric at Reid's house and passed on the details of what had happened in the village. She warned him that Reid would be asking questions and that things were out in the open. *Literally* in the open. The whole village had witnessed the incident.

'No, no, no!' She could hear the utter anguish in his voice. 'I can't believe Donny would *do* such a thing. And I can't believe he thought Reid had any part in an affair, not after what Kate did. He knows how hard it all was. Shit, I'd better get to the police station.'

'I don't think that's a good idea. We want him out of there, not staying longer. And if you go and tell him the truth now, he'll react and then he'll be arrested. Is Evin okay? He doesn't need to be hearing this from people. Do you need me to come and get him?'

'No, no, thank you. He's fine. Well, as fine as can be expected under the current set of circumstances. He's sitting in the garden with Chewie. Kate's coming tomorrow to take him. Evin's heartbroken that he'll be leaving Chewie behind. Poor kid, he's begged her on the phone to let him take the dog, but she's adamant. Apparently, *tough biker boy* is allergic.' He sighed heavily down the line. 'Oh God, Jules, this whole damned thing should never have even happened.'

'I know. But now we have to deal with the fallout.'

'We? None of this is your doing. You shouldn't even be involved. I'm so sorry.'

'Look, I just want to see that boy happy. And Reid too.'

Kendric sighed and whispered, 'I'm really worried about Reid and what this will do to him.'

'I know. I hope he's okay, too. I want more than anything for Kate to change her mind about taking Evin,' she said hopefully.

'And pigs might sprout wings and take to the skies.'

34

A message pinged through from Reid at gone midnight. I'm home, was all it said.

Juliette desperately wanted to talk to him; to check he was okay; to apologise for her part in the secrecy surrounding Kendric and Kate. But she knew he would be angry and upset. She knew there was a very good chance he blamed her for keeping things from him. Why wouldn't he? Her heart ached and her stomach knotted. She'd been on the verge of admitting her feelings to him. She'd been on the verge of hoping there was a future for them.

But now, it was all gone. In a matter of days, she'd be returning home.

* * *

The following day, Juliette was distracted by the knowledge that Reid's ex-wife, Kate, was arriving, and everything was about to come to a head for him and Evin. She wished she could be there to support them, but she didn't want to intrude, especially when she didn't know what kind of reception she would receive. Much to her relief, the post arrived and amongst a pile of junk mail was a parcel from the shop over in Kyle of Lochalsh.

As soon as it was closing time at the museum, Juliette paused at the main entrance and gazed across to the display cases, each piled high with items that contained the memories and imprints of the people who had made Glentorrin the thriving village it was today. It was incredibly sad to think that in a matter of months these items would have to find new homes, or be returned to their owners, never to be put on display again. With a deep sigh, she locked up and went back through to the house.

After pacing the floor, she could wait no longer. She had to head up to Reid's. She just hoped he wouldn't be annoyed at her turning up unannounced. She gift-wrapped the Hungarian Vizsla ornament that had arrived and headed out.

Another warm evening enveloped her in its embrace as she walked along the lane. Sunlight cast patterns on the water's surface and the light breeze caused ripples to dance along to the inaudible music of late summer. The village was alive with tourists snapping photos of the picturesque setting, and Morag was obviously doing a roaring trade on ice creams as the queue was stretched right out of the main door.

As Juliette passed the pub, Stella waved as she cleared the tables outside, and then Archie from the outdoor shop saluted and shouted hello from his bicycle as he headed away from the village on his evening ride. Everything felt so normal now. So familiar. The sights, the people, the sense of belonging. Three months had felt like a lifetime and a second all at once. It was going to be strange waking up in Mistford again and not seeing the villagers through the museum windows, getting ready for the day each morning; not walking over to Caitlin's for a fresh croissant and a few giggles; not heading to The Coxswain for a wee bit of dancing and Stella's famous haggis.

A cloud of melancholy began to descend, and Juliette had to quickly shrug it off. She was on a mission for now and that had to take precedence.

When Reid's house came into view, there was no sign of Kendric's car, but there was an unfamiliar vehicle parked outside. She presumed it was Kate's. It appeared Kate was still around. Juliette had mixed feelings about meeting her but she was relieved she hadn't missed Evin. As she approached the doorstep, the front door opened, and Chewie came bumbling out at speed. He headed straight for Juliette and, reminiscent of their first meeting, almost knocked her off her feet.

'Get back here, you *stupid* animal!' an English voice called from the direction of the house. A woman appeared a few seconds later, jogging after him, red-faced and perturbed. When she saw the dog fussing around Juliette, she shielded her eyes from the sun. 'Sorry about that. He's a bit mental,' she said with an eye roll.

Juliette surreptitiously assessed the woman who had once owned Reid's heart. She was quite beautiful from a distance. Dark hair that fell in waves down past her shoulders and a curvaceous figure that most women would kill for. She wore skinny cropped jeans, tan wedges and a cream shirt, nothing special, but she seemed to have that effortless beauty about her that made Juliette feel dull in comparison.

'It's fine. We're friends, aren't we, Chewie?' She laughed as she scratched the dog behind his ear and received an appreciative lick in response.

The brunette eyed her suspiciously until realisation apparently dawned on her. 'Oh. Are you that... *Shiny Sheila* that Evin talks about non-stop? The one who saved that wretched dog from drowning?'

First it was bloody Janet and now Sheila. Juliette tried not to take offence. 'Ah, you mean *Sparkly Jules*, and yes, that's me.'

The woman approached her and gave a sweet smile. 'I'm Kate, Reid's ex.' She limply held out her hand.

On closer inspection, Juliette could see that her make-up was applied a little too thickly and that grey roots were beginning to show through in her hair. The perfect mask was flawed, and Juliette felt relieved and more relaxed in knowing this.

She shook the proffered hand. 'Jules,' she said with a forced smile, trying her best to remain impartial even though the urge to shove the woman out of the way was strong.

'So, you're the latest poor soul to be lumbered with all the old crap in the museum, are you?'

Juliette frowned. 'I'm not lumbered. I happen to love the place.'

The woman scrunched her face. 'Ugh, all those grubby things that have been handled by goodness knows who? Bleurgh.' She shivered dramatically. 'Well, each to their own, I suppose. And it'll be something far more useful soon once it's sold, no doubt.'

Juliette's nostrils flared and she tried to keep herself in check. 'I think it's a shame. Those pieces are incredibly important to the people of this community.'

Kate shrugged. 'Well, as I said, each to their own. What can I do for you, anyway?'

'Nothing, thanks. I came to give Evin a gift and to see how they both are in light of the last few days.'

'Oh, you mean the Donny thing?'

'Yes, I mean the Donny thing. His lies and betrayal, to be exact.'

Kate folded her arms across her chest, her stance becoming defensive. 'It wasn't *all* lies.'

Juliette tried to keep her opinions to herself. She really tried. *So* hard. But nope, they had to be expressed. She mirrored the stance of her nemesis. 'I'm afraid pretty much everything that horrible little man reported back to you was lies.'

Kate tilted her head and smirked. 'And *how* long have you lived here?'

'I don't live here, but I do know a confession when I hear one. I heard Donny admit to everything. And I've spent a lot of time with Reid, so I know what he's been going through too. Donny stomped all over his heart *and* his life completely unnecessarily.'

Kate pursed her lips. 'Look, I know you mean well, Sheila, but you don't know as much as you think you do.'

I know that you slept with your husband's brother, then you ran off and abandoned your son. And I know that you broke the heart of a kind and generous man. And that you think you can come in and play the hero, her conscience screamed at her.

'It's *Jules*. And, yes, you're right, I *do* only mean well. I know it's nothing to do with me, but I hate to see someone plastered with dirt without reason. It sticks. And that seems unfair. I'm still shocked that you're actually taking Evin away, seeing as it wasn't a court-instructed thing.'

Kate huffed in apparent exasperation. 'It's got nothing to do with you. This was a decision made by Evin's parents. It's what's best for him. He needs a stable home with two parents and that's what he's going to have from now on. And anyway, Reid will still get to see him. He realises that the boy is better with me.'

Juliette snorted. 'I highly doubt that that's how Reid feels.'

Kate jutted out her chin. 'Look, have you come to stir up shit? Because I haven't got the time. I need to finish gathering mine and Evin's stuff.' She gave a fake smile this time.

'No, I haven't come to stir up shit. Like I said, I was only calling to drop off a gift and check in on my *friend*. I'm just concerned about how he's handling today.'

Kate waved a dismissive hand. 'I can take the gift for *my* son and, don't worry, your *friend's* fine. Can't say the same for his brother though.' The little smirk wasn't lost on Juliette.

'What's happened to Kendric?'

Kate narrowed her eyes. 'Let's just say he's gone home with a black eye and wounded pride.'

Juliette clenched her teeth. 'I can't believe you're finding amusement in this. And I'm sure Reid *and* Evin are anything but fine. I hope you're happy with yourself.'

Kate stepped forward and hissed through clenched teeth, 'Don't judge those you don't know anything about, lady. This has nothing at all to do with you.' As if realising she was verging on threatening behaviour, she straightened up and fiddled with her hair, feigning innocence. 'And, anyway, Reid'll probably be glad to get shot of Evin. He's a little monster when the mood takes him. He'll be glad of the tidiness and the peace and quiet. It should be *me* you're worried about. I've got to put up with all that now. It's a good thing I love the little sod.' She had the audacity to follow this with a laugh.

Juliette gasped at the way Kate referred to her own son as if he was a badly trained animal or a possession to be easily discarded. Even if it was a joke, it was in very bad taste under the circumstances. Her nostrils flared involuntarily. 'As you said, it's none of my business, but I can assure you Reid is in no way glad to *get shot*, as you put it. He's heartbroken, Kate. You *left* Evin without explanation. He's been happy with his *dad* ever since, because that's what Reid is to Evin, his dad, and no amount of paternity tests will change that. And I happen to know Evin wants to stay here. So, now that you know the truth about Donny's lies and the whole situation, maybe you should rethink things? That way you won't have to *put up* with him.' She immediately clamped her mouth shut. A feeling of déjà vu rattled around her mind from the time she delivered those horrible home truths to Reid. She needed to learn to keep her mouth shut and her nose out of other people's business.

Juliette held her breath and waited for Kate to slap her or, at the very least, hurl abuse at her.

Kate scowled and curled her lip, but she spoke through gritted teeth once again. 'Well, maybe you should go home, eh? And keep out of things that don't concern you. And, for your information, I'll be rethinking nothing.' She snatched the gift from Juliette's hand. 'Bye, *Sheila*,' she spat and turned to go back to the house. 'Come on, *dog*!' she shouted harshly at poor Chewie.

After hesitating and glancing up at Juliette to see if perhaps she had a better offer, the poor animal reluctantly headed after her into the house.

* * *

Back at home, Juliette paced the floor. She contemplated calling Millie, Caitlin or her mum, but was worried about tying up the line in case Reid tried to get through. Rain pounded at the windows and thunder rumbled overhead intermittently; more the typical weather for September.

The later it got, the more agitated she became until she forced herself to open a bottle of wine and sit down. She clicked on the radio and tried to distract herself with music, but her mind insisted on wandering, regardless.

It was almost ten o'clock. *Kate must have gone by now*. She picked up her mobile and considered shooting off a text to Kendric to find out what had happened but thought better of it; she didn't want to appear to be taking his side. She was just considering to whom she should reach out, and what to say, when there was a knock on the front door.

Juliette placed her glass of wine on the table and dashed down the hallway. A slumped silhouette was visible through the glass and she presumed it was Kendric, out on a drunken self-pity party again. She unlocked the latch.

She gasped as she was greeted with the sight of a rain-soaked

Reid, wearing a thin T-shirt and jeans. He looked frozen and was shaking violently. 'Come in! Quickly! You'll catch your death out there!'

He staggered through the door and dripped all over the tiling. 'I'm s-sorry. I j-just didn't know what to d-do,' he stuttered and dripped a little more.

'Don't apologise. Go on through to the living room and I'll go get you some towels.' She ran up the stairs to the bathroom and grabbed a couple of bath sheets, as well as her fluffy robe, and ran back down again. She found him standing in the centre of the lounge rubbing his hands up and down his arms. 'Look, you're going to have to get those clothes off. I don't have anything suitable, but you can pop this on. I'll leave you to it and go make some tea.' She handed him her pale blue spotty robe and some towels.

'Can I m-maybe have something s-stronger?'

'Sure. I'll get you a glass. Is wine okay?'

He nodded.

When she returned, he was standing with one bath sheet around his waist and was rubbing at his hair with the other. She glanced at the robe that was folded up on the chair and he cringed.

'I'm sorry, but I couldn't even get it on.'

When he removed the towel from his head, she was greeted with the full frontal of his naked chest. A smattering of dark hair sat across his pectoral muscles and droplets of water still glistened on his skin.

Juliette closed her eyes for a second, willing herself to forget his attire, or lack thereof, and shakily placed the glass on the coffee table. 'Have a seat,' she gestured to the sofa, and he sat down closest to where she stood, so she sat beside him. 'What's happened? You could've called instead of coming out in this awful weather.'

He shook his head. 'I hope you don't mind, but I had to see a friendly face after the shitty day I've had.' He ran his hand over the wet strands of his hair and his brow crumpled. 'I know you're aware of the Kate and Kendric thing.'

Her heart sank and her stomach dropped as if she was on the downward portion of a rollercoaster. 'Shit, Reid, I'm so sorry. I didn't mean—'

'No. Don't apologise. You should never have been put in that situation. I can't blame you for staying out of it. None of this was your doing.'

Relief flooded her to the point where the room began to swim, and her eyes began to fill with tears. 'I felt so awful. I wanted to do something to help you, but I couldn't think of what.'

He turned to face her and took her hand. 'Hey, stop. Don't beat yourself up. I'm not upset with you. I mean that.' He quickly released her hand and she had the urge to reach out and touch him, just to make sure he was really here and had really forgiven her. He continued, 'Anyway, Kate left with Evin around half an hour ago. He was refusing to get in the car at first. Then, he ran away and Father McAllen found him in the graveyard. He phoned to say Evin was there, sitting on the bench in the rain, clutching the little dog statue you got him and talking to his *grandma*. Father McAllen said he heard him saying, "Grandma, if you're really watching over me like everyone tells me you are, please can you make it stop? Tell them I want to stay with Dad. I'll be lonely without him and I don't want to leave Chewie." It was heart-break-ing, Jules. He was begging her to step in and stop his mother from taking him away. His grandma died ages ago. I was terrified he was losing his mind, but then he said you'd told him that you found it helpful talking to Laurie, so he wanted to get his grandma to help us.' Reid shook his head, pain evident in his crumpled expression. 'Why did this have to happen to him? Hasn't he been through enough?'

The desire to hold him was almost overpowering, but instead

Juliette leaned forward and placed a reassuring hand on his arm. 'I'm so sorry. I wish I could've done something.'

He placed his hand on top of hers and his lips curved upwards for a split second, but it wasn't really a smile. 'You tried. I heard what you said to Kate earlier. She took delight in telling me how you'd had a go at her. I was impressed with how you stood your ground. You're pretty bloody amazing. But then, I've told you that already, eh?' He dropped his gaze to the floor and shook his head again.

Anger at Kate knotted Juliette's stomach. 'I just wish she realised that this amount of stress and anguish isn't good for Evin. *Or* for you. And now that she knows Donny's stories were blatant lies, she should have the decency to reconsider her actions. Especially in light of the fact that *she* was the one who left in the first place.'

Reid sighed. 'She's too stubborn. Too proud.' He gave a humourless laugh. 'You know, I found out she wanted to come home around six months after she'd left us; I heard that little snippet from a mutual friend. Apparently, the biker had lied about his wealth. But she wouldn't pick up the phone. Scared of losing face. So, she's stayed with, and tried to get pregnant with, a guy she apparently doesn't even love. She even married him. Crazy.'

Juliette caught a strange expression in his eyes and had to ask, 'Would you have taken her back?'

His response was quick and firm. 'Absolutely not.' He shrugged. 'The trust was broken. There was no going back for me. Regardless of how much it all hurt and how much I loved her. I wasn't prepared to take that risk again. Definitely not for Evin. But look where that got me. He's gone anyway. All I can think about was the way he sobbed as they left. Reaching out of the car window and calling to me. And Chewie howling. God, the noise he made. He knew something was wrong with Evin and I had to fight with his lead to stop him from chasing the damn car.' He rubbed at his eyes, his jaw clenched, and she could see he was struggling with the anguish of it all.

Her stomach roiled as the image of Evin, distressed and reaching for his dad, assaulted her mind. And that poor, helpless dog. She shook her head to try and dislodge it. 'What about Kendric? What will you do now?'

He huffed the air from his lungs through puffed cheeks. 'Honestly? I have no idea. The strange thing is I feel... numb. It happened a long time ago and he was so, *so* sorry. He sobbed. I've never seen him like that. He explained the reasons behind it all, and I tried to understand, but... It hurt. It hurt like hell. He's the one person in all this that I should've been able to trust. But how can I now? He's shattered that with his actions. He's my *brother*, for God's sake. And yet... on the other side of it all... he's my brother. Do you know what I mean?'

Juliette nodded. 'I do. You still love him even after what he did.'

He nodded. 'Talk about a double-edged sword.' He closed his eyes briefly. 'I want more than anything to forgive him. I just can't do that right now. I hope that one day I can.'

'Give it time.'

'It's all I can do. I'm just glad that Evin knows nothing about it all. Once the paternity test comes back, we'll deal with it then, if we need to. Thankfully, my heartless ex has decided to give me that much. As for the rest of the stuff going on...' He sighed heavily. 'Well, the café is sold. So, I think I'll maybe rent out my house and use the money I get from that to rent a flat closer to where Evin will be. Kate warned me off doing so, which to my mind makes it even easier for me to go ahead.' He gave a wicked smile.

'And what will become of the museum?'

'There have been two offers. But both are low. And both are from big-name chains who want to cash in on the pretty location. Make it something more commercially viable for the tourist industry.' He cringed. 'You can see it now, can't you? Pictures of coffee beans in sacks and modern barista equipment adorning the walls, instead of photos of the people who made the village what it is. *The Lifeboat Coffee House.*' He sneered.

'I wish I could help there too. I'm sorry, I just...' She lowered her chin, guilt twisting her insides.

He reached out and lifted her face with one finger. 'Hey, I totally understand. Your life is in the Cotswolds. There's no need for you to apologise and I should never have made you feel guilty about that.'

She wanted to explain. To tell him that it wouldn't be the same here without him, so the thought of owning the museum, whilst it would still be wonderful, wouldn't have quite the same sparkle. She wanted to say that he'd got things wrong before, that she did have feelings but that she'd been trying to hide them or ignore them until they went away. After all, this could be no more than a brief holiday romance, and surely people in their thirties just didn't do that kind of thing... did they? But instead she remained silent, watching him watching her.

For a few moments more, they sat there, eyes locked on each other, his thumb grazing her cheek. She parted her lips and waited... Would he kiss her? Would she let him? But all too soon, he removed his hand and sat up straight.

He swallowed hard. 'Maybe I should go home, get into some dry clothes.'

And, just like that, again the spell was broken.

35

Juliette felt the chance slipping away from her. 'Look, Reid, I'm not in a rush to kick you out. I can hang your clothes in the airing cupboard. They won't dry completely, but in a couple of hours they'll be dry enough to put on and walk home in. I'll even lend you a brolly.' She smiled at the mental image of him walking through the village with her bright red umbrella complete with little black love hearts.

'Oh, no, I don't want to put you out. You were right, I should've just phoned, really. It's silly but... All I wanted to do when they'd gone was talk to you. Oh God, that makes it sound like you're my bloody counsellor or something. That's not what I meant though. I just meant—'

She held up a halting hand. 'Honestly, it's fine. You can stop explaining now. Why not have that glass of wine? At least wait for the rain to stop.'

He seemed to ponder her words for a few moments and then said, 'Oh, why the hell not?'

After hanging the damp clothes in the airing cupboard, she returned to the lounge and poured them each another large measure of the ruby red liquid. Reid took a gulp and placed his glass on the coffee table before slumping down on the sofa again.

'I think you're being very brave,' Juliette told him, hoping she didn't sound trite.

He scrunched his face. 'Hmm. I don't feel it. I've cried so much lately, I have no clue what people must think of me. I feel like I've regressed to become a sulky toddler.'

'The people who matter know that you've been through a horrible time and they'll totally understand. Anyone who says they wouldn't have cried is lying. I can assure you. And I'd be more worried if you hadn't cried.'

He shook his head and clenched his jaw. 'Just seeing Evin like that. I felt so cruel. Like I was making him go.'

'Evin knows that's not true.'

'I really hope so, Jules. And I hope *she* doesn't go filling his head with rubbish out of sheer bitterness. I can't believe I ever loved her. I can't believe she's the same person I fell for. You know, it doesn't matter how beautiful someone is on the outside, if the inside doesn't match, they may as well be a bloody gargoyle.'

'Yes, I totally agree with you there.' She thought back to when she saw Kate standing there in all her glorious perfection: amazing skin, gorgeous figure, a sense of style. Until she got closer and saw the flaws. It was true that beauty only ran skin deep.

'I close my eyes and all I see is the pain on Evin's face. How betrayed he must've felt. Kate was screaming at me to help her force him into the car. But I wouldn't. I couldn't do it.' His voice wavered and he cleared his throat.

'And Evin will have known that was because *none* of this is your doing. That you didn't want him to leave.'

Reid didn't respond, instead they sat for a while without speaking and just listened to the radio presenter telling the listeners which tracks had gone up or down the charts. Juliette had lost touch with music until her visit to Glentorrin. But now it was part of her daily routine: radio on, kettle on, breakfast/dinner plated up...

'How are you feeling about heading back down south?' Reid asked out of the blue, evidently exhausted from going over his trauma.

A deep sigh left Juliette's chest as she contemplated her answer. 'I'm not too sure. Mixed emotions, I suppose. This trip has been so wonderful. I've learned a lot about myself and about people in general.'

'Really? What life lessons has Glentorrin delivered?' Reid rested his elbow on the back of the sofa and his head on his hand, all his attention focused on her.

'I think I've realised that I'm quite a strong person, after all. I had my doubts before I came. I'd been recovering from depression and dealing with grief and wasn't sure if I'd cope with going it alone in a new place, even though I desperately wanted to. But now I've done it. And I've loved it. And I've discovered that I love history even more than I thought.' She laughed. 'But I've learned that people need to be listened to. You can't judge someone until you've really delved into their minds. Walked a mile in their shoes, as the saying goes. You have no clue what someone is going through until you find out for sure.'

He narrowed his eyes. 'Do you mean me, by any chance?'

She felt her cheeks warming. 'You're in there for sure. I mean, at first I thought you were just a grumpy sod with no sense of humour.'

He laughed out loud. 'And now you *don't* think that?'

'Absolutely not.' She gazed around the cosy room with its oak beam mantel, tapestry curtains and claret walls. 'I'm genuinely going to miss this place. The cottage, the museum, the music, the friends I've made. The dancing. I never imagined I'd enjoy a ceilidh so much. But it's one of the fondest memories I have. Amongst others.' She knew what she meant by that but wouldn't elaborate, so she hoped he didn't ask.

'So, what do you make of the local radio station?' he asked, pointing at the little portable unit where it played to itself on the mantel shelf.

'I've loved it, to be honest. It's been nice to listen to something completely different to the traffic news about Gloucester. And I love the accents of the presenters.'

He tilted his head. 'The accents, eh? What do you think of mine?'

Her stomach flipped. *It's like melted chocolate and sends my insides to jelly.* 'It's not bad,' she lied.

He raised his eyebrows and laughed. 'Not bad? Gee thanks. I bet you wouldn't say that if I looked like Gerard Butler or James McAvoy,' he teased.

She was trying to decide how to respond without giving herself away when the acoustic guitar of Lewis Capaldi's 'Hold Me While You Wait' began to play.

Reid closed his eyes and leaned his head back briefly. 'Oh God, this song. It gets me here,' he said, placing his hand over his heart. 'Every single bloody time. I get goosebumps. It's like he's had an insight into my soul. Like he read my thoughts and wrote them down.' He shook his head.

Juliette wanted to say so much but wasn't sure how to put things into words. 'Mine too. He expresses how hard it can be to overcome the fear of not being enough, don't you think? And that when you do give your heart away, especially if it's been broken before, you open yourself up to getting hurt again. It's terrifying.' She sighed deeply and closed her eyes, hoping Reid was reading between the lines and understood what she was trying to express. 'Finding out that your feelings aren't returned must be such a heart-breaking thing to experience. Maybe it's better not to know? Not to take the chance.'

He swallowed and nodded. 'Aye, maybe. But maybe sometimes it's a chance worth taking?'

They sat quietly again for a few moments as the song played, and Mr Capaldi sang about the agony of unrequited love and the pain of feeling insignificant and alone.

Eventually, Reid stood and peered down at her. 'It's a bit different to a ceilidh but... would you like to dance?'

Juliette glanced at his attire, then back up to his face and smiled. 'You're wearing a *towel*.'

He shrugged and held out his hand. 'I'm game, if you are.'

She put her hand in his and let him pull her to her feet. She felt a little silly at the prospect of slow-dancing in a living room with a man dressed only in a bath sheet and a giggle escaped.

Reid took another step and slipped his arm around her waist. Suddenly, their amusing situation wasn't quite so funny any more. The lyrics took on a whole new meaning as they moved together, slowly and in sync in the confined space. She rested her head on his bare chest, his heartbeat thumped a steady, hypnotic rhythm against her cheek, and he placed a tender kiss on the top of her head.

She lifted her face to make eye contact with him and there was a pleading look in his eyes. He wanted to speak but was holding back as the music floated around them, enveloping them in warmth and melancholy.

A line appeared between his brows and he chewed his lower lip; sure signs of conflict. 'I... I know I said things about the timing, and I know you're leaving soon, but...' He swallowed nervously. 'I'd like to know how it feels to kiss you properly, at least once before you go. And to have you kiss me back. And I'd like to just forget about all the stuff that's happened today; to feel something good rather than utter uselessness and despair.'

Without breaking eye contact, Juliette slipped her hand around the back of his head and into the strands of hair at the nape of his neck.

Taking this as an invitation, Reid lowered his face until his lips gently touched hers as they swayed. She felt his heart rate increase as hers did the same and she closed her eyes. He deepened the kiss. His hand found her hair, and the arm around her waist tightened, pulling her closer still. She smoothed her hand around his shoulder and held him.

His lips were soft yet demanding; new, yet somehow strangely familiar. Shivers travelled the length of her spine as her desire for him grew. It had been so long since she had been held like this. She'd thought she'd make it through life never craving such a feeling again, but now she realised she was wrong.

Reid moved his mouth from her lips to her neck and back again; the towel was doing little to mask his own desire. 'God, I want you so much,' he whispered.

She responded breathlessly, 'I want you too.'

The expression on his face, when he pulled away, told her that she'd surprised him with her admission. Before he could say anything, she took his hand and led him to the stairs, where he kissed her again, passionately, deeply. They walked silently up to the bedroom, leaving the music behind. Juliette was completely lost now to the need deep inside her, and the way Reid followed willingly as she pushed open her bedroom door made her forget everything but the two of them.

Once inside, she stretched up and removed her top, slipped down her skirt and stood before him in just her underwear. She should have been nervous, embarrassed even, but the way he looked at her, the longing in his eyes, gave her a confidence she thought she'd lost; she left behind her inhibitions and let him devour her with his gaze. It was empowering to let herself just *be*; to give herself over to her desires.

He touched her cheek. 'You're so beautiful,' he whispered. 'But are you sure you want to do this?'

Her chest heaved, but it was lust rather than anxiety. 'I'm sure. I want to feel all the things I've been missing. I want to feel wanted again.'

He stepped towards her and traced his fingertips along her collarbone and down the curve of each breast, causing her breath to hitch and her pulse to quicken.

'You're definitely wanted, Jules,' he told her, before pulling her into his arms and connecting their lips once more. This time his tongue entered her mouth and she moaned at the feeling of his hands touching her. She allowed her hands to roam his body too and revelled in the way she felt shivers as she stroked her fingertips down the planes of his chest. She let go, giving in to desire, and with one swift move, Reid's towel was discarded and they tumbled onto the bed in each other's arms.

36

When Juliette awoke, she found herself alone. She held her breath and listened in the hope that Reid was possibly in the kitchen making coffee. But the place was silent. She scanned the pillow and bedside table for a note, but there was nothing. Had he just left without a goodbye? Surely not.

She stretched and climbed, in her state of nudity, from the bed. Thoughts of the previous night interrupted her, and she paused for a moment, allowing herself to remember the feeling of Reid's weight on top of her and the way he kissed a path between her breasts down to her navel. She tried not to melt as she remembered the intimate connection of their naked bodies and the way he sent shocks of pleasure racing through every fibre of her being. She hated that she wished he'd stayed so they could experience it all over again. And she hated that she was upset with him for simply leaving.

But the thing she hated most of all was that, when she had looked up into his eyes, there had been something more there; something more powerful than lust and desire and need; something that outshone the way he made her insides quiver with the ecstatic joy of climax. And she felt it too, right down to her soul. She couldn't call it love, but it was a deep bond, perhaps borne out of their commonalities. But whatever it was, it had left its mark on her heart and now she was going away and would have to forget about it; move forward and get on with her life.

The only problem was, she didn't know how.

* * *

She'd showered and dressed and then scoured the kitchen and living room for signs of a note from Reid. She checked her phone; perhaps he'd messaged instead?

Still nothing.

She made coffee and sat in the garden. There was a distinct chill to the air, but she was still warmed from memories of the night before. A realisation hit as she listened to the birdsong around her; she had no regrets. For once there was no feeling of guilt. Just a sense of calm. Perhaps she was finally moving on? Not forgetting but feeling whole again.

She guessed this serenity wouldn't last, however, there were only two days left of her stay and she'd have to pack her belongings into her suitcase at some point. But for now she wouldn't think about that.

Unlocking the museum door, Juliette stepped inside. It hit her like a ton of bricks that this would be the last time she would stand behind the desk; the last time she'd smile at people as they walked through the door; the last time she'd be able to see the photos of Hamish's wife and her own mother. A lump of emotion tightened her throat and tears spilled over, leaving damp trails down her cheeks. She would probably be the very last museum guardian at the Lifeboat House Museum too, which compounded her sadness.

Such an incredible place that no one had the time to invest in any more.

Her mobile rang and, grateful that her best friend had forgone the video-call option for once, she answered Millie, quickly trying to disguise her despondency. 'Hey, Millie! How are you, lovely?'

'Erm, why is your voice all wobbly? What's happened?'

Bloody hell. She's telepathic, I'm sure. 'Nothing, I'm fine. Everything's fine.'

'Nope. Not convinced. Truth please.'

'It's just because this is my last day in the museum, that's all. Feeling quite emotional about leaving.'

'Hmm. I buy that that's a part of it, but what else? You forget how well I know you.'

Juliette huffed and sat on the chair behind the cash register, her head in her free hand. 'I slept with Reid.'

'Oh my god!' Millie squealed, almost rupturing Juliette's eardrum. 'I knew it! I knew it would happen! I said to Harry that you felt something real for him.'

Juliette feigned amusement. 'Pfft. It was just sex, Millie. A one-off.'

'Who are you trying to convince? You don't *do* things like that. And you don't cry over someone if it's just sex. So, what really happened? Was it awful? Is he crap in bed?'

'Good grief, Millie. That's all very personal.'

'Says the woman who I've shared a bathroom with. Spill it, Fairhurst.'

'Okay! He was incredible. I didn't want it to end. And I wanted more of him. Is that better?'

'Definitely. So, what's the problem?'

'He left without saying goodbye. Didn't leave a note or anything. I don't know if he saw it as a one-time thing and I'd feel stupid and needy asking him. In fact, it's out of the question. I absolutely *can't* ask him. I'm supposed to be heading home tomorrow and I have no clue how to feel. Apart from guilty.' She closed her eyes when she realised the feeling had returned with a vengeance.

'Guilty? No, no. Stop that. Laurie isn't here, sweetheart. He's gone. But you *have* to live. You must go on and enjoy your life. And eventually it would be wonderful if you let yourself love again.'

'I just feel like I was already betraying Laurie with my attraction to Reid, and now we've had sex I just... God, I'm a mess.'

'Oh, sweetie. You have nothing to feel guilty about. You haven't betrayed Laurie and you must stop thinking like that. But I can tell you really like Reid.'

'I do. And now I feel like he used me. Or like I read the whole thing wrong.'

'Look, honey, just get through today. That's all you need to do. If he comes to see you, then great, you can talk. But don't chase him if it's going to hurt you more. If he doesn't come, then... well, you're coming home tomorrow anyway, so you can try to put it all behind you. Are you heading to your folks for the night?'

'Yes, I think I need to see them.'

'Great, well, I'll come up on Sunday morning, so I'm here when you get back to Mistford. I've still got the spare key. Harry has gone to New York on business, lucky sod, so I'm free to look after you. And you can tell me everything.'

'Okay. I'll see you soon. Love you.'

'Love you too. Be strong.'

Juliette hung up, composed herself, took a deep breath and prepared herself for her final day in the museum.

* * *

Thankfully, the day was busy once again. Juliette wondered what any new owners might do with the place once a sale had completed.

Would Reid's imaginings of coffee bean posters come true? She hoped it would be something that at least kept the character of the building, but she sincerely doubted it. And maybe it was a good thing she wouldn't be here to see it.

At the end of the day, she closed up for the very last time and walked around the museum in the quiet absence of the day's visitors. She let her fingertips trail along the glass cases and inhaled the smell of the place, trying to commit it to memory. The old Lifeboat House had been put to wonderful use as a museum and she felt privileged to have been a small part of it. The sad thing was it would make such a wonderful quirky coffee shop for some huge chain. But what a shame that would be. The Lifeboat House had gone from saving lives to giving people a chance to learn about lives they could only see in such a place.

There was a knock on the locked door. Juliette wiped her damp cheeks and walked across to see who was there. Could it be Reid? She hoped so.

'Oh, hi, Caitlin. I've just closed up for the last time,' she said with a quiver of her chin.

'Oh, honey, c'mere.' Caitlin enveloped her in a warm hug. 'I had a feeling you'd be sad. I know I am. I can't believe you're going back south. It's always felt like you were supposed to stay.'

'Ah, it's just not meant to be. And I'm a great believer in if it's meant to be, it will be.'

'Aye, my granny used to say, "If it's for you, it'll no pass you by." But I hoped this was for you. I really did.' She let go of Juliette and stood back. 'Anyway, pub tonight. A wee farewell drink. How about it?'

'That'd be lovely. Thank you. Have you seen Reid, by any chance?'

She frowned and chewed her lip as if realising for the first time that she hadn't. 'Actually, no, which is odd. You must've heard from him though?'

'No. I haven't seen him since... well, since just after Evin left.'

Caitlin frowned. 'I haven't seen anyone walking Chewie either.'

'Do you think they've gone away or something?'

Caitlin shrugged. 'Your guess is as good as mine. Anyway, I'll let you go home and get sorted. I'll call for you around seven? We can grab a bite at the pub.'

Juliette nodded. 'That'd be great. See you then.'

When she stepped inside the cottage, she checked the answering machine. Along with a message from her mum, there was the one she'd hoped for. Although the content wasn't what she wanted to hear.

'Hey, Jules, it's... it's me. It's Reid... Look, I wanted to explain why I dashed off like that. Kate had been trying to get hold of me while you and I were... Anyway, Evin ran away. I had to take Chewie and leave to help her find him. I didn't want you to think I left because of... (*a deep sigh*) The good news is we found Evin. He's had a rough time and I need to focus on him now. What happened between you and I was...' He sighed again, clearly struggling to find the words. 'I'll never forget it. I'll never forget *you*. But in a way, it's probably a good thing I was called away. I'm useless at goodbyes. Especially when I really don't want to say them. And I didn't want to say goodbye to you, Juliette. But I understand that the other night was something you won't want to repeat. A once in a lifetime thing. And I'll treasure it because of that. I understand that your heart still belongs to Laurie. I really do. And I understand that your life isn't here. It's in Mistford. And my life has to be wherever Evin is. So, I'm letting you go.' His voice broke and he cleared his throat. 'I've left you a gift at the pub with Stella and Joren. Please don't open it until you get back home. It's not for anyone else to see but you. I wish you happiness, Jules. You deserve happiness, more than anyone I know. Take care.'

When the message ended, Juliette's face was wet with tears that had fallen silently as she'd listened to the pain in Reid's voice. Her shoulders juddered and her heart ached. She wanted to have the opportunity to tell him he was wrong. That she did want to be with him. That it wasn't a 'once in a lifetime thing' for her, regardless of what he had presumed. She hoped Evin was unharmed and that Reid would be able to mend himself and be happy. But the pain she felt was too reminiscent of the loss she'd experienced before.

* * *

Caitlin arrived at seven, and after she held Juliette and let her cry without needing explanation, Juliette washed her face, applied some make-up and they made their way to the pub.

'It's hard to believe that tomorrow is the last morning I'll wake up here. This past three months has gone by in a blur.'

'Yeah, it doesn't seem like two minutes since I was meeting you and now, I feel like I've known you a lifetime.'

'Well, a hell of a lot has happened, that's for sure.'

'You could say that. Poor Grace is devastated that Evin has gone.'

'I bet. They'd become fast friends, bless them.'

When they arrived at the pub, Caitlin held open the door and Juliette walked through. Suddenly, there was a cacophony of party poppers, blowers and applause. A sign hung above the bar which said,

So Long Jules, Haste Ye Back!

Juliette brought her hands to cover her mouth and widened her eyes as the shock of it all grabbed hold of her. The Toilichte Hens began to play *The Dashing White Sergeant* as everyone clapped along, and she was hugged from every which way.

Stella and Joren had put on quite a spread of food and there was a huge cake in the middle of the buffet table with the words *Sparkly Jules* in edible glitter – she had to fight the tears at that point. Greg McBradden showed up and played a few of her favourite songs and, as before, his demands for no one to join in were lost as everyone was in such good voice. The place was alive with music, laughter and singing. Juliette was grateful to everyone for making such an effort, but, in reality, she would've preferred to slope off without the fuss. This was too hard; too emotional.

Morag found her and pulled her into her arms. 'Oh, lassie, I'm going to miss you so much, my dear, dear friend. Promise you'll come and visit. You'd be more than welcome to stay with Kenneth and me. We'd love to have you.'

Even though Juliette adored the couple, she was unable to tell Morag that it would break her heart to return, so she smiled and said, 'I would love to, thank you.'

'It won't be the same around here once you're gone. Too many changes for my liking, and I'm quite adaptable.'

'Any news about Donny and Leanna?' Juliette asked, on the subject of changes.

'Oh, therein lies a drama. Donny has told her to leave. He's decided to turn the café into something else. Everyone is reckoning the new owners of the museum will be a coffee shop chain. Goodness knows what he'll do though. He hasn't been into the village for a few days. Probably too ashamed to show his face, and rightly so, if you ask me. But, apparently, Reid refused to bring assault charges.'

The mention of Reid caused her stomach to flip. 'That sounds exactly like something he'd do. I hope he's okay.' Juliette's heart sank; for Reid, for herself and for Evin. There was even a tinge of pity for poor, disillusioned Donny. But one thing was certain. She'd be heading home without a proper goodbye from the man and little boy who'd stolen her heart.

37

Juliette was swung and swayed by Archie, Kenneth and even Joren. She tried to enjoy the night for what it was; tried to put Reid out of her mind. Of course, she didn't succeed. However, she was touched that so many villagers made the point of coming to say goodbye. Hamish popped in but didn't stay long. Clearly, the fact that the co-op were forging ahead with the sale was breaking his heart.

He handed her a gift. 'My grandson works in graphics,' he explained,' So I had him do this for you. It was a bit sneaky and I'm surprised you didn't catch me out.' She opened the gift and burst into tears.

In her hand, she held a framed copy of the photo of her mum and her grandparents beside their beloved croft house. She couldn't speak, she simply hugged the kind old man and whispered thank you when the words would come.

When she pulled away, his eyes were glistening with tears. 'It's been a pleasure to know you, Juliette Fairhurst. You remind me so much of my darling Mary Ann.' He dabbed at his eyes. 'I must be going. My grandson is waiting outside. You take care now. And be happy.' He cupped her cheek in his wizened hand, and she placed hers over it.

Towards the end of the party, Kenneth and Morag presented Juliette with a framed photograph of her group of friends that was taken on the day of the Highland games. It would be taking pride of place on the mantelpiece when she got home, along with the gift from Hamish, and she would look at both with such fond memories.

Caitlin gave her a little photo album with selfies taken on their various shopping trips, walks and nights at the pub, and Archie presented her with a tartan blanket from his outdoor shop. Along with these, she received a variety of cards, chocolates, shortbread, single malt and even a vacuum-packed haggis from Stella and Joren.

They were such a wonderful group of people for accepting her into their community and making her feel a part of it. Their generosity and warmth had helped her to heal and to finally feel able to move forward. She knew she would always be welcome to visit and would be greeted fondly if she did, and that meant the world to her.

After all the dramatic changes in her life over recent years, this was the most positive one, and she would be forever grateful to the community of Glentorrin. The fact that she had fulfilled a dream of visiting Skye and she'd been able to run the museum were the icing on a most beautiful cake. Add to all this that she had used her own experience to help someone in need meant that something good had finally come from losing Laurie. Things with Reid may not have ended how she expected or hoped, but knowing she had gone a little way to do some good made her smile.

Before she left the pub at the end of the night, Joren handed her another wrapped gift. It was a large, flat box wrapped in brown paper and tied with a bright red ribbon. He kissed her cheek and said. 'This one is the most special. You're not to open it until you get home to Mistford. Not my rules, *Reid's*.' He held up his hands.

She nodded, unable to speak due to the emotion clogging up her vocal cords, and she hugged him tight, in lieu of hugging the man she wished was there.

* * *

Saturday morning arrived too soon, and with a heavy heart, Juliette climbed from the bed and looked out of the window. The sky was dull, and the breeze was kicking up leaves and other detritus. She had arrived at the height of summer, but it was the cusp of autumn now; the weather was changing, the leaves were already losing their verdancy and beginning to carpet the ground; the air was nipping at ears and noses, breath was becoming visible as it condensed in the air and soon, coloured lights would replace the bunting. She knew the place would still be beautiful in the cold and it tugged at her heart that she wouldn't get to see it.

Today the lacklustre sky, with its grey hues and rain-filled clouds, matched her mood. Overhead, seagulls were fighting against the gusts and for once there was no sign of Gus, the fisherman. The prospect of fighting the increasing wind was not a good one.

A man she'd seen around but didn't know walked, head down, determinedly into the oncoming, prevailing wind, and on the end of the lead he held was his little dog, whose expression told Juliette that he'd rather be tucked up in his basket with a juicy bone than walking in such inclement weather. The darkening clouds moved rapidly inland as if they too were trying to evade the worsening weather.

She gazed over towards Caitlin's shop, where the lights were on, and beside it, Reid's former café, where they were not. She wondered what he was doing. She hoped he was having a positive day, wherever he was.

Juliette took in every little detail, committing it to memory and wondering if she should have done more to secure her dream, instead of giving up so easily. There were ways and means – if she'd had the guts to take a risk.

Once she had brought her case and bags of gifts downstairs, she hovered at the door to the museum, her hand resting on the handle. She wanted one last look but knew it would only serve to darken her mood further. So instead, she turned away and left the cottage to load up her four-wheel drive and slammed the door.

She had one last walk around the house to check everything was in order and said a bizarre goodbye to *Florence the Philodendron*, whose blooms were apparently a sign of a contented plant. At least she hadn't killed it/her. With one last glance, Juliette stepped outside and locked the door behind her. She took a final stroll along the street to Morag's shop to drop off the keys and, as she arrived, she was greeted at the door by Kenneth, who hugged her tightly.

'Safe journey, hen. It's been a pleasure to have you here. Come back any time.'

'Thank you, Kenneth. And any time you fancy a change of scenery, you're more than welcome to visit the Cotswolds.'

He thanked her sincerely and walked back inside the shop.

'He's quite taken with you, like the rest of us,' Morag told her as she appeared in the doorway. 'You'll be missed so much.'

Juliette hugged her and tried not to cry. 'I'll miss you all too. So, so much.'

'Hey! Save a hug for me!' came Caitlin's familiar voice from outside. And when she arrived, she joined them in their embrace.

'I finally have a best friend and you're moving away and leaving me.' Caitlin sniffed.

'Oh, don't say that. I'm trying hard not to blub.'

Morag laughed. 'Well, you're better than me. I've already started.' She laughed through her tears and wiped her eyes.

Caitlin placed a hand on either side of Juliette's face. 'Take care of *you*, okay? And remember that if ever you get sick of the beautiful, picturesque place you live, you can always come back to this old hole.' She grinned and her eyes shone.

'I will. And please come and visit me too, okay?'

'Don't worry, me and Grace will make it down south soon. Maybe Christmas!'

Juliette nodded vehemently. 'That would be absolutely fab. The Cotswolds are so pretty at Christmas. Like something off an old chocolate box. Grace will love it.'

'Can't wait. Now, Morag has put you some breakfast together that you can easily eat as you drive, seeing as we knew you wouldn't have eaten—'

'What makes you think I haven't eaten?'

Morag, with hands on hips, chipped in, 'Well, have you?'

Juliette laughed. 'Well, no!' She was tempted to add '*Mum!*' to the end but refrained.

Caitlin grinned and held out a paper bag. 'See! And I've brought you some shortbread. There's some for you and some for your mum and dad.'

'You're so sweet,' Juliette said as she hugged them both again. 'Thank you, both. I never expected leaving to be this hard, but I really should get going now; long drive ahead to my folks' house near Durham.'

'Well, as my Kenneth said, safe journey. And let us know when you're there safely.'

Juliette nodded, no longer able to form words.

Caitlin wiped her eyes. 'You know, friends come and go in this life. But the ones who make you laugh and the ones who it hurts your heart to let go, those are the ones that mean the most. You're that for me.'

Juliette hugged Caitlin again and sobbed into her shoulder. Eventually, she took the food packages, kissed both women on their cheeks and turned back to walk to her car.

She took one long last look at the Lifeboat House Museum, the place she had temporarily called home and the place that had stolen her heart, before climbing into the driver's seat and starting the engine. Morag and Caitlin waited outside the shop to wave to her and, as she pulled around the corner at the end of the village, Stella and Joren waved too.

Juliette drove along the road and stopped at the end of the lane that led to Reid's house. She wound down the window and listened. It was eerily quiet, except for birdsong and the sound of the breeze rustling through the trees. Her heart squeezed in her chest as she remembered the times she had walked up and down this pretty lane, but she was determined not to be sad. She hoped Reid was well. That he was reunited with his boy and that he could move on and find happiness.

She wished that for herself too.

She started the engine once again. Instead of Dexter's CD, she flicked on the radio, deciding she'd listen to the local station until she was out of its reach.

Juliette was just crossing the Skye Bridge and memorising the view from up there when the radio presenter announced the next song. All the strength she'd tried to muster was swept away in one fell swoop as the opening bars to Lewis Capaldi's 'Hold Me While You Wait' floated from the speakers, and once more she was transported back to that one special night with Reid as the heartfelt words wrapped themselves around her semi-healed heart.

38

The homeward journey was just as stunning as the one she had made to travel to Skye, only this time she skirted the Cairngorms National Park on a tree-lined A road, with a mountainous vista beyond, just visible above the tops of the silver birch and alder trees. On through Pitlochry, Dunkeld and Bankfoot. At Perth, she pulled over and managed to eat a little of what Morag and Caitlin had packed for her but did so in silence. She couldn't risk listening to the radio in case she was yet again presented with songs that reminded her of things she needed to forget. Once she had eaten, she set off again, determined to arrive at her parents' house before nightfall.

Around five in the evening, she pulled on to the driveway of the house she had grown up in. Her dad's Volvo and Dexter's motorbike were sat side by side in front of the pleasant, detached home, which was located in a cul-de-sac of nineteen fifties red-brick buildings, all similar in appearance, with their bay windows and slate tiled roofs. The arched porch over the front door was adorned with a stunning hanging basket of evergreen plants – gardening was something her mum was fond of and every spare minute was spent pottering. Everything looked just the same and that was such a comforting fact.

Juliette pushed down on the front door handle and opened the door before stepping into the smartly decorated hallway. 'Mum! Dad! I'm here!'

Seconds later, amidst coos and kisses, she was enveloped in a family hug – something she really needed. As she was held at arm's length and told how well she looked, she tried her best to put thoughts of handsome Scottish men called Reid out of her mind for good.

Eventually, she held out the brown paper bag that had accompanied her all the way from Skye and managed to say, 'I brought some of the best shortbread you'll ever taste.'

'And I can vouch for that!' Dexter agreed. 'Melts in the mouth, that stuff.'

'I'll go and put the kettle on,' her dad said. 'Then you can tell us all about your trip.'

It felt so good to be home – even though there were memories of her time visiting there with Laurie at every turn. Sometimes even a grown woman needs her mum and dad.

* * *

Millie had arrived at the house in Mistford an hour before Juliette, just as she had promised. She had filled vases with flowers, put milk in the fridge and had even brought home-made lasagne and fancy cakes to welcome her home. She had been hugged to the point of breathlessness and cried on by her best friend, but there was no getting away from it; for Juliette, being back in Mistford was strange.

The house didn't feel like home. Nothing had changed, yet she felt like she was checking in to a holiday cottage. Bizarre that she should have the feeling *there* but not at the cottage on Skye. She had been away for three months though, so perhaps it would take a little acclimatising for things to feel normal again?

She hoped that's all it was.

She unpacked her belongings and sat on her own bed for the first time in months. The smell of Laurie's aftershave had faded in her absence – if it was ever really there at all. Perhaps it had been a figment of her imagination; a way of holding on that bit tighter to the man she'd loved for so long.

After a quick shower, she dressed in yoga pants and a baggy sweater – things she would never be seen wearing in public, but, seeing as she only had Millie for company, it was fine.

They sat and ate the lasagne at the kitchen table, chatting about the museum and the people Juliette had met there. She told Millie all about Caitlin and Morag and how they'd been so good to her. She revelled in sharing stories of her dancing abilities – or lack thereof – and even attempted to show Millie a step or two. They had ended up in a knot, giggling profusely. She told Millie about the Highland Games and, of course, the muscular men in kilts that she knew her friend really wanted to know about. In fact, they talked about every*one* and every*thing* Juliette had encountered – with one major exception.

Millie grabbed a corkscrew from the drawer by the fridge and, focusing her attention on opening the bottle so she didn't have to look directly at Juliette, she asked, 'Have you heard from Reid?' She finished opening the bottle of Pinot Noir under the guise that it was seven o'clock *somewhere*.

Juliette didn't feel like talking about *him*. But she knew how concerned Millie was and didn't want her to worry unnecessarily. 'Not since the message he left. It's fine though. I'm putting it behind me and moving on.' She waved a dismissive hand as if doing so would demonstrate her point further. She omitted to mention the wrapped parcel that she was yet to deal with. She knew it was one of Reid's paintings, from the shape and size of the package, and she knew she would love it. But she also knew how much it would hurt to see whichever one he'd chosen from his collection to give to her.

Millie poured crimson alcohol into two glasses and eyed her with suspicion. 'It can't be that easy, honey. I know you really liked him.'

'Well, it wasn't meant to be, so what else can I do?'

'I don't know. But what I *do* know is it's given me hope that you'll love again in the future.'

Juliette smiled despite the ache in her chest. 'I think it's made me realise a few things too, so it's been a good lesson, if nothing else.'

'Like what?'

Juliette shrugged. 'That being in a relationship isn't what I need or want right *now*. It was all too soon.' There was a little truth in there... but *only* a little when she really thought about Reid.

Millie sighed and placed down her glass. 'Well, you know my feelings on that, so I won't repeat myself. And I think you *did* want a relationship, so don't let this put you off completely. Not all men are going to be unreachable. And I think maybe he was scared too.'

Juliette pondered this for a moment. 'I think he probably was.' She shook her head to shake away the images forming in her mind of Reid beside her in bed, his fingertips gently tracing her jaw. 'Anyway, how are things going with you and Mr Dreamboat?'

Millie rolled her eyes. 'Don't do that. I know what you're doing, Jules. I want you to *talk* to me.'

Tired and exasperated with the world at large, Juliette growled, 'I *can't*, Millie, okay?' Guilt niggled at her for the way she had snapped. 'And before you ask why... It's because I feel like such an *idiot*. I feel like I let myself get close to someone too quickly and it backfired on me. I feel like I fell in love with the whole damn place and that maybe, looking back, it was a huge mistake to ever go to Skye.' Her voice wavered as her words came out in a rush. 'Because they say you can't miss what you've *never* had. I had Laurie and look what happened; I had a little taste of a different life with the Lifeboat House Museum, which is something I never expected. And I was *so* close to falling for Reid, Millie. So bloody close. It's stupid, but it's true. The more I got to know him, the closer I got to Evin, the more we talked about our pasts, the stronger my feelings grew. It all happened too fast and I couldn't control any of it. And now, all I ever seem to do is look back and yearn for things I can no longer have. When will I learn? When will I get it into my head that I'm not *supposed* to be completely happy again? That I'm far better sticking with what I know. Staying as I am and *where* I am; alone with my books, my job and my memories. Why can't I make it sink in? Why did I let myself hope?'

Millie took her hand. 'You did all those things because you're *human*, Jules. And you *want* to be loved and to love again. You may not be ready to admit that to yourself, so it's my job as your best friend to tell you, you did nothing wrong. You need to let go of this guilt you're still carrying. Laurie wanted you to find love again. He told you so, didn't he? He gave you his blessing. You're too young to live the rest of your life as some bored, lonely old spinster, for goodness sake. You deserve to be happy. You deserve to find love and you deserve to give yourself a break.'

By this point, Juliette's eyes had given up the tears she'd been stifling since her return and Millie had enfolded her in her arms to let her cry out all the anguish she'd been bottling up.

* * *

Before she climbed into bed, Juliette lifted the wrapped parcel from her wardrobe and smoothed her hand over the paper. Paper that

Reid had touched and carefully tied a ribbon round. She'd held onto it for days now, unable to bring herself to open it; because, once she did, it really would be over. It was the last thing she had that connected her to him, and seeing it might break her again.

'Time to rip off the bandage,' she said to the empty room. And, after inhaling a long, shaking breath, she pulled apart the edges of the paper until the canvas was face down on her lap. She was about to discover which of his wonderful paintings he had chosen to give her. Was it the one of the village in all its summer glory? Was it the one of the mountains topped with snow? Or maybe the bridge they had walked and shared coffee beside? Slowly, and with a trepidatious breath, she turned over the canvas and gasped.

Tears streamed relentlessly down her face.

The canvas before her showed Juliette sitting by the inlet, a serene smile played on her lips, colourful bunting was strewn along the walls and railings, the sky overhead was the vivid blue of summer, and cloudless. The museum stood behind her, as beautiful as she remembered it. Her yellow summer dress was slightly rippled as if caught by a light breeze, her hand was outstretched and, balanced on her finger... a robin.

39

The weather was definitely cooler, and daylight hours were becoming noticeably shorter. It had only been a week since she had arrived home from Skye, but it already felt like months for Juliette. She had placed her new painting over the fireplace and had purposefully searched up Lewis Capaldi's songs on the internet. Why she was torturing herself, she wasn't sure, but since Millie had gone home, she'd wondered if her friend was right about the fact that she wanted a relationship with Reid. She'd been trying to make herself believe that she didn't, but the more she tried, the less convinced she actually was.

After countless occasions of picking up the phone and dialling Reid's number only to hang up, she eventually let it ring long enough for it to go to voicemail. She was partly relieved and partly disappointed at only hearing his voice telling her to leave a message.

'H-hi, Reid, it's... it's me, Jules. I just wanted to check that Evin is safe and that you're okay. And I wanted to thank you for the beautiful painting. It's...' A lump lodged in her throat. 'It's wonderful. It has pride of place on the wall above my mantel. I can't stop looking at it. It reminds me of... well, you and happier times, I suppose. Anyway, that was all I wanted to say, so I'll go now. But thank you again. I'd love to hear how Evin is. And Chewie,' she added with a small smile. 'Bye for now. Take care of yourself,' she whispered and then hit the end-call button.

It was only a matter of days until she would be back at the university. Back to real life. Skye was already becoming a distant memory, regardless of how many times she revisited it in her mind. As she slept, she dreamed about being at the museum, happy amongst the displays and Tiffany lamps; smiling as she chatted to visitors with excited expressions. Glancing out of the window to see friendly faces passing by. She woke feeling happy and excited, only to realise she was hundreds of miles away and all alone.

Dexter had stayed with their parents for longer than he'd originally anticipated, and she missed him too. Millie was loved up and loving life in Notting Hill with Harry. Dexter had been right; he was a great guy. They had made a brief visit and he had treated them to dinner. He was good fun, just what Millie needed. Caitlin was keeping in regular touch but thankfully seemed to be avoiding the elephant in the room: Reid.

'Grace is loving reading Harry Potter. I'm so glad you encouraged her to give it a go. I'm tasked with making a themed birthday cake, so I've been trawling the internet for ideas. I'm thinking I'll go with the sorting hat. I mean, I'm a baker, how hard can it be?'

'Mmhmm. Yes.'

'I think she'd quite like a Hermione cloak and wand for her birthday, but she hasn't mentioned it yet, so I'm not sure what to do really.'

'Mmm.'

'I suppose I could do a bog-standard round cake and just put some icing figures on the top. What do you think?'

'Hmm.'

'Yes, and I thought I'd hire the whole movie cast to come and deliver it by hand. Maybe get some owls to carry in a banner that says *Happy Birthday, Grace*.'

'Mmm, great idea.'

'Jules, where are you?'

'Sorry?'

'You're not listening.'

'I *am*. Cake... Harry Potter... and... *stuff*.'

'And the movie cast?'

'What about them?'

'Yep, not listening at all.'

Juliette sighed deeply and rubbed at the crease in her forehead. 'I'm so sorry. I'm just... My mind's all over the place.'

'And your heart?'

'Back on Skye, I think,' she admitted.

'I'm so sorry you're feeling that way, Jules. But maybe that's your subconscious telling you it's time for a change?'

'Even if it is, I have no clue what to do. I loved my job before... well, before the Lifeboat House. And now nothing compares to it.'

'Oh, yes, I meant to mention...' She hesitated. 'It's sold.'

Juliette's stomach dropped and she sat up straight. 'Oh. Who bought it?'

'No one knows for sure. But there's a rumour that it's someone from down south. But there's been lots of coming and going, so I'm guessing we'll find out soon. I'm so sorry it's not you.' She wasn't the only one.

'It wasn't meant to be.' Juliette hoped that one day those words would sink in and she'd believe them. But the fact was, she'd kicked herself on many occasions for not making further enquiries.

Too late now.

'Anyway, I'd better go. Grace is just finishing off her homework and then she'll want to tell me all about what's happening to Harry and the gang, no doubt.'

'Okay. Give her a hug from me. Night night.'

'Aye, will do. Night, Jules.'

Juliette checked the clock. It was only six thirty. Much too early to go to bed, even though it was worryingly tempting. She wouldn't let herself fall back into old patterns again. She stood at the kitchen sink and gazed out of the window at the little cottage garden. Birds were picking at the seeds on the hanging feeders and there was a pale Titian glow created by the setting sun. As she waited for the kettle to boil, she replayed her conversation with Caitlin. '... *maybe that's your subconscious telling you it's time for a change...*' Was she right? The more she mulled it over, the more she let her mind wander to thoughts of Reid. His smile, his voice, the way she'd felt in his arms. Perhaps she had pushed him away by being too reticent to say how she really felt? It was too late to change things now though, wasn't it?

She picked up her phone and flicked through the photos she had taken of Glentorrin until her eyes stung with tears and her heart ached with regret. Maybe it wasn't too late? Maybe Reid had been right that night when they had been listening to Lewis Capaldi, and chances were sometimes worth taking.

She lifted her head again and gasped. A little robin sat on the window ledge. Was it another sign from Laurie? Tears overspilled from her eyes and she smiled as the tiny creature paused to watch her before he took flight and became a silhouette against the sky.

That was it. That was all she needed. Tomorrow she would look into revisiting Skye and finding out where Reid was living. She had to at least find out if his feelings for her matched her own for him.

With a sense of relief, Juliette flopped on to the sofa, picked up her book and thumbed the pages to find the last one she read and stared at the words. Nothing was registering. She read the same page over and over again, and was about to give up when the door-bell chimed.

Dex must have decided to come back down south.

She placed down her book and walked to the front door. It would be good to have him around again. Maybe he could drag her up from the doldrums and tell her if she was being ridiculous in considering going all the way back to Skye on a whim.

With a smile and arms open to welcome her brother, she yanked the door open.

'H-hi, Jules.'

'Reid!' He stood before her in jeans and a leather jacket over a fitted pale blue T-shirt. The beginnings of a beard graced his angular jawline and his blue eyes looked unencumbered, sparkling in the light of the porch lantern. Her heart tried to escape through her ratty old sweater top, which no amount of smoothing down would help to unwrinkle. 'What on earth are you doing here?' She hadn't heard from him after leaving the voicemail about Evin and the painting, and had spent so much time since trying to convince herself she would be fine and that she'd move on, that she hadn't considered the possibility he might simply turn up on her doorstep.

He cleared his throat. 'I think... I mean, I *know* I owe you an explanation.'

'You'd better come in,' she said.

He followed her into the living room, glancing around at her home as he walked. 'Wow, you looked absolutely stunning on your wedding day,' he told her with a warm smile as he pointed at the black and white shot of her and Laurie's special day.

'Thank you. Please, have a seat.' She sounded incredibly formal even to her own ears. Like he was some market researcher that she'd never met before. The truth was that she didn't know how to act. The urge to run into his arms had been almost overwhelming and she'd dug her nails into her palms to keep herself grounded.

He sat awkwardly and shook his head as if he was having an internal conversation. He glanced at the painting above the fireplace and his cheeks coloured red. 'You've hung it. I wasn't sure if you would.'

She looked over at it too and her heart skipped. 'I left you a message to say I had. And it's beautiful, why wouldn't I hang it?' she whispered, but it was a rhetorical question.

'I've missed you.' And then his brow crumpled. 'My phone, it got damaged and I lost some messages, contacts and things like that… I didn't get yours, I'm so sorry.'

As he hadn't immediately taken her into his arms, she wasn't sure what to make of his arrival. She closed her eyes and sighed. 'Why are you here, Reid?' she asked as she gingerly lowered herself to the opposite sofa; keeping a little distance was vital for self-preservation.

He huffed and widened his eyes briefly. 'Where to start. So much has happened. But… first, I want to say how sorry I am. At around two in the morning on the night we… the night that—'

'We had *sex*. You can say it out loud, Reid. We're adults.' She was aware that her reply was out of character and a little blunt, almost to the point of childishness.

He raised his eyebrows. 'Okay… okay… so, on that night, at around two in the morning, I received a call from Kate. My phone was on silent, so I missed it, but I got up to go to the bathroom and there was a text message. Evin had run away.'

Her heart pounded and she panicked momentarily. Was this the reason for his visit? Was something wrong with Evin? 'Yes, you said so in your voice message, but you said he's okay…'

'Y-yes… Thankfully, he's fine now. But… erm… So, they'd stopped at a service station on the way back to Manchester, that's where she lives with that *bloke*, and Evin had got out of the car and just disappeared. He'd been gone for hours and I'd been blissfully unaware. The guilt I felt was immense, Jules. I grabbed my clothes and left as quick as I could. I grabbed Chewie because I knew Evin would be desperate to see him, got in my car and set off. All the time, I was thinking, what if something happened to him and I was too busy enjoying myself to be there. I hated myself so much.'

'But you didn't think to leave me a note or... or wake me? I would've understood, Reid.'

'In all honesty, I couldn't focus on anything else. I was frantic. I just wanted to find him.'

She did understand and inwardly chastised herself for being selfish. 'How long did it take?'

'All bloody night. The police were involved. It was horrendous. I've never been so scared. When we did find him, he'd fallen down an embankment and landed in some bushes. He'd broken his ankle. He'd been stuck there, terrified, cold and in agony.' He rubbed his hands over his face. 'It broke my heart.' His voice trembled, the memory too recent and raw.

Juliette sat with her hands over her mouth. 'Oh no, the poor boy,' she whispered.

He nodded. 'I know, it was horrific. He was rushed to hospital and his leg was operated on. I slept in my car with Chewie while Kate stayed at the hospital with him. It should've been *me* there. Anyway, a couple of days later, he was allowed home. But she insisted on taking him to Manchester. In the meantime, I received a call from the clinic about the paternity test.' His eyes shone with happiness and tears. 'He's mine, Jules. Evin's been mine all along.'

Juliette let a sob escape. 'Oh, thank God. That's wonderful.'

'It is... it really is.' He lowered his attention to the floor, trying to hide his emotions. 'So... to cut a long, painful story short, we arrived back in Manchester. *She* wasn't too happy that I'd tagged along, but there was no way I was leaving him again. I told her about the paternity test, and I think she realised she couldn't stop me from being close to him. So, I stayed in a dog-friendly B and B and visited Evin the next day. He wouldn't talk at first, just clung to Chewie, but then... he kept apologising and begging me to take him home. Kate overheard all this and pulled me aside.' Reid lifted his chin and the smile on his face was in total contrast to the saltwater over spilling from his eyes. 'She said that after he'd run away like that she was worried he'd just keep doing it. But I think, in all honesty, she was finally seeing that he didn't want to be with her. Not permanently. He loves her, I know he does, but *she* left him, and he knows this. It's bound to affect him. I think it finally sunk in. She told me to take him home, Jules.'

Juliette rose from the sofa and rushed across the room to where Reid was already up on his feet. She threw her arms around him, relief flooding her veins. 'That's wonderful! I'm so happy to hear that. You must both be so relieved. You can get back to normal.'

Reid pulled away and gazed into her eyes. 'Not exactly.'

She frowned at his response. 'But... *why*?'

He shrugged. 'The café is no longer mine. No income, apart from my paintings, and they tend to sell more in the summer.'

'Ah. Of course. But you *will* go back to Glentorrin?'

'I think you should sit.' His tone worried her, and she did as he requested, sitting beside him on the same sofa this time.

'That sounds ominous.' She forced a laugh and tried to smile.

He took her hand. 'Jules, I have so many things to be grateful to you for. You were only in Glentorrin for a short time but... as I've said before, the impact you had, not just on me, was massive. So positive. Okay, there were some painful moments too, but, on the whole, you helped me so much. You taught me that it's okay to ask for help, a lesson I really needed to learn. You taught me what it is to stand up for what you believe in. To not give up, no matter how dire a situation feels. I owe you so much. Your friendship alone meant the world to me.'

The word *friendship* cemented in her mind that this was his way of saying a proper goodbye. A goodbye he hadn't presented her with before. A goodbye she needed for closure. But it hurt all the same. Reading between the lines, it sounded as though he was moving on completely, taking Evin and starting over somewhere totally new to them both. Somewhere far away. She couldn't blame him. She bit her lip to try and stop it from trembling.

He continued, 'So, thank you. I hope you know how special you are. And I hope that one day you'll allow a man into your heart to prove that to you over and over again.'

She took a deep breath. This was it. *Thank you and goodbye. I'm moving on. Glentorrin isn't for me any more now the business is gone. Et cetera, et cetera.* At least he had saved her the embarrassment of travelling all the way to Skye to find this out. She realised she didn't want to hear him say the words, after all. So, she stood. 'Honestly, I'm so glad things have worked out for you and Evin. And I know the two of you, and Chewie, will be stronger than ever now. I know that, wherever you go and whatever life you choose, it will be wonderful.' Her voice wavered and her words fell from her body in place of the tears she was holding back. She'd said too many goodbyes already. She could live without this one.

He stood to face her. 'You didn't let me finish.'

She gave another forced laugh and held up her hand. 'No, but I know what you're going to say. I'm just not great with goodbyes, that's all. It's probably best if you just get going, eh?'

He lowered his gaze to the floor. 'You want me to leave?'

She nodded but couldn't speak.

He didn't move and instead walked towards her. He was too close for comfort now. 'Jules, I have to say something else. I know how you feel now, and I respect that, but I need to just say one last thing.' He took a deep breath and fixed his gaze on her. 'When I left that morning, I didn't get to say how I was feeling... about *you*, I mean. I think it may have appeared that it was *just* sex because of how I left things. And I know that in doing so I ruined everything. But you should know... It meant *everything* to me. I know how much guilt you carry and how hard it was for you to let me get close to you. And I'll forever be in awe of you. I thought I saw something in your eyes that night. Something that spoke to me more than words could. I thought we connected, and I don't mean just physically. I hate that my leaving spoiled any chance we might have had at seeing where we would go. And that man I spoke of earlier, the one who you eventually let into your heart, I wanted that to be me.' His voice wavered again. 'I wanted that so, *so* much. But I want you to know I totally understand.'

His words confused her, and she shook her head. 'But... you came to say *goodbye*.'

He smiled with no little tinge of sadness. 'No. I came in the hope I could convince you to come back with me.'

She gasped.

He held out his hands and let them fall to his sides. 'I've lost my heart to you. It's as simple as that. It happened so fast that I didn't even realise it until I thought you were gone for good. I came here to be the knight on a white horse. To sweep you off your feet.' He closed his eyes and tilted his head back. 'I really am one giant cliché, aren't I? You don't need rescuing. It was me that needed that. And you did it. You rescued me.'

Juliette couldn't speak. Reid's eyes were filled with hope and anticipation, but she said nothing.

'Look, I know how ridiculous this all sounds. We've known each other a matter of months. And for the first part of that I was a total dick. So, I really do understand. I guess I just hoped that maybe you'd be willing to take a chance on me again but I understand you just want to be friends.' He leaned towards her and kissed her cheek tenderly. 'Be happy, Jules. Always be happy.' He turned to walk away for what she knew would be the very last time.

The recent appearance of the robin on her window ledge sprang to mind, so too did Laurie's words. '*Go out and live. Fall in love again. You have so much love to give. Don't waste it. Learn to throw caution to the wind. Learn to fall like you did on that day in the library. Promise me...*'

'Wait!' she blurted as Reid's fingertips wrapped around the door handle. He turned to face her, a pained expression in his eyes. 'Don't go. Not yet,' she said.

He shook his head. 'I don't want to go. But this hurts too much. I'm not strong enough to be friends. I hope you can forgive me for that. I'm just not—'

She rushed into his arms and kissed him with all the passion she could muster in the hope he would realise what she was trying to communicate.

When confusion crumpled his brow, she decided it was time to follow Laurie's final wishes. Throw that caution to the wind. 'Take me with you,' she told him.

Reid released a noise from his chest that told her he couldn't quite believe what he was hearing, but he pulled her into his arms anyway. They held each other tightly, laughing through the fog of tears, kissing and gazing at each other in disbelief.

Eventually, Reid pulled away and placed a gentle hand on either side of her face. 'Is now a good time to tell you I've bought you a gift?'

She widened her eyes in excitement. 'You have? What is it?'

'It's a museum.'

It was Christmas tree day at the Lifeboat House Museum. Juliette had brought every single decoration she owned and Evin had appeared with another huge box. Chewie sat by the tree, a tinsel scarf around his neck and a set of reindeer antlers on his head. The boy and his dog were like a double act and she was pleased with how Evin had progressed after everything he'd been through during the summer. Caitlin had called to say she would be over soon with Grace and Cleo and that they were bringing some Christmas-tree-shaped shortbread and a cheeky bottle of sherry. Juliette couldn't wait.

Bing Crosby crooned in the background and the smell of pine was so fresh and uplifting, even though the tree's arrival in the museum had been a different matter. Watching Reid struggle through the door with the massive evergreen had been hilarious, he'd painted the air blue with expletives as pine needles made their way into his hair, down his back and even ended up in his underwear. It had all ended in giggles though and Juliette knew it would all be worth it.

Being back at Lifeboat Cottage had been incredible so far. The place had done its job of saving people again. Juliette counted herself as one such lucky person. Reid had been inspired to paint again and his paintings were selling like hot cakes at a variety of galleries around Skye. His latest exhibition, *A Robin in Summer,* featured the painting of Juliette at its heart, which she was initially a little embarrassed by. But the success of the exhibition had meant so much to Reid that she had decided to embrace her newfound fame as an artist's muse.

Thankfully, Reid had been happy to take things slow. Juliette lived in the cottage by the museum and Reid remained back at his house with Evin and Chewie. On the day they had returned to Skye, Reid told her that he wanted a future with her, but that he wouldn't rush things; that she could move in with them at whatever point she felt ready. So, as a surprise for Christmas, she had purchased a special wooden keyring, complete with sparkly jewel adornments, with the words 'Reid, Evin, Jules and Chewie's Place' carved into it. She hoped he would get the message.

Her friends and colleagues back home in Mistford had been shocked when she announced she was leaving. The first month of working her notice was painfully slow, but she knew she had amazing things to look forward to. And now she was in Glentorrin for good, Dexter seemed to think her spare room was his personal crash pad. Every spare weekend he had, he jumped on his bike and made the gazillion-mile journey under the guise he was simply visiting Juliette. But she saw through it. She knew he was living in hope that Caitlin would miraculously realise she was head over heels in love with him. Her poor delusional brother.

Millie and Harry had asked if they could visit and Juliette had the distinct feeling that Harry was going to propose. Call it women's intuition. Her mum and dad were going to be arriving the day before Christmas Eve and Reid had bitten the bullet and called Kendric during the week. He had decided to extend an olive branch. Juliette knew it would all take time, but she had faith they would eventually build bridges and get back to being true brothers again. And whilst she could certainly not condone Kendric's actions, it was clear he was devastated at how much he had hurt Reid.

Morag, Caitlin and Juliette had taken up where they left off. Their long walks included putting the world to rights and lots of giggles. Kenneth cheekily likened them to the witches from Shakespeare's 'Scottish play'.

Leanna and Donny had moved away from Glentorrin. They had somehow reconciled and sold the café to make a fresh start on the mainland. The café was bought by... the co-operative! They said it was a little easier to run than the museum and things were going well. The museum was also thriving under its new ownership.

Hamish had been delighted at Juliette's return. He'd hugged her and cried when he discovered the museum was staying open. He thanked her for her hand in this and for the fact that his wife's memory would be kept alive. Meanwhile, Juliette's mind was whirring with plans for the museum. She'd got a little idea up her sleeve that involved Kendric and his TV show featuring a certain sweet elderly gentleman and his love story. She just had to choose the right time to broach the matter with Kendric. She guessed Hamish would be delighted to share his stories.

As Juliette sorted through her decorations now, Reid walked in. He was wearing a Santa hat and the loudest Christmas jumper she had ever seen; both literally and figuratively, thanks to the 'press here' button that instigated a terrible rendition of 'Rudolph the Red Nosed Reindeer'; the latter having a light up nose for full effect. She wondered whether he should dye his newly acquired beard white and finish the job properly.

'Hey, my love. I've brought you a mug of hot chocolate. I

thought you'd appreciate it seeing as you've been working so hard today.' Her stomach still flipped at his accent.

She took a sip of the sweet, steaming liquid and as the rich flavour hit her taste buds she sighed. 'Mmm, delicious. Thank you.'

He planted a kiss on her cheek and went to manoeuvre the ladder so he could stick the garland around the top of the room. Juliette still had an aversion to ladders so she left him to it. Laurie was ever-present in her mind and heart. She still wore the locket he gave her but these days she could remember him without guilt. She would always be grateful to have shared part of her life with him but she knew she had his blessing and now looked to the future with excited anticipation.

The weather had been quite dramatic that whole week. There had been a few snow flurries, but nothing had settled; then there had been a spectacular thunderstorm that they all sat watching through the window, huddled in the dark. Although to some, snow was an irritation, Juliette was looking forward to seeing the ground blanketed in white. The shops and houses around the inlet were already trimmed with coloured lights, Juliette's included, and the place looked wonderful. So festive.

'Sparks! Can I put some tinsel around the chair in the kid's section?' Evin asked. His original nickname for Juliette had been chopped down as he had easily settled into having her in his life more permanently. He had even made her a clay pot at school and painted the name on the front. It was supposed to be a Christmas gift, but he couldn't wait and she adored it.

'Absolutely!' she replied. 'It needs to look like a fairy has sneezed all over the place in there.' She laughed.

'Challenge accepted!' He saluted her and she giggled at his enthusiasm.

Being a mum had been a dream Juliette had held ever since she fell for Laurie. These days Evin filled that void she had felt for many years. He was respectful, caring and sweet, just as she hoped any child of her own would be. They often took long walks together when Reid was painting, and played with Chewie on the big field. Evin's laughter was one of the best sounds she'd ever heard. He had come along in leaps and bounds at school too, finding the confidence and strength to put the bullying behind him. Reid insisted this was Juliette's influence on his life and she hoped he was right. Because although it was only early days she loved the boy as if he was her own, and knew she would do anything to keep him safe.

Sometimes, in quiet moments at the museum, she reflected on her life choices, and when she was feeling extra vulnerable, she worried that she may have dived in headfirst with Reid, when she had previously insisted to herself that she would never fall in love again. But then she would look at Evin and Reid, Caitlin and Morag, and even Chewie, and be reminded that what she'd actually done was fulfil Laurie's wish just as she had promised.

Some men rescue women from lofty ladders, some whisk them off to London, some take them on exotic holidays. But for those who don't need rescuing and fancy trips, there are those men who do something completely different. Juliette's? He had bought her a museum and a chance at a shared future and she couldn't be happier if she tried.

ACKNOWLEDGMENTS

Well, this has certainly been the strangest year hasn't it? Writing is one of the things that has helped me get through the uncertainty of 2020. I would like to start by thanking my husband, Rich, and my daughter, Grace, for putting up with my constant second guessing of myself. I'm so lucky to have the two of you grounding me.

I wouldn't be where I am today without my wonderful mum and dad and I want to thank them for making the huge step to follow us to Scotland. Having you both so close by means the world to me.

Thank you to my wonderful friends Claire H, Claire M and Caroline for your encouragement and for listening to me waffle on about my story ideas and book stuff until your ears were sore!

I'm so grateful to my incredible agent Lorella Belli. Thank you for taking a chance on me and for sharing your abundance of publishing industry knowledge. I love working with you and look forward to sharing a bottle of Prosecco again at some point in the future. Thank you so much for all your hard work and for believing in me.

I'm so very excited to be working with Caroline Ridding again and I couldn't be happier to be embarking on a new chapter (pardon the pun) with Boldwood Books. After following their successes, I feel honoured to be a part of their team. Thank you too to Caroline, Jade and Rose for making this book so polished, and to the whole Boldwood team for your enthusiasm and support.

Last, but certainly by no means least, I would like to thank every single person who has read my books. When I set out on this journey, I could never have anticipated the number of wonderful people I would come into contact with. But I'm so grateful to now call so many of you friends. Your feedback, reviews and messages are so energising and inspire me to continue creating these fictional worlds with their romance and happy ever afters.

Thank you all,

Lisa